T0267304

BECAUSE OF NOTHING AT ALL

Also by Paul Sunga
Red Dust, Red Sky
The Lions

BECAUSE OF NOTHING AT ALL

PAUL SUNGA

GOOSE LANE

Edited by Bethany Gibson.
Cover and page design by Julie Scriver.
Cover imagery inspired by Tanzanian batik
fabric found at www.kallistiquilts.com.
Title font in Deacon Flock licensed by
Chequered Ink.
Printed in Canada by Marquis.
10 9 8 7 6 5 4 3 2 1

Goose Lane Editions acknowledges the
generous support of the Government of
Canada, the Canada Council for the Arts,
and the Government of New Brunswick.

Library and Archives Canada Cataloguing
in Publication

Title: Because of nothing at all / Paul Sunga.
Names: Sunga, Paul S., 1956- author.
Identifiers: Canadiana (print) 20220193371 |
Canadiana (ebook) 2022019338X |
ISBN 9781773102467 (softcover) |
ISBN 9781773102474 (EPUB)
Subjects: LCGFT: Novels.
Classification: LCC PS8587.U57 B43 2022 |
DDC C813/.54—dc23

Goose Lane Editions is located on the unceded
territory of the Wəlastəkwiyik whose ancestors
along with the Mi'kmaq and Peskotomuhkati
Nations signed Peace and Friendship Treaties
with the British Crown in the 1700s.

Goose Lane Editions
500 Beaverbrook Court, Suite 330
Fredericton, New Brunswick
CANADA E3B 5X4
gooselane.com

Your money might buy you rich shoes,
but you will always walk on the same poor dirt.

Contents

Office of the Analyst, Canadian High Commission in Nairobi
Re: The Turkana Incident

Initial press releases:

Ministry of Home Affairs, Republic of Kenya
PRESS RELEASE, May 2, 2016
Kenyan security forces are investigating a possible
abduction of Kenyan citizens and foreign nationals in
Turkana County near the Kenya-Sudan border region.
The missing persons include Canadian government and
UN officials.

United Nations Mission in Nairobi, Kenya
May 3, 2016
Press Release
Unidentified armed men have abducted an Ethiopian
national employed by the IOM, along with Canadian aid
officials. The abductors are as yet unidentified.

US Department of State
Office of the Coordinator for Counterterrorism
Terrorism Report
May 4, 2016
Foreign fighters, including al-Qaeda operatives and
Indigenous violent extremists, continue to pose a threat
to regional security throughout East Africa. An incident
in Turkana, Kenya, appears to be the 77th abduction
of international workers in Africa this year, possibly by

Islamists. There are estimated to be roughly 200,000 foreign aid workers in Africa at this time.

GoC Notes:

1. In Ottawa, this file, marked URGENT, was initially passed to the Minister of Global Affairs on April 30, 2016. Subsequently, the Minister resigned (for unrelated reasons), leading to a delay in the response to the situation. The response of the Ministry is currently being reviewed at the behest of the new Minister, particularly as it resulted in the abduction of a government official and the death of a Canadian engaged in official government business.

2. Turkana, to the west of Lake Turkana, is a tenuously administered district of northern Kenya inhabited mainly by nomadic Turkana herders. The northernmost extreme, where this incident is thought to have occurred, is the Ilemi Triangle, an area disputed by Sudan, Kenya, and Ethiopia. Daytime temperatures in Turkana can exceed 45°C. The entire region has recently suffered a prolonged drought.

3. As of yet it has not been possible to generate a complete report of the incident, since there is insufficient access to both electronic communications and the principals.

AK – Analyst, Global Affairs, Nairobi

PART ONE

THE IMPERATIVES OF MONEY

CHAPTER 1
Money Manyu
Dandora, Kenya
1991-1995

When Money Manyu held himself to account, as all must eventually do, he thought of the reasons for his choices. There were many reasons that went far and deep, to his beginnings. Ultimately, he considered himself to be an economic agent—not a terrorist, and not a killer.

It was because of profit, the invisible hand. Because of supply and demand.

Because of how he started. Because of how he went. Because of the accounting that must be done.

Because he was a sufferer who saw opportunity. Because in the end there was no opportunity. Because of what he did not know.

Because of *one thousand now and nine later, and possibly much more.*

Because the way he started was in the Man U Healthy Child Centre, where they dispensed ugali—porridge so stiff it stuck in the throat. So he decided, no. It meant hungry, while the others ate. They took his bowl to share among themselves while Matron looked on with her grand jegi swinging over them, saying he might starve or live, it mattered not. She had sixty-two others to see about, and every one of them had to decide to live or not, that was the way of the Lord. *And just as your name is Money, you can go one way or the other, up or down, wealthy or poor. Asset or debt.*

He chose not to eat, if only to show Matron that his mind was independent. It was the first choice he could remember making.

Because no matter which way he turned, there were other kids, all of them the same. He might pelt his feet down and travel far and fast, hide himself, leap bravely into the waters of the Nairobi River and wade, and still, there on the other side, more kids, shoving, falling, hurting, yelling, sinking, yanking at his trousers to laugh about his broken ndiki. Forty-seven, fifty-seven, sixty-eight changing faces, changing names. The babies unnamed until the director decided to label them in hopeful and practical ways that only he would think of, names meant to guide them to good destinies. Cute, Timely, Wailing, Beautiful, Slightly Lucky, Very Lucky, Fortunate, Persistence, Jurisprudence, Truth, Righteous, Struggle and Freedom, Mercy and Equity, Contract and Commodity. Inflation, Royalty and Profit. Gold, Shilling, Sterling, and Euro. When the director was in a less visionary frame of mind, he named them Solicitor, Engineer, Medical, Prestige, Influence, Power. Capital, Barrister, Doctor, Accountant, Banker. Money.

Baby Power had liquid, blind eyes that put Matron into a trance so that she carried him about on her hip, then slept with him nestled into her soft joogz. But Baby Power vanished in the dark of one night, and that was the end of Matron. She searched for Baby Power and was wazimu and had madness. One evening the director found her crawling on the floor, overtaken by the spirit of lost and blind Baby Power. After, Matron went away, gone to Baby Power. Some days later an older girl named Mercy casually asked the director the whereabouts of Matron and Baby Power. He answered with a smooth smile.

—Ah, by the way, by the way, they were sent back.

—Sent back where, Bwana?

—Ah, by the way, to their people. They were sent back to their people.

Others were sent back to their people, to places so far away no one ever saw them again. One by one and two by two. Brothers and sisters came and were sent back, kids with narrow chests and coughs and thin legs, with their lost eyes. Sufferers, some with ribs jutting, malarious, their guts infested. They wanted to stay. They would try to be normal, chase the rag football with the others, never running well, never touching the ball because of cramps, tired, diarrhea shit, vomiting, sick, sick. Always sick. Some stayed for a time, only to be sent back later. Others faded gradually, overrun by fevers, their skin gone yellow, angry red, cold. Infected, spat blood, too bad. Others shat so much they went from narrow to empty. Or starved, shat, choked, then sent back. *Brain fever malaria typhoid. Slim disease sorcery medicine. The poisonous spells of the Mungiki fevers.*

Because of those who were sent back. Because of his brothers and sisters. A person needed to fight for wellness, commodities, profit.

They fail, Director Bwana explained with a broad smile, *in order to mock the wealth of opportunity.*

Chici comes down the lane, heavy in the belly, her baby ready to pop out of her thing. She comes along slowly, climbs the stairs, sinks down with the baby half out, the baby trying to be born right there. No one knows this chici with her spindly legs; she is not from here. But her baby fights like a rat, stuck, gasping at the sour air. The kids watch quietly, knowing that the baby is them and that the mother is their own mother, a mother no one knows, this young mama who wails for someone to help because the baby is stuck. A girl named Purity comes, sticks her hands in, gets hold of the baby, but it's slippery with blood and mess so that Purity lets go and runs away wailing to Bwana D with hands bloody. Bwana comes out and shoos the children away. Later that mother is gone, *sent home to her people*. But the baby gets a name because what else is there to do, and the baby stays for a time, infected, HIV, howling through the dark nights like a cat on fire, mad for its bad luck.

Others come at night to the Healthy Child Centre, sniffing, troubled, quiet of words or explanations. Girls with footballs already in their bellies, who give birth here and there, stay for days, weeks, then gone, their footballs left squalling behind so that the new mothers can be sent back to start their lives again, or sent home to their families, back to their places.

Because of babies, babies, so many babies left behind. Behind the walls, in the ditches, in the river, in waste bins, in the latrines. If they were lucky, Director and Matron brought them in, collecting them in bags, babies in rubbish, babies jettisoned, only to be collected before they sank, and others who washed up, unsinkable, blinking and choking away the muck of the Nairobi River.

II

Because when the children went out the door each day, they had a choice: uphill or down.

Uphill: the grandeur of the main road with its God Help You Market and the Disco Bar (Dancing Always), the line of stalls that sold tomatoes, papayas, rags harvested from the dump, the engine parts to any car. In the distance, the hazed towers of Nairobi town, and beyond that, Nairobi National Park: simba, twiga, hippo, crocodile that no motherless kid has ever seen.

Downhill: a skidding run. Easy running, easy skidding, follow the flow of the drain, the windblown trash, the legs of children spinning, to the muck of the riverbank, then the river itself that struggled through the overflow of the dump. Beyond that, the bank, the water, the opposite bank with the dump spreading out as far as the eye could see, dotted with lazy ghosts who moved about in the drifting and acrid clouds.

Because that was the choice, uphill or downhill, a *wealth of opportunity* on a slope from the Nairobi River to the main road, a sloping football match with a rag ball, down to grassy banks where children hope for a fish while the dump seethes.

A wealth of choices: ugali or not, grow or not, learn or not.

A wealth of opportunity for illness and fever and sick, sick and the days of childhood crawled along, like lost bugs on a traffic street.

III

Because of New Matron who finally arrived with creaky leather shoes that talked, saying *why-o-why-o-why-o-why*. As her shoes talked, so did Matron herself, a river of words, even when there was no Bwana Director around to hear, only sixty-six children too hungry to sleep.

—Where is he? Where is that man? Why am I left alone with nothing? (*Why-o-why-o-why-o-why.*)

New Matron was not like Old Matron who had great jegis, her ancient skin as soft as flowers. New Matron had the arms and the chest of a boy, all wire and bone. Hard to say if she was pretty. Her shoes talked through the house, her hands flitting over the heads of the kids in their beds, her fingers so swift and light the children wondered if another bat had gotten in.

—Where is he? Where does he go? Why did he disappear? (*Why-o-why-o-why-o-why.*)

The children tittered and someone squeaked, —Disco Bar, Dancing Always.

But she did not understand. She went on walk-talking through the house, passing through the door into the lane, jogging up to the main road, panting, her shoes talking, talking, saying *why-o-why-o-why.* She dropped into her chair and was surrounded by hungry kids because the evening meal had been missed, the cupboards bare. New Matron smelled sharp, like a rubbish fire.

—And where o where are the staff? And where o where is Cook and the food for dinner?

She took up a child and placed it on her lap. She hugged it and sang about a goat on a hill, enough to make the children settle. A few fell instantly to sleep, as though they had awaited that moment to escape the discomfort of their growling bellies.

Because later, in darkness, in night, New Matron tugged Money from his bed. She led him by the hand, out of his tousled sleep, out into the chill air of the veranda, where he was pulled up and pressed into the hard boards of her chest, and he went limp against her as he looked at the distant fires flickering in the dump across the river. Other children, a band of poor sleepers, followed behind, as though tied together with strings. They wandered out, half awake, not heeding her flagging insistence that they return to their beds. Matron sighed and spoke in a soft voice to Money that everyone heard.

—Little man, your mama was my friend. She brought you here when she was diseased and knew she would die. But I am telling that she was a young and beautiful sister with a beautiful heart, and that is all I can say to you. She left you here, for you to grow in the charge of Bwana, wherever he is. So I give you this message from your dead mother, that is all I have.

The other children murmured agreeably, their sweet breath filling the air, their lidded eyes dreamy with this story. They nodded as though they knew the ending to the story, or because it was their story too. They were Money and he was them. The dead mother, whoever she was, she was their dead mother too.

Money struggled out of her lap to stand on his independent feet, among the others, then drifted inside where he found his bed cold and dark. He lay with eyes open and head stuffed and stiff, as though they had put ugali in there, instead of into his stomach.

IV

On the way to school, eight motherless kids passed the Methodist Church, the Catholic Church, the Glory to God Church beside a wall painted with the picture of a chubby boy drinking Milo, his cheeks like two mangoes. (*Who is that boy? He lives in the church! Is he Jesus?*) And on past the Milo-Jesus, past the Viagra Taverna ("Where a Man Can Kill His Thirst"), where cars were stopped and rich men got out with full bellies proudly before them, faces slick from nyama choma dinners, eyes glazed, and their women with swinging hefty buttocks. And on past the market stalls where the kids lingered over a tray of fresh mandazi. No coins to buy fat bread.

Because school, classroom, yes teacher, Bwana, headmaster.

School bell. After school an old man laid out by the side of the road, battered and stiff, got tangled in fast traffic, in bakkies, lorries, Rovers, Land Cruisers, Hilux, Isuzu, rubbish vans. His dried cheeks sucked back into his head as he puffed his last air. Dusty silver coins spilled from his pocket.

—Is he dead?

The kids hovered in ill-fitted school uniforms, boys in short pants, girls in skirts, edging closer until the man blinked open his eyes. He smiled, dreamed he was rescued by angels. Then he noticed Money and the smile faded. No angel, this. And Money saw the eyes of all the dying things he had ever seen. Fish, cat, rat, dog by the river with eyes gone dull and hazy. The eyes of the man rolled, pushed toward death by the disappointment of seeing Money there, and Money shivering, leaving the other kids to dying-man-mandazi coins.

In the morning that old man was gone. Maybe got better, walked away home. Or hauled away to be stuck in the dump or the river, or maybe stolen by animals or collected by the Mungiki, the Hordes. No one knew.

Late for school bell, running, then stopped up wondering, going back to search the place where the old man had lain, again. Back to school, late, lessons begun, turn around and back.

New Matron, her voice cool.

—Missed school and formal education, which you will need as much as anyone. So now appointment with the director.

Then waiting outside the office on the hard chair, feet dangling. Then a voice deep enough to shake walls.

—Come.

The director of the centre sipped his morning tea, his shirt dark in the armpits, his neck creased with fat, his shoulders sloping piles of broken concrete. He looked up and said sit. He put his hand up to forestall Money's words and closed his eyes and drew from the teacup held between a thick thumb and finger. They said the director never slept because he watched over the orphans, Matron and Cook, and the boys of the staff. His eyes were tired. He had a head like a tired bull, with a tired brain to match. His back was as wide as a van, and his legs were quick with a football.

After a long moment the director placed his teacup in its cracked saucer and squinted up.

—Now what? Why not at school where you belong? Must there be the old-style disciplinary steps? Traditional discipline? Like our forefathers?

—Yes, Bwana. But no.

—Yes-Bwana-but-no? Anyway, I understand you well enough, you. The answer to your question is that the old man you saw has returned to his place.

— Dead?

—Of course not dead, you little spider. You think people give up life so easily? Now hie thee back to the classroom. Take this note so you are not beaten to smithereens for your troubles. And, by the way, by the way, wait. Do not let schoolmaster oppress you or your brothers or sisters. And, by the way, by the way, do not associate with the children of Mungiki. You know the ones. If you befriend them, you will end up in their clan. It is the wrong one. If you do that, woe betide you...

Because of an old man, Matron and Director. Because of the Mungiki and their tricks.

CHAPTER 2

Avtar Kestner, MD, PhD
Refugee Camp Number Two, near the Kenya-Sudan Border
April 22, 2016

The High Commission of Canada driver pushed open the door to Dr. Avtar Kestner's room, peeked in, listened to the sound of Kestner's rough breathing, and stepped inside. When Kestner woke up, the driver was hovering over his bed.

—Driver? What in hell time is it?

—Ah, Sah. Good I came to check you. May I say, I'm very pleased to see that you survived. The time in hell is late. Past one, Sah.

—Past one? Swahili time or...

Kestner fumbled for his phone. It was a little after seven. He blinked up at the driver. Although the interior of the room was dim, the driver wore curved, reflective sunglasses.

—What do you mean by 'pleased to see I survived'?

—Yes, Sah. Because of the reasonable grounds for doubt, to be perfectly frank. But now I see it is only because you overslept, not that you expired. A tremendous development, and we can therefore mobilize as we must.

—I don't wish to mobilize this morning.

—Ah, I can see that you suffer. Too, too much spirits consumed! Body dysfunctional, mental disorientation, metabolism, dysmenorrhea, et cetera. Now, let me guess. You are feeling a painful brain, a terrible intestine and whatnot.

—You missed your calling. Dysmenorrhea? Really, but for one or two dubious calls, you could be a physician. We should swap. I drive; you diagnose.

—Ha ha. I think we should not swap. You may know the saying 'Small deeds are great in small man's eyes, and great deeds, in great men's eyes, are small.'

—I'm still dealing with alcohol consumption as a cause of dysmenorrhea in a male.

—Ah, Sah! The line comes from a Muslim poet, very great in Arab literature. Al Dawlah, Sah. I think they do not teach the Muslim poets in Western countries.

—Possibly, probably true. And what might Al Dawlah have in mind?

—He has in mind that you are the great man in the theatre of life and death, yes? And I am the small man, although great or small, these are choices we made, you and I respectively, just like your choice last night to…how to say? Damage your liver with the spirits. Yet, somehow, whatever our choices, we must fulfill our roles and duties and timetables, et cetera. Otherwise, we might arrive late at the airstrip at Lodwar. Then, miss flight, blame driver, retrench driver. They love to blame drivers. But then, this is the role of small men, one might say.

The driver folded his hands, pushed his glasses higher on his nose, and settled himself on the metal chair, as though he had satisfactorily completed an essential task.

Kestner pulled his blanket up to his chin and stared at the water stains on the wall. It was his daily Rorschach test, the figures horrific at that moment. Besides the metal chair and regulation cot, the room contained a rickety wooden worktable and a cramped toilet room. A narrow window, filmed with dust, looked out on rows of tin and plastic and canvas shelters.

—No one in their right mind would stay in the place.

—Yes, Sah! If you were a holiday-maker making an online

review of Refugee Camp Number Two, perhaps you would give it poor rating.

—No more than two stars.

—Ah, Sah, you are generous. Only one star from me.

—'Service is sad, the rooms rustic. Selection of wines is appalling.'

—Yes, Sah. 'Pool hours are not posted…also, no pool.'

—'Luxury suite is a large prison cell.'

—Ha. 'Polo fields are managed by hyenas.' But, in fact, Sah, you know, your room is a very much luxurious compared to the quarters I share with two other drivers. No private toilet as you have. The men share, which makes it very dingy. But why did they send you to prison, Sah?

—Prison? No, they did not.

The driver looked about thoughtfully.

—You know, if this were a Kenyan prison cell it would contain twenty men, several of them in need of medical care. There would be no toilet and no window. That is what prison is like in East Africa, even now.

—So I've heard. Those sunglasses make you look like an insect, did you know that?

—No, Sah. But perhaps this is a hallucination caused by alcohol, Sah. Delirium, delirium what-and-what.

—Delirium dysmenorrhea?

—Ah, Sah, but you laugh.

—Not a bit.

—Or it could be that I am the very insect. Low down, scritch-scratch to survive. Creeping here and there. Although, in truth, insects have an ecological role. You must pay no mind to dark glasses, as such. You see, they help drivers see the road without damaging the parts of the eyes like cornea and retina and sclera. Conjunctiva and rods and cubes and what-what.

The driver bent and plucked Kestner's briefs from where they had been kicked under the bed. He took them up by the finger-tips, folded them, and offered them up to Kestner. He held the briefs in both hands, the palms raised high.

—You must not forget these, Sah.

—For the love of god, Driver. Is this the way you behave with all your clients?

—Ah, yes, Sah. I am happy to say I do not discriminate based on race or sex or sexual preference or disability. Except for women though. And maybe the high officials, of course.

—I was mistaken about you—in fact, you should be an actor. Moonlight on stage, dysmenorrhea diagnoses in clinic by day.

—Sah, you mock and confuse me. What should I do? Physician or actor? Which is better?

—Neither is better. Driver is better, come to think of it.

—Are you about to manifest emesis, Sah? You know, your skin colour this morning is very wrong.

Kestner lurched to the toilet where he looked to close a door or curtain but there was neither, so he dropped onto the toilet anyway. The driver politely turned away while on the shelf opposite the toilet a row of cockroaches leered. Parents and children, extended families, all in miniature sunglasses, attentive and implacably entertained.

The driver looked out the window.

—Sah, are you nervous that the *entire* hospital staff will be awaiting your presentation in fifty-seven-point-five minutes from now? You must be excited to be punctual so we can finish and leave this luxury holiday. After that I promise we will drive at top speed so you can embark on the plane.

—Why don't you go get coffee and breakfast for yourself. You can fuel the car and give it a thorough wash while you're at it. You say the *entire* staff will attend?

—Yes, Doctah. Just so you know, Sah, I did as I thought best, Sah, because of your *indisposition*. This morning I personally woke each member of clinical staff, Sah, and took the time to explain to them the significance of this, the last day of the review of the great and wonderful Refugee Health Program. I went beyond duty, if truth be told. I explained how you might be melancholic and perhaps clinically depressed and in need of clinical psychiatric care if they neglected to attend.

—Now why would you say that?

—Sah, I went further. I mentioned electroconvulsion therapy. Because of the, ah, the *important nature* of your, ah, disappointment, and your last night *excursion*. I believe the mention of electric therapy got their attention though, Sah. They laughed at me, Sah, but they will attend, I am sure.

Dr. Avtar Kestner sat on the toilet listening to his driver, his aching head held gingerly in his hands. At the moment his condition was treatable and certainly diagnosable: the screaming meemies, snakes in the boots, the rajas, the slippery slope. He thought of two new terms: *delirium dysmenorrhea* and *cockroachia galoriens*. A chronic condition since he had discovered that Levigne was gone. The problem now was that he was incapacitated and no longer able to properly function. Impossible to gather information for the review. Impossible to analyze it. Impossible at the moment to formulate even a single preliminary conclusion for the review. For the last four days he had been capable only of drinking away the evening. Interviews he had conducted were full of gaps. The project reports he tried to read were incomprehensible. He had tried nonetheless, in states both drunken and hung over, to produce the presentation he was about to deliver in a few minutes' time.

On the floor of the toilet was a familiar plastic canister of liquid. He looked upon it dully—an old acquaintance who made the walls of his stomach twitch. The canister featured a jaunty label with a badly rendered profile of a chicken, a scribbled expiration date and the words Black Rooster, Proud Product of Sierra

Leone. He did not touch the canister, aware of the family of eyes that watched from the shelf. Instead he located his dependable black work journal by the sink, its pen in place, hooked, as ever, over the open entry.

April 21, 2016, Refugee Camp Number Two. Black Rooster Whisky (?), 250 millilitres, estimated, score: 2/10. The harshest of rides. Reminiscent of being dragged behind a car over a gravel road.

The cockroaches waved their antennae as though to cheer him on.

He did not manifest emesis.

A tepid shower and a rough towel later, he was at a wooden table in a bleak meeting room, his journal laid open beside his laptop. The room, which served as a further patient examination room when required, was sharp with the scent of disinfectant. Outside the window, the clinic intake area and street, temporary housing and tents. Beyond the camp perimeter, a sky laden with the soil of eastern Sudan.

The driver appeared, his dark glasses like little movie screens.

—Yes, Sah. You look better! Now your skin is the regular colour of a living human person. Not quite, but somewhat. Sah, what is the name for this skin tone?

—Hepatic yellow might be right.

—Now is the hour of professionalism, is it not, Sah?

—Yes, you're right.

—The hour to polish and burnish and rise like chaff to the top, yes?

—Cream. Rise like cream.

—Sah?

The wind carried Sudanese grit the colour of old blood. It settled on the tables and chairs, on Kestner's laptop, and on his skin. Tents flapped as though they were stranded, injured birds attempting flight.

He added a note in the margin of his journal.

Parkinsonian tremor. Neurotoxicity? The heebie-jeebies. Myodesopsias, the floating punctuation is a distraction. Not known whether they be periods or merely commas awaiting the next phrase. A question: why would a whisky have an expiration date?

He kept writing, filling the margin. This small logic appealed greatly to him at the moment.

Acute gastritis, precipitated by the fine elixir of West Africa. Although subject to investigation into other etiologic factors such as Seiko Levigne and a week of piripiri sardines and rice. Ten days of Seiko-less whisky cups, unexpectedly and miserably because she is gone and vanished and we have no idea where

A woman entered the room. She was a refugee in the camp, dressed in a tie-dye T-shirt under a faded cotton thawb. The driver fussed about, directing her to set out tea for the meeting. The woman was anemic, her focus wavering, her limbs weighted with lethargy. Sickle cell disease, typhoid, malaria—it was probable that she suffered parasites, malnutrition. She limped, straining to push a wheeled cart carrying foam cups, packets of sugar, sliced white bread, a plate of unnaturally pink jam, and a large steel boiler.

The driver grew impatient. He shot Kestner a complicit grin, shrugged, gave the woman a few small bills, shuttled her out, and set the tea things out himself.

—These refugee people, Sah! How will they live in a modern

economy? Coming to Kenya from wild places where there is no electricity or microchips or search engines. No Facebook, Sah! How will they survive in the modern world? They will try, Sah, then give up hope and fall into despair. Truly, they are the wretched of the Earth.

As he talked, the driver plugged the tea boiler into an extension cord and ran it to an outlet. When he returned, he took a slice of bread, spread the pink jam upon it, and ate it with a frown. The colour of the jam made Kestner think of hematuria.

Out the window, in the new section of the camp, recent arrivals queued for water. A woman tended a cook fire that was buffeted flat by gusts of wind. At the clinic intake gaunt figures with crude slings or on roughly made crutches had formed a line.

—So much human need here. It never stops.

—No, Sah.

—The clinic could run for twenty-four hours a day if they had the staff.

—Yes, Sah. In fact, last night was like the wedding of a politician's daughter. So many new arrivals with their new troubles. Impossible to sleep, thinking of these guests and their medical troubles. The medical team here is too busy. But they will come to your presentation, do not fear. The British. The Dutch and others. The British surgeon likes to talk as he drinks, Sah, much like you. He has a beard that reminds of Karl Marx, and similar way of speaking.

—Similar to Karl Marx?

—He advised me that I must always speak up, to express my opinions, even as a lowly driver.

—Really? Marx said that?

—No, Sah, not Marx. The drunken surgeon, Sah. He said, even if my opinions differ from those of my superiors. He made the case that if people like me did not speak, there will be no justice in East Africa. Although, Sah, I wonder if maybe he is a communist, after all.

Kestner's mind suddenly clicked into place. He started tapping at the keyboard, creating a slide.

—I am not usually thinking of British surgeons as being communists. I suspect they are monarchs.

—Monarchists, you mean?

—And the Chinese who have come to our country. Those Chinese are genuine communists—but they talk very little about it. At least ones I have met.

—They need the Marxian advice of the British surgeon.

—Perhaps.

—What of the Americans?

—No, Sah.

—You must have heard that there were Americans here as well.

—No, Sah. I have not met Americans. I have no opinion of them.

—I was told there were two Yanks who were here just before we arrived. They told everyone they were here to work on the camp computers. Everyone thought they were spies since none of the tech problems were fixed. They left around the time that the project director left. I keep wondering about that.

—I know nothing, Sah. I never met that director. But I only hear that these days in America every someone thinks they are an expert.

—How could no one know where the director went? How could she leave the camp the day before her project review was to start? She left without telling anyone, not even her assistant. It's not like her.

—You are obsessed, I think, Sah. Obsessed with this Project Director Levigne.

—No one knows why she left…

—I would know nothing, Sah. As you know, being a driver is a very low position. No one tells anything. You carry on with your duties like a blind snake.

—Blind snake? Did you say *blind snake*?

—Although, I have heard that women have private reasons. Sometimes they do a surprising thing. Although the caveat, as such, Sah, is I am not a married man. I have heard that women have privacies of which we men should not ask. Sometimes it is the case that the men struggle, Sah. But I heard she is AWOL, which is a term we use in the army. It means absent without—

—Yes, I know what AWOL means.

—No one can say for certain what is in the mind of a woman. They say that Director Levigne was a good leader, that she took an interest in every person she met. That is what I heard.

—She just disappeared. I reported it to her organization. The people there told me it is a private matter.

—Yes, Sah. You have mentioned this too many times.

—I know.

—Especially you talked about her last night when you were, ah, quenching your, ah, spirit, Sah.

—My what?

—We must always be open to the evidence, yes? Madam disappeared so maybe she is not such a good director as they say. Or perhaps Madam Director will one day explain to you an amusing anecdote explaining her absence. But I think she is a special friend to you. Though as driver, it is not really my, ah, affair, is it Sah?

—Where did you say you were educated?

—Makerere University. I studied humanities, Sah. My studies were focused on the human condition, as such, including—

—I hear it's an excellent school. Wild parties in the undergraduate dorms. Black Rooster flowing freely.

—Aha, Black Rooster! Ho, ho. Ah, no, Sah.

The driver lapsed into a brooding silence as he watched the broken figures queuing outside the clinic. After a minute, he cleared his throat.

—But, you know, Sah, even the schoolchildren in this country read the internet about Britain and America and all the countries. They know much. Even the children become cynics, even while in primary. Some of them graduate believing in nothing at all. Others believe in stupid things like computer games and YouTube of cats sitting on toilets.

—You don't approve of the internet. You're leery.

The driver shrugged.

—Well, no, Sah. Not leery, as such. Why would one be leery of technology? But it is desirable for children to begin their lives with proper beliefs. Ah, but Sah, I am distracting you. I am prone to talk too much this morning. More than usually, I'm talking, talking. Like some kind of exhibitionist.

—I think you meant *extrovert*.

—Yes, Sah. Like an American.

—So, you do, in fact, have a thought or two about Americans.

—No, Sah. I never think of those men.

—Who?

—Those men…the American president and vice-president. What and whatnot.

—You're sweating. Are you feverish? Or are you just worried about getting us to Lodwar on time. It's remote country for a driver.

—No, I never worry, Sah. I only plan.

The driver ran to the toilet, clutching his stomach.

Kestner turned his attention to his presentation. The slides he had prepared the evening before dismayed him. One read 'Program director has vanished. We are appalled, confused, disoriented, and depressed.' He deleted that and worked back toward the beginning.

The driver came out of the toilet, his forehead beaded with sweat.

—Nothing, Sah. Call of nature. But a violent and urgent call.

—You've got a long day of driving before you. At least the dispensary is well stocked with Imodium. Diarrhea is one thing that the program seems to have got right. I should write that as a finding, at least.

—Yes, Sah. I am fine, of course.

—Of course.

— Although, if I may say, it is impressive the way these camp doctors and nurses toil. They toil like camels! Like donkeys! They are camel-donkeys serving Kenya and Africa, for the good of the poor and ignorant and ill and war-ravaged. To think they choose to be here instead of modern places. Why? They leave pompous hospitals with grand reputations in prestige places. Kenyatta National, the Aga Khan, Kolkata Ruby General, Amsterdam Medisch Central.

—Pukka hospitals, those.

—Basel University Hospital, Clinical Central Cira Garcia, Chicago Rush Memorial.

—In pukka places.

—Royal Victoria, Karolinska…

—You've kept a list.

—Why do they come, Sah? Families, they leave behind. Friends they leave behind. Important patients left. Good salaries left behind. They come for how long, Sah?

—Depends. Some for a few weeks. Others stay for months or years. Did you say *pompous hospitals?* I like that. I've worked at those.

—But why, I ask? These professionals perform their work with the dirt flying in the wind, the wind blowing into surgery mask, into surgery incision, while the patients die of sadness so far from their home villages. How can they do it? It is a kind of powerful dedication.

—Maybe they have practical reasons. Marriage breakups. They might be escaping personal problems in their homes. There are so many marriage problems, these days. And financial messes. Here they simply work, and, at first, life is straightforward. Wake up, work until exhausted, provide salvation to the most wretched of humanity, crash. At the end of the month, save your pay.

—Yes, Sah. As I thought. Dedication of the highest order. They think of higher things than mere money! One can see this. Even though money is always a thing much needed and much problematic for ordinary men. It is a sower of chaos, truly. The sower of dishonesty, deception, corruption. Such a small thing, this money, yet we all must have it. And always there is not enough.

—True.

—And to think that these dedicated and principled camel-donkeys will arrive here soon, Sah. You must write a very *stirring* review about these dedicated people.

—Yes, yes. Let me concentrate on that for a moment.

—Oh yes, Sah. Don't listen to me. My mind is a distraction. This is what my teachers told me: *his mind is a distraction unto itself.* This is why I am the driver only, not an actor or physician that you suggest. But pole sana, Sah. This morning I talk like a what—an *exhibitionist.*

The queue for the clinic stretched along the wall of the building, winding through the compound into the windy street. A team of Turkish orthopaedic surgeons and physiotherapists and surgical nurses had arrived for a week of dislocations, comminuted fractures, malformations, rickets, osteomyelitis, tumours. Kestner dashed out more slides, paused to watch the growing clinic queue. He went to the side table and poured hot tea into a foam cup, drank it off, poured and drank another with lumps of sugar. The driver stood by singing a muffled song from *My Fair Lady.*

People stop and stare. They don't bother me…

Kestner flipped the pages of his journal, searching for the key points he should make. He continued to be distracted by the writing in the margins. Levigne had collaborated with him on these, the *Purple Whisky Reviews*, as they sat next to each other in planes and cars. He thought of her shy laughter when they were in public places, her mirth careful and private.

The Knot: a calamitous distillation to be imbibed over the course of a week, rather than a single night, preferably commencing on a Friday. Briny, clean, finished with the ash of a blazing ship foundering in an icy gale in the Celtic Sea. A decent 7.5 out of 10 for the Knot. If unavailable, easily replaced with the little heralded and barely distilled Black Rooster, elixir of S.L, best before 2014

He looked balefully at the title slide: Midterm Review of the of the Refugee Health Program, Camp Number Two. *But who was he to review anything?* Thirty-four consulting assignments successfully completed for the Government of Canada. Program design missions, midterm reviews, final evaluations, in places overcrowded or remote, dusty or dank. Efficiencies, poverty, parliamentary oversight, logical framework, babies wasted, mothers bleeding, in countries spread halfway around the globe. There had been no situation similar to this one. And he, the official witness of all this suffering, with his own private suffering, of a liver that spewed metabolites, his breath a cocktail of aromatics, alcohols and aldehydes, esters possibly, ketones evidently. For the next hours he would reek of his excesses, exhaling Black Rooster, speaking Black Rooster, sighing Black Rooster, perfuming the air with the degradation products of Black Rooster.

With a keystroke he deleted everything and began anew. He skipped the technicalities and wrote about the dedication of the medical and support staff. When he looked up a while later, the driver was in the corner texting, his glasses gleaming.

—Ali? Since the schedule's tight, please go ahead—pack up

the car. We'll hit the road right after the meeting. We shall have to make it a short presentation.

—Who, Sah?

—We. The team.

The driver looked at him then went out, head raised, his spine stiff.

A minute later the clinical staff began to arrive. They flopped into chairs, exhausted. Sharma the pediatrician, Larsen the technologist, Rose the scrub nurse, Kamau the infectious disease specialist, Bernier the internist, Unwin the drunken surgeon, Ramirez the Cuban anesthesiologist, the Romanian head nurse whom everyone only ever addressed as Head Nurse. The incoming Turkish staff had been spared, apparently.

As they arrived, Kestner wrote: *commitment and bravery... challenging international situation...monumental medical contribution...*

David Mason-Tremblay, the Canadian government man on Kestner's team, came into the room on the balls of his feet, his skin glowing, as though he had woken early, swum laps, worked out in a gym, and had a massage. He approached Kestner as he surveyed the clinical staff in attendance.

—Doctor, good doctor Kestner, you survived the night!

—Whatever do you mean? Good morning to you too.

—I'm amazed to see you in functional form after that. How are you?

—I was overtired last night, that's all. My apologies if I wasn't very good company.

—I can't drink like that. I would die. What was that horrendous stuff?

—You didn't drink that, did you?

—I didn't. Remember? I stuck to beer. My guru advises abstinence, which is impossible in this job. Abstaining would kill me quicker than anything. But, as a good Canadian bureaucrat, I compromise. So one beer while doing yoga, a second as a reward. Where's that Mihret, our wonderful gender adviser? I hope she's not upset after last night.

Mason-Tremblay went off to seat himself in the front row, wearing a bemused smile.

Kestner dashed out four slides in quick succession. He suppressed panic or bile (he was not sure which) as he glanced up now and again at the filling room. He stopped writing when the team gender adviser appeared in the doorway. Mihret Gebriel, though she only ever went by her first name, never failed to attract attention. She lingered at the doorway to better inspect those in the room. Once satisfied, she glided forward to a chair at the other end of the room from Mason-Tremblay. She dusted the chair with a white handkerchief before sitting. She directed a breezy smile at Kestner and Mason-Tremblay as her habesha kameez settled about her like a cloud. Mihret turned and exchanged warm greetings with a trio of nurses who sat behind her. It was as though they were old friends.

Kestner had only a vague memory of Mihret coming to his room the night before. He began to write once more.

The condition of the refugees at this camp is well documented in the Feasibility and Inception Reports and elsewhere: the refugees in these camps are traumatized, malnourished, injured, exhausted, and ill. Highly dedicated health care is a major foundation of their return to normal life.

Junior clinical staff crowded in — interns on health studies placements with NGOs, students, junior nurses. They settled onto gritty plastic chairs, queued for tea, giggled, celebrated the minor respite from the pressures of the clinic. A few attended to their phones: messages from distant homes in distant countries. Families, lovers, ex-this-or-thats. Beyond the window the refugees squatted, grouped according to tribe: tall Nuers and Dinkas, and others who sat separately. They were prepared to wait for hours or days. There was nowhere else to go, villages and fields and animals abandoned to the invading men with their boots and guns. A tall Nuer woman had one child by her side and another on her back. In her arms she carried a third: a tiny head with huge eyes poked out from a goatskin sheath. The faint bleat of the baby was drowned by the rattle of the wind in the roof.

The Refugee Health Program is essential to the safety and well-being of a high-needs regional population. In general, international support for the Refugee Health Program is commendable. The attention of the international community attests to the importance from humanitarian, political and security perspectives...

At 0900 hours, international time, Dr. Avtar Kestner, Review Team Lead, presented the Summary Findings of the Midterm Review of the Refugee Health Program, Refugee Camp Number Two, Turkana County, Republic of Kenya. He opened with a proverb that he thought was from the Turkana people.

Only a medicine man gets rich by sleeping.

He did not try to explain its meaning since he was not certain of it. Two hours later the review team rolled out through the camp gates onto the dirt road that gave onto Route A1. The driver pointed the Government of Canada Range Rover down the middle of a highway that was empty but for the kites and vultures that soared on the updrafts. To the north were dry ravines and stunted acacia trees, in hues of rust and tan and black. In the distance, hazy ridges. An old woman appeared by the road. She raised a solemn salute, her hand devoid of fingers, her knuckles a mass of gleaming scar tissue.

II

An hour later the Range Rover came to a stop in front of large, white-painted stones arrayed across the newly paved highway. A drippy arrow on a piece of plywood pointed to a diversion. The driver searched the empty road ahead. He got down, took out a tool bag and disappeared under the car. He came back to the driver's seat, mopped his head with a towel, wiped his dark glasses and put them on. The road was deserted.

—Unfortunately, we have a diversion, Sah.

—I don't see the reason for the diversion, do you, Driver?

—Ah, no, Sah. But I can say, there are many reasons for diversions, not all of them apparent.

Mihret leaned forward.

—Are you quite all right? You look unwell. Should someone else take the wheel?

The driver straightened up.

—No, madam. That would be against regulations. I am perfectly fit to drive. It is my profession.

Mihret turned to Kestner.

—I cannot miss the flight. I am anxious about my schedule in Nairobi.

Kestner searched down the empty highway.

—Driver, why not drive around the stones? If we run into anyone, we'll explain that we're on government business and need to catch a plane.

—Ah, no, Sah.

—I beg your pardon, Driver?

—I said, no, Sah. I cannot because of regulations, standard operating procedures, or SOPs, as we know them. The SOPs oblige us to adhere to all government advisories. This is for insurance purposes and mitigation of risk. If there is the possibility of hazard, then we must do as advised by the officials. There may be jambazi—the bandits. There may be military operations with live ammunition. So many government things happen in these remote areas, Sah. Then the government must implement the shut-ment of the road. Unfortunately, we are not always privy to the wherefores and whys. We simply accept, that the authorities have deemed this stretch closed. We must heed, Sah.

—The signs don't look very official. Can you call someone to verify?

—Ah, no, Sah. This is the typical way the government shuts the road. We must follow the diversion, as indicated.

The driver took off his glasses. Sweat poured in rivulets down his face. His eyes were yellowy. Suddenly he dropped his hands, his eyes rolled back, his head pitched forward on his chest, and he slithered sideways in his seatbelt, unconscious. The passengers gaped. Mason-Tremblay said, —Did he just have a stroke?

Kestner lay the driver out flat on the seat. He examined him briefly.

—Malaria. It's the not the first time.

Mihret wet the driver's towel from a water bottle and dabbed at the driver's face as Kestner went to his luggage and found chloroquine tablets. He and Mason-Tremblay eased the driver onto the ground, laying him out in the shade of the wheel of the vehicle. He stirred but kept his eyes closed. After a moment he croaked out a few words.

—Schizonts, Sah. Schizonts are uprising today.

He held out his hands for the chloroquine tablets, washed the pills back with a mouthful of water and lay back, panting in the wavering air. After fifteen minutes he struggled to his feet, put his glasses back on, shook himself, and returned to the driver's seat.

—The schizonts are capable of destroying human schedules, Sah. They are wasters, those ones.

He put the car in gear. It dropped from the pavement onto the diversion marked out by periodic splashes of white paint. The diversion ran parallel to the road for several hundred metres then turned sharply northeast, away from the highway, along a ridge. The splashes of white paint gradually vanished yet the driver confidently followed a faint track over sand, rock, and scrub, down the bank of a sandy riverbed, up the opposite side, into a narrow defile between two stony caputs, over a pan of rock that looked to have been poured there.

When they stopped again, Route A1 was an hour behind them. Warning indicators lit the dashboard, the engine rumbled. The driver let the Range Rover roll down a last grade into a dell. He switched off the ignition and sat for a long moment, swallowing air as the others looked on.

—Now what, Driver?

The driver pushed up his glasses.

—It seems a further mishap. I will investigate, surely, but the indicators say the engine has failed. This is a very bad mishap. We are not lucky.

—How could the engine fail? It's a new car. Where the hell are we?

—Turkana County, Sah. Kenya, Sah. In a misfortunate place, Sah. Who can say where misfortune strikes. Misfortune is beyond the human mind to know, is it not? Although I dare say that places of misfortune are more abundant in my native country than in Canada. Who knows why this is so? Perhaps there is correlation between misfortunate incidents and high temperatures found in equatorial countries. It seems that this idea might bear scrutiny.

Mihret leaned forward from the back.

—Take some water, Driver, so you don't have another seizure. Let us wait. We should let the engine settle. Perhaps the car requires a moment to correct.

—No, madam. Engine will not settle because it is finished. One only must look at the indicator. One only must sniff the air. This smell is the smell of engine failure. It is burned steel, an indicator of misfortune.

—What about our flight?

—Sometimes flights are missed. Who knows when misfortune causes flight to be missed? 'Deep in a man sits fast his fate.' Only the higher-ups, like Allah and maybe others like Hindu and Jewish and Buddha, only God can influence, and then, only if you happen to believe in them. Ha, ha. So many people do not believe!

— Please, Driver, this is not the time for this...

—Yes, madam. But think of it. Such is this strange life! Here we are provided with the best expensive vehicle, with every technological equipment. Software, hardware of excellent top-European quality, as such. One hundred thousand US dollars for this machine. More in Canadian! This amount is a gold mine in my country. It is virtually a gold mine rolling on wheels. Automatic everything including air con, premier stereo music, electronically adjusted suspension—

Kestner broke in.

— Ali. Please. Never mind all that. Let's see if there's anything we can fix. If not then we need to put in a call for assistance, that's all.

The driver paused for a moment. A stream of sweat ran along his brow onto his glasses.

—But who is this Ali you keep mentioning, Sah? Do I know him? Is he a friend of yours?

—What do you mean?

—Sah, I am not Ali. I am Salim.

—

—Salim Mohammed, in fact.

—Salim! Yes of course, of course, you're Salim. I know you're Salim. Pole sana, Salim. I was distracted.

—Yes, Sah. My name has always been Salim, Sah, through-out this entire mission and from the day I was ushered into the world. I have never been Ali, although I do have a fondness for that name, as such. But I do not know any driver named Ali in the High Commission carpool, although there are certainly many Alis about in Africa and the Mideast. But there is perhaps one driver named Ali who works for the Swedish, now that I think of it...

Salim mopped his face. His voice was shaky.

—In fact, Salim Mohammed is the same name as my uncle, and it is because of that man that I came to be named. Although in truth I never met that uncle because he passed from this world at a young and promising age. They say he would have become a politician. But who really knows what will become of a man? We start out young with much hope and promise, then encounter stumblings in our path, stumblings placed before us as though someone above is wishing to test our quality. 'As if predestination overruled.' So wrote Milton.

— Milton Friedman?

—Truly astonishing it is, Sah, that you and I have known each other for more than ten years. Twelve assignments, I believe. It is a long time, no? I am always the same Salim Mohammed every time. Your driver and your assistant and, I might venture, your friend.

—Yes, friends.

—But our friendship is unequal. You do the important and expensive work in the grand theatre of life and death, whereas I drive where I am ordered. But as Allah is my witness, I am Salim, not Ali, Sah. You must recall that time, that bar that was full of sex workers, and you were so drunk...

Mihret broke in with a firm voice.

—Driver, I implore you. Everything will be fine if we remain calm. It is time that you turn your mind to your duties.

He took a deep breath and looked out the window.

—Yes, missus. Of course.

Kestner stared at his watch.

—Salim, please accept my apologies. I'm very distracted these days. You might have noticed. So many strange things have happened.

—No, Sah. I did notice. Especially last night when you were so very corrupted by alcohol.

—Aside from that, please accept my apologies. We all have challenges from time to time. One sometimes gets under the weather.

—Challenges. Under the weather. Yes, Sah, I understand very well. These are very fine words. Yes, Sah, and the absence of your, ah, *associate*, Madam Director. Perhaps you yourself have a health challenge, like a medical disorder. Although it is you who are the diagnostician, Sah, not me. I am merely the driver, small in endeavour, weak in thought. Perhaps you have early dementia or some-such. My grandmother had this. She always called us children little fuckahs, in the end, instead of by our names. At least you did not call me a little fuckah, Sah.

—How long before we can drive again? How far are we from Lodwar?

—...or a brain tumour or some-such.

—What?

Kestner stared intently at his watch. It was a Rolex, a blatant little slur against the international development goal of poverty reduction and health equity. Somehow, with his immense personal wealth, he had not been attentive to this when he acquired it. Only later did he guiltily cover it with his sleeve in the presence of his host country counterparts. He should have bought a cheap knock-off. At that moment he was also acutely aware of the abdominal sensations that had assailed him of late, his Little Doubts, he called them. Inflammations or growths or parasites or their larvae, jitter-dancing in his viscera. Today they attended what felt like the region of his pancreas, as though they were autonomous, crouching in corners, listening to the unfolding of the misfortunes of the outside world before activating. This day they had chosen pancreas.

Salim, however, was not finished.

—Only the Almighty knows how long we may survive in good health. Suddenly, disorders like brain tumours and dementia arise. Or other problems. Myriad problems, many of them difficult to diagnose—like this vehicle. A machine only, yet so many things could be wrong. Mechanical or chemical or electronic. I think these things are not designed with the Turkana heat in mind. Some EU engineer designs them, I think, in a cool office in Europe. Maybe a rich but unhappy EU engineer with soft and clean skin and expensive spectacles...

—Maybe it's something simple like the fuel line, said Mason-Tremblay.

—Let us call for assistance. It is times like this when one calls for support.

—No cell service on mine.

—Nor mine.

—...but impossible for this EU engineer to imagine this place where conditions are so irregularly hot and rough. Turkana. In fact, a rough and temperamental place where forgiveness and mercy are strangers. Filled with hard animals and hard people with unpleasant teeth.

— The satellite phone. Use that.

—A tough land filled with tough things. Unforeseen things. As if it were a different planet. So then EU car gets a malfunction and a disorder. Like brain cancer, Sah. Like heart disease. Malaria, Sah. Schizonts uprising. Intracranial pressure. ICP.

Salim sweated and stared out the window as he went on, unable to stop.

—Oh yes, it could be the fuel line. Or even the fuel itself. Or fuel filter. Or fuel injector. Or ignition. In fact, as to your suggestion, clearing the fuel line in the field is an excellent and logical possibility, if that is what you are thinking. But it is also in direct contravention of the SOP because of the high risk of fuel spill and unanticipated ignition and explosion and fire and possible grievous and life-altering burn injuries. Like, for example, skin grafts. Liability and disfigurement, loss of social and professional status. Then the matter of insurance. I am wondering, does not one require hospitalization for brain tumour? The satellite phone is not functioning. I tried.

III

Kestner jumped out of the car. He stood panting in the heat for a moment, then began to walk back along the diversion route. After three more steps he stopped. The air was like fire in his airways. He squatted to avoid fainting. The ground was volcanic there, shot through with glittering crystals. He realized it was the remnant of an ancient caldera.

Mason-Tremblay came out of the car with a container of sun lotion that he proceeded to smear on his skin. He glanced at Kestner.

—That was weird. Are we supposed to repair the car ourselves? What are you looking at?

—Nothing. Just rocks. Nothing.

—You're into geology? What about car engines?

—I haven't looked under the hood of a car in years. I think that one was a '65 Chevy Impala with a V8. Anyway, I never got it to start, I seem to recall. After I looked at it, it caught fire.

—A '65? That was way before I was born.

—That's right. I suppose it was.

—If a person's heart skips a beat or two, should they worry about it?

—I don't know what's wrong with that driver.

—What if it skips a beat or two for five minutes and then it just stops?

—What?

—The heart, the heart.

Kestner looked at him, and Mason-Tremblay bent over and plucked at the crystals embedded in the earth.

—We're going to miss our flight, you know.

—Looks that way. I've known that driver for years and never noticed anything peculiar about him. Something must have happened.

—All those years. All that time you had his name wrong?

The caldera was enclosed by a ring of grey basalt. Beyond the rim, the expanse of riven land stretched away toward mountains to the northeast. To the west were twisted lines of low trees where water had coursed during the rainy season. The two men stood and strolled up the grade slowly, over patches of sand and rock. They stopped to examine the curvaceous track of a side-winding snake. Predator pursued creature, devoured it, left a scat. Along came snake. Mason-Tremblay scuffed at the furrow made by the snake.

—I almost refused this posting because of snakes.

—Was there a snake experience in your past?

—No. The whole point is to not have the snake experience. If I have the snake experience, it's too late, isn't it?

—Don't worry. They stay under cover during the day, to avoid the heat. Although in Nairobi you might encounter one or two at diplomatic functions.

—Diplomatic functions. Ha.

Mason-Tremblay peeled off his shirt and flapped it in the air to dry it. Kestner looked at the younger man's pale torso. He refrained from comment, even as his mind robotically proceeded to review the main points of the pathobiology of skin cancer, which became intermingled with the problems of decompensating liver, erratic driver, broken car, lost, late, missed flight. He thought of ionizing radiation, light skin, cell membranes darkening with oxidation, reactive erythema and inflammation, mutagenesis, resistance, failure, dysplasia, neoplasia, disfigurement, surgery, chemotherapy. In fact, he preferred not to be assailed by processes of disease. Lately he wished more than anything to escape the graphic confirmation of humans as neglected gardens that dumbly await inevitable failures. In his briefcase he carried paracetamol, doxycycline and ciprofloxacin, Imodium, ibuprofen, oral rehydration salts, chloroquine, tincture of iodine, ASA, suture, and cutting needle.

He turned away from Mason-Tremblay's skin and searched across the empty terrain. The sun had dipped toward the horizon, turning the western reaches into an inferno. Mason-Tremblay flapped his shirt in the air and laughed.

—They said, 'David! Field missions, field missions! The best and most wonderful, satisfying part of the job!' They said, 'David, you will love it! Real development work, meet local people, learn the local culture and language, see the real beneficiaries of aid!' They were right. I love it. Here we are in the middle of nowhere. What could be better than this?

—The first time in the field can be difficult. Give it a chance.

—No, I mean it. I love it. I loved the cute kids in the refugee camp, the clinic, the fun people. Even now, this situation. It's one of those real bona-fide African adventures.

— I'll be sure to tell Anton Kuric what a tiger you are. Now put your damn shirt on before you burn.

In the distance a small group of stick figures moved over the terrain. The group moved erratically northward, then southward, then stopped, then resumed a meandering course, as though inebriated or lost or confused. Mason-Tremblay snorted.

—Whoever they are, they're nuts.

The two men turned back to the Range Rover, which now cooled in the shadow of the rim. Salim had not moved from the driver's seat. Mihret rested in the seat behind him, her eyes closed. When Salim saw the men returning, he tried the engine again. The engine belched a cloud of smoke and died.

—Sah, I am quite sure another vehicle will come.

The driver took out the satellite phone. He pressed buttons, then tossed it back in its compartment and remained stonily quiet.

Along the diversion track came a band of ragged children and a starved, mangy dog. The eldest of the five children looked to be ten years old while the youngest was the size of a three-year-old. They were half starved, their skin roughened by scabies. The smallest one, who trailed the others, preferred to hop from one foot to the other. One child wore oversized track pants bunched around his waist, tied with a of strip of hide, but the others wore no pants at all beneath torn T-shirts with logos. Higher State. Budweiser. Nike. Sun Holidays. The children paused when they saw the travellers. They moved cautiously to the lowest spot in the dell and began to dig lethargically, assisted by the dog. When the effort failed to produce water, they made a circumspect arc around the strangers and whistled discordant notes. The dog panted behind, its tongue lolling out.

Mihret spoke to them in Swahili. They replied with three blank stares and a shy smile. They moved to the long shadow cast by the Range Rover where they commenced a game of stick and rock. In the game, stick hit rock or rock hit rock, and this was the only sound in the dell for a while until the dog pounced on the stick and ran away with it, ending the game. The players flopped to the ground.

Kestner looked at them. *Ascites, kwashiorkor, parasites, stunting.*

The shadows deepened in the dell. The air cooled. Mihret sat in the open door of the car while Mason-Tremblay perched atop a large rock.

As the last daylight faded, Salim walked to the rim of the dell. When he returned, he announced that there were vehicle lights on the diversion road. A minute later a clanking and ancient urine-coloured Mercedes lorry with a snub-nosed front end hove into view and stopped in the dell. The windows of the cab were high and narrow, the back end framed and covered in heavy canvas that beat the air like a slackened mainsail. A slogan was printed across the upper windscreen in large, partly degraded letters: IN GOD WE TRIST.

Salim climbed up to the cab window and spoke to the driver, then came down. The lorry driver dropped to the ground behind Salim.

—These kind people have agreed to take us onward. Room for everyone and everything. We must only get into the lorry, be patient about our missed flight, our missed appointments et cetera, et cetera, and whatever happens we must take calm and measured breaths. No cause for any worry.

Salim set about transferring the luggage while the Review Team looked at the lorry and its driver, who was, at that moment, scuffing the ground as he circled the stricken Range Rover. What they could see was a man half in shadow, his face constructed of asymmetrical angles and dents, as though of beaten metal rather than flesh. He thrust his hands in his pockets and chewed.

—Touring in Turkana County, Kenya. How nice! But now, bad luck followed by good luck for you, yah? Good luck, bad luck, good luck, one after the other.

—What do you mean?

—I mean, good luck is drive about in expensive luxury vehicle. Made in foreign land by foreign hands! Brought to Kenya by ship! Bad bad luck is luxury foreign vehicle breaks because not so luxury Turkana County. But then? Good luck come again. Old very un-luxury Mercedes ten-tonne to rescue, 1960 model, very tough, very un-luxury. This is the typical luck for adventurers who wander from the city in East Africa. Here in Turkana the tourists from rich countries suffer because of no conveniences, yah? Microwave, call centre, lottery, ski tow, Fed-Ex, takeaway Chinese noodle, bank machine— where are they?

He grinned at them, kicked the tire of the Range Rover, peered inside.

From the window of the cab of the lorry came a hesitant voice.

—So from what you say, these people, they had good luck, then bad, then good. So, it must mean, again, bad luck should come next?

Everyone peered up at the window, which was dark. The man on the ground spat.

—Never mind that noise. That is the Somali, my partner. Pole sana. My apologies. It is what they call co-dependent relationship. You know it? Very common here, between people. Even between nations. Like Kenya coming to the aid of Somalia as part of African Union obligation. Although, sometimes, we are forced to use discipline. They are like children, the Somalis. You will see.

When Salim had finished transferring the luggage, he opened a compartment at the back of the Range Rover and pulled out meal packets and drinks. He paused to watch the children as they squatted on the ground before him. He handed the eldest child a wrapped sandwich, which was accepted and carefully examined, the plastic wrapping stroked and poked. Salim took it out of the child's hand and ripped the plastic away and handed over the sandwich. He removed the plastic paper of the other food packets of sandwiches and pieces of chicken and samosas. He popped open bottles of soda and handed them out as he glanced up at his passengers.

—Ravenous jackals, these ones. My faith instructs that it is our duty to bless the hungry children with our food. That way we might be forgiven for our errors.

—I hope your errors were not so very bad.

—We all make errors, is it not so? Moral mistakes, madam. It is human nature. It is why there is religion.

The driver of the lorry stood listening in the background. A moment later he reached over, plucked up a sandwich, stuffed it whole into his mouth. The man chewed messily, took a bottle from a child, swigged, took another sandwich, and ate that too. He looked at Salim, gulped at the soda, wiped his mouth with his hand.

—Ah yah. Hungry always beat morals.

He laughed.

—They say when you feed a starving man, his hunger grows.

When the starving man eat, he can become a danger because he might go greedy, not want to stop. Anyway, these little desert mice, they can eat anything, by the way, by the way. Food, food packages, all. Then rubber tires. Then vehicle, engine, all. They can even eat the one who fed them.

The driver finished his soda, belched, and handed the empty bottle to Salim.

—Ah, pole sana, Bwana. Pole about bad manners. Maybe because I spend too much time on the rough roads of our nation.

—Never mind. Hakuna matata.

—Yes, never mind, Bwana. I have complications. The road is too rough. Too many rough things to see on these roads. It is worse than internet, worse than YouTube, Al Jazeera, *New York Times*, Twitter feed, Google. So difficult for humble man to have nice manners. Pole! Come, people, we can go on in peace, make the journey together. Welcome people of foreign nations. Karibu in Kenya! Plenty of space for you in back of double cab. No problem. It is not the luxury of new Range Rover, but we can move from place to place, over every land, every desert, no problem.

The Review Team and the government driver climbed the steps to the high door of the cab. The back of the cab had a wooden bench covered in a sheet that featured drawings of camels. In the driver's seat sat the Somali. He averted his face and said not a word.

The lorry rumbled out of the caldera, through a gap that led to a cracked riverbed and east.

IV

The passengers fell asleep where they sat, even as they were tossed gently about on the bench amid a clangour of steel and the roar of the old engine.

When Kestner awoke later, he listened groggily to the drivers.

—You know nothing, Somali. Nothing! About stars, about diesel fuel gauge, nothing. About people, nothing. Wewe ni kitu.

—Not here!

—Yes here.

The lorry had come to a stop. The passengers stirred awake to the cab doors opened on a nightscape of moon-shadowed terrain. Cool air flowed through the cab. The moon was sharply lit, the edges serrated, hanging perilously over the desert. The only movement in this scene was of the slow mastication of the lorry drivers, who stood below staring up at the passengers.

At that moment the passengers experienced fleeting premonitions. There was a strange familiarity, or perhaps an expectation of the unfolding of a plot. This plot did not include a flight to Nairobi, a frosty glass of beer, a hot meal, a calming shot of Glenmorangie, a bath, clean sheets. Nearby, an insect clicked thrice then stopped.

Mason-Tremblay's voice was dry.

—Why are we stopped? What's going on?

—What is going on? A good question! Nothing is going on. This is nothing. We are nothing. You will forget about us. One day you will forget you met two men of average nothing with no remarkable anything. Two nameless nothing men...

A wisp of a cloud drifted across the face of the moon. The passengers noticed a combat weapon, an AK-47.

—Get down. Time to talk. Time to plan. It is not often that we have chance to plan.

Mihret and Kestner and Mason-Tremblay climbed down to the rock slab on which the lorry had stopped. Kestner finally said, —Okay. Maybe you should tell us the plan.

—Good idea. Best not to waste time on formalities, introductions, preambles. We should work together for the next days. Like a family.

—Work together with you?

—With us, of course. Who else?

—Work together on what?

—Economic matters. Economic projects.

—What projects?

—In fact, you are the project. Easy for you to work on it since you *are* it.

Kestner had an overwhelming urge to run at that moment. He did not. Instead he laid two fingers on his wrist and counted his pulse. The pulse was erratic, his heart readying itself to run.

Mason-Tremblay spoke up, his voice plaintive.

—Is this a joke?

—Ah, no. Does it seem a joke?

—We're government officials. Did you know that? We come here as friends to your country.

—Good. Very good. Everybody need friends.

—I play golf with the minister of foreign affairs. I've had dinner with the minister of defence. You might want to think about that. Sana matata. Salim, explain to them who we are and who we know.

Salim was only now, slowly making his way down from the cab.

The gun bearer said, —When I listen to your voice it makes me very tired. I feel like I worked all day with no food.

—You have no idea who we are.

—Maybe now you should shut up so I do not fall asleep. By the way, by the way, your voice is tiring, like listening to a poor woman complaining in the market about the cost of food. Your voice—it lacks imagination.

—The police will search for us. The army. Governments. Do you understand?

—I think it is you who do not understand.

The gunman laughed. His laughter went on longer than was natural or plausible, and it worried the passengers. He handed the gun to his companion and went to the back of the lorry.

—I cannot listen to this zuzu mlami.

The other driver, now holding the AK-47, stepped forward. He pointed the gun at Mason-Tremblay.

—Myself, I am Hassan. You are as of now the prisoners of Hassan of the Islam Front.

The other man yelled from the darkness, —Islam-IC Front, dwanzi!

—Islam-IC, yes. He is right. Islam-IC Front and he is—

The voice in the dark came back.

—I am none of their business. They can think of me as a nothing person of vast wealth and vast violence. And they can note that superficialities are notwithstanding.

—He is so much wealthy they called his name as Money.

Money stormed back and hissed at Hassan. —Why did you say that? Was it a good idea? Did you think before you said?

—I did think. Where I am from, honest people use their honest name. But maybe...of course not, no.

—Try to use that rock we will generously call your brain. As for you people, you are, as this genius says, political prisoners, although you previously thought of yourselves as government officials. Now you will understand the complicated life in Africa, where one minute you are one thing, the next minute you are forced to be something else. Sometimes high, sometimes low. One minute government official, next minute prisoner. Fortunes change. As of this moment you should think of yourself as dollars, euros, shillings—cash value. Maybe one, maybe one-point-five million, depending on market forces. Maybe you are like me, worth only a coin or two but not more than that, because no one wants to pay, so no market, no demand. Modern principles of modern economics.

The prisoners were quiet.

—I will say this one time so everyone understands it well: I have many reasons to use violence. You hear me? Violence is my special friend. But to you, it might be a hazard. So be clever and do as instructed, and you might be fortunate and avoid violence. If everything goes well, everyone will be fine, you will go back to your homes. Maybe one day it will be a good adventure story you can tell your family. If you understand then you can show it by giving your name and country and handing over your personal documents, identification pap-*eh* and so on...

—We won't cooperate.

—Oh no? So boring. You make me want nap. How about this? How about you crawl home from here without toes on your foot, with trail of blood for the ants to drink.

—All right, all right. Take it easy. No violence. David Mason-Tremblay, Canadian government.

—Ah, so much better. David Boring-*Tremblaar*? Truly better. Such a young and average intelligent mlami who weeps like a lonely woman. Let me see. You were first-class student in expensive school. Your teachers would praise you, saying, 'Oh, that Boring-Tremblaar, so smart and good.' Except even your teachers knew you were boring. So, my estimate is one and half million US dollars for Boring-Tremblaar? Sold. Now, next one. You, lady.

—Mihret. Ethiopian. I work for the UN. My father's name was Gebriel.

—Your father? Father is not here, is he?

—He passed away.

—Oh. So sorry. All fathers pass away and leave orphans behind. Very terrible and tragic. Since he is dead, I will call you Ethiopian Sheba. Good, yah? Know what, Sheba? Only one and one-half thousand US dollars on open market for you. Sold! But I hurt your feelings? Why so little? Because UN don't care about you, and Ethiopian government don't care about you. And by the way, Ethiopian Sheba, just so you know, when revolution comes, all the princesses from Ethiopia and France and America and Kenya and everywhere will become slaves, and all the sex sellers will be the new rulers. Is it fine with you?

— And what? Do you think your words shock me?

—Ai. She is tough! Tougher and braver than Boring-Tremblaar! Must be a princess from Ethiopia Highlands. Now you, mister.

—Avtar Kestner. Canada.

—Kes-*neh*, Kes-*nah*. Canada. Canadian doctor, yes? See, I know. But when I look at you I am confused. You do not seem like Canada. What kind of Canada looks like Mahindu-Bollywood-Japon-Pilipeen what-what and what. What in hell? Oh, wait. I know. Man met woman. Mishap occur. What is it they say? Mash-up! Out come mash-up. Mash-up goes become doctor.

—Delightful.

—Sad fact. Canadian government only pay half, quarter for the mash-up. See, what they do is this: pay a little bit Japon yen, some Chinese renminbi-what, bit of rupee, dollars, pesos and what-what, and what. All your life you thought being mix-and-mash-up is fine, except now it comes to how much of chedaz they pay for your life. You did not know because nobody said it out loud. They pretend. But now you know! And next one, you.

—Salim. Driver service only. Kenyan only.

—Driver service only. Kenyan only. Belly-to-fill only. Hyena bait only. Now all of you except Kenyan only, give over your pap-*ehs* and so on.

—And cash and money cards.

—Yes. And cash-*eh* and, like Somali say.

—And devices, like iPhone, Blackberry, Nokia, Toshiba.

—Yes, yes, yes. Comput-*eh* and food-*eh*.

—Apple, Dell, Microsoft, Samsung.

—Please shut up, Somali. All of you remember this: violence, the thing you hate, that is my best friend, better and more reliable than this noisy Somali.

Money collected the passports, wallets, laptops, papers and stashed everything roughly in a nylon duffle bag while Hassan hastily bound the hands of the captives with frayed twine. He herded them back into the cab. Money climbed up after them with the AK-47 poised. He put his back to the windscreen to face them with his gun casually against his leg while Hassan took the wheel.

They drove on as the dawn sun boiled onto the horizon. Mihret loosened the twine on her wrists and shook it away. She let the bindings drop to the floor, looked at Money with a flat expression. He smirked back at her like a penniless man inspecting the expensive offerings in the market.

—Ethiopian Sheba. Ha.

Mihret arranged her shawl so that her hair was concealed, then sat up straight to absorb the pitching of the thing labelled IN GOD WE TRIST. Next to her Mason-Tremblay slumped dejected against the stanchion. On her other side was Kestner, then Salim. The lorry wallowed up the side of a dune of soft sand, along the crest, and down again, lumbering into shadows.

Wedged against the door, Kestner preferred not to look too carefully at the gun and averted his face from the muzzle. He had doubts, particular Little Doubts, he wished to divert or suppress: elevated blood pressure, minor dysrhythmias, unresolved significant relationship, failure as husband and father, arterial walls ragged and fat-streaked, sexually and prostatically compromised, he was quite sure. And the liver, the liver, the liver—he visualized a lumpish bump, a messy, fibrotic, rubberized mass, decompensated from repeated toxic assaults. He dwelled for a long time on the matter of liver.

Four degrees, including an MD and a PhD. What made him what he was? What made a man into a consultant commanding three hundred thousand a year? A mind brimming with the inconsequential: abstracts of the reports of important medical scientists, bureaucrats whose names he should forget but instead remembered; the sum of learned expressions taken from anonymous policy and research papers; shards of the biographies of persons he had noted or knew; a torrent of discombobulated concepts, frozen-in-place concepts, anatomical structures from cell to system; processes, functions, and dysfunctions locked in from repeated examinations for which he must prepare and excel. And more: summary updates on the proceedings of the major UN bodies, and announcements of conferences in a dozen or so health disciplines. Yet the memories of his estranged family, fading residues only.

This was the sum of Dr. Avtar Kestner's analysis, his intelligence of the moment.

What did he know of the tides and winds that created criminality? Twenty years and twenty-five or more different countries in five continents, programming public health for the multilateral and bilateral agencies—the World Bank, the WHO, the donor governments—programming for millions of people of countless ethnicities, tribes, languages. MD, PhD, mentor, teacher, professor. Yet here he was, ultimately valued at the price of a Range Rover.

CHAPTER 3
Money Manyu
Turkana County, Kenya
April 22, 2016

One thousand now. Nine thousand and maybe more than that later. Along came an opportunity with the added possibility of control, and an acceleration of time and chance. But from the beginning it was too easy. Anything that was too easy made Money nervous.

It might be a matter of the particular batch of qat they were chewing through. Perhaps that batch was collected from a mountainside where lightning had struck or by a road where a motor had spilled oil. It could be that he and Hassan unknowingly chewed, jaw by poisonous jaw, *qat stupidity, qat thrill*. It could be that they were in a qat world in which they only thought they had control of events. A man could chew themselves into believing anything about himself.

Nothing was ever easy. If it was easy, something was wrong.

He was irked by the presence of the extra man, this driver. How had no one explained that this prick of a driver would remain with them? The job was to bring the three: two foreign men, one Ethiopian woman. Why was the driver not mentioned? Why did the driver not get out of the way, instead climbing aboard like an uninvited monkey? Who was he? Someone called Salim, a stupid monkey who did not know when to come and when to leave. It made a complication. How should they treat this monkey? Was he worth something? Was he paid for his part? *Two thousand now...*

Money plunged the vehicle down a grade into the black maw of the Turkana night, fighting the wheel. He squinted at the faint splash of light formed by the headlights. He had insisted on taking his turn driving, but he was not good, the machine ancient and ungainly. It fought him like a belligerent mule. The wheels pulled one way or the other, the lorry wandering into places he did not wish it to go. The transmission cursed at him and resisted his control. For all that it was a robust beast, overcoming the rough terrain, the heart roaring without fail, and the tortured gearbox singing. He sweated, fought the lorry while trying to appear calm and normal so that Hassan, this Somali, would not notice. After a while it became obvious that Hassan pretended not to notice. To make this yet more annoying, when Money finally yielded the driver's seat to Hassan, the Somali yawned and deftly drove as though he had done so every day of his life, looking far more relaxed behind the controls than he did as a passenger forced to endure the jerking and pitching as Money fought with the machine.

Money preferred to watch over the passengers with the gun in his hands. He was alert, his fingers were alert; there was satisfaction that now *he* was the director and CEO. It would be appropriate, he reflected, for the others to hail him as Bwana or Sir.

As the bearer of the gun he was free to scrutinize the captives and examine them, learn about them. This was how he had gotten on during his life, by observing people and learning them, the rich, the foreigner, the mark. This was his skill. Watch carefully, learn the weak places so that when the time came, he was efficient and the result was good. Most of all he needed to know if and when others might resist. At some point everyone resisted, then one must be prepared to do what was necessary.

He was ready for that. Violence when necessary. He had learned that lesson.

As he sat with the gun, his back to the windscreen, he gave in to the temptation to stare unabashedly at the woman with her enormous eyes and carven jawline and unblemished white garment. It was a weakness, he knew that. So unmarked was this woman. So proud. Her skin and her garment glowed, even in the darkest hours, as if she were created to keep men from ever sleeping. Only on the internet had he seen a woman like this. He had suspected that the internet women were not real. Yet here was one: Ethiopian internet mosquito princess, put on Earth to sting men and leave them scratching.

As he looked at her, a bitter taste arose. She would never allow herself to be sullied by low people and their dirty plots. In other circumstances she would not even notice a person like him. Ah, but now she had been forced to notice low and crooked Money, had she not? For a moment he fantasized that he was one of his own captives, so that he might rescue her from himself, perhaps to bestow simple blessings upon him.

Yet it was too late to be dreaming of princesses. Money laughed bitterly at himself. His only wife would be hunger. That wife owned him the way a big mama owns her skinny husband, and she would belabour him whenever she had the chance.

How many men had lost themselves chasing a pretty face and a smooth belly? Yet here he was, a man with the gun, a man who knew about violence, and here was a beautiful woman. He had other sensations when he thought of it this way, then the struggle between his higher and lower parts ensued, until the higher beat a hasty retreat and he was uncomfortably ruled, which he well knew would lead to pain and ruination, and he would go from pleasant dream to poison to rage. If only he might talk to her privately, that she might know him better. He closed his eyes, then opened them and forced himself to avert his gaze. He looked at Hassan.

Hassan, Hassan. This Somali was another problem, a pesty, annoying thorn in the foot. The way the Somali nursed the controls, talking, coaxing the vehicle. How could the Somali see so well through the darkness to find the right direction and best path forward among the ridges and riverbeds? Money had long ago lost his sense of place and direction, yet Hassan drove on with only the cascade of stars to guide him.

They swept forward into a dirty blanket of a night. As Money looked out over the dark land, he was convinced that modern civilization was at an end. In this post-civilization world, the lights had gone black, the villages were taken over by flies. There was no sanctuary for human beings in this world, no home for the weary. Home was only a story for believing children.

II

Back in those days, a journalist from the *Daily Nation* appeared in the lane outside the Man U Healthy Child Centre. He did not enter the place but rather took a long time to move up and down the lane, collecting himself, his throat burning in the acrid smoke that drifted in from the dumpsite. He was young and clean, with a neat shirt and pressed jeans that attracted the attention of the Man U staff. The staff were young men who might claim to be youth workers but were actually touts whose job it was to protect the lanes and the neighbourhood. They were known in the streets as the Man U Gang. They were in a state of war with the powerful and roving Mungiki. So when the journalist appeared, the staff surrounded him, their thumbs stuck in baggy trousers slung low on their hips, their T-shirts torn and disreputable, cigarettes dangling, one hand concealed so that anyone would assume a blade of one sort or another. The journalist had been in the streets before and recognized the look of gang boys everywhere in Kenya, and everywhere on the planet. He took out his pad and pen and prepared himself to interview. Just then the director of the orphanage, the man he wanted to see, came along with a face as tense as Nairobi traffic.

—You there. Hanging about wanting something. Do you seek trouble or are you in trouble already, like most of the young people hereabout? Because either way you will be assisted by these social workers. And by the way, by the way, they are always happy to oblige.

—Ah, no. No need for social work. But, yes, perhaps in trouble already—sent to request an interview. With the director of the Man U Healthy Child Centre. We have reports of this wonderful community institution. Is it you?

The director's smile shifted slightly.

—Wonder community institution. Ah, who requests such interview, by the way?

—*Daily Nation*, Kenya's most widely read journal.

—Ah, *Daily Nation*. Yes, I read it to know which nation we are in, day to day. Is it Kenya today, or some other?

Bwana Director smiled and his face slackened, as though he were nothing other than a humble and expansive bestower of community childcare. He posed for a photograph with his teeth stuck forward, his lips well-shaped. Then he proceeded to seat the journalist on the step, surrounded by everyone, and provide, for the record, the tale of the Man U Healthy Child Centre.

The story the director told was this: the Man U Healthy Child Centre began as a clinic built by the British during a cholera outbreak. After the epidemic settled down, the British departed, leaving behind a skeleton staff of a manager, a medical assistant, and a housekeeper. These three went on with the work, educating the community about cholera, about the hazards of doing their business in the river or in plastic bags to be tossed anywhere. They worked on *latrinization*, trying to convince families to construct tiny outhouses when the families lacked enough money for daily food. Most people laughed at that. Then the HIV epidemic rolled in, and the parents began to die, leaving children behind. The medic went away. Only the manager and the housekeeper stayed on, converting the clinic to an orphanage, pleading for support from local community organizations and from Muslim masjids and Christian churches and Hindu mundirs.

—And what of the rumours that there are criminal gangs associated with this orphanage? Is there truth to that?

—Rumours. Shabby rumours.

—What does it mean to live in one of Kenya's most impoverished communities and to be one of Kenya's poor, living in Dandora?

The director gave a great bark of laughter.

—We? We are not *the* Poor. In fact, *we* are the wealthy, endowed with strength and liberty, and, by the way, blessed with a wealth of opportunity.

He took the journalist by the arm and pointed across the river, at the smoke and the mountainous heap that was the dump, with its dim figures scrabbling like beetles on a corpse.

—Those. *Those* are the Poor.

The newspaper article appeared in the *Daily Nation* alongside a photo of the director standing outside the Man U Healthy Child Centre. The headline read: Man U Healthy Child Centre: Orphanage or Gang Headquarters?

The director was enraged. He stalked into his office and closed and locked the door behind him. When he emerged two hours later, he announced changes. The Man U staff would never again be referred to as a gang. It was thence forth a business, an economic entity. A corporation, in fact. And he, the director, should be referred to as the CEO.

One of the staff giggled and said, —Sawa, Mr. President.

The director looked about at the staff and gave no reply. He returned to his office. His door clicked shut.

III

Hassan eased them to a stop without a word. It was midnight. The Somali climbed down and walked away to mind his private business, leaving Money to watch over the prisoners. They peered at him in the dark.

—You, Ethiopian UN woman. Get down so we can talk privately. Everyone else remain seated. Just her. We have UN business to discuss.

Money waited for the men to voice an objection. He peered through the dark at them. He had learned enough about them to understand that if there was resistance, it would be weak. He waited for Kestner to speak, and Kestner finally cleared his throat.

—If you harm her, you will pay dearly. You will wish you had not.

Money clicked back the safety of the bolt-action gun. Kestner said nothing more. The woman shifted in her clean garment. She spoke slowly, as if speaking to a dull child.

—Why must I speak to privately?

—Because I say, that is why.

—Are you sure that this is the right thing to do?

—Call me Bwana from now. Only that. Do as I say at all times. If I say talk, you talk. If I say sing, you sing. Just so that you understand clearly: if I decide to kill you in this Turkanaland place, no one will know. Look around. Where are we? Like we are in the middle of the ocean, under the water. No civilization, no police, no authority. You have no one to help you. You have nothing.

—Nonetheless, I ask you this question. Are you sure this is the right correct course of action?

—Correct course of—

He choked off his sentence because he had not foreseen the

princess becoming a schoolmistress. She was too calm. It was as if were her clean garment to be soiled, the soiling was anticipated. She would deal with it, clean away the stain. She would wipe her tears. She would go on. Now she gathered her garment about her and opened the door and stepped down the ladder without faltering. Money followed her. On the ground he nudged her before him, away from the cab toward the back of the lorry and then past that so that they were alone in the scrubby bush. Above them the sky was laden with bright riches, and before him was the unspoiled garment. He put the gun aside and stepped close to her so that she filled his senses. Her scent was warmed by the most delicate anxiety, of light sweat on perfumed skin. When he looked at her face the dense column of stars in the middle of the sky, the Avenue of Ismail's Sheep, surged brighter, like a gigantic and observant divider between right and wrong. If there was a God, this column of stars would be it, present, towering, an unblinking witness.

The woman was not afraid. Her breathing was regular, the whites of her eyes barely showing. Her eyes remained on him but it was calm observation, more than a prey animal's fear of the predator.

—You don't know a man like me. Why do you think you do?

—Of course, you are right. I do not know you.

—People like you so easily pass judgment. You love to judge.

—People like who? Normal people make judgments. So what?

—You know nothing about me. You don't know how my thoughts go, where they come from. If you see me smile, you don't know if it's really a smile. It might be something else. How would you know? If you see my fury, you don't know that either.

—Perhaps you are not so full of mysteries as you think. But I can tell you this about myself: I am not a child, and I am not a plaything for you or any man.

—Why are you not afraid?

—Of you?

—Look all around. We are alone. In this place I am president. I am secretary-general. No one can interfere. I am the president and I am nothing. Any action I take is meaningless, you understand? I lose nothing.

—Yes. It depends on the kind of man you are, doesn't it? We are what we are. Sometimes the product of our families, sometimes of environment. So, your mother and father, your predecessors—these people are behind you, even if they are no longer alive. Whatever deeds you do come from them.

—My mother and father! You know what, Ethiopia lady? A woman like you can drive a peaceful man to violence. A woman who talks like Solomon and acts like a princess. A rich and wise Ethiopian woman living in Nairobi.

But Mihret refused to be afraid. Her eyes reflected the light of the column of stars that seemed to keep growing in brightness. She was looking at him, not as though he were a kind or gentle man, nor as a threat, but only as though he were another flawed man whom she must placate. She could be a mother or auntie or matron or sister.

Money took up the old gun, and turned to find Hassan, the Somali, standing silently, two metres behind him. Hassan spoke to the woman and not to Money. He chose his words carefully, his voice quiet.

—Please, madam. Come back to the vehicle. We have a great distance to travel this night.

Mihret followed Hassan back to the cab. As they climbed the steps to the cab door, Money heard the Somali say other soft words to her. He could not hear what Hassan said, but it sounded like an apology.

Money swallowed everything—his own blood, his heat, his ideas—slung his weapon, and cursed the star-strewn heavens. He had only wanted to talk to her privately, after all.

IV

The director—the CEO—brought in the new girl. Everyone said her home was in the street, but no one was sure what this meant. They overheard Matron say it to the director.

—But Bwana, she is a street girl...

On the day the street girl arrived, she hung around near the CEO's office, ready to fight the other kids. When no one challenged her, she came and went as she pleased, day or night. She preferred to sleep out on the open veranda. Matron told her she must sleep in a bed, like a proper girl, or else she would be made to leave the place, to either find her way back to her people or to her demise in the street, it was up to her. The girl cursed at Matron and stalked away a short distance, then she turned, sat in the shadow of a wall and put her head between her knees. After a time she came back and made a crushed, wordless sound that made Matron give her another chance.

In the morning the girl was curled up on the stuffed chair that was set to the side of the room where the children slept on mattresses. She stayed that way, deep in an exhausted sleep, oblivious to the movements and voices that bustled around her and the sunlight that slanted through the doorway. Her long eyes and smooth brown skin made Money stop as he passed by. He was suddenly flustered and looked about to be sure no one noticed. He went on his way, but his feet hesitated, and his eyes helped themselves to her again, and his face burned as though he were ill. He was supposed to be somewhere. At school or missing school. It would have been better if she were an ugly or skinny or damaged girl with scabies and bumpy skin, but she was not. She smelled like a fragrant weed by the riverbank. There was no sickness or injury on her, no sick worry that creased her face.

Money prodded her, not too gently, with his toe. Her eyes opened and looked at his foot. His voice came out in an unintended hiss.

—Go somewhere else, girl. No room for another kid. No beds. No food.

He shook himself and went out into the lane so that he would not have to look at her any more. He was furious and confused, all the while fighting burning eyes and heated brain. His legs were jittery. It felt as though a lump of dried ugali had lodged in his throat. No appetite, but that was normal. He could not sit in one place, so jumpy was he, so he scuffed his sandaled feet down the lane to the river which, at that moment, stank worse than a corpse, as though it were a river of dead things rather than a river of water. He stayed at the riverbank looking at the flowing water, smelling the stink, until the end of the day when he took a meandering course back up to the road, to the school. The schoolmaster squinted at him and looked for a piece of chalk to throw, so he turned and ran until he reached the market, then back to the river to sit in the mortal stink again.

Hours later, when he returned she was there, primly sitting outside at the corner of the house, watching the children play. He walked near her, wanting her to see him ignoring her, went inside then came back again, but she was gone. She returned hours later in the night. He smelled her come in. He heard her speak to someone, a child, chiding it as though she had had that right.

Troubled, he lay himself down late, in the adult hours, wishing for sleep, even as his eyes insisted on watching out for her. It was a strange feeling, perhaps a kind of anger or hate or violence; he did not know. His brain smouldered and heated blood surged back and forth inside him.

In the flickers of light that strayed into the house, he watched her form as she found a place to rest. He crept over to the corner where she lay.

—Why you don't listen? Why you don't go away? I told you: no room here for another kid. House is full. I will tell Director to send you back to your place.

She made a muted sound in her throat that made his chest ache. He did not want this shame that ached his chest and burned in his head.

—Are you a baby to make that wet noise? Did you know where you have come? Do you know? We are Man U. *Wealth of opportunities*. A business organization. Not a home for lost girls.

She said nothing, the whites of her eyes gleaming. He went back and lay in his place.

In the morning, she was gone, although he was sure his eyes had been on her the entire night. He went out to steal mangoes that day; it was mango season, the shapely red and orange ones awaiting in crates near the stalls of the vendors. He succeeded in one mango. When he returned for a greedy second, the fat son of a fruit vendor snagged him and pummelled him to the ground.

That night when the girl returned, empty tins and bottles occupied the place where she had slept so that when she put her hand out things tipped over and rolled and crashed. Something sharp nicked at her bare legs. She growled and went straight to Money's bed.

—Are you the one who did this?

—I told you. Go back or you will be sent back. This place does not want you.

—What place to be *sent back*? What place? There is no *sending back place*. No place needs a girl like me.

She stood over him breathing hard. He watched the shape of her eyes, the way they changed as she spoke. Abruptly, she shoved him aside, dove into his bed beside him, and wrapped her arms tightly around his chest.

—Now what will you do, big man? So big and strong and rough. Man U big man.

Money fought to free himself. He grunted with the effort, struggled with everything he had. It was not enough. He squirmed and puffed and kicked, but she would not let go. He caught his breath and silently fought and kicked to escape the hot fragrant torso pressed against his back. Her arms were tireless, like thick ropes.

Suddenly he was finished. Exhaustion overcame him as suddenly as if he had tripped and fallen into a deep spot in the river. He went straight to down to sleep. In the morning, when he woke, the girl was still warm against his back, her breath against his cheek.

She did not speak to him when she woke but went off, out of the house, to return late in the evening. When she returned, she searched out Money in the dark room, to pounce on him, snake her long arms around him, crush him into submission. He could not object too loudly. If he complained, he would be humiliated, perhaps beaten, hung by his feet, mocked before the director. *A girl beats you each night?* He fought, less and less convincingly, and afterward slept, muscle-weary and dreamless. He slept through a loud dispute among the Staff, through a raid in which something or someone was stolen away by enemies. He slept through storms, an election riot, and through the raging of the CEO. Matron came by and noticed how he and the girl slept. She only shook her head and giggled.

The director came and handed the new girl a tilapia fish he had bought in the market. He said, —Aketch, my dear, go to kitchen and make it for my meal.

She prepared the dish carefully with herbs and onions. After that she prepared the same meal for the director once a week, bringing it to his office. He made her sit by him while he ate the fish and drank a cold bottle of beer. Afterward she emerged with the empty plate and a look of satisfaction on her face.

The long rains came, and cold winds clattered the zinc roof. Aketch returned late one night with a dripping little boy tucked under her arm. She shucked off his wet clothes, dried him and stuffed him in the bed beside Money. She dried herself and stuffed herself in as well. She told Money, —Watch over this lost puppy if you know what's good for you. He's called Richard, do you hear? And he is your new puppy, a gift from the generous citizens of Kenya.

Money stared at her in the dark, his eyes burning. He would rather not see the boy who lay sobbing and knuckling back his tears. Money turned his back and stared into the dark. Part of him wished the Mungiki would come and put Aketch in her place. They would know what to do. He knotted his gut hard against the urge to comfort this Richard. The harder he knotted, the smaller the urge.

By morning the new boy was asleep as though he belonged there, as though this were his own home. Money inspected him. The boy Richard seemed to be nothing, really. A round head attached to a neck, smooth brown limbs attached to a torso. In the days that followed, as the new boy fled from his tormentors, Money noticed that Richard's legs were not only smooth, but they functioned far better than his own. They swept that boy along, the legs making graceful arcs as he fled the other boys. Money noticed saw that this Richard was like an expensive little Mercedes-Benz car rolling along the downward part of the road. His hair was fine and loosely curled so that Matron could not restrain herself from touching his head and petting him. Richard was a high-quality item, made with great care. He did not belong in the great wealth and imperfection of the Healthy Child Centre. Even his sounds were well made, as he wept into the night for someone called *Moo-ah, Moo-ah*. Pleasant and handsome sounds that Money was often forced to stop by putting his hand over Richard's mouth or around his throat, patiently explaining that if the handsome sounds did not stop the Mungiki would hear him and come and snip his pecker with scissors. Later, when Money found Richard whimpering alone at the river, beaten and muddied by the older children, he was forced to cuff Richard's head until he came to his senses and took Money's hand to be led back to the Man U Centre for dinner.

For a time Money slept with two others, the three curled in a ball during the rains, the girl's ropey arms squeezing Money against Richard to meld them into one so that Money would have to care for Richard forever. Money saw her plan though. Sometimes he was one of the tormentors by day, sleeping companion by night. Then Aketch would grow impatient and torment Money in turn. Then, at other times, Money held Richard in his arms to stop him from weeping, telling him not to worry because someday he, Money, would be Bwana Director and CEO, and Richard would have all the milk and sweets and gifts and new shoes a child could want.

At times, the problem was heat and bad air. On one such evening, the Man U Centre became intolerable, crowded with children screaming for various reasons. Some screamed, others wept. The air was thick with the smells of diapers, sweat, and old food. Aketch led them away, to try their luck in the lanes. She showed Money and Richard a gap under a wall into the Viagra Disco Bar. They crawled in under the tables and watched overheated beer drinkers and the television that played English football, American comedy, Italian game shows, Indian song and dance, until an hour later Richard fell asleep on the legs of an adult, at which point they were thrown out.

They sat by the road, counting the traffic going in each direction, making marks and comparing observations.

—If more go down than up, then we win. We get mandazi.

—Yes, but if more up than down?

—Then no mandazi. Hungry.

After a time they were ready to give up trying to escape their discomforts. They went down to the river where Mungiki kids were fishing. Everyone forgot the warnings of matrons and guardians and siblings and parents, and fished together like brothers and sisters. They trapped a swimming thing that was so deformed it made everyone silent as they pulled it out of the water. They made a fire, roasted and devoured it, one bite each.

—Maybe it was a fish. Maybe something else.

—Maybe it was the last fish in this river. Because of pollutions.

—It is special medicine. Everyone who ate it is the same, like a family.

Everyone agreed. They agreed on a special salute to signify their sameness, then solemnly went their separate ways, back to their various problems. Bullied, sick, worried, lonely. Aketch said they lived in the Sick and Worried Child Centre, and special dark medicine would do nothing to change that.

Money and Richard crawled into bed, and Aketch sat up telling them stories that night. She told the story of how she took car rides into the city, and this was full of danger. But she knew how to fight and how to run, and she knew the better areas of town where she could get food and coins from well-dressed foreigners.

—I will save my coins until we have enough to buy a farm. We will keep animals there: vervets, crocodiles, cows and chickens, goats. And a baby zebra for Richard to ride.

PART TWO

IMPERFECTIONS IN THE MARKET

CHAPTER 4
David Mason-Tremblay, Global Affairs Canada
Turkana District
April 23, 2016

On the floor of the cab David Mason-Tremblay found a pink workbook, a pencil, and a pink plastic piece that he determined was a hair clip. The cover of the workbook was titled *Masomo Exercise Book*. *Zawadi Odhiambo* was written in pencil in the place for the owner's name. He flipped through it. The first two pages had sums, a drawing of a bird, a teacher's red corrections. The remainder of the pages were unused. It appeared that Zawadi Odhiambho had started school, then soon lost her exercise book in the back of the lorry. Mason-Tremblay wondered whether she finished her school year and what became of her afterward.

The sky to the west was ripe with crushed apricots. Mason-Tremblay said, —We will pay you well if you would just take us to Lodwar. More profitable for you if you negotiate with us, right? You have my word. On behalf of the Government of Canada. On behalf of Queen Whatever. On behalf of the United Fucking Nations.

Money looked at him. He gave a flat and short laugh. He pointed a finger and cocked his thumb.

—You think I am stupid. You probably think all Kenyans are stupid.

—I never said that. No.

—Ha. Sometimes even I think all Kenyans are stupid. But hard for us to self-evaluate, yes? Someone cannot say of themselves,

'I am stupid, I am genius.' If you are stupid, you think you know things that you do not. If you are stupid, you have poor judgment. On the other hand, if you are genius, you think you might know or might not know, but as a genius you also think about the uncertainty of what you know, right?

—I was just pointing out that there are better options for you. Easier options.

—Or you can be stupid because you make assumptions and do not think that maybe your assumptions are wrong. Where did you get this book? It is a schoolbook. Give it to me.

Mason-Tremblay handed over the exercise book. Money flipped through the pages and handed it back.

—Who is this Zawadi? How do you know her?

—How the hell should I know her?

—Why you have her exercise book?

—I found it. She must have lost it.

—You don't return the lost possessions to their proper owners?

—Of course I would if I knew how to find her. Maybe I will return it if you let us go.

—Ha. So clever. You white people, always talking about maybe this, maybe that. Maybe People, that is what you are. How about this maybe. Maybe you like to walk instead of ride. Maybe you walk through wild animals and heat and sand. Maybe without those nice shoes you wear. Look at them. What is the meaning of such shoes? What kind of style is it for a man?

Mason-Tremblay looked at his feet.

—Walking shoes.

—Walking shoes?

Mason-Tremblay shrugged.

—They were on sale.

—Ah. You saved money! But you never thought that the shoes you wear send a certain message?

—What?

—Different shoes mean different things, yah? Your shoes send a message. Like your shoes here send message like, *maybe* 'I am a not very cool dude.' Or 'I am not good at husband because I have no sex style.' Or 'I am incapable so do not hire me.'

—I'm not married.

—Of course not. If you had a wife, *maybe* she would run away with another dude with more shoe sense. For the reason of sex.

—Where are you taking us?

—You are like an old person. Always worried. No wife, no girlfriend. Why worry? No one to miss you.

—We'll double whatever you're being paid.

—Ah. But you know. Girlfriends, they know about shoes. And hair.

Money chuckled. He fished out dark glasses and Mason-Tremblay's phone, which he held up.

—Tell me something. How do they make these things?

—I'm a international development manager, not a tech person.

—When I see things like this, I want to know how they function.

—Phone waves. They shoot out waves and then the satellites pick up the signal—something like that. Microchips and code and silicon. I'm the wrong person to ask about science and tech.

—Are you not educated? College, university? Expensive tuition, maybe thousands, paid by Mama-Papa.

—They were very insistent on higher education.

—How much they pay to see you again?

—They're middle-class people. They're not rich.

—Middle-class Canadian? Let us see. Summer house, winter house, two car, two toilet. Middle-class son must win diplomas, degrees, baccalaureate, doctorate.

—It was expected.

—Mama-Papa work hard their whole life, yes? Earned every dollar! Now rich!

—As a matter of fact.

—As a matter of fact, then, *maybe* they will pay, yes?

—They're old. Retired.

—Old and retired and rich Canadians! They will pay. How about you call them, then I talk to them, friendly-like. Explain things.

—I'm sure they would enjoy that.

—On mobile satellite phone.

—It's dead.

—Ah, and you cannot fix because you did not learn tech. All those Mama-Papa dollars for university, and now you cannot phone them. Very sad. Maybe you know some other useful thing for East Africa, like sanitation economics or mine construction or agriculture?

Mason-Tremblay cast a look of appeal at the others. Kestner stared fixedly out the window at the bleak landscape. Mihret glanced at him and looked away.

—*Maybe* you just go in university so you can say you know things. But really you learn nothing important. Like about poor and rich. About death.

—I can't at the moment think of what I learned, especially with a gun pointed at me. You're right.

—Gun is not pointed, okay? How about this: maybe this thing that happened to you, this being abducted by jihad people, maybe this is the first real lesson you have in your life. Imagine that! African poor man teaching Canadian rich man. Tuition is free, you pay nothing. Maybe you can even take notes in Zawadi's book. You can write how you met the Poors, and all they think about is death jihad and death gangs and death weapons and death diseases like brain worms and brain fevers. You can write how babies come out of the *sufferers* all the time, and they keep coming, next baby, and another baby. Hungry sick babies with no mama, no papa. Baby who need a name, food, school uniform, book, and pen. So the Poors keep getting more and more desperate, all the time.

Money stopped, suddenly furious, his eyes popping. He barked at Hassan, Hassan hit the brakes hard, and they stopped. Money loomed over them with his gun.

—Best lesson of all is next. We will do *economic experiment.* See, poor sufferers, all they do is walk, walk all the time. But the rich? Do they walk? Do they even remember how? Do they know about natural dirt and foot holes and stones and shit and snakes and biting things?

He switched to Swahili without pause, addressing Hassan. Hassan was upset. He got down, walked around the lorry muttering, then came back and got behind the wheel.

Money waved the gun at the captives.

—Experiment is on. Get down. Let the economic scientist see if you can walk.

The prisoners did not move until Money released the safety, aimed out the window, and squeezed the trigger. At the sound of the gun discharging, the passengers scrambled out the doors and stood attentively on the ground. Money climbed down behind them. He directed them to the back of the lorry. At the tailgate he hoisted himself and sat with legs dangling, the barrel of the gun glinting in his hands. He banged the floor with the gun stock, and the lorry lurched forward in low gear. The walking experiment was begun. Above the roar and grind of the motor and gears they heard Money talking into the velvet night, giving his lesson.

—All you people, you talk all the time about human right, human wrong, but you know nothing about human anything, because if you did you would know that humans are hungry bellies who all want the same thing: to be rich so they can stop worry about empty belly. Now you are thinking, *I am better than this hungry Money and his internet economic idea...* Who is poor, who is rich? Who is prisoner, who is entrepreneur? We all follow economic rules. Supply and demand. Free market, open bidding, free flow of goods. Rule of supply and demand means people make demand for things like food and water, school, clothes, shoes, place to sleep, blanket for rainy season. Then when they have these things, what happens? They demand more! Like bicycle, fancy dress, metal roof. Then more things like car, phone, house, holiday, furniture. Everything they see, they demand. Now along comes entrepreneur! He sits and thinks how he can use this greedy demand to be rich. But economics is one thing, East Africa is another different thing. Sometimes the economics is more like no latrines or water pipe that goes through communities that have no water supply of their own. Then, the Poors, they get thirsty, take a hammer, break into the water supply. Sometimes they steal. Sometimes join Mungiki. Other economic rules and equations happen. Law of Violence. If capitalists fail to recognize those laws, if they fail to kill and steal, they gain nothing. If I went in the USA, I would fit in there. Entrepreneur, risky capitalist, captain of industry. One day I will go. I will get rich. By the way, by the way, you must not tell them my past, if you go to that country. If you do, the violence will find you.

The captives walked for a long and dreary time, and they were unable to reply for the fumes and dry air, and they were no longer able to hear the voice because of the concentration required to keep from falling over.

CHAPTER 5
Avtar Kestner, Consultant and Field Team Lead
Turkana District
April 24, 2016

As field lead, Kestner had been briefed about Turkana. It was a turbulent part of Kenya, the nearby civil war in Sudan having displaced Turkana herders eastward from their traditional grounds. In the dry Sahel lands west and north of Lake Turkana, the Turkanas clashed with other groups: the Daasanach, the Omos, the Pokots. The various sides acquired arms, raided and counter-raided, stealing and losing cattle from each other. The Kenyan Defence Force saw fit to drop barrel bombs from transport planes as a pacification measure.

As he plodded along behind the lorry, stumbling through holes and rocks, Kestner peered into the dark lands around. There was no light nor any sign of human settlement, the land apparently devoid of people.

‖

An article in a Canadian newspaper had referred to him once as "Dr. Avtar Kestner, expert on East African health care." It had made him wince then, and he winced again to recall it. Around that time he was introduced in a CBC interview as a "seasoned government adviser with great expertise on developing nations." He had resisted the impulse to send a corrective note. He had resisted telling them that he was simply a provider of services, an expensive hack, liked by agencies and government because he did what he was asked without ruffling feathers. Great expertise in doing what was necessary to keep getting paid. Great expertise in the many forms of scholarship. Lectures, conferences, seminars, research, teaching sessions, talk, talk, and more endless talk. Thousands of words congealing and vanishing and not in any way related to simple matters like surviving abduction, or keeping feet in motion across a trackless wasteland at the point of a gun wielded by a furious and deranged product of developing twenty-first-century economies.

The great expert, adviser to governments. Great and rapidly tiring former physician, frustrated Romeo, piteous Lothario. Aging stumbler in the night. Great expertise in solitude, whisky, dissolution. The great expert, his expensive assumptions sullied and dispelled by the simple reality of a pointed gun.

Great. Expertise. He scoffed aloud, and Mihret glanced at him through the darkness.

The ground sloped upward, and they climbed forward on crystalline stuff that crunched underfoot like sugar.

Kestner's legs flagged. His feet were blistered and swollen. Yet what were these but trivial and superficial conditions of the moment, decorations of the profound condition: mortal anxiety, regret? The Dance of the Little Doubts.

III

Please confirm security status and qualifications of Dr. Seiko Levigne, program director...

Fifteen months after he last saw her, he sat in his rented room in Dhaka, Bangladesh, and keyed out the words of this short and, he imagined, devastating message and sat staring at his screen long enough to finish one large serving of whisky. (To be specific: Carew's Yellow Label Malted Whisky, product of Bangladesh.

A stone-in-the-boot drink. 5/10, with a bonus point for the enjoyable paradox of a product distilled and bottled in a Sunni Muslim nation.) He stared at the words he had written and fortified himself before hitting send. As soon as the message was gone, regret. It was not in any way part of his official reporting; his monitoring contract had ended months before. Driven to it, he told himself, an irksome and undeniable sense of professionalism.

The response from his director came immediately across the time zones:

All okay, status checked. Care to elaborate????

No. Indeed not. No further elaboration. Move ahead, onward and forward. The next job and the next one after that. Other countries, other contracts, desk managers, directors, analysts, consultants of all breeds and ages. The government in Ottawa fell, and a new one came to power. His missions continued as though they were independent functions out of reach of the political changes.

If anyone were to ask, he had, at least, a record that showed that Dr. Avtar Kestner had flagged an error and a flaw: Seiko Levigne, professional fraud. Seiko Levigne, if that was her name, *liar*.

Immediately afterward he had an overwhelming desire not only to have his message back but also to have Seiko Levigne back. There was more to her than this. She wished him to discover her secret. But he had failed to do so.

Or was this the simple lonely projection of a lonely man?

A few days later he was presented with the contract for Refugee Camp Number Two and the opportunity for redemption. The contract had clear terms of reference: lead an independent evaluation of the Refugee Health Program at Refugee Camp Number Two, western Kenya. The donors, five governments and three UN agencies, were legally required to have independent parties carry out performance audits. But Kestner took the contract for his own reason. Then Levigne vanished, and the reason vanished.

In Turkana, in the small hours, he willed himself to keep walking, one step at a time. In the darkness, in the exhaustion, he lost track of time. There were moments when he thought he was dreaming. The lorry stopped. They heard Money's voice, explaining things like a reasonable man.

—In the dark, in the night, in the desert, walking. If your people saw you now, they might not know you. They would say, 'Who are those people and why are they walking like that?' They would say, 'But this is wrong way round, because look who is walking and who is riding and holding gun.'

Money laughed.

—Wrong way round! They would deny that it was this way. 'Why is that African man holding that gun?' They would reject the holder of the gun—'Ah, that is a lie, that could not be! What is that thing with a gun? Is that a man or something else?' They would deny that Money exists. Even Kenyan officials would deny that Money is real, that he exists. They would say, 'That gun holder, that Money, he is not entered in our ledgers so therefore he is an unofficial someone.' Unofficial, Unrecorded, Unregistered. Unofficial Man doing Unofficial Things in Unofficial Economy. Unofficial People, all my type. Like economic side accident. Like someone made mistake, spilled coffee. Something went wrong. But what? A human life that was not meant to be. A life that is not correct. No one wants to know about it. Unofficial People, they come and mess the economic equation. No one knows how many Unofficials are around, because no one wants to count a thing they don't like to see. Meanwhile, Unofficial People, the Poors, they keep sexing and populating and crowding up the place with Unofficial Hungry and Unofficial Shit with Unofficial Smell, all over Dandora and all over Kenya and all across Africa and other poor places. There they are, invisible lies and illusions, in real blood and flesh, a real thing, big inconvenience. What happen when you let Unofficial Man loose in the world? He might get a chance, then what happen? Worst economic thief of all time come. Arms trade, drug cartel, sex trade. American Dream. Free enterprise dream, business entrepreneur dream. Big thief dream for Unofficial Man. If I was American I would go all the way to be CEO, maybe with a gun and drugs to help me succeed.

Money banged on the floor with the gun, and the lorry started rolling. They marched up a grade while Money sank back into the shadows with his legs stretched out in front of him.

Kestner walked, one step followed by the next. Walkers at the behest of the Unofficial People. Surrounded on all sides by dim presences, by clouds of diesel smoke.

If violence were to befall the UN official or the government man, it would be he, Kestner, to blame. By the memo of understanding, he was responsible for the security of his team. It hardly mattered who did what. Incidents like this happened in remote places, to people he did not know, unfortunate fools without the faintest idea. It happened. It might be considered a data point on the spectrum of human behaviour. As he walked Kestner went back trying to remember the outcomes of abductions. Imminent rescue. Mishap leading to injury or worse. Torture. Months in captivity. *Years* in captivity. Captivity with medical care or without. In a cellar. In a hut. A tent. A hole in the ground. A tunnel. In the open desert. Handed off from place to place and group to group, the captors criminal, military, religious, violent, mad. All of the above.

Kestner peered through the murk at his young colleagues. They had relied on him to keep them safe. He wondered about the woman, Mihret, who seemed to float, the material of her diaphanous gown luminescent. She glided along without effort, it seemed, but he could not see her face in the darkness. All during the mission she had been as quiet and watchful as a child. From time to time she touched her scarf to her brow. Despite everything, when they stopped, she had perched on a nearby rock, apart from the men, her face averted, wrapped in white, her habesha kameez settled about her like snow.

They passed over rough ground, staggered upon stones worn to a polish. Knees sore, fatigue in the quadriceps femoris. Hamstrings, gastrocs, and ankles. Beneath that, deeper, were errors, misgivings, his own private Little Doubts, roused from the corners in which they hid. They were the source of a different kind of pain. It was visceral, dull, and inquisitive. He waited for his Little Doubts to grow bored and retreat to their den.

It had been more than three years since he had seen his daughters. Canada, home, was an abstraction. They seemed to fall away from him when he thought of them, distant objects that receded, as though his thoughts pushed them away. Violence, violence of the rumoured sort. There would be the obvious victims, the people deemed wrong on all counts: Indian, Canadian, semi-Jewish, old, alcoholic, obstinate, feckless, dishonest, ill—a victim, warm for dark demise.

All the world would be wrecked into sand, and one day, far in the future, that too would be rendered into atoms.

CHAPTER 6
David Mason-Tremblay, Development Officer,
Government of Canada
Turkana District
April 24, 2016

At dawn the economic experiment of the Rich walking on poor dirt came to an end. The Rich were allowed back into the cab where they collapsed on their seats, exhausted and fretful. Money declared that the experiment was a resounding success and his hypothesis was correct.

The lorry lurched forward, along a sporadic track that passed through sand and scrub, over rock formed in long, twisting ridges running north and south along the Great Rift, along the separation that was creating a new continent. As the sun rose, flocks of brightly plumaged birds scattered out of the acacias. A great horned eagle swept up out of an old collapsed hut, rising majestically on the updraft. To the west were the shadows of the steep and verdant mountains of Sudan.

Mason-Tremblay's mind fluttered in his discomforts. He smiled at Mihret. She did not smile back, but looked at him with steady eyes.

Money waved his gun.

—A Canadian man like you might be worth a million dollars. Very expensive. Why is this? Maybe because you are perfect, unscarred man. Never hungry in his life, never fought over rotten fruit for meal. Never drank water from a dirt puddle. Never had parasite worms filling your belly instead of food. I know what you thinking. You thinking death is equal for everyone. Democratic-like. Universal-like. So, let me educate: say a village man dies in Kenya. His wife chaps him so she can run to another place with her city lover. She tired of old village husband. Tired of village farm life with no money, only work in the field every day. Goats sleeping in your house. Neighbours come and bury village husband, that's the end. Now, say same thing happen in the USA. Normal man, good-bad like everyone. US citizen man. Then US wife with her factory hairstyle, she come and shoot him so she can run away with her lover, just like Kenya wife. But now what? Now police come in cars, uniforms, then television news come, internet news come, government come. Everyone wants to know about that man's name and job and his cat and what the cat like to eat, about the wife and where the hell she is. Everything. Put it all on internet. Put it in US court. So what did we have: two dead human beings. No difference? Except Kenya man is in Africa and US man is in California-New York. Of course. Later on, Kenya man, his neighbour come and steal his farm and kids while US man, they make Hollywood movie, radio song, Facebook, YouTube. Everyone makes millions of dollars. Everyone happy, gets new luxury car.

David Mason-Tremblay had never experienced parasitic worms. He could not imagine having worms of that kind. But here he was. Victim. It did not square with his understanding of the world. Young, handsome, ambitious David, of superior education and intelligence, or so he was always told. His life trajectory, as he had rolled along the smooth track of his years so far, had been opportunity after opportunity. He could have chosen sciences, business, law, or music, tennis, golf, or hockey. The choicest lifestyles were laid out before him, a banquet of choices.

How could an elite person, nurtured in a plentiful and generous home and community and offered a full range of career and lifestyle choices, end up at the disposal of an drug-addicted terrorist, a person from the bottom rung of a poor society? But then, of late there had been a noticeable shift. There were moments when he felt disadvantaged *because* he was elite. It was a paradox. Up was down. The social scales had shifted, the entire world now smiling on women, people of unusual gender, people with brown and yellow and black skin. The formerly downtrodden were now at an advantage, simply because they were downtrodden. Although he was entirely sympathetic to these changes, at a personal level it was disorienting. People now saw his eliteness and made him feel deficient because no one had ever been cruel or abusive to him during his life.

Money laughed and Mason-Tremblay cringed.

—Sometimes I think they gave to me the wrong life. But when I think of that, I feel hope, you know why? Because a mistake like that can be repaired, even if I make repair myself. You know that feeling? That you got given the wrong life? Me, I think I am a repairman.

Money looked at Mason-Tremblay for a long moment.

—I was wondering: you think God is American?

‖

None of this would have happened if Mason-Tremblay had remained in his old brokerage job. His only concerns in that job were the prices of shares, the false schemes to drive the price up or down, and convincing people he knew to invest in those schemes. Liquidity flowed in and out, fortunes ebbed and flowed. One needed only the agility of a surfer to cling to a wave of riches and to be bold when swamped. And a beautiful, leased, red convertible Porsche and a spacious apartment over the river to maintain the illusion of success and confidence. Until the disappointments came along on the tides as well, the stocks not behaving as they were expected, investors losing money, losing confidence. In fact, he was not sufficiently interested in the details and the mechanics of it all. It was quickly apparent that the painstaking analysis and forecasts and dissections were as often wrong as they were correct. As a result, he was perpetually uncertain of which direction the tide was going, when to buy or sell, or when to keep his opinions to himself. He repeatedly lost his own money and those of the unfortunates who entrusted him with their investment portfolios. After a time, his family found excuses not to place money with him. Then, in one colossal run of bad luck, he lost everything and bailed out of the market altogether. From time to time it was necessary to remind himself of that terrible moment.

So onward and forward. Mason-Tremblay had not needed to exert himself. School had been easy. He was a good, if not brilliant student, but always popular with his teachers and the other students. He was known to be easygoing, cooperative, polite. He prided himself on understanding what others wanted. In some ways, he was celebrated. He was considered by all to be one of those individuals who slide onward and upward by dint of charm and a general acquiescence. His classmates called him Slack Man. His parents referred to him as the Prince of Leisure, with great affection.

But later, and especially recently, he wondered privately if he were fundamentally lazy. At times he felt this lassitude in his limbs and in his mind. It worried him greatly. When he was hired in government, he found that many of his colleagues drove themselves until exhausted, for reasons he could not ascertain. He spent most of his work hours reading short messages on screens, even though this did not constitute productive or thoughtful work. He suffered ennui. He suffered from a lack of ambition.

The lorry jarred against the rocky ground, and he glanced at the sculpted and beautiful face of Mihret. It was hard not to look at a face like that. But she did not look back. She stared fixedly at the passing land. There was a set look to her face. She was either unaware of Mason-Tremblay or did not care to acknowledge him. Her face was as impassive as an obsidian sculpture.

Mason-Tremblay nudged Mihret and leaned close to her.

—Will you be alright?

Mihret glanced at him, shifted away from him slightly, shrugged her shoulders, covered her mouth and yawned. He went on.

—Do you have any idea who these people are and where they might be taking us?

—We're going north. If you keep going north you reach my home country of Ethiopia…but who knows? They are unpredictable, these people. They are liable to do anything…

Money stirred and looked at her.

—Yes, lady. I can hear you. But you are wrong. Where we are is in the middle of a major crisis. Country does not matter. Kenya or Sudan. Maybe Ethiopia. Does not matter. We don't know where this crisis is going, but we know there is no solution and not even a proper road. No government takes an interest, and no international somebody dares to assist. You will not see anyone, even the lowest, darkest, dimmest people. No one lives here and no one will come here, because no one knows how to solve the crisis. Is that enough information? Good, then be quiet your talking, or I will come and give you my unwanted attention.

Mihret looked at him evenly. She betrayed no emotion, as though to say that she had already experienced his unwanted attention and it amounted to nothing.

The track gave into a riverbed, and they pitched forward into high gear, the dust billowing out behind them.

After a minute Mihret stretched her arms.

—Please, can we not stop for a rest? We need water and food. Also, nature's business…

They stopped. Money and Hassan climbed down and conferred, Money with great animation while Hassan listened, his brow creased. They circled the lorry, the heat of Money's voice floating in querulous waves behind them. Hassan took out a long scarf and tied and retied it several ways on his head. He had no reply to Money's words. They opened the cab doors and let the captives get down.

—Stay calm and do not do stupid things, okay? Go and do your private business there among the rocks. You will not try to escape because you know why? Because number one, I will kill you, and because number two, you will be dead. And because number three, you wealthy rich people cannot walk anywhere. You are like infants. You will fall over and be eaten by ants or choke on your own spit. Also, there is no place to go and no water and no food, and you will die after walking around in circles. There are hungry animals in this place—hyenas, leopards, and lions. There are vultures and other things that will gouge your eyeballs as a delightful snack, even before you die. So go, go! Go for five minutes, and if you do not come back we will abandon you here or I will shoot you, and either way you will be unnecessarily dead. But you must come back because I made a wager you would come back. If I lose wager, I get angry...

The captives clambered down into the sun and trudged away from the vehicle. There were no trees in that place, the only cover formed by the large boulders strewn about the steep bank of the riverbed and hillside. The prisoners went four separate ways.

Mason-Tremblay could not find a satisfactory spot to relieve himself. His bowels were cramped and distended. Precious minutes went by as he wandered among the rocks, disoriented, checking here and there for a private place. He worried that Mihret might inadvertently look up to see him humped over in his labours like an ignominious defecating dog. It would ruin everything. He climbed the hill away from the riverbed. When he looked down at the ground, he froze. Immediately before him, a large snake resolved out of the sand and rock. He stood blinking at the thing. The snake blended with the background, its skin patterned in the same colours of rock and sand. All but the eyes, which were eerily white in a large triangular head, was perfectly camouflaged. The snake was a metre and a half long and grotesquely thick. It lay still, slightly curved, directly in his path. For a moment Mason-Tremblay wondered if it was dead. But it was not dead; the eyes were cold, but not dead. The slotted retinas narrowed by the merest amount. It watched him, and waited for him to take another step.

Mason-Tremblay inched backward until he was at a safe distance, his heart bounding ferociously. The snake continued its wait. It was a puff adder. He had seen pictures of them. What had he read? *Puff adders kill more African children than…* than what? Other snakes? Traffic accidents? Malnutrition? Malaria? He had heard the same about hippos, leopards, dysentery, water buffaloes, lightning. *Terrorists kill more people in Africa than…*

In the distance he heard Money's voice, flattened in the overheated air.

It would be impossible to move his bowels now. His heart still gyrated like a rubber ball. The grotesque thickness and passivity of the puff adder had shaken him. It was portentously alien, like this entire country, this entire continent. What else was out there? As he studied the ground carefully and picked his way along, his nerves popped and sputtered. He tramped his foot noisily so that the many other snakes he imagined awaiting his tread would be forewarned.

It occurred to him then that the best thing for him to do was to simply withdraw from this awful situation, whatever it was, and forget snakes, the old vehicle, the addled drivers. He should save himself, go it alone, make his way back to the city alone, return to his sweet garden, open the door with his key, summon the girl Khadija to prepare a hot bath, bring him a cold beer, and serve him a hot meal. Collapse into bed and awaken in the morning, take his first coffee thick with hot milk, the way he liked it, on the patio, followed by a session of yoga and then a long sit, with the doves cooing and the starlings rummaging in the foliage. Begin life again. In fact, what was to stop him from resigning his post entirely, right then and there? It was the perfect time. He could revert to bystander, a reflective sojourner. Anything but an abducted government officer.

He nodded his head. His hands shook a little as he conjured the scenario: announcing to colleagues and abductors alike that he had been fired, or that he resigned, and that either way, forthwith he was no longer in service to government, and therefore of no value to anyone. They would be forced to let him go on his way, and he would find his way home. After a few days, he would catch a flight straight home to Ottawa, tell Julia what had happened, find a new job in finance, real estate, management, anything. Release himself. Why not? It was a joke, this entire business. He was not needed here. They would forget about him and he would forget them. *Promise. I swear I was never here.* Leave behind the awful circumstances that drove poor people to their desperate schemes, forget the dull anonymity of government offices and the uncomfortable protocols and their confusing jargon. Forget Kenya, forget Africa, forget this awful Turkana with its woeful lack of amenities. Forget the refugee camp that sucked at hope like a bad debt.

It had become quiet, the air whistling softly among the rocks. There was no sign of the others. He climbed the sharp slope away from the riverbed and found a spot to conceal himself after ensuring there were no snakes nearby. He took a deep breath to calm his galloping nerves and shaking hands. It might be best, he thought, to remain hidden among the rocks until they gave up looking for him and the lorry pulled away. Perhaps the terrorists were too high on qat to notice his absence.

The sweat ran down his arms onto his shaking hands. If only he could find a flat place where he could perform his entire yoga routine, starting with the downward-facing dog. Masterji, were he here, would suggest several positions and encourage slow breathing. One nostril, then the other. The answer, as always, was yoga. He needed yoga; they needed yoga. If Masterji was here, everyone would calm down, inhale, slow, stop thinking. At least he might sort himself out so that he would know what he should do. Maybe he could be the one to lead the terrorists in a yoga session. They could relax, view the world in a new light, make friends, return together to Nairobi where he could collaborate with them on a book. Later, film rights. Better still, he could start to teach yoga, like Masterji, whose real name was Marty Fontaine. Like Marty, he could lead people to better, healthier, more mindful existences. Dream of abundance, and you will profit from life. That was Marty, or some other guru. Marty, somehow, drove a 7-series BMW.

He climbed further so that he looked upon the riverbed and the yellow lorry. He could read the windshield slogan. IN GOD WE TRIST. There was no sign of a road or village. No herds or farms.

That the hijackers were capable of murder, he was certain. The one called Money might be deranged. Yet what did it mean, precisely? Deranged, disarranged, disordered, dis-balanced. He had no understanding of such a person. The man was one of the faceless millions of desperate, disadvantaged, hopeless. What might a person like that do next? He probably had nothing to lose. He half expected to see Money stand atop the cab and aim his assault rifle at the prisoners, for amusement, for target practice, for some pathological understanding of justice. Mason-Tremblay clambered higher, felt his muscles respond to the exertion. One triumph: his shoes, a bargain, had proved perfect. Breathable, tough, with soles that were the product of scientific investigation and translation into a marketable good.

Below him, the two men atop the cab searched in the opposite direction using Mason-Tremblay's own field glasses. Anyway, he always carried them and had not found an occasion to use them. Nikons, purchased on sale. A bargain at eight hundred Canadian dollars. The two men took turns with them. Behind them, not far away along the riverbed, a bright movement caught Mason-Tremblay's eye. It was Mihret, her flowing white garment flying as she went. She disappeared between the rocks, came into full view again, moving, running. She was sprinting. It was an admirable sprint, athletic, her stride fluid and long and effortless—the woman was born to run—and she covered the ground rapidly. She came into open space, clearly visible, a distinct target and well within the range of gunfire. At any moment, they would turn, stop talking and shoot at her. For twenty seconds, thirty seconds, then a full minute, they did not turn, and there was no gunfire and no eruption of the engine, and in that space of time Mihret flew over the ground, escaping, vanishing around the bend in the river.

The woman's courage and physical prowess were stunning to behold. He had the absurd notion that he should draw attention to the flaw in this scene that only he had witnessed. He had the crazy urge to tell someone. For her own safety, perhaps, he should inform the others that the most unlikely of their captives had hightailed it. Or perhaps to let them know how stupid, how utterly incompetent, they actually were. He giggled loudly. This was the kind of thing that must drive terrorists mad. Fooled by a beautiful woman.

He scrambled along on the ridge with his excellent shoes gripping the rocks. From another vantage he glimpsed her briefly once again, through a gap in the rocks, still sprinting at an impossible pace, now safely out of line of sight of the abductors, devouring the distance. He wanted to shout out, or laugh, to share in her triumph. She did not pause in her flight to look back.

David Mason-Tremblay, market imperfection, man of the new millennium, leapt away down the side of the ridge after her, his eyes ever watchful for snakes.

CHAPTER 7

Salim Mohammed, Driver, High Commission of Canada
Turkana District
April 23, 2016

Salim had piloted the Range Rover off the road, along the diversion track, willing the last of the engine oil to drain from the loosened oil plug. Every hole and bump shot pain up his clenched rectum, up his spine. He was acutely attuned to each shift in direction. Like some hyper-directional creature, he was, while his skin shed his body water, bathing him in his own duplicitous poisons. It was as though his body, his sweat glands, were in rebellion and wanted nothing more than to display for everyone the full extent of his treachery.

One thousand now and nineteen to come. More possibly. No expense would be spared for this important task...

It was a nightmare too elaborate and overpowering to escape, except, perhaps, with the intervention of the Almighty. In this nightmare he had fallen under the influence of the terrible and insatiable Shaitan. Peaceful sleep would never visit him again. *What hath night to do with sleep?*

Twenty thousand and perhaps you will serve the Almighty. No expense was too great for that.

But it was a wonderment: here was an educated man, practical and religious, a man who might admit in a moment of truth to minor weaknesses, a man who might confess to cracks that had appeared in the wall of integrity and honesty. How could such a man find himself in the service of Shaitan instead of the Almighty? Innocence of heart. Decent. A dependable, well-read man, sensitive and learned. Reliable. At one time he would have considered himself a pious man, with a proper regard for the Beneficent and Great, however the cracks. But he was none of those good things after all. Cracks become fractures, fractures become Great Rifts.

It had always been necessary, therefore, to attend to patching the cracks. An occasional private penance might do the trick. Like assisting the young or old, or rendering dutiful service here and there. Taking care with his salat, his prayers, five times daily, or three times, or at least one. An expert and professional patcher was he, redeeming himself in expedient and inventive ways. Except now, this devilish nightmare, this trap that no human could possibly escape. Would any man ask for such a fate? Yet it was dealt to him—a bad hand of cards tossed his way in a game he did not know well. He had not, by any means, intended to be part of this game, nor had he wanted to be appointed to its terrible tasks. He had no wish to make such a bargain with these criminals.

It was too late, and few choices were left to him. He kept reminding himself of that. He understood chance and luck and fate and the cosmic jest called probability more than most. Anxieties roiled through his chest, and he had premonitions of disaster so strong that he felt his blood vessels would burst.

One wondered, at these times, if one's prayers were taken up, heeded. Was anyone listening?

In the name of Allah, the Merciful.

The root of the problem was gambling, drinks, card games on late, hopeless nights. He was no better than Kestner when it came to bottles and glasses, which was why he did not object to helping his client out of his drunken situations from time to time. He understood about the lonely, hopeless nights of men. Of bottles full and empty.

But he should have worried more for himself. One stupendously long losing streak had done it. He had tried to fix his losses by taking larger and more frequent chances. Then the debts exploded, and then the borrowing became precarious.

He could not remember how he had discovered gambling and cards. Who invented these evil things? Games, they called them! Games of weakness! Games of haram!

May Almighty Allah give us all the ability to act upon His commandments and abstain from His prohibitions. Aameen.

He had been forced to go to the users, the Mungiki. Forced to dodge and feint as his debts spiralled. Finally, this nightmare, as though he had reached out his hand for help from Shaitan himself. He had brought it upon himself and broken his word and his honour. He was not practical or good or pious. Not really. Not at all.

He wondered why and why not. Why had it happened to him? Why not some other weak link in the human species, to be caught and enmeshed in wrong choices, sin, evil and unholy and polluted and corrupted death. Why, why, and why not? Here was a man stupid at the same time that he was intelligent, who seemed to not know at the same time he knew very well the ways of Shaitan. Highly educated and useless was he, schooled in literature and philosophy, along with unhealthy doses of the modern sciences, such that it produced in him a tangle of contradictions, never resolved, constantly in battle in the corners of his thoughts. How could he have been awarded a first class in Anthropology and Evolution and still call himself Muslim? How could he write in his essay that religions were *intersubjective ideas held by certain people in certain places*, yet still proceed with daily supplications to Allah? Perhaps this was why one abandoned one's studies, left a degree incomplete. Perhaps this was why there were fallow grounds for Shaitan to sow.

He considered himself a man who, by his aptitudes, was destined to be a scholar, perhaps a teacher of poetry. A gentleman.

Yet he was considered by Kenyan society to be fortunate to find a salaried job and nothing more. Ultimately, his fate was to be a man of long roads, a driver, not a man of paper. His was to be in service to foreigners and diplomats, ferrying around *wealthy rich fuckahs* who seemed to think of themselves as superior beings from the High This or High That, creatures who draped themselves in pomposity and self-regard. His lot was to attend to those most fortunate of creatures who happened to be born in other, gladder places than this but somehow never seemed to realize or acknowledge their good fortune. Who instead regarded he, the driver, as an inferior, a half-wit, a failure, or, still worse, who would not regard him as anything at all beyond telling him where to drive while they lorded their important and fortunate work over him, patronizing him with ignorant jests and anecdotes. And this Dr. Kestner was not even the worst. In equal measure, in fact, he detested and admired Kestner, with his streaked tonsure and sombre eyes and distracted thinking, a man taken to lonely drinking so often that now he could not remember a driver's simple name, yet was heeded by high officials in international agencies and governments.

Ultimately, though, another *wealthy rich fuckah*.

Finally, the engine had failed at the perfect spot (although it had gone an impressively long time in the heat with the oil drained out). He had stopped and feigned and dodged and feinted and lied and Madam Ethiopia had looked right through him so that he thought he might melt under her scrutiny. Luckily, she became distracted by more pressing matters, namely the ragamuffins who alighted like innocent birds, as though the Almighty Allah had sent them down to provide an important moral test. Or maybe it was Shaitan. Or both, he could not tell. Magic birds, angels, djinns. The children alighting with filthy faces and ancient eyes that swallowed the soul of the flawed and corrupt. The children regarded each of them without judgment: the white man whose skin was actually red, the Ethiopian madam, the car, and all the other things that would captivate tribal children. They innocently took in all this news and reported it, no doubt, to the realm of the Almighty. *And they feed, for the love of Allah, the indigent, the orphan, the captive.*

He watched Madam Ethiopia pour motherly syrup upon the desert children. Salim sighed. One moment a woman like that would warm you by calling you brothah, and the next, freeze you and put your koko in a vice. There was little point in reminding her of what she already knew—that the children were locals. If anyone should worry about the approaching night it was not the children but she, though she did not yet know it.

How tough was Madam Ethiopia? What would become of her? The thought that he might be a responsible for her humiliation and belabourment by ugly criminals prompted further stabs of pain, from his rectum up to his chest. No one had explained to him that there would be a woman. This madam, she was a great one. She was one of those who came from upright country people. Capable and independent and formidable. He had worked with women like her. They were far superior to corrupt urban specimens such as himself. He knew it, and the women knew it. They moved to a different music, looked out for the children, the old, the community, the nation. Wise and as tough as leather by the time they reached fifty.

He answered her queries like a good boy.

—Ndio, Mama. Sawa, Mama.

He felt very strange, his rectum twitching as though that immodest part of his body sent a rebellious message about his bad choices. The message travelled sharply up his spine. Since when was rectum the boss? What did it know? At that moment he sorely wished to be alone so that he could sort thought from emotion. Why did the seconds crawl, each one with its own flaw? Why was freedom so unavailable that he could not, at least for a moment, step aside and sit quietly and think about what he was doing? It was happening too quickly and uncontrollably. The mist that formed made it hard to focus, and so his mind pounced on details to avoid thinking about the significant questions.

The light was failing. Let the darkness come. Better the darkness to conceal guilt. What did the holy book say? *And from the evil of darkness when it overspreads.*

When the lorry arrived in the caldera, he had to force his feet to climb the steps to the cab door. He peered in the open window, to behold two human mistakes, two terrors who peered back through their predatory eyes. He choked on his words.

—You have something for me, yes? From Bwana Rosie?

—Like what? You expecting an award for your deeds? How about Chief of Order of Golden Heart. Would that be good enough?

There were two. He immediately hated both men. Ugly A and Ugly B. Ugly A, the nasty one who did the talking, flicked back a blanket that lay along the floorboards, uncovering a gun.

—Only one thing we have. Only one thing we need.

Salim had said nothing as he clenched the door handle and looked back at his passengers, who waited, unknowing, below him. He diverted, for some reason, and began to spout like a grandmother about lost children. It was the only sensible thing he could muster at that moment, even though as he listened to his own quavering voice, he knew it was wrong. As he jabbered he took in the shoddy interior of the cab, the army gun (he knew nothing about weapons), the plastic sack of qat, the reek of sweat and nerves and unwashed bodies. These men were unclean; why did he think they would be pious or righteous?

He coughed out this and that nonsense, rambling. The men gaped at him as though he had lost his mind. He most certainly had.

Ugly A spat out a wad of well-chewed qat.

—Why you chattering about desert brats? Do we look like nursemaids? Do you see titties on this chest?

—I was thinking of what the Prophet would say about lost children. Are you sure he did not send something? A letter, perhaps?

—Who? The Prophet or Rosie? Which one? Anyway, the answer is neither. Neither the Prophet nor Rosie cared to send you anything but us. We are the only message.

Ugly A followed this with a disrespectful and ironic laugh that was not easy for Salim to hear. The laugh had the instant effect of sending more rectal pain shooting into his head, giving him a cracking migraine.

Nothing. No message, no money. He thought there would be something he could take in his pocket so that he could be done, escape and forget, his part of the bargain kept. *Nineteen thousand to come.* They could have sent along even one thousand to show good faith.

Shaking, Salim climbed down from the cab. He avoided the Canadians, momentarily unable to face them. But he could not so easily avoid Mihret Madam, whose eyes saw all, even in the faltering light. He went to her with as much of an appearance of purpose as he could muster.

—Hapana, madam. No, they say we cannot carry the children. It is, of course, against the guidelines to steal children away from their home environment. Anyway, madam, the driver said he knew these children. They belong to people around here. To remove without the permission of their families would be foolish. It would be tantamount to abduction in the eyes of the law.

At this he stopped, astounded to hear the words that spilled forth from his mouth—there seemed no end to the new things he was learning about himself. These words, these choices he was making, they were like an anvil being hit by a hammer, right next to his ear.

—As such, these drivers are law-abiding citizens. They have assured me of that.

She looked in his face and knitted her eyebrow. It was a thing about these villagers. They knew how to look at a face. They knew that a face reveals all, if one looks closely enough. Dishonesty, corruption, unholiness, greed, rotten hearts. They might examine a stranger for an uncomfortably long time as the madam did now, looking upon his face to see his imperfect character written below the surface.

—Who are these men, and what is this ancient contraption they drive?

He hated himself as much as he hated the men. After all, he was one of them. He was Ugly C. He could not answer her so did not try. He turned away as if he had not heard the question. He busied himself with collecting the luggage and setting it in the back of the lorry. The two Canadians and, finally and reluctantly, Mihret Madam, climbed up into the second row of seats in the cab. These people who relied on his integrity, his honesty, waited as innocently as lambs at slaughter. A rivulet of urine spurted down his leg into his shoe.

Yet, yet, *awake, arise or be for ever fall'n.* How was it possible that he could go on with it, further, deeper, into this morass. The fibres of his being rebelled as he went forward, perpetuating the lie he had begun.

He took a moment to look at the desert children a last time. They were already asleep in the open rear section of the Range Rover, scrawny bodies thrown at awkward angles, mouths askew, limbs unhinged, reckless among their dreams and the clean synthetic lining of the interior. They slept as though at the breasts of their mothers. How wrong it was for them to be secure in their sleep that way. There were no secure places in these times. Security was an illusion. He got into the driver seat of the Range Rover and put his head on the wheel. Perhaps he should wave the others on and simply wait there with the children, for whatever was in store for him.

‖

Salim Mohammed, a man unmarried, a man unfamilied, a man uncoupled in any way, despite higher senses, fine intellect, a love and appreciation of fine art. Particular life things had not happened, although, in his moments of honesty, he could not imagine himself entwined in the limbs of a woman or as a father of children. He would not let himself think of why. (But it was never women who made his heart ache for company. He refused to think further than that. A man could be slain like a dog for thinking beyond that.) But poor husband material. Poor life material.

And then? Then, of course, a man loses his way when the map of life is stained with sin. Card gambling and betting and drinking and losing money over money and borrowing and owing and all of it haram. He was a solitary, literary, sensitive, university-educated, almost baccalaureate. A man who could not control his urges.

It matters not how strait the gate, I am the master of my fate.

And so it went on, as always, his thoughts like cocks in a fight, battling back and forth, stupidly and stubbornly. It was a kind of three-way cockfight, though, his innocence, his modern education, and, aloofly on high, the Supreme Principle, all battling for his soul.

Better to reign in Hell than to serve in Heaven.

Or perhaps this was the prerogative of Allah.

Allah, and the others who conspired to send him the most troublesome, the most horrendous nightmare of a scenario in which to act. He was indeed an actor in a play; a great Shakespearean play like *Macbeth* or *Hamlet*, and he was the character of...

What had they said?

One thousand now and nineteen to come. Maybe, possibly, more.
You must simply follow the diversion. You must simply drive away
from the road. North, north. Then your part will be done.

Your part would be done? How would this happen? How would
he be rewarded?

He was yet a good man, a man who should have been a scholar.
So what if there were cracks now and again. He was Salim and
Salim understood risks. He knew when to place a bet and when
to not. (Or did he really?) What was he to do? Quit and beg on
the streets?

All was as Allah decreed. By the will of the Almighty who once
more reveals the Order of Things. Why could he not be satisfied
that it was the will of Allah and leave it at that? Who did he think
he was, with his minuscule place in this universe of worlds ruled
by unknowable forces? Why could he not be at peace, like the ants
and bugs that one spares or destroys with a flick of the foot? Do
they lose sleep for their fate, for the vagaries of higher powers? He
could not think it through. All he knew now was that he had put
himself in league with the servants of Shaitan and their hell-bent
deeds. He had not imagined this dirty sensation of giving oneself
over. Or what might come after. He had assumed that after he
had done what was asked, he would take his reward and be free
to continue on his way, finally, unburdened by debt. He would be
judged on his day of reckoning.

Then there was the Range Rover. That had given him a pause.
Even while he might resent being a driver at times, he so loved
the beautiful machines that were put in his charge. The touch
and smell of the material, the sophistication and precision of
the engineering—it was as though he'd been sent a personal memento from Europe, a place where boundless resources
were concentrated to a fine point in the aesthetic precision of
the machinery. The new cars he drove, paid for by the people of
Canada, or Sweden, or the UK, or whomever he drove for, were

tastes of the great river of wealth that flowed out there, in other places, just beyond the fingertips of the local people. As a driver he had occasionally thrilled, dreaming he was part of it—until he woke up to the fact that he was no more than a slave to it. Still, he could weep to think of how he had destroyed a beautiful machine like that. In the end he could not think of a way to avoid what he had set out to do, and the act of destruction had become yet another boulder to bear.

That beautiful, precision, fucking Range Rover cost as much as he would make in ten years. In a brutal way, the machine was ten times more worthy than he.

It was too late, far too late. Too late for honesty, trust, integrity. Salvation.

Wealthy rich fuckahs. He giggled at his own madness.

There was a moment when he could have walked away, hedged his bet, limited his losses, vanished in the darkness, spared the Range Rover. Then that moment was gone because *nineteen thousand and possibly much more to come.*

Then the lies. And more lies. How did he lie so well? He might lie to men, yet how could he lie before the Supreme?

When the Review Team accepted the ride in the lorry, the die was cast. Emotionally drained, he fumbled his way into the cab and squeezed himself into the worst part of the bench, against the door, his muscles squirming, his rectum shooting sparks into a wracked brain. He stank! It was his duplicity that stank, and he was sure everyone could smell it.

Then the ugly lorry with its ugly drivers started to drive, and he pulled a muscle in his neck just thinking of looking back.

III

Salim knew the territory west of Lake Turkana as well as he knew the other regions of the country, with the exception of the military zones to the east. In his years of driving he had come in contact with many of the diverse tribal people of Kenya. He prided himself in knowing who was who among the ethnic groups. He knew their circumstances and hardships. He had seen with his own eyes starvation, banditry, insurrections led by private armies, the government bombings of tribal lands. Early in his driving career, when he was still in possession of a certain charm and still had hopes, he had befriended many locals and so learned bits of traditional wisdom about certain plants that could keep a person alive, about the habits of the creatures who would hunt humans in the wild lands. In the old days he had driven rich clients across the game reserves, feigning expertise. Then, in the years after 9/11, things had quickly changed. Strangers fanned out across the land. Extremists of every sort. Jihadists. Then the CIA agents, newly minted American spies. More extremists. Veterans of foreign wars. The villagers and herders become suspicious of strangers. Sometimes it felt as though foreigners had taken over the nation. There was suspicion in some places, and paranoia in others; on the coast, a new sharper edge of desperation in the way people conducted their business. The concepts of trust, honour, and integrity were quaint notions from another time. The drivers drove faster, stopped less. They heard things that made them drink and gamble harder than before.

Embassy drivers always knew more than they let on. It was a part of their craft. Knowing the routes, knowing the cautions, even if they were kept officially in the dark. They did not sit behind the steering wheels listening only to the engine and wheels after all. At times they traded scraps of intelligence from overheard mobile phone conversations in the back seat or a quick debriefing between passengers, in barely coded language that fooled nobody. Or the frank and open ramblings of a fatigued client with a belly full of fine whisky, returning late from the club or the official evening reception welcoming the new French ambassador. Even the High Commissioner himself let his guard down.

But *wealthy rich fuckahs*, all those clients.

So when they heard about the mission to Refugee Camp Number Two, all the drivers but Salim turned off their phones. They knew about it. Salim had already been placed, whether he accepted the mission or not. Later, he shivered to think there was an unknown higher person in the labyrinthine corridors of the Canadian High Commission who knew everything and oversaw his movements.

Salim could not rest, his mind crowded with questions about fate and will and the Supreme. How was it that he was responsible for right and wrong while all fates had been determined long ago, at the beginning of the world? How was it that he felt guilty about what had not yet occurred? As he drove his clients away from Refugee Camp Number Two, the questions were ploughed aside by the challenges of faking, lying, boldly sabotaging the vehicle. In the rear-view mirror he caught glimpses of his own broad, white smile of betrayal, his face like a sweaty wooden mask. He glimpsed the smooth expressions of the *wealthy rich fuckahs*, so certain of themselves with their power and fat pay and assumptions and blind eyes. Salim smiled his best holiday smile while behind it his jaw clenched, his teeth ground, and his smile was really just a cheap mask offset by plastic shades.

As they rolled forward, he kept going back over his buried instincts, his thoughts like admonitions from the Almighty. At one time he had known how to be good and honest and clear! He had known! He had known how to be a good man but then, he also understood what a man had to do to keep himself. He knew he was alone in that. Yet it was as if Allah were speaking to him, showing him the correct and the incorrect.

One thousand now and… who knows how much.

IV

There was a tickle on his scalp, as though a tiny spider scampered there, nothing more than that. He ignored it. Over the months the spider crawled about at certain moments, as though to remind him. Then it disappeared, and he forgot about it. Wages came and bets were placed and wages went. The more the wage went, the more he sought to borrow. Pure logic, the logic of gambling. Lose lose lose, then put more money in to stay in the game, desperate to win back. Drink drink drink, in order not to worry about the empty wallet. Depressed on the weekends because of dissolution and haram. His university degree might have been in drinking. He would have graduated summa cum laude, because every varsity night he was at it, hour upon wretched hour, a lonely wastrel in the company of other wastrels, tilting glasses of Ndovu or Tusker and staring at bad hands of cards.

He was not entirely surprised on the day that Rosie's messenger, a lanky and not unattractive lad, waited outside the gate of the High Commission. The boy followed him closely along the sidewalk until Salim finally turned on him so he could see who he was.

—So my brothah, today you are my shadow. What an honour.

The spider ran along the crown of his head, telling him something he should already know.

—I'm here only because Rosie of Mungiki wishes you to remember him, not to honour you. *Brothah.*

—Rosie?

The boy handed him a piece of paper with an address. Of course, Salim knew exactly who it was. For some time he had feared to sit down with a pencil and tot up the amount he owed.

He went to see this Rosie the next day and had to suffer through the man's terrible breath and unhindered gas, and the awful touts who hung about like cheap Ramadan decorations. Then came the proposal which was not really a choice—he knew this—and all of it was tacky and shoddy and made to seem like a salvation.

—You are a man of vice, yes? Do not pollute the waters by denying what is already known. Then comes the time to pay your accounts, yes? But you are such a fortunate fellow. Well placed as a driver, so a wonderful opportunity for redemption in the eyes of the Almighty. You will make common cause with others who wish to demonstrate devotion and faith, while you address your debt. It will look pretty. In one stroke you are holy and free of debt. Allah will not mind. He might praise you roundly.

—My vices? They are nothing very haram, really. Small games of cards to pass the time. Small wagers. Child's play compared to—

—Do not pollute the waters. As always, we are here to help others. That is what the Mungiki do.

Rosie flicked his fingers to rid the air of the words Salim was about to voice.

—Hold your tongue. You are a believer, Salim Mohammed?

—Of course, of course.

—Then you will know what should be done. Allah the Merciful works in alliance with men such as us. For our part, we provide chances for men to redeem themselves. And your part, your part, your part. That is all anyone can do in life. Your choices are limited.

Salim opened his mouth to speak once again but was stopped by the flicking of Rosie's fingers. Salim closed his mouth.

—Sometimes, Salim Mohammed, we are too small to understand great matters, and it is best that you do not think about it or ask too many questions. But we offer you one thousand now and nineteen thousand to come. American dollars, you understand. One thousand now and nineteen to come. Much more possibly. No expense would be spared for this important task. That is *twenty thousand*, and perhaps you will serve the Almighty, and perhaps he will take note.

Rosie had no eyebrows, which was disconcerting. Blank baldness over bloodshot eyes. Salim went out of Rosie's dim office, leaving Rosie alone at a metal table pouring coffee from a plastic pot into a plastic cup.

He did not sleep afterward, knowing dimly that this was the end of the road for one embassy driver. He was quite sure it would be the end of him altogether. From that time and forever more he would never again sleep an entire night through. It had been a good and enviable and well-paying job. There would never again be peace for his soul, and he would be a tortured and conflicted person, and there was no way out of it. He was about to be lost. He was already lost. Could he at least think over the offer? He knew he could not. It was the Mungiki, and they would not be denied.

He eyed Ugly A, the one called Money. He had spent his life avoiding such people. Salim had not realized how deeply he could detest another man. He did not speak to them. He wished not to know anything about these dingos, these jambazi. He attempted to ignore them as a petulant child tries to ignore its family. The dark helped him hide his distaste, his hatred, which was surely written on his expression. Ugly A, with his name of Money. Bony shoulders and the chewing jaw incarnations of all his debt and all the evil paths he had taken. His repugnance was so intense it made Salim shudder. He hated them. He hated himself.

Hell was verily leaping up to claim him even before he departed this life. Hell was the mute apology he suppressed. Hell was the regret that spidered along on his scalp, denying his repose. Hell was abandoning a new Range Rover in the middle of the wasteland.

Humdullah.

He feigned sleep as the lorry blundered over the land. Later, he shut his eyes when the gun came out, the foreigners sitting taut as guitar strings. Salim froze in his place as Money's voice fell on them with terrible, devilish force. He girt himself, preparing for his moment of exposure. But nothing happened. The moment passed, and no one sold him out. But later, they made the foreigners walk in the dark, and he remained frozen and mute in his seat. It was clear to him, moreover, that the Uglies were stoned or mentally ill, or perhaps both.

He stayed that way, a piece of frozen fish, dead, unable to witness the ordeals of the clients he had betrayed. *Wealthy rich fuckahs*, to be sure, but what crime had they committed? They knew nothing of gambling debts. He squirmed in his seat and stoppered his ears and closed his eyes. Half of him fought the other half. A few tortuous hours later, the captives were put into the bed of the lorry. Salim thawed some and came back to life. He tried to organize his thoughts so that he could make a plan, knowing that it was too late for that. Anyway, planning was not his forte, evidently. His planning went to the point of vowing that if they came near any road or settlement, he would take the chance to depart. He could make it look to the Review Team as though he had escaped. Ugly A and Ugly B would be rid of him and he of them.

He determined that they travelled out of the government-controlled part of the district. If one went north in Turkana, at some point it was beyond the reach of government, or at least the Government of Kenya. He observed a scattering of tracks and as the light increased, a scan of the horizon told him there were no settlements and not one herd animal. Still, he could get out by himself. He knew some Turkana words. He could talk his way through.

Just as he was putting details on this plan, the Ethiopian woman made the men stop. The Somali turned to him.

—Go watch over them. Make sure they do not have stupid ideas.

So he had gone out like a good servant of the ugly majambazi, thinking that this was the chance he needed. He was afraid of being shot, though. The light was painfully bright after the long night, and large stones were oddly glassy. As he followed the others he had second thoughts. Perhaps it was better to go back and have his word with these ugly gun shooters. Perhaps they should know of his plan. But these weak-minded and flawed plans were never going to secure a place among the angels.

Then, just as he was set to walk away, his plan began to un-ravel. He watched the Ethiopian madam fly like a white-feathered bird. She spread her wings, that one. It was clear that this was not merely some lady-mama-madam. She was a physical specimen as well, strong and fast. She took her opportunity boldly, with no hesitation. He saw it and for a moment pretended to himself that he was mistaken; she was not doing what he thought. It caused him to hesitate. Perhaps he should follow her. Perhaps he should go in the other direction. In the meantime, he relieved himself in the rocks as he thought about his position. Or he could inform the Uglies. This would earn their trust. Maybe there would be an extra reward. Had not the Somali told him to watch? Not only that, but what if the woman were better off in the lorry? She carried no water. There were wild animals, wild people, no roads. Or would she be better off? The Uglies were mentally ill, rough unknowns, their mouths stuffed with qat. What if…what if…

Stunned, he watched her until she was out of sight around the bend in the riverbed. His entire being seemed to stutter, his mind trying to process, his mind fighting reality. His mind told him he should sit on one of the shining rocks and weep. At that moment he heard a footstep. Dr. Avtar stood looking at him as though trying to read his thoughts.

—What part did you play in this, Salim? That's the worst thing about this. I know you're part of it. After all these years.

They were, at that moment, behind a massive rock that looked to have fallen from the sky. Behind them was the riverbank.

Kestner sank into a crouch and laid his hand on the ground, still looking at Salim. Salim's voice was as parched as the air.

—You have no idea of my life.

—Was it for money? At least tell me who these men are. You owe me that much.

—No, Dr. Kestner, I do not think I do owe you. In fact, I do not know these men.

—You listen carefully to me, Salim. You can fix this. Come with me. We can work something out.

—Ah, Sah, no. Come with you where? We are in the middle of wild lands with arid drought and wild animals. Lions, leopards, hyenas in the night. There is no water in this unprecedented drought. Everything and everyone has died or gone away from this place.

—I'm offering you this chance. Look, we get out of here, find a hotel with a casino, have a cold beer over the tables. We talk things through. What do you say? I will keep this entire episode to myself. No one needs to know a thing.

—Ha ha. Yes. You are joking.

Suddenly he could not meet Kestner's gaze and had a bad moment in which panic seized him and made him want to scream. The man was taunting him. Why had Kestner mentioned casino? He had never been in a casino with Kestner. He mumbled a reply.

—Sudan border region is not a casino. It is a place of war and misery. No authority of any kind, for any man. Except perhaps Allah.

—Ah, yes, Allah. And what of the others?

—Others than Allah?

—The team members. Have you no regard for the woman in our group?

—Ah, yes, they. Well, to tell the truth...to tell the truth...as such...the truth is that madam has taken her chances. She is impulsive, that madam. Those Ethiopians, Sah, they are exceptional people.

—What do you mean, taken her chances?

—She ran, that one. Where can she go? We should find her and bring her back safely.

Kestner stood suddenly. He grimaced at Salim, barely glanced in the direction of the lorry, and turned away to run in a half-crouch, along the riverbed. Salim watched this, frozen. Kestner was not fast, like the madam. He was going off in the opposite direction that she had taken. Salim winced. In fact, the doctor was horrendously slow and still within range of the gun. But Kestner too somehow, with the grace of God, vanished among the boulders and corners of the bank.

Salim looked back. Stupid majambazi. What were they doing? Instead of being vigilant over their captives they seemed to be having a difference of opinion. He could hear the voice of Money. Somali this! Somali that!

Salim spat into the ground. Stupid majambazi and just as stupid wajinga! He ducked his head, took a breath, and counted out ten drops of his own sweat as it splashed onto the parched ground. Then he stood up and sprinted after Dr. Kestner. As he went, he felt a sensitive spot between his scapulae where the bullets would strike. But it did not happen, and suddenly he was past the bend in the river. He could see Kestner ahead of him with his plodding run. It took only a minute to catch up to him. Kestner had concealed himself behind a rock and stood there panting, looking at the open sky, counting his pulse in a whisper, one hand monitoring the opposite wrist.

—You've come to drag me back, I suppose. I suppose I will have to fight you.

—Sah, think carefully please. I appeal to your reason and logic. This is not a wise or safe decision. As you are the team leader, you must listen to your driver, even if...

But he stopped talking.

Kestner meanwhile whispered the number ninety-two. He looked at Salim, caught his breath and stood and bolted another fifty metres up the river. But so slow! How could his feet be so heavy?

Salim swore under his breath and followed again. He was breathless when he caught up. He attempted to speak to Kestner, but Kestner looked at him and restarted his whispering count, then ran again, a dodging course away from the lorry and along the river.

A wave of fury passed through Salim. There was a brief instant when he searched the ground for a loose rock to use as a bludgeon. *Wealthy rich fuckah!*

Was this not also written, this fate, this determination, beyond his puny powers? Whom did he detest more, the ragged qat-eating pretenders of Islam, or the foreign Canada doctor who did not have the decency to know his name after all these years, who could not even remember after all the times he had helped him when he was exhausted, lost and drunk, when Salim offered his help like an equal brother?

He sprinted after Kestner, enraged, determined to take some action. He got his hand on Kestner's arm and hauled him to a stop.

—Please, Sah, enough. You must stop. They will soon look this way, Sah. It is the first direction those men will look.

—Tell me your part in this, Driver. Tell me the entire plan. Who are they? Who's behind this?

But Kestner did not wait for a reply. He shook away Salim's hand as though it pained him and he ran, and Salim swore and caught up with him, and as he did so they heard the gunshot that cracked open the air over the desert. They both dove onto the ground.

For a moment they lay in a pool of breathing and heat. Salim could not assemble his thoughts. His head had taken up the heat, melting his thoughts. He looked around at the ground for spilled blood.

Kestner staggered up and ran. He managed a hundred metres. Once again Salim went after him, slower now, hesitant now, half doped by the heat, half wishing to be shot. His feet snagged on his guilt and confusion, his movements ungainly. He stopped by the bank finally, his hands on his knees, inspecting the ground. Water had flowed through that place long ago. How long, it was impossible to know. A year, ten years, ten thousand. It was impossible to imagine water flowing in this place of bones. He stood up, his breath coming in rags. He caught up to Kestner. There was nothing to say. He had no answer for Kestner or himself or anyone. *One thousand now and ten thousand years of guilt.* They were in a tight hollow, a metre and a half high, that was carved into a sandy bank.

They heard the wheezing pistons before they saw the lorry slewing down the middle of the riverbed with Money dangling by one hand from the door frame, shouting, his rifle loosely pointing at the tops of the hills, at the sky. The gun discharged, and the explosion hung like a pertinent question. They were near enough that it seemed impossible that Money did not see two figures crouched in the shadow of the bank.

Salim half stood to reveal himself, unsure of whether he would be shot or if he wished to be found. But strangely, Money did not notice him. In a moment the lorry bucked about in a wide arc in the soft sand and lumbered ponderously away in the direction from which it had come.

Mind gone one way, body another. Salim did not breathe or make a sound.

Kestner moved again. Salim stayed back a moment, then followed. After a time, they found themselves jogging side by side along an exposed bank. In a place where the riverbed narrowed, they stopped, listened, dashed across to the opposite low bank, and clambered up and onto a barren plateau littered with the bones of animals large and small. The ground was broken by three dead acacias.

They stopped and listened, breathing.

—Don't think about beer, Sah.

—Fizzy and cold and long.

—Yes, Sah.

They scrambled to the rim of the river valley. Dark clouds formed in the distance, and the air was unsteady. They came to a plateau of cracked clay. In the distance, on a promontory, was a solitary tree, old and blanched and leafless. They aimed for it out of instinct. A while later, before they reached the tree, Salim hung back. He turned around, scanning the horizons.

At that moment his way became suddenly clear. He was meant to escape, rescue Dr. Kestner from captivity. This was a tremendous relief. There was redemption, as long as he accepted it. He gave a great sigh as he watched Kestner's plodding progress toward the tree. Then he looked at the tree more closely. Any predator would use it as landmark and vantage point. He scanned the shadows and the skeletal tangle of branches, half-expecting to spot a leopard sleeping in the low branches in the heat. But there were none. Perhaps his instinct was wrong. The tree beckoned, as though in its deadness it could still offer shade and protection.

Somewhere there were chances. Always, wherever he looked, there were chances and gambles and bets and debts.

CHAPTER 8
Money Manyu
Northern Turkana
April 25, 2016

One thousand dollars in hand, the captive escaped and one thousand to repay, except that only a paltry few hundred remained of the first one thousand. Instead of nine thousand, the Mungiki would chase him down, looking to get back the one thousand before doing away with him. Assets lost, one thousand owed. It could be that the Somali, Hassan, was one of them. It was impossible to know.

The state of the local economy was this: capital assets had flown, and now they had no marketable items. A vast wasteland to search for three marketable items and one unanticipated flaw. Two poorly fed, poorly clothed eaters of qat in an old dinga, an old piss-coloured tank, running deficits of food, fuel. Deficits of strength, ability, and intelligence.

Money was furious for letting himself be sucked into talking, talking, not thinking, thinking. Sucked into revealing his worth by parading great intelligence and great knowledge to the wageni, the foreigners. How he had wanted to impress them! But why? Who were they to him? Was he a child? Why the need for recognition by these rich people? Because he had no idea of who they were or how much they knew, or how they had become slick with wealth, every detail of them strangely luxurious, from their gold fillings to their clean nails, from their anointed skin to their crafted shoes, jewellery, watches. All things they casually displayed or neglected or lost. They cared not if their wallets were stolen—they knew how to get another, better wallet, with even more cash and cards than the old one. They cared not! Careless of wealth! The wealthy careless!

Yet, he was bothered that these people were in danger of perishing in this furnace of Turkana. If they were to die, it must be on his terms, not the terms of the scorpions and vultures and leopards. His lovely control over the situation had vanished as quickly as the excitement caused by a chew of stale qat.

After an hour of shouts and insults and the stupid discharge of the gun at the sky and rocks, Money fell into a sullen silence, his squelched fury worsened by Hassan's calm demeanour. It was as though Hassan had expected the captives to escape all along. All while the Somali's brow and eyes remained as clear as that of a hopeful child. He happily shifted gears, taming the heavy machine better with each hour that he was behind the wheel. They rolled up and down the river twice, then Hassan found a natural ramp up onto the plateau where they could view the surrounding land. If they had found tracks, it would been simpler, but they saw no signs. The sand was deep there, and there were dunes that held no footprints. There was broken rock, and solid rock.

They stopped after a time to fill the army canteen with water from the barrel. They sat in the shade of the big back wheels to cool and drink. Hassan pulled out figs and passed them to Money.

—They will not go far without water. We will find them soon.

—Are you stupid? Look at this place. We should give this up and go back to the city and lose ourselves and hope we are forgotten.

—There are those with long memory.

They got in and drove on, ploughing through dunes. They came to a track that disappeared into granular sand. Hassan rapturously declared that the hand of Allah surely ushered them onward. It made Money's head ring to see Hassan's beaming face and hear him invoke the name of Allah. No one ushered anyone anywhere and nothing was easy, Allah or no. Only he, Money, seemed to understand that there would be an accounting for all men's actions, sooner or later.

They came to a shallow valley, and an incline of deep sand. In this the wheels suddenly sank. The old engine laboured, and the wheels churned themselves steadily down until the axles hit the ground. Hassan opened the door. He looked down at the sand and wheels, then reached into the bag of qat and filled his cheeks and sat back and sighed. After a moment he put the lorry in gear and gunned the motor.

Money made a heroic effort to control himself, to detach brain from boiling blood. Blood said: what a tremendous service it would be if he were to rid the world of this disease called Hassan. Blood said: Money is the magistrate, the policeman, the prime minister in this stranded lorry. Only two men will ever know if Hassan is missing, and one will not know it for long. It was only a Somali, after all. Magistrate Money would deserve to be thanked, rewarded for this service of ridding the world of a Somali terrorist.

Hassan thoughtfully stuffed a wad of qat into his cheek and gunned the old motor, the transmission complaining, sand flying. The lorry, however, shivered itself into a pit of its own making, front wheels and back.

He used his foot to remove Hassan from the cab. He might have used the gun instead. As it was, Hassan was sent pitching out through the open door with an expression of surprise and regret. His neck might easily have broken if not for his cat-like reflexes and the soft sand he landed in. He landed like an elite football player would land after being fouled. He absorbed the shock, rolled once, then lay as though stunned. After a minute his jaw resumed working on the unfinished ball of qat that had remained in his cheek.

Money took the driver's seat and shoved the worn gear lever, producing a rending of metal on metal. Hassan called out, —This is not a motorcycle. Clutch is big and heavy and slow.

Money switched the motor off and put his head against the wheel. He tapped at the broken fuel gauge. For a long moment they were suspended like that, waiting in a pool of thick, silent air. Hassan remained lying on the sand as though he had accepted his place and chose not to disturb it. He took the opportunity to gaze upward at the expanse of sky and the spaces beyond. When he finally spoke, his voice was weary.

—Violence is of little use here. Somehow, the world made you violent, I can see that. I do not know all the things that happen to men to make them this way or that, violent or not. Men should be good because God is good. In my heart I forgive you. I know you are not a bad person.

Money banged his forehead softly on the steering wheel. Why must he listen to this? He spoke his reply into the wheel.

—Bad? I am not bad. I am not good either. I am bones and meat and worms in my belly. I am another thing in the desert. Now get yourself up and make use of yourself to dig before I shoot you dead. Then you will be also a thing in the desert. A dead thing.

He sat and took up the gun, climbed down, and walked back to the tailgate, remembering the clangour of tools that so irritated him as he had sat watching the prisoners walk. He was aware that behind him Hassan was slowly getting to his feet and shaking sand from his clothes. Money kept an eye on Hassan's movements, and Hassan seemed to know this. Hassan moved slowly, as though he were injured or tired.

The benches in the back opened into storage bins containing spades, ropes, cables, blocks, a full array of tools, oil and grease, a kerosene lamp, two emergency tanks of diesel, a long stick with marks for gauging fuel, old engine parts. Money found a spade. He found a neatly stowed pair of heavy leather workboots, oiled and repaired and thick soled. He carefully took out the boots and put them beside the spade.

Hassan came behind him and looked at the boots.

—Good boots for hunters. They look to fit.

—Fit who? You? It would be a waste since after you lying dead I would have to take them off your stinking dead Somali feet.

—You are a disrespectful person. Violent and disrespectful both. It is bad manners. Still, I am more than ever certain you are not really bad. Not all of you anyway.

—You should be a shutter, not a thinker or a talker. Better you shut while others do the think and talk. You took too much of qat, you know? Qat prevents shutting and leaves only talk and talk until finally war. Kenya-Somali war.

—You ate the qat as much as me, brother.

—Who made me your brother, Somali?

Money threw Hassan the spade and glared at him until Hassan shrugged and picked up the spade and went to the front wheels. A moment later Money heard Hassan digging, and his tensed muscles relaxed slightly. He could not kill Hassan. Hassan was a piteous qat-chewing Somali with nothing, not even boots. He took the boots and climbed into the back where he sat on a bench. Inside each boot Money found a folded sock. He pulled the socks on and found them uncomfortably hot and itchy. He determined to ignore the discomfort. He slid on the boots and laced them. It took some concentration to do this, and when he was done he noticed that it was quiet.

He leaped down with his gun, landing on the earth with the boots. Though they were hot, the boots were fortresses that made him large and weighty in the world. He towered. He swaggered as he moved along to where Hassan was supposed to be digging.

The boots sank impressively into the sand, leaving solid, treaded prints.

Hassan had dug the sand around one wheel and lay sweating in the shade of the fender as the sand slowly slid back into the hole. He stared up at the great order beyond the sky.

Money looked at the hole and spat into it.

—How could you turn your back on our prisoners? How could you let four fat people fly away? Are you stupid? Are you crazy? Our only job was to deliver them. Now what? Gone and we have nothing. Now what? No payment for you, no payment for me. The Mungiki will kill us for failing them. I know them. They think nothing of killing. They kill because they like blood, no other reason.

—Ah, you are too anxious. Those people won't get far. There is nothing here, no villages, no water. We will find them. I know places like this. Waterless places like this are like my native home. We will find them, and you will get your payment. You will see.

—Maybe yes, maybe no. They were smart, those Mungiki. They bought us for a trivial amount and a promise of more. And being stupid and hungry we said, 'Oh yes, Bwana,' and believed them. You ever think, Somali, that maybe you allow yourself to be tricked by thieves. They know your price, how much you worth. Here is Hassan-Somali, one thousand US dollars and a bad promise and you can own him. Where is your thousand now, Somali? Let me see it.

Hassan smiled proudly.

—It was six thousand they offered me. Six hundred they gave. They said I could have more, maybe much more than that. If I get more, I leave Kenya and go home to find my family, take them out of that place, to Europe or Canada.

—They gave you six hundred?

—US dollars. I will be rich enough when we deliver the prisoners.

—Six hundred.

—We will find them. You will see. Places like this are home to me. It is as if someone was lost in my very house. Most people, you can guess their path. Men think the same way, most of the time.

—You think criminals are dependable men for you to do business, Somali?

—They were ferengi behind that Rosie. I saw them. They had so much money that six hundred is only the money in their pocket for a day of amusements.

—Having money not the same as paying money. Those people, the reason they have full pockets is because they steal from stupid people like us.

—Why would they not pay? They are rich.

—In fact, you are poor because you are a genius. Geniuses like you deserve to slave for others, like they do in your country.

—This is a bad thing to say.

—I will say worse and do worse, so you can prepare yourself. Because you are brilliantly wrong. I *am* a so bad person. One day you will see.

Hassan looked into Money's face for a long moment.

—Maybe, maybe. About myself, I am not violent. I only pretend for certain purpose. But if you insult me too badly, I am not afraid to do what is necessary to protect my honour. When I think about my life, it reminds that there is little that can stop me from doing what needs to be done. I should be dead. I do not fear hunger or pain or death or the loss of my people. My family, my mother and father and brother, are already gone. I am left alone to make my choices, to find a way forward for my wife and children. Yet, still, I wonder: what makes a man violent and disrespectful? Maybe your family? Maybe your father beat you too hard or maybe your mother was indecent.

Money grinned. Better to deal with this than piety and daily, prayerful considerations of the Wonderful and Merciful Allah. *This*, he could manage.

—Yah, you are a genius, Somali. All what you say is brilliant. Indecent mother and beating father. Just as you say. Violence and corruption and bad family and no parents. So now you know the story about me. Very good. Does that make you feel better? You say my mother an indecent, like maybe commercial sex woman, and I cannot argue—I do not care about her. But, if turn around the other way and *I* say *your* mother sells her belly to strange men, you take that badly, neh? Because *your* mother, *she* is holy to you. I know. She is a saint and a beautiful korona. Hey, Somali, I hope you not the type to have the sporty dreams about your own mother.

Hassan grimaced, and his eyes blinked rapidly.

Clouds billowed up to the south. A while later the clouds were gone, only to reappear on another horizon, darker than before. During this time, the lorry tilted like a dead monstrosity in the growing hole in the sand. It was a stubborn creature with its hooves dug in, its head pitched up. Night was coming on with masses of up-gusting air.

Money's hands shifted up and down the gun, feeling the parts of it. He kept his eye on Hassan when he could. There were things he now noticed about Hassan that he had not noticed before: the thick muscle that curved over the Somali's shoulders, the voice that rarely faltered or hesitated, the unchanging mood, his single emotion, the large, flat, rusted blade with the stained wooden handle that was belted to his waist. The blade, at least, Money understood. It was Hassan's special companion, his friend, of which Money had his own. But Hassan took pains not to make a display of it. This was merely a practical and rusted fact of his life, without complicated emotions attached to it. Nothing to conceal, but nothing to celebrate.

They stopped chewing qat after a failed attempt to build a rock base to run the wheels out of the hole. The rocks pivoted, rolled, sank, slipped sideways.

Every now and again, Money's blood was so frothed with heat

he wondered that it did not erupt from his pores. He went to the back, lit a cigarette, and smoked it, his mouth dry. Cigarettes were nearly done. Water was flat, tinged with a sickening chemical sweetness. His skin crawled, the nerve endings like disturbed insects with nowhere to alight. The cigarette did not calm his blood. They never did.

He looked balefully upon the captured luggage of the escapees. Money reached over and opened the duffle of papers and valuables. He pulled a mass of stuff out onto the floor and riffled through it: billfolds, passports, papers, all of it reminding him of nine thousand, maybe much more. It was a disaster. A failed enterprise. *Unfinished business.*

The credit cards were slick, embedded with special chips and wires. He put them carefully aside, wondering about the technology. Perhaps they tracked the owners: he was not sure of this. There was an amount of cash, which he found far more familiar, but it would not do. The foreign currency, the dollars and euros, was immaculate compared to the Kenyan bills. Of course. Like the place. Like the people. The Kenyan shillings, though thin and shabby in comparison, bore a trusted familiarity. When he handled stolen bills like this he felt a lift followed immediately by nausea, as though he had eaten hungrily, but it was the wrong food.

Suddenly he was aware that Hassan stood at the tailgate, quietly observing him. He had come up on him silently.

—This is not something you should do alone, brother.

—See, I was doing the counting of our financial. Otherwise, maybe I forget why we are here in the middle of kuzimu.

Money quickly shoved everything back into the duffle and pushed it along the floor toward Hassan.

—Go ahead, your turn. Later we divide. Enough for both, equal, no matata. Democracy, man.

Hassan did not touch the duffle. He lazily hopped up, stood, and strolled along to the bench closer to the cab. He walked past

Money as though Money were no threat at all. He lay on the bench opposite, in the shadows. He spoke quietly.

—There is a hunting camp nearby. I smell roasting meat. We rest for a while. Later we go out into the quiet night to see who and what.

Hassan turned on his side, apparently ready to sleep. As he did so, he slung his knife around to his chest, wrapping it in his arms as if it were a precious child.

The evening colours slid from purple twilight into black night. The air shifted about, undecided as to its intentions. A sliver of a moon came and went through a sky broken by clouds. Gusts blew up the remnants of past failures, of creatures, of families, of entire communities. Money found neither sleep nor dream nor rest. He rubbed the grit that had settled into his eyes, saw malignant little devils, little shetani, borne along in the gusts.

After an hour the air suddenly quieted. Hassan rose and moved past him and dropped as quietly as a green leaf falling to the ground. Money was only aware of the faintest movement, as though only a fibre belonging to Hassan had flitted by on the breeze. He suddenly knew that, if he wished to, Hassan could kill him easily.

Money sat up and re-tied his boots as the sliver of moon winked on through the broken sky. Then the two men walked out, side by side, sniffing the air for direction.

After a few minutes Hassan reached out and touched Money's arm. Money stopped.

—Your step is as heavy as a camel with those boots. They will hear us before we see them. They will either run away or kill us. Maybe you should remove the boots if you cannot make them quiet.

—Yah. I keep boots on. These boots have work to do, Somali.

They went on through the quiet night air, through the scant shadows of scrubby acacias, until they caught the scent of smoke, from a fire that might be burning hot, then the scent of roasting meat with it. They followed the scents in an arc away from the lorry until they saw the reflected dim orange glow of the fire sunk into a cleft in a hump of land. They circled it at a distance, losing sight of it when it was directly before them, then seeing it again when they looked to one side. They came closer and saw movements, dark shapes. When they focused directly, they saw nothing but the firelight. They circled inward, Money towering with strength in his boots.

When the herder leapt out at them, they were ready. The herder had known of their approach. He had tracked them then attempted to dive at them from behind, brandishing a short spear, the whites of his eyes gleaming. But Hassan swivelled, swept aside man and spear, and wrapped his arm tightly around his assailant's throat as he pulled him silently to the ground. He might just as easily have slashed his throat or strangled him but did neither. When the herder stopped struggling Money bundled him to his feet, and they shoved him along until they were standing at the edge of the circle of firelight.

The band consisted of three other men and a group of women and children who sat and lay on the ground, goggle-eyed, observing the strangers. They were Turkana people, patchy and stringy, garbed in a mixture of hides and shreds that had once been the clothing of richer people. A goat, roasting on a steel spike, dripped fat over the fire.

Hassan pointed the AK, and the herders shifted back from the fire. They had a healthy understanding of guns. They settled carefully to watch as Money carved hunks of meat that he alternately passed to Hassan or ripped into it like a hungry dog. The women began to lose their patience as their meal was consumed. They decided, without saying anything, that they would not be shot by the gun after all. Or perhaps they were hungry past the point of caring. These women were scrawny and tough. They leaned in close and proceeded to jeer. A cagey woman with deep ruts for eyes and a naked, breastless chest, stood and took out her knife. She stepped up, carved away a shoulder of meat, and took it to distribute amongst the children, all the while issuing guttural curses, some of which caused bellows of laughter from the others. She came for another portion while making gestures that referred to the genitals of the interlopers. She swivelled her scrawny hips, waved the knife in the air. When Money had enough of this, he stepped toward her, glaring. She screeched as though poisoned, ran in circles, gestured about the evil eye, the evil heart, the evil stomach, then collapsed in a fit of demented and drunken laughter. This emboldened the others. They came forward with their own knives, directed insults at their own men for their insufficiencies, had a difference of opinion and began to land blows on each other, bellowing with laughter, shrieking out long, inventive phrases.

Hassan and Money tore off last pieces, withdrew from the fire, and retreated back to the lorry. They set turns on watch, but both quickly fell asleep, their bellies full.

In the morning they tried placing rocks around the wheels again. This time the rocks held and the old tires gripped easily, released somehow, and the lorry lolled out of the hole like an elephant climbing out of deep mud. They drove on again, northward and east, through the empty terrain, wheels churning, slipping, digging in, the old wheels ceaseless and slow now, as though driven by a force other than a steel engine made by human beings. They were on the riverbed, then climbed a bank down through yet more dried waterways and bushy low acacias that went on for miles. A day later Hassan spotted two sets of shoe tracks, the edges fresh and sharp.

—Only two! Look, one man, one woman missing.

—Two is better than zero. Besides, it is only one who matters.

Money no longer cared. His reasons, and the urgency of the job, were ebbing away. He was aware of the danger in that. It was beginning to feel as though he were being punished, stuck in the wastelands with the Somali and with nothing to show for it but trinkets and pocket change. The chances that they could locate and recapture four people in all this trackless land amounted to nothing. He knew the odds as well as any survivor. He would wait a while, then see what could be done.

For the tenth time Money contemplated how to jettison Hassan so that he could take off with the loot they already had. He wanted to get away, go back. At very least he would be shed of that particular affliction named Hassan. Perhaps he would track the Ethiopian Sheba, place her on the throne beside him.

With his head hung out the door, the rushing air seemed to blast the effect of the qat from him. It was clear that he had no idea of the direction in which to find their quarry. It was a mistake to underestimate people, even lazy and rich foreigners. His mistake was in not imagining that they were, in the moment, simply desperate humans with survival instincts. It was a revelation to him that the rich could fight for life as hard as the poor. Even the fattest of maggots has the survival instinct.

He let his body dangle out the door, his hand wrapped in the old strap, and he scanned the terrain. He glimpsed a movement among the rocks and hammered on the roof. They ploughed to a stop in a cloud of dust and smoke. He could not see a thing but pointed the gun in the general direction and shot. A panicked ibis rose into the air.

Hassan smacked the fuel gauge with his hand. The gauge had given a full reading briefly, then settled at various random levels. At that moment it read nothing.

—Soon we will be walking about the desert with nothing in our pockets, looking around like lost desert children. Anyway, if Allah wills it, let it be so!

—Forget Allah. Shut up and let me think.

Hassan looked at him.

—A Muslim would not say the things you say.

—Maybe they ran in circles until they die. It will be a lesson for them. A lesson for dead. School is over, children. No school tomorrow.

—Yes, or maybe they will find their way back to the city and police and army and whatnot. But I do not think so.

—Just shut and let me think.

Hassan sighed and pulled out his prayer mat. It was a special mat with a compass sewn into it to get the direction of Maccah accurately, a gift from his brother.

Money gaped at, mouth twisting, wondering how many things about Hassan he did not know. It was possible Hassan knew more about this job than he, and this was an uncomfortable thought that made Money angry. Over the days he had chewed too much qat, said too much, assumed too much. Now he felt he had been taken up in something more complicated than he thought.

As he watched Hassan, he said, —Eh, Somali, your name is not Hassan, is it?

The other man shook his head. He looked at him with complete and utter lying innocence.

—I am Hassan, of course. Who else would I be?

—Your friends are not who you said.

—I may not call them friends. I may not know them, but they are my brothers. But I hope they are my brothers. Do not worry. You have done a good thing. Allah sees it. He will praise you for your work. Jihad. It's a good thing.

—Allah will never praise me for jihad, you know why?

—No, why?

—Because I never praise Allah or anyone else. And anyway, you should go to your friends and tell them we lost our prisoners and the big plan is bust. Time to give it up.

Hassan shrugged.

—It is not their plan, but our plan. You and me, brother. When we catch our prisoners, we will turn them over to those people and their organization. They will be very grateful for our good work. You will be rewarded and then you will have so much great wealth and also freedom.

—You know, there are kinds of wealth, and kinds of poverty. Right now I am feeling the worst kind of poverty, which is the poverty of intelligent companion.

He thought of seizing the gun to use it on this Hassan once and for all. As he was thinking of it, his enthusiasm flagged. Hassan's simple and unadorned lying certitude, his fake prayer mat and his fake Allah. All of it nervy. It had elevated the Somali and made him seem more important than he was. And then there was the question of this organization Hassan had mentioned. And then too there was the question of all the other things that Money suddenly did not know about Hassan and their plan and about the escaped captives.

Hassan unrolled his prayer mat on the sand. It seemed to Money that the area of the prayer mat was cleaner than the ground around it. It was a place that was uncorrupted and free from the trickery and confusion and criminal activities. He was irritated that suddenly Hassan had assumed such self-importance. A part of him was envious.

—Eh, Somali, whatever your real name is called. Do you have many wives like a real Muslim man, or are you too *impoverished*?

Hassan was praying with great concentration as though trying to make up for all the days in which he had not prayed sufficiently. He tried to ignore Money while he took his time finishing his prayers. Then he just sat with his legs crossed.

—I think our people are close. We will find them today.

—How exactly do you think this? Any logic?

Hassan did not answer but stood up and pulled out the gun. He checked the magazine, taking the bullets out one by one to inspect them.

—You see this gun. They gave it to me. But I made the bullets myself. These bullets I made — they fly straight if I shoot them.

But if someone like you shot the bullet at me, it would fly crooked. I put extra things in these bullets to make them obey. Bullets like this, sometimes they explode if the wrong person shoot.

—You never killed anyone. That is plain for anyone who has eyes. Crooked bullets! A comedian, this man.

Hassan grinned and showed his straight white teeth.

—Maybe not, maybe not. But who knows what a man can do? As for your other question, I am not rich enough for many wives. Anyway, I only need one wife. She was a special gift of my brother who died.

Hassan cradled the loaded AK in his lap as he climbed onto the winch mounted on the front of the vehicle. He climbed up onto the short bonnet, leaned back on the windscreen, and called to Money to get into the cab and drive slowly to the top of the nearby ridge. Money got in, gnashed it into low gear, and the transmission whined them slowly along, Hassan on the deck before him. When they were at the top Hassan gave a signal, and Money killed the motor. They sat for an hour watching over the lands. Then Hassan pointed. Far in the distance two spots moved in the glare of the sun. Money started the motor and they drove until they lost sight of the spots. Then they both got down and walked and searched the ground. It was early in the evening, and sunlight slanted across with rays the colour of new blood. After a while Hassan handed Money the AK to carry. Money took it gratefully; he much preferred to cradle the weapon in his arms, rather than watch Hassan all the time. Once Money held the gun up and pointed it around.

—Somali, with your smiling face you think you fooling people, that you are smart like a genius. But I know you are a greedy, just like everyone. You are no different than other Somalis. And those seventy-two virgins...

Hassan glanced at Money and said nothing. He kept his eye trained on the ground. This seemed to invite Money to continue.

—But listen, I have something important to tell you. See, seventy-two virgins means seventy-two teenager who won't stop talking. *Chak-chak-chak* all night long. *Chak-chak* about each other and they never shutting their mouths except sometimes maybe complain this and that, and cry and quarrel about stupid things. And you, big Muslim man with your big Muslim heart, you be running to buy them clothes and feed them, sleep with them, keep them quiet. You be talking and crying yourself all night after that. Twenty-four-seven of no peace for you. Twenty-four-seven all the way to eternity.

Hassan stopped walking.

—Is this really what you think about me? Is this what you think of Muslim heaven?

—Oh, yes! Who will take care of the seventy-two noisy chickens if not you? Hassan, brother, you better go quick to market and carry big money before you martyr yourself, eh?

Hassan spoke quietly with his head bowed.

—You should know something about me. I have one wife. She is humble and good. A woman who lost her family. One good wife is enough for sons, and I have two. This means I am a father of men. You should not say such things to a man who is a father of men. It is not correct, and it is not permitted.

Money laughed but said nothing more. He might have gone further, but for some reason he stopped. Hassan was a father of men. Even stupid people could be fathers. Then they have that purpose of being a father.

They went back and drove. For a while the lorry moved at a better pace along a vein of hard sand at a river bottom. Then the riverbed narrowed, and they encountered obstacles, and there was no way out. They considered going back but managed to plough through the banks, climb a slope, and squeeze the giant machine around an obstacle course of boulders. The riverbed became shallower, or at least the land around it dipped in that place. They came out in an unfamiliar terrain of salt deposits and obsidian rock that was like blackened, shattered glass. They rolled forward for a time, then stopped. Hassan climbed out on the roof and squinted in the sun. He pointed ahead of them.

—Hyena tracks. Looks like they track something. I think they track our people. See? We rest here and find them at first light of morning. Tell me, my brother, will our prisoners find us just and fair?

He looked at Money quizzically.

—There will be no violence. Is it agreed, my brother?

Money shrugged. He went into the back of the lorry to lie on the bench staring through a gap in the canvas canopy at the sky above. So much sky, so much emptiness.

One thousand chances now and eight thousand later. It was a sum. Mpango mzuri, a sweet deal, a gig, a chance for something big. Perhaps, perhaps, but *by the way, by the way...*

How does it come about that a man must make risky choices? Reasons for everything in the sky, in the universe, but *by the way...*

II

Because of *by the way, by the way.* Because of the children. Because of the abundant wealth of childhood and this place where he was sorely lucky to be raised—the Man U Healthy Child Centre.

One night a girl named Lovingly stumbled over Matron Mumbi, who was coughing blood into a jar, collapsed in the kitchen, her eyes wrong. They ran and brought the director. He had just returned from a trip, *a conference.* But Bwana Director did nothing to help Matron. He had been drinking spirits at that moment. They saw the bottle on his desk. In his drunkenness the director lost his temper at the situation confronting him. In his drunkenness he noticed things he had not noticed before. He saw that Matron had become skeletal, and her skin ravaged. He realized that she kept a jar in her pocket in which she stored the blood that she coughed. Now the jar was clenched in her hand. Director took it up. His eyes made a drunken effort to focus on the bloody fluid. He took her face in his huge hand, and he tried to concentrate on her sick eyes, and just then a sharp light flashed over his face, which gave her a moment to brace herself. With one hand she took back her bloody jar, and with the other she seized his leg, for this was her only support, as he began to fire questions at her, one after the other, each one more unanswerable than the last, and each followed by a blow. They were small questions at first and resulted in cuffs about her head. There were questions about her jar, her blood, her filthy frock. Then came harder questions and harder blows. Had she been seeing men? Did she think about men? Was she lonely at night? Where did she get her medicines? How did she pay? Where did she get money? How did she account for herself? How did she account for her existence? As the questions became more difficult, especially as she was coughing violently, he became more enraged and raised his hand. She curled herself into a hardened millipede ball, elbows tucked over her vitals, one hand clenching the jar of blood. He tried to loosen her grip but could not. Then he staggered, dragging with his leg this miserable and resistant millipede ball into the middle of the room so that the children saw clearly how well he could pass or shoot. He wanted to show this fallen matron what would happen to her. But she lay there sick and quiet and tight. After a while she let go his leg and her jar and lay on the floor in complete surrender.

Money and the other children crowded around her but dared not touch her.

One day the director, the CEO, would be called to account for the things he did.

Matron Mumbi went to the NGO clinic and was seen by one of the NGO nurses. When she came back she was clean and in possession of TB medication. She told the director that if they did not repair the holes in the roof and buy proper beds, she was leaving. Director listened silently then stood and threw his bottle at her feet.

—Advocating on behalf of your charges. This is what you are supposed to do, is it?

—I am matron.

—So why all the rubbish, the sickness, the addiction. Rubbish! All she can talk of is rubbish!

He stalked outside to the road, calling her Our Rich Lady of Nothing and Our Lady of TB. He went to the Disco Bar (Dancing Always), which lately had come under new management and was now the Viagra Taverna (Where a Man Can Kill His Thirst). He returned late that night to burst through the door into her quarters. One or two of his assistants awoke and tried to stop the director but knew better than to try to restrain the big man. He was left to decide for himself in a drunkenness and rage whether he should beat the matron once and for all. Matron watched him with eyes that said she was ready to be beaten or even killed; it was all the same to her. So he did not beat her. He stood wavering as if in a wind, then his body slowly deflated and he turned, clumsily tried to replace the broken door in the frame and went out into the night.

Matron Mumbi was helped back to her quarters by the children. The welfare of Matron and all the children were entirely reliant on the mood and whim of the director. That much had been made obvious, although no one said it. After they put her to bed and closed the door to her quarters, they heard her singing quietly.

Money and Aketch remained outside in the cool night air for a long time, until the singing stopped, and they knew Matron had gone to sleep.

During that long period of growing parts of Money grew faster than others. It was all unequal and unbalanced. People noticed; some covered their eyes or their laughter. The faster-growing parts jutted at unnatural angles, for no good purpose. It was not

attractive, and he knew it. This unbalance was not an encouragement for a young man with an unfortunate other private problem
to now have this unequal problem. But he thought, *I will improve
myself*, and he set about to acquire a knife. A good knife. A good
knife would correct the people and impress girls and bullying
staff members, the corporation, the children of the Healthy Child
Centre.

It could not just be any piece of steel, this knife. It required
a certain threat to its shape. He had no luck trying to steal one
from the older boys. A knife he copped from the kitchen was
made for ugali, ugali, ugali, and nothing else.

He scoured the fringes of the dump. One day he spotted a
large naked blade without a handle protruding from the muck. As
a blade it was notable —flat and grooved, with a long edge. It was
the very knife. Alone, late, at the riverbank, he honed the blade
against a rock, his hand clumsy. When he was done, parts of the
blade could cut, and others were nicked and rough. He used the
blade to carve its own wooden handle, then he tried the grip and
carved more and got it to be good enough, then he bound and
taped it together and went around with it strapped to his body,
the handle exposed for anyone to notice. He might be unequal,
but he had become *dangerous*.

Aketch scoffed when she saw the knife, but he was convinced
that she was actually afraid. The other children allowed him
additional space. Where they once would call to him or laugh at
him, now there was respectful silence. They were not so quick
to follow him as he went about his business, a business that at
that time had assumed some complexity. For he greatly desired to
find his place among the staff in their duties to maintain *security*.
Instead of school in the morning, he broke off and trailed those
older boys, the staff, or if they were doing nothing, he observed
carefully their actions, their way of dressing, their expressions. If
he was in a bold mood he might venture to sit at the periphery of
their circle until they grew annoyed and swatted him away, which

they unfailingly did, berating him for missing school, as if they had not done the same thing.

But they too noticed his knife. They were not cautious and worried about it like the children. Instead, they mocked the knife, and for their own entertainment, chased him, caught hold of him, shoved him about as he was trying to wield the blade, and dispatched him off in the direction of school as though he were a child. As though he were nothing.

And said to himself, *I have my own mind and I am not nothing.*

The second time they attended to him by capturing him. They confiscated his knife effortlessly. As a lesson in lieu of school, they ripped away his trousers to expose his broken and private thing. Money wept in furious humiliation. He was forced to wait until darkness covered him before he searched and found the knife discarded in the ditch, not good enough for them to keep, and made his way back to the Man U Centre. The third time he tried to join them, they were stoned and angry. This time their entertainment was rough: they gave Money a minor beating — mere love pats. After his bumps and bruises subsided, he kept a distance while he followed them, his gaze and his thoughts fixated and dull as holes in a cinder-block wall. He trailed them to secret night spots, to the places they rested and pleasured: the Viagra Taverna and the markets and places in between that he had not known. At night he slept where he found himself, his knife against his thigh, teasing him.

A day came when the CEO received a political summons. He took off for the town with his staff, a pack of dogs called by the whistle of some unseen master. Money watched two bakkies appear, and everyone piled in and roared off singing election songs.

He waited for their return. Hours later an illness took hold of his guts, then came an oily rain, and the roadside went slick. He crept under an eave and slept, then woke and slept, dreaming that they brought him in a bakkie to a market in Nairobi where everything was plentiful and easy and where the roasted chickens dripped with oil and piripiri. When he woke again, he was disoriented and raw, and the worms in his belly squirmed for roasted chicken, as though they were making ready to abandon him, leap out of his body, run away, and find another, more provident owner. He was sick, his head a fly circling a dead thing. He was a sick death fly, wanting, wanting, always wanting.

When the staff returned, it did so in disarray and without the CEO. The staff were in a foul mood. They limped on broken shoes, moaning over their new bruises and bleeds. Their clothing was torn. They had been hired by one side to dish out beatings and threats to the voters. Then someone in the governing party heard about it and sent soldiers. Things went the other way, and the beaters were beaten.

They stumbled across Money where he had waited concealed in the shadows. They caught him and slapped him roughly, took away the knife he waved in his hand. They hauled him up and lashed him to a post, his head down and feet up, and they left him while they drank beer.

There he remained, head down, strung up in the public street, knifeless, as he watched through furious, bulging eyes his inverted tormentors pass among themselves bottles of beer and spirits. Eventually, they drunkenly quarrelled and fought as Money screamed curses at them. They were forced to cover their ears against his shrill attack, then they left that place, leaving him stranded. A girl came to pump water at the standpipe, saw him, covered her mouth, and ran away. The air filled with an acrid smoke from the dumpsite while a gaily decorated starling perched briefly on his foot. Children from the dump came, the starling flew away, the children danced around him for no reason, then ran off singing insulting songs. No one dared cut him down. He was meant to be left so that he would burst like a melon. Voices in his head bounced about, forward and back: *Mungiki, Mungiki. Are you a Mungiki? Are you a Lethal?*

The fearsome Mungiki, the Hordes, came along the lane and stopped at the post where he hung. They looked him over, then went on to the standpipe and harassed the few women there, demanding payment. Since they had no money, the women switched allegiances and confessed their affection for the Mungiki. They were allowed to take away home a grudging amount of water. The Mungiki climbed utility poles as though they were vervets and played in the tangled electric wires, hooting as they did so. Money listened to the voices of these Multitudes, these Enemies, and he felt he was ready to abandon his own wretched people and switch over like the women.

Are you Mungiki?

Maybe. My own family, my Man U, they dangled me for the sun to devour, alone.

The Mungiki whispered in his ears, and the day was turned night with their messages. How could it be dark so early? Voices meant for night, carried in black air, across the dump, and through the lanes, and into his ears.

Come with us. We have new food. We have new water. We have new motors and other new phones. New computers. Come be Mungiki.

He lost consciousness, dreamed, conceived his own death.

When he came to, the sun was in his eyes, and someone hovered over him. It was Aketch with Richard in hand, and with them, the old imam, Mzee Ibrahim, and his young protege. The protege cut Money loose and set him on his feet, whereupon Money collapsed.

They carried him to Mzee Ibrahim's place near the mosque.

Mzee Ibrahim's house was neatly constructed of bricks and wood. It had carved doors and glass windows. Outside was a compound with a date palm and tomatoes on vines and a vegetable patch laid out under the smoky sun.

The imam directed his protege to see that Money was bathed and given a hot meal. Afterward, the younger man brought out a wooden box that contained trousers, shirts, and used shoes, all donated from rich places. He handed Money trousers that fit and shoes that were too big. Mzee Ibrahim came in and asked Money if he felt whole. He bade him sit and talk to his helper. Being tied to the post had an effect on Money. He began to talk more than he liked, about mad things that he had not known were in his mind. He told the man he had second thoughts; he told him he wished he were in school, in front of a teacher. Until that moment he had not realized how much he missed sitting in the classroom and reading. He said he was dirty and wanted to cleanse himself, and that he wanted to turn his back on foreign and unknown liquids and on the Man U Healthy Child Centre, because he hated them now. He would join the Lethals or the Mungiki or other gang. Perhaps the Mungiki had better food. He could go from gang to gang and find out. He said all of this and more.

He was brought out to the compound where the old man sat with a steaming cup of thick, milky tea in the shade of a tree. He slurped noisily while pinching his nose.

—May Allah smile upon you. You look much improved, good enough to go to paradise. Or at least to mosque. But tell me first how you came to be hanging from a post with your head toward the earth and feet toward the sky, an unnatural position for a boy. What did you do to your enemies?

—Those ones? My brothers. They were playing a game.

—Ah. Rough game, that.

Money shrugged.

—I hate them. Where is the girl and small boy?

—We gave them something to eat and sent them home. They would have waited here for you, those two. You are fortunate to have a sister and brother like those two.

—They are nothing, just children without mothers. Orphans. Worthless orphans.

—Yes, I know. All your siblings are orphans. Even I am an orphan. Even Muhammad is an orphan.

—Is not Allah his father, like the Christian god?

—Ah, no, my friend. Allah is not like that. Allah is not a father but the Absolute and the One. In fact, Allah is not man or a woman or a person of any kind. Not a he or she. This Allah cannot be a father if not a human being, yes?

—Allah is an orphan?

—Not like that, my boy. Allah has no beginning, no end. He is eternal, unlike human beings, unlike orphans. Orphans like you began somewhere, with a father and mother. Then those people were lost to the AIDS.

—Why did Allah do nothing to save them?

—Ah. No one knows this. You can say that what happened was written by Allah, that is all. If he sounds like a person, it is the limitation of our human language, that is all.

It made Money nervous to think about something with no beginning or end. His brain fought the ideas like a broken computer.

The imam's movements were as quick and nervous as a worried bird searching for seeds along the ground. He cleared his throat and said nothing to Money for a long time. He slurped at his tea, his eyes twinkling behind his spectacles.

—But your baba was a Believer, a Muslim. Did you know?

—The CEO, a Muslim?

—Ah, not that baba, no. Of course, it is possible he is a Believer inside himself. He has become something different, that one. What I meant was, you are Muslim by birth. But you were diverted away from the path of light provided by devotion to Allah. I have seen this happen before.

—I don't care about it. So I can be a Muslim too. Why not?

—Yes, yes. Of course.

—I don't care about it. It makes no difference...

Mzee Ibrahim's neck tensed, and he spilled his tea. He stopped talking and decided to ignore Money. He bent his head to his book, his eyes blinked rapidly, his lips silently forming the words he read. After a while he went into his house and came back and handed Money a slim packet. Inside was a factory-made knife with a decorated, moulded handle that fit the hand and a convenient hole for a tether to be passed through it.

—How you know I lost my knife?

—You see? Allah can make new from old, good from bad. One day you may find that you need the guidance of the Prophet. Then, when you decide you are ready to believe, come find me. And remember what I said. You had a real father. A real mother too, for that matter. But that is another story.

Because, because.

Hard to understand the particulars of what Allah had set out for him. It seemed as though nothing could be certain in those days: vans careened past on the main road, rubbish flying in their wake, engines howling, while the old Nairobi River crawled by, its waters diminished by the disrespect shown with its passage through the city.

Perhaps this was to be paid back in some way, this Muslim upside-down rescue, this new knife. This instruction. If it was a debt, then he would hang it about his neck; it would join the other debts to make a necklace he wore each day.

There was no way to know the true burden of one's debt, no way to see the wealth of opportunity.

One thousand reasons now, eight thousand reasons to come.

Money sat up and pulled the boots off and shook the sand out and wiped them with a rag. He removed the socks, folded them, and placed one sock atop each boot. Then he left the boots near Hassan so that Hassan might find them and try them on his feet when he rose. Money was quite certain that the boots would fit.

PART THREE

THE MOVEMENT OF CAPITAL ASSETS

CHAPTER 9
Avtar Kestner
Northern Turkana
April 25, 2016

Kestner ran. This, in and of itself, was a brilliant, sympathetic gift. It was as though he soared, catecholamine-fuelled. Fight or flight response fully activated, a miracle of survival. Propelled by the prospect of a bullet in the back. After a few minutes of running, he dared to hope and dared to exult because he ran, he escaped, and the bullet did not come. Then Salim came in pursuit and they ran like dogs.

It was an epic day, of blinding light, of heart-stopping heat. But Kestner ran, he soared, on into dusk, into night and into the next day, until thirst became dehydration and would not be set aside. Then time slowed to a trickle, as sluggish as viscous blood, the hours marked by the succession of parched mouth, dark yellow urine.

He remained dispassionate at first, as he made sparse clinical observations of his own bodily functions in the absence of water. He dispassionately observed his compensations, his decompensations, and inevitable exhaustion. His muscles were shrunken, his thinking weirdly disconnected from his emotions. He had grand literal flights of fancy, of soaring away. He had bookkeeping of the mundane and minute, of estimates of blood volume loss (per hour and per day), estimates of the limit of the range of tolerance for dehydration. He had molecular visions, of coalesced macromolecules jumbled into primordial muck. His thoughts were bogged down by dysfunction of his liver, his brain, his heart. It would be a disorderly descent toward acute kidney failure. Hematuria the bright tint of dyed jam.

Salim snagged his shirt and looked at him so that Kestner found himself staring at two sick reflections of his sick self in the double mirrors of Salim's dark glasses.

—Sah, I want you to know that I know I am a dead man. They will kill me now, for certain. But I will not go gentle into that dark night.

— I don't know what part you played in this, Driver. I don't know what part you're playing now.

—Yes, Sah. But I will not go gentle.

—No, nor me.

—Sah, I am here to help you survive. We must find water not only to drink but to bathe our heads and soak our feet. They say the water in the desert is the sweetest of all drinks, even better than whisky.

They moved onward, plodding over the bright plain, scanning the land behind for their pursuers and scanning the terrain for signs of water. *Water had been in such abundance.* Had he known that one day he would be in such deficit, he would never have left Lac Verde, where the water torrented during the snow melt, saturated the land, the forested hills, overflowed streams that cascaded into the lake, charging it full and clear. Had he known then, in the Canadian summers of his childhood, as he shivered, wading into the weed-shadowed lake, diving into silent depths. The hills around, the Gatineaus, had a thousand ponds and lakes and streams, water in abundance, bejewelled, aquamarine, dun, silver, and black.

If he had known as he swam out to the distant island, duck-diving into mysterious darknesses, deep in a distant northern lake.

‖

Eight years old, his stomach a knot from too many days that were uncertain, unfamiliar, uncalculated, wrong. There were no places where he belonged. He inhabited the life of an unfamiliar boy, a new boy in a strange home. He was lost, and it was impossible to retrace his steps backward. The new life, the new boy, was silent and watchful. He wished his mother would put a halt to the rush of newness that she brought on them both. But he said nothing, daring not to interfere, knowing already, at eight years old, her fragility, and because he loved her unreservedly, and she was so beautiful and young and lonely, and she needed and if she did not get, she would die and it would be his fault. So he suffered without complaint the knots in his stomach, the unfamiliarity, and the stranger's life, in which he was perpetually a visitor, an unwelcome guest, the new boy, the new student, the new member, the stranger in a strange family where he did not know things. There were new smells and foods and the old house and the tent on the cold lake, and he said nothing.

His mother would have life and laughter, but he would not because he must remember that which was left behind. His father, his home. The confusion and the hard words between his parents that he could not understand. Someone must remember this, so that it would not vanish entirely. It seemed no one wanted to remember. She said, on the occasion when he quietly asked, that he would see his father again one day. But he never did. Then even his own memories of his father's home faded, crowded out by the new life.

At first he hated the lake and its cold depths and the forest. Then he thought that he could be alone there. If all else failed he could dive and swim away, leaving behind the unfamiliar life. He would find himself surrounded by weeds and rocks and fish and shadows. At first, he was afraid of the depths. Levi gave him fins and a mask and snorkel and showed him how. He followed the instructions quietly, took it up, and discovered that with fins he could follow the turtles and fish, and this was another refuge. He heard the turbulence of his body as it torpedoed through the yawning chasms, looked upon bottom places on the lake shallows that he thought no one would ever have set eyes upon but he. At night he dreamed fish dreams and loon dreams. Mornings on days when it was cold and quiet, he plunged back into the water. He felt his mother's glance following him, for she knew what he was. So he was what she expected him to be, and this was what he wanted.

The forest around the lake was immense and mysterious. He imagined it to stretch northward, unbroken, toward the tundra, the frozen Arctic of the stories of Mowat and Service. Among the real trees of the real forest, he wandered, transformed into the first boy on Earth, placed his feet silently on trails made by wild creatures, and ascended, an explorer, to the stony ridge where he would sit in his solitude, a primal boy, a boy of the water and the forest heights.

When they were not at Lake Verde, they were in Ottawa, and he was skeptical of the open spaces and greenery of the new place, which seemed not so much like a city at all but a continuous parkland with stone houses and concrete office buildings scattered throughout it, and at the centre the gothic tower of Parliament, which he assumed from the outset was evil, haunted or inhabited by other ancient terrors.

Throughout all, the shambling figure of the new man, now stepfather, this Levi, this man with power over his mother, who brought laughter to her. Levi, the owner of the cottage and lake, who spoke brief words to the new boy. At the end of that first summer he realized that Levi followed him into the lake each day with his own fins and mask, to swim at a respectful distance.

III

They fled through a muted dawn, through the open land of scattered acacias and cacti, through a rent in the earth made by water, over an ancient lava flow. As they went, the sun climbed to a corner of the sky where it stalled—when they looked to it for guidance it had not moved, locked in position.

Salim, the driver, was nearby, Kestner sensed, but he did not look to him, his senses occupied by directionless heat in which he heard the hissing conversations of the Little Doubts, those granules of his internal ruin.

He was a thoughtless and waterless creature under a stalled sun. The kidneys would not have the capacity to recover from this day that went on forever.

They halted in a knot of thorny trees that bordered a great slab of flat rock. Salim came along behind and pointed silently in the direction from which they had come. There were followers, at a respectful distance: a band of discreet forms. These followers appeared for a moment, dispersed to meander at oblique angles, vanished, then reappeared and stopped and waited, as though they only faintly believed their effort would result in a reward.

Kestner was spurred on by these new and courteous pursuers. But he needed to rest frequently as the day went on. They stopped in any place that offered shelter from the sun. He napped at one point. When he awoke the sun had not moved. It remained fixed in a corner as though it were perpetually morning. They searched for water.

As they walked, Kestner drifted, and Salim would touch his shoulder to remind him that he was there to redirect him. Kestner's mind would not be redirected, though. His mind detached, abandoning the plodding and futile effort of walking into a vast and monotonous space. Strange visions shouldered forward as the stalled sun struggled to free itself. There, he spotted his destiny ahead but a little distance, an end in which he lay desiccated and weak, encircled by the opportunistic and the hungry, their teeth snapping. Then that vision gradually lost its unpleasantness and mingled with memories of childhood. A kind of lassitude settled over him.

As a boy, he would eventually return from solitary adventures in the woods, scratched, sun-blackened and wild-eyed, saying nothing, hungry. His mother stroked his head, never admonishing, while Levi tilted his head, shrugged, and spoke his gentle baritone to her so that she smiled. Levi with his massive chest of fur, a bear in swimsuit and tennis shoes, hauling rocks, cleaving stumps, axe or mattock in hand.

Cool nights in the forest, on a mat in the corner of the tent, distant from the adults and Levi's beautiful teenaged girls, Alexandria and Tannis. He lay awake to the stirring of the night wind in the leaves, rain suddenly bouncing on the canvas roof, then stronger rain, hissing on the lake. Later, peace, the sudden hooting of an owl.

Kestner and Salim arrived at an ancient and dust-blown riverbed, the banks barely discernible but for the places where they had given way. These places were a deep rust in colour. Jutting from the bank were strange stones that looked like branches and when Kestner grasped one in his hand he knew instantly that it was fossilized bone, a mammalian humerus to be exact. Beside the humerus he found the occipital bone of a large animal—perhaps a lion by his guess, the foramen magnum stoppered with a distinct shade of stone. Nearby, half embedded in the bank, sitting upright, as though watching over the millennia, was the blackened upper vertebral column and sphenoid bone of an erect hominid. Both men halted at the same moment in sudden, mute recognition.

They were delayed at that place, dreamy and fatigued, drawn out of the moment, made trivial by the presence of the fossil.

Salim finally shook himself and stepped away from the bank.

He peered out over the land. The hyenas had settled about a kilometre away, under a patch of brambles. They called out periodic, pessimistic messages. Salim frowned and wiped his glasses on his shirt.

—Ah, Sah, but look at the friends you keep.

—Yes. Too many friends have I.

—You see, Sah, no use to be consumed by worries. Better to be consumed by friends.

—Ha. Said the hyenas.

—Ha ha. Yes, Sah.

Kestner put his head between his knees. He would have liked to remain there, to patiently tease the skeleton from its place. It would take months of painstaking work with tiny instruments. The simplicity and slow pace of the task was alluring. Who was it, locked in stone for the ages, waiting for liberation? Yet there was not an iota of energy left, and that was a pity. The skeleton would be left to the dusty, sweaty, sun-stroked paleontologists to come and find all over again in ten or a hundred years.

Nearby, Salim studied a patch of soft ground, explaining something to himself.

—Animals, animals. Tracks going every way. There must be a water hole.

A family of rock hyrax emerged near the skeleton through cracks and burrows. The hyraces spoke long sentences and trilling vocabulary, the stories of their rock, the skeleton, the hyenas.

Kestner and Salim walked out in the wavering air to a depression in the middle of the channel. Salim probed the ground with a stick. It crumbled into powder.

—In another season, perhaps quite soon, this place might be filled, even flooded.

—Hard to picture that.

They followed camel tracks along the riverbed for several kilometres until Salim grabbed Kestner's arm and pulled him toward the bank again.

—Sah. Do you hear it?

Kestner heard nothing but the ebbing of his own blood and the disquiet of the Little Doubts. He followed the direction of Salim's backward gaze and saw a hyena on the ridge immediately above them. It positioned itself in an open spot where it could observe them. It lay on its belly, a sphinx overseeing the proceedings. Salim took up a stone and threw it. It was a bad throw, of the kind that any predator would take note. *Feeble, inaccurate attempt.* The hyena blinked one eye as the stone fell nearby. It did not look at the stone at all but kept watching the two men.

Salim collected another stone to carry with him. With the other hand he hauled on Kestner's arm and pushed him forward, and Kestner resisted, weakly shrugging Salim's hand away. Dehydrated yet indignant when he remembered what had happened, and now stuck with this betrayer, who still took it upon himself to push and shove his client, entirely forgetting his duty and his place. Why throw stones? The hyena was a beautiful animal, vividly spotted, impartial in its baleful regard. Why? They were all three, two men and a hyena, under the same sky, at the same moment, in which the temperature had risen to new heights and the global climate disaster unfolded, finally. It was a tipping point: hyena, dehydration, erratic driver. It was a catastrophe fully unleashed.

Kestner put his hand up. He needed to find his wallet and phone. They were missing, and he only noticed it now. Renate was not in sight. Nor Seiko, nor anyone important. He looked back at the ridge. The hyena had moved elsewhere.

Here was a situation. Missing wife, missing wallet, missing phone. Somewhere, someone would be asking about the final report on the health project at Refugee Camp Number Two. He should be in Ottawa, not here. Wife, wallet, daughters, phone. Was it possible to misplace a family in a single moment of inattention?

When Kestner collapsed, his momentum carried him headfirst into the powdery ground of the riverbed. In his semi-conscious state his head dashed into a pillow, and it was a relief. For a blissful moment he was in the cool, lush gardens of the diplomatic mission of the UK, attended to by elderly Hindu women with finicky British accents who bore knishes with light cheese in them. He would try to eat the knishes for he was ravenous, although he knew it was impossible because his mouth was parched. The knish would suck the remaining moisture from his body and kill him. As he passed out, the hostesses served Renate and Mihret, who seemed fast friends, while his daughters and the Turkana children played together in the periphery.

When he came to, a pleasant shade was over his face, which Kestner came to realize was Salim. As a face came into focus, Salim's words swam up out of the ground.

—...must arise, Sah. They are coming near.

Kestner struggled to sit up, thinking of the hyena. Instead he heard the familiar whine and rumble of the ancient diesel engine. IN GOD WE TRIST. He smiled. Trist, triste, tryst, Tristan. Isolde?

—Sah, we must run. If they catch us, they will be angry.

Kestner could not rise, much less run. He waved his hand weakly at Salim. Then, he was out again, in the grey of in-between, then water was running into his mouth, and dribbled into his airways, and he sat bolt upright, choking. The water he drank tasted bitter, not of Glen Moray but of diesel oil. He drank despite a distant echo from a remote part of his mind concerning hydrocarbons and nephrotoxicity.

He was lying in the back of the lorry, under the canvas. There was not a hyena to be seen. The escape had failed, the clever effort for naught. The lorry shifted into gear and rolled forward. Near the open gate Money sat cradling the spade-handled AK.

—Look at you. Maybe it would be better I should kill you to save you from killing yourself. See? When Money is kind and good, what happens? People abuse Money. Now fuel and time were wasted. Why? Because of pride. Now maybe we miss our important meeting with important buyers. All because of bourgeoisie and elite and adventuresome attitudes. Look at you. Damaged goods.

—Where is Salim, my driver?

—Ah, that one. He ran. Seems he is confused. He did not feel safe.

—Ran?

—We only saw his tracks. Perhaps he ran just before we came. Perhaps the big hyena caught up to him. We saw also those tracks.

—Now what will you do to me?

—Do to you? Everything is very simple, if you understand the marketplace. We deliver our goods. Those Mungiki, they follow market principles instead of religion.

—What does this mean?

Money shrugged. He looked out at the empty terrain.

—Yah. They are not like the Somali, who goes on his hands and knees and makes petitions to the Almighty. They are only profit makers, that is all.

CHAPTER 10
Mihret Gebriel
Northern Turkana
April 26, 2016

At first, Mihret was disgusted. She detested dirt and ignorance and desperation and the pettiness of crimes and all the exposed ugly entrails of poverty. It brought on an urge to chide complete strangers about civil behaviour. She wanted to humiliate her abductors, see them shackled before a magistrate, thrown in jail. She wanted them to know that she found them only loathsome, not fearsome.

It was a question of God-fearing decency. Moral standards. God helps those who help themselves.

But over the hours she found herself sinking into a self-critical pattern that was a familiar one; she had become a member of the elite, and like many other elites she forgot her privileges. Then she berated herself for forgetting that, and for her lack of empathy for those less fortunate. If they were dirty and ignorant, she was intolerant. It was not the example the Son of God had set. She should know enough about the poor and the unfortunate, the misbegotten and the desperate. These were men she had encountered enough in her life. Her disgust gave way to embarrassment for the men and their situation. Men like that were easily recognized; hungry irregular men, riding their evil conveyance that looked to have emerged direct from gehenemi. IN GOD WE TRUST, it was supposed to be named—named by the devil himself—and they could not get even that slogan right.

Some of her anger deflected away to the incompetent ferengis. Any normal Ethiopian woman would have taken more care to ensure the safety of the mission at every step of the way, even after the abductors arrived. Instead she had remained silent, habituated within the walls of the UN offices to let others, especially Europeans and Americans, stick their noses out to be swatted. In her short career she had gone from being an outspoken and independent leader, despite the objections of the men in her community, to a silent bureaucratic survivor. *A docile cow led by a weak string,* was what her father would have said. Perhaps. She had learned to be attentive to the rank and importance of those around her who rushed everywhere without thinking, usually destroying themselves in the process. The white ferengi were the worst, with their overblown confidence in their limited abilities, their patronizing attitude toward African women, their bland and misguided assumptions. By the time they learned to abandon their conceits, they were old, and it was time to leave the continent and return to their homes. She was not expected to say anything about any of this. Anyone could see that. She was merely the gender equity adviser on the team, required by the policies of foreign governments to be present on every mission, looking out for women. A box to check. A pretty, brown-skinned decoration.

She had learned much else since coming to Nairobi. She had learned to avoid probing personal questions and how to make strangers maintain a respectful distance. Her colleagues remarked that she preferred to be left alone. Because if anyone looked closely, they would see that which she wanted no one to see: she was not at peace. Luckily, in the world of the international bureaucracy, in the big city world of organizations and foreigners and the rush of international this and that, no one took the time to search the corners of the face of a stranger, no matter how friendly or fine. It was an Old World practice, carried out in villages: to know a person by their face. To look into the eyes and search the soul—to recognize the tormented, the dishonest, the thief. On careful scrutiny, close-up, all was evident. In her home, they look into the eyes, searching, rather than fill the air with words.

Beneath her calm exterior, she was a piece of leather stretched in too many directions, pulled thin by the questions that had no answers. Pride pulled her north. Ambition pulled her south. Her lost child and husband. After everything that she had been through, she wondered sometimes whether her soul was intact.

The least she could do was summon understanding and patience for other tormented souls.

Yet, the moment she was alone, out of sight of her captors, she bolted, knowing full well what might become of a woman held captive by such men—or other men she had yet to meet. As she ran, she braced herself. She kept her mind on her certainty in order to keep her fear at bay. She followed the soft riverbed as long she dared, then she climbed the ridge. After a time she found herself suppressing the word *lost*. She was confident in her direction but had only a faint idea of her position. The kilometres passed beneath her quick feet.

For the first two hours she was simply relieved to be free, but after that the word *lost* was in her mind, and then in her mouth, and she was saying it out loud, and when she suddenly realized it, she became anxious. She was too alone in this life, and it was not as it should be. Now she spoke when there was no one to hear. Only the wind and the acacias listened to her voice.

The ground, at least, was friendly. That she found her footing so well gave her confidence. It was familiar soil, after all, even these thousand and more kilometres from her home. Her shoes were strong enough, and when they gave out, her feet would be strong enough. As a girl she had walked an hour to school barefoot, over hot sand and stone, every day, dedicated to the walk, to the school. Only when she was older did she make herself sandals, copied from another girl.

Good feet, good heart. Good feet, good heart. It was a saying of her father's. She said it aloud instead of the other word, *lost*, and so she went on, covering distance with a trot as steady as her heartbeat.

As the sun descended toward the horizon, she searched for safe places to rest. In the western sky, a stain of blood. She came to a cluster of three dorobo trees and tried to fix a nest in the branches, but after some frustrating minutes gave up and curled herself at the base of the largest tree. She was about to fall asleep when she noticed a yellow scorpion making its way along her sleeve, then looked around and saw others were moving in the semi-dark, up and down the tree. She lay awake the rest of night on the open ground, her confidence troubled. An hour later she heard a grunt that she decided could only be leopard or lion. If it were leopard, it was on a nocturnal hunt some kilometres away.

Mihret had not slept under the open sky for years. She had forgotten the mysteries that were traced in the night sky. As she watched the stars wheel around her, she remained alert to the leopard on its hunt. Finally, there was a squeal as it dispatched a prey animal. She spent the rest of the night worried about what the leopard had killed, what had made such a sound, and what she would do if the leopard decided to hunt again. She had no defence, only faith and humility before the Almighty.

She prayed and watched the sky. She imagined things, her mind playing tricks. In the middle of the air, outlined by the stars, she saw the face of Yeshi, her daughter. She reached up to touch the face and found it cool and distant.

Mihret had begun her journey as a wilful girl with an inquisitive mind who wanted an education. Her father was a schoolmaster who impressed upon her the importance of schooling. He was not in favour of the traditional life for a woman. It was good enough for the previous generation but not for his youngest daughter. Her father told her she must go as far as she could, and if possible she must lead other women out of darkness.

She was an excellent student. As she made her way through early school and into secondary and the number of girls in her classes fell away, she grew bolder and more incensed that other girls did not fight for their education. Mihret observed her two elder sisters proudly finishing secondary school then quickly reverting to local traditions. Mihret wanted more. She graduated at the top of her class, but soon other things happened that blocked her way. Her mother arranged a marriage to a distant cousin. His name was Yessef; he was her age, and he liked to laugh, and he had a university degree and had lived as a student in Addis. She liked him well enough, in part because he had done the things that she herself wanted to do and had done them easily and matter-of-factly and everyone in his family was proud of him. Already he was called upon in the village to help decide the disputes over land and cattle and water that had become all too common. The courtship was a distraction but she went along with it. She agreed to marry and within the year she became pregnant and delivered Yeshi, a baby with gigantic eyes and a joyous laugh. Yeshi became her world. She dreamed about Yeshi. She lived for Yeshi. She wanted to be an example that would push Yeshi to go far, and in so doing, she realized she was not finished with her own plans. Mihret told her husband she must apply to the university in Addis to complete her degree. He was opposed. He told her she belonged with him and their child. He was trying to farm the family land and needed her in the village. Mihret had seen the village life and what it did to women. She did not want it, and she did not want her Yeshi to have that tradition and limited outlook. With her father's blessing and funding she and Yeshi moved to Addis, leaving Yessef behind on the farm. She attended university while her daughter went to city school. Mihret went back to being the wilful and inquisitive girl.

When she was in her final year Yessef came to the city and

took Yeshi away. Mihret came home to her empty flat to find her nanny in tears and her daughter gone.

Yessef did not take their daughter back to the village farm. It turned out he had hated the village after all. In fact, he had left Ethiopia altogether, which took Mihret some time to discover. They had gone to Kenya.

Mihret did not hesitate. She needed her daughter with her. She trailed them to Nairobi.

That was three years before. Things had happened quickly in the city. Someone she met was impressed by her impeccable English, natural grace, and calm nature and told her about the position at the International Organization for Migration. She decided to stay and apply for the position. She was successful.

She changed. She met and worked with people from all over the world. She met high officials, including heads of state. She carried herself with solemn dignity. She made contacts, read books, was invited to sophisticated international social events. All the while she searched for her daughter. She asked everywhere after a man named Yessef who had a beautiful daughter named Yeshi.

She was known as an honest person and a strong woman. She did not share her pain as much as she might have. She was slow to make friends with the Swedish and Swiss and French and Kenyan and Indian colleagues she worked with at the IOM.

She heard finally, from a girl who worked in another agency, that someone with her husband's name worked for the Canadian High Commission.

She considered what she should do. She could go there as an IOM officer. She could phone to make further inquiries. Then she wondered how her husband, if it were he, would react. Perhaps he would move on again. Perhaps he would refuse to see her and send Yeshi away.

She came and went from work, preoccupied, perplexed, and

alone. At her office she was given progressively more responsibilities. She now carried the additional burden of those her organization would assist, of the thousands of other women, her sisters, who were separated from their families by hard circumstances. Separated from their husbands. Separated from their children. She saw that it was happening everywhere, that families were broken by wars, famines, floods, and droughts. There were thousands of mothers like her, bereft of their loved ones yet continuing with their lives.

One day she found herself in front of the Canadian diplomatic mission. She got down from her taxi and sent it away. She was determined to know if it was Yessef who worked there. She hesitated outside the gate. As she stood, an official car, its flags rolled and sheathed, emerged from the grounds. She could see nothing through the darkened glass. The car contained a foreign world beyond her ken. It would not contain her daughter, she knew, yet she found it to be an affront. All she wanted was a hint or a sign to tell her how she could find Yeshi.

She withdrew to the shadow of the exterior wall of the compound and waited. Cars came and went, important cars bearing the flags of other countries. Meetings were going on, a busy day was proceeding in the world of international relations, foreign aid, global security, poverty reduction programs. A man wearing a white shirt and tie conducted the security ritual of inspecting the engine compartment of each car then using a mirror on a long handle to search for bombs strapped beneath. After he gave his assent, the gate would slide open, and she caught a glimpse of the interior of the compound, a place entirely sequestered. Inside were mowed, trimmed, green gardens. An oasis. A realm of great power and wealth was out there beyond her. She was mesmerized to see its physical form. With moist eyes she observed it from her insecure spot. For a long while she remained outside the gate, watching and thinking.

There came a pause in the comings and goings, and the guard in his white shirt noticed her. In a moment he came toward her with a sheet of paper and pen.

—Madam, I see you waiting by the gate for this past hour. Is there someone inside you wish to see? Do you have an appointment?

—No. Yes. Oh, I am sorry, it must look odd. I am Mihret from the IOM, but I am not here on IOM business. Is there an Ethiopian someone who works here in Canada? He would go by the name of Yessef.

The guard went to his shed to speak on the phone, wait, speak again. Then he came out.

—You know, there was a someone on the staff with that name. I remember him. But he left several months ago. They do not know where he went.

She went on. She returned to her flat, her worries, and her work.

A short time later she received word that her father was on his deathbed. It was sudden, the onset of his illness abrupt, his blood corrupted, his body rapidly failing. Before she could allocate her work and apply for leave, she received another message that he had died.

She intended to remain on the family farm for a week. But it was complicated. Her mother was in a state of shock, unable to express her grief and incapable of taking over the management of family affairs. It was left to Mihret, as it often had been, to oversee the farm. Her brothers and sisters were petty-minded and only seemed able to squabble among themselves. Who should get the best part of the land? Who would get the animals and farming implements? How should it be divided? The two sisters lived in a nearby village and were occupied with their families. They were poor. Mihret was the only one who had become educated, moved on, lost her child and husband. She found that her sisters, who had once chided her for her single child and absent husband, now harboured complicated feelings of judgment mixed with envy because of her apparent liberation. There were some notable comments about her morality, which Mihret chose to ignore. No one inquired about her life beyond knowing that she worked for a UN agency and was therefore rich.

Her mother gradually regained her senses enough to understand what was going on in the house. She helped Mihret mediate the sibling disputes. Together they managed the burial.

Meanwhile a severe drought had persisted in the woredas to the east and north, in Tigray and Afar. A famine had been brewing already. It became a silent crisis. At first, the men were forced off their farms to seek work or food. As the shortages worsened, families began to leave their homes in search of relief.

That year, the year of her father's passage, was a time of upheaval. The villagers blamed the local demons, the agenint, and invoked their faith to defeat it. Some blamed the government and pointed to the repression of political dissent. Mihret looked at the cloudless skies, the deforestation, the overworked soils. On her return, after her long absence, she travelled though forested lands, the savannahs to the south, to places rich with animals. She saw how depleted and tough was her home woreda. The local people would not admit that their ancestral land was deforested, dying and impossible to farm. Every season, they doggedly planted seeds in the faint and stubborn hope of a bountiful harvest of tef, but every year the wooden ploughs snapped off in the desiccated and rocky ground. Every year the farmers, old beyond their years and as parched as the soil, harvested diminished crops while their families ate less and less each year. There were days when she looked out in the fields and was sure only skeletons guided the wooden ploughs. Skeletal oxen and skeletal goats and the skeletal farmer himself, hauling his own plough through rocks and dust.

She watched the drama unfold on a vast stage in which migrants struggled across the countryside, starving and dying. They did not utter words, these people, but she saw in their eyes the pain and shock of those who must witness death moving among them with a free hand, stealing their elderly and their children. They fled before it, enfeebled and defeated while the land burned under an unearthly wind. Before them they drove the remnants of their herds. Even the animals were resigned.

In Mihret's community strangers appeared near the farms and around the towns. These wandering strangers were silent, their words stoppered by their upended hopes and growling bellies. The wanderers were a trickle at first, and they were offered assistance by the farmers. But the trickle grew to a river. The locals changed and withdrew their welcome and began to worry about their own grain stores and herds. During the night they could hear them arriving, their feet shuffling through the dust, a procession of ageninti, demons. In the morning there were ganen children with their skeletons revealed, children who had forgotten how to play or talk but only stared with huge-eyed wonder. There were ganen mothers nursing infants from flaps of leather that were once plump breasts, mothers who carried their dead infants at their breasts, some attempting to nurse the tiny corpses. Ganen fathers with vacant minds and vacant glances, who had lost hope for the future of their families and their clans.

The locals talked. Some actively tried to send the ganen people away. What could one do? Should they sit by and let these starved demons come and occupy their lands? There were those in the community who would force them to move on, violently if necessary. The village leaders advocated self-preservation and showed little sympathy.

All of this was futile because as they were being harangued, beaten, chased away, the starved and dying only stared with hollow eyes, and croaked out words that sounded alarmingly like the voices of the carrion-devouring kites and vultures.

Mihret watched and listened. The country was ailing along with all the people in it. *What could one do?* Indeed, what could one husbandless, childless woman do to help a whole country? People said God and Christ would help, but God and Christ seemed to sit back and watch, despite prayers from the devout.

She went among the refugees. The starving, the half-dead spoke in their own, unfamiliar tongues, when they spoke at all. But Mihret looked into their faces. She studied eyes. She knew these people. She saw that these were farmers who wanted only the most basic mercy—and did not even expect that. They wished only for a chance to survive. A chance for their children to live a life. What could anyone with a heart do but make room for them, open the grain stores and fill the water troughs until everything was gone?

Humbled in her circumstances, grieving for her lost father and child, she opened the granary of the family farm. She told her mother. Her mother nodded and awakened from her grieving to instruct her siblings to listen to Mihret because she knew what must be done.

Mihret came to realize then, that despite her situation, she was fortunate and wealthy. Her own farm and family were strong. She split her stores to ration the *tef.* She monitored the animals, counting the cows that still produced milk and those that could be slaughtered to feed the family. She counted the farm workers and newcomers. There was still sweet water in their deep well.

When those starving people discovered Mihret would do her utmost to assist them, the word spread, and they came in numbers. They made places in odd niches on the margins of her farm and waited for death or salvation.

Mihret went to the town and emailed the regional office in Nairobi, telling them she would be delayed. She then wrote a brief report on the situation including estimates of the needs of the displaced people in her area and copied it to the Ethiopia country office in Addis.

Two weeks later white-painted World Food Program vehicles came along the little dirt track into the area. They unloaded water and bags of grain and rice and oil at the farm and went back. Lorries followed later carrying tents and blankets and simple stoves and water and grain for the growing colony of displaced persons.

Mihret was busy from sunrise until late in the night, directing the making of the coffee as the sun rose and managing the tent colony growing on her land while fending off the objections of her siblings and the kebele chairman, who was old and obstinate and did not like to be advised by a woman. If not for the quaint and sometimes irritating view that she was of noble blood, nothing would have been possible.

Weeks passed, and then she knew that she had to prepare to leave, the demands and her personal worries overwhelming her. She enlisted the help of the most likely of her younger brothers who agreed to take care of the farm as well as he could. She explained to her mother that she had a job, she had other duties, that she had to continue to search for Yeshi. Her mother tried to dissuade her but released her in the end.

Mihret arrived back in Nairobi in a state of exhaustion. Two days later her agency assigned her to the Canadian-led review of the refugee health program.

CHAPTER 11
David Mason-Tremblay, GoC
Turkana District
April 26, 2016

He looked upon the length of the riverbed to where it hooked around a headland to the south. He saw no fleet figure, no flowing white garb, no beautiful woman running. Nothing moved under the midday glare.

David Mason-Tremblay moved on, walking swiftly, jogging in places, his certainty shrinking. When he would stop to rest, it was eerily quiet, as though the land were holding its breath. It had been hours since he had watched Mihret sprint away, and all these hours he had kept on, thinking she was nearby, around the next bend in the river. It was possible that she had diverted from the river. He was aware of this but shunted the thought aside because he did not wish to think his assumptions were wrong. He kept pressing back that possibility. If he admitted it were true, the logical extension of it would be that he was off track and alone and lost. So he kept on, persistent in his belief, pushing himself harder. He still carried the exaltation of his successful escape.

In the places where the ground was soft, he noticed a great many tracks, large and small, but none that would be Mihret or any other human. They were animal tracks. He had no idea what they might be and did not have the time to try to sort it out. He pushed on, took himself in a roughly westerly direction, guided by the afternoon sun, to stony ground that overlooked the riverbed. He came to a hump of branches and mud with the remnants of a fire near it. The hut, even though collapsed, renewed his confidence. He had no idea if the hut was a month or a year or ten years old, and he did not want to dwell on that. He preferred to believe that whether he found Mihret or not, the hut signified that he was sure to encounter friendly local people who would help him. So he pushed on.

At the moment, he wished, more than anything, to catch up to Mihret. In principle, she was nearby. She could not have travelled faster than he, an athletic younger man. He looked forward to the relief she would show when he came upon her. She would be afraid and alone, confused perhaps, worried. She would be ecstatic to see him.

But he had challenges. He stopped now and again to listen and look back lest he be found. And the heat. He had never experienced such heat. When he was offered this posting, he was told that Nairobi was cool and temperate and he was very wrong to think Africa was snakes and heat. No, not Nairobi. But here he was, well away from Nairobi, and what was it? Snake and heat in one day. Unlike the snake, the heat followed him. The skin on his face and head was blistered, and he did not dare touch it and did not want to know the details of why it burned so, even though he had fashioned a skimpy turban with a piece of material torn from his shirt.

He cut away from the riverbed, along a slanted plateau that ended in a hillock where he felt the breeze on his skin. The view to the west was vast, the sun filling the sky as it began to settle toward the horizon. He kept on for another hour and saw large birds wheeling in the distance. He ran toward that place, arriving exhausted and out of breath. On the ground were the remains of a kill, a large antelope with magnificent spiral horns. Its bloody bones were scattered, tatters of sinew hanging from them, the birds rending at the sinew and bone. Directly in front of him was a footprint of a very large animal. He saw several prints in the clay, with four digits and a complex, lobed foot. He stared at it a long time and concluded that it belonged to either a lion or leopard.

This made Mason-Tremblay pause. He sank to a squat, the blood draining from his head. The predator would not be far, perhaps sleeping off the large meal. If it were a lion, there would be a pride. But the more he looked at the ground, the more tracks he saw and the more confused he became. He knew nothing about wild animals or their tracks.

He stood suddenly and looked around. There were large acacias on a nearby low hill but no other cover. He hurried away from the kill, suddenly wishing to put it far behind him. His heart laboured in the heat. It was important to stay calm and focused, and he was not. He thought to call out to Mihret, in case she was within earshot, but he suppressed the urge, thinking of what else might listen to the anguished cry of a lost human. As he trotted forward, he had the eerie sensation that the sky over him was watching and passing judgments. He glanced up once or twice, expecting to see someone who could provide hints or directions. He saw only the sun watching, and the contrail of a northbound jet. He stopped to look for the silver outline of the jet, kilometres above the earth, and took some comfort from that. Should someone look out their porthole, they would see the earth where he stood.

He hurried on, following a path made by a herd, over a cracked and fissured water basin that was entirely clear of trees or rocks. He stopped now and again to look back and listen for the sound of the lorry called IN GOD WE TRIST. His feet were blistering in several places. He was aware of being newly schooled in old lessons: his body was not as impervious as he had thought; energy was not limitless; water was crucial. It had been six hours since he had escaped, and he had set a fast pace the entire time. A new sensation, of panic, bubbled within. He fought it down and tried to work things through. He knew something about survival, did he not, from the many days spent skiing and hiking in the British Columbian interior, in the hills and valleys of Quebec? He was an advantaged person. Although of late he had begun to wonder if his advantages—athleticism, Brad Pitt-ish looks, advanced education—might work against him. They meant nothing out here, where simple survival was the measure of a man. The instruments of testing were heat, desiccation, predators, unmapped terrain.

The sun melted into the west like a golden chandelier. At the bottom of the sky, it was a pool of fire. He did not stop his quick-paced step. He decided that he should descend to the riverbed once more. He cut away to the north toward the river ravine he had kept to his right. But when he came to the lip of the ravine, he found that it was not a riverbed but a shallow depression with a blind end and several large burrows on the opposite slope. He did not wish to know what sort of creature made such large burrows.

Now there was this choice: either retrace his steps in hopes of locating the riverbed once more, or forget the riverbed and head south. At that moment he gave up, finally, the idea of finding Mihret. He looked down at the ravine, sick with apprehension. An annoying and remote vision came to him, of sitting in a pub drinking a beer, telling some attractive woman the story of his harrowing experience. He imagined trying to tell the story of how he was hunted by lions in the Turkana wastes. He would try to explain that a man could have everything and still be foiled by the lack of drinking water. It had the potential to be a very good story. An admiring female might be impressed.

He began to run, and briefly he had the weird sensation that he would at any moment be released from the confines of gravity, from all earthly ties, to float upward through the sky to where it opened into the deep and endless indigo of space. He stopped and squatted and looked about in the half-light, afraid. He breathed deeply for a moment, stood up, and resumed walking toward the last of the sun, his pace slower now.

Less than an hour later, there was only the residue of light in the west that declined by the second. At this time he heard a voice. He froze in mid-stride and did not move a muscle. A moment later he heard it again, distinct this time. He shifted this way and that, trying to locate the source. He called out: —Mihret! Ms. Gebriel!

The voice went silent. He walked carefully in the direction from which the sound had come, toward a shadowy depression, to find an old Turkana woman on a stubby handmade stool, alone, her spear and staff on the ground before her. She was in an attitude of meditation or prayer but had stopped to listen. After a moment she resumed, speaking in a stream, her eyes closed tightly.

Mason-Tremblay approached her carefully. He looked about for a vessel that might contain water. When he saw she had none, he sank slowly to the ground a few metres from her. Her skin was dusty and dry and very thin, her limbs like ropes. Copper ornaments resembling leaves pierced her lips and ears. About her neck were necklaces, thirty or forty in number, with beads that looked to be worn grommets of laundering machines. Mason-Tremblay opened his mouth to speak but managed only a croak. He wondered if he had blundered into the death ritual of an old person.

The old woman opened her eyes and blinked in surprise to see the red-skinned man squatting before her. She looked at him in disbelief, then struggled to her feet, only to collapse backward, her mouth working. Then she howled. It was a penetrating, piteous howl that made the hairs on Mason-Tremblay's neck rise. She grabbed at her spear. Mason-Tremblay backed away. He pantomimed that he drank from a glass. Her eyes grew wide. She howled again.

A half-grown albino boy appeared, running, firewood spilling from his arms. He immediately put himself between Mason-Tremblay. The old woman pulled out a rough blade and held it up. She stood with a grunt. She whispered at the boy, and he held his knife up.

Mason-Tremblay's throat was parched.

—Water. Maji?

The boy stared.

—Maji. Please.

He cupped his hands together, licked his lips.

After a moment the boy stepped back. He went to the woman and guided her back to her stool. Then he took up a goatskin gourd, took Mason-Tremblay's hand, and dripped water into his palm. Mason-Tremblay's knees buckled. He sank against a large rock and a tide of grey swept over his vision.

The boy and the woman watched him and whispered to each other. Then the darkness deepened, and Mason-Tremblay could barely discern the boy as he gathered the wood he had dropped. The boy made a fire, the old woman hissing instructions. The fire flared up immediately. The boy came back to Mason-Tremblay to place a shred of dried, gristly meat beside him. He gave Mason-Tremblay water again, this time filling his hand twice.

When his mouth was wet enough, Mason-Tremblay chewed the meat. His mouth was still too dry to swallow. Sleep overcame him. He awoke later in the midst of a field of coloured stars that reeled through the depths of space. He was thirsty. The fire had burned down to embers. At first he thought he was alone, but then he saw the lumped form of the old woman, huddled and asleep on the other side of the fire. He heard the tapping of a stick on rock nearby. The child was awake, watching over the camp. Mason-Tremblay slept again until daybreak.

When he opened his eyes the old woman and the boy were studying him. They had bundled together their possessions and were ready to move on. After a few minutes, the boy spoke to Mason-Tremblay, which he took to mean he was invited to go with them. The sleep and the minute quantity of water had stolen something from him, rather than nourish him. He followed along, distinctly aware that he would die otherwise. Should he die, he wished to be with people. He thought of the bones of the antelope strewn over the ground.

He stumbled after them, his eye drawn to the peculiar, smooth gait of the old woman, who was obviously not ill. She carried a short staff in one hand and had her belongings slung along her side. She walked erectly and quickly. The boy wore a ragged cape of woven grasses on his shoulders, a hyena hide around his loins. On his feet he wore old canvas sneakers. The boy was sleek and well-fed, his limbs smooth as polished ivory tusks. Again they shared with Mason-Tremblay their food and water. He clung to this sign that they were compassionate, in spite of his foreignness.

It occurred to him as he walked with his scalp and feet burning, over the torched black rock and sand, that this was a monumental mistake. He was hardly committed to the ideals of bilateral aid, poverty reduction, sustainable practices, gender equality, or any of the other policy planks of the agency. Wars, starving refugees, droughts, climate change—these sorrows of the world were too immense in scale, and therefore too abstract to touch him. His colleagues fretted over a cyclone twenty thousand kilometres away in a place inhabited by people of foreign race and language, a coup staged by misogynist armed men. He watched his caring colleagues, and listened. It was difficult for him to empathize. At times he wondered why it seemed as though the emotions his colleagues expressed were absent in him. He faked it as much as he could, hoping to appear as one of these people he so liked and respected. Ultimately, his upbringing was to blame. His mother, Julia, was a tough-minded Alberta Tory who was strident in her belief in self-sufficiency above all. He still heard her sharp opinions reverberating through the house, that corruption was afoot, that she knew that the weakest, least competitive members of society had come to rule the country of Canada because of socialist governments, because of immigrants, because of welfare. In public she expressed a muted tolerance for other creeds and colours. She refused to even talk about the demands of the province of Quebec. The idea of government redress of broken treaties with Indigenous people drove her to fury. She applied for and then mailed her government pension cheques to her Member of Parliament each year, along with scathing and virulent screeds against governments that tried to buy off citizens. When Julia Tremblay heard that her one and only, her beautiful tennis-playing, water-skiing, water-polo team captain of a son, had quit the financial firm and applied to join the federal government, she was nonplussed.

—Why the hell can't he stick to normal things, like a normal Canadian boy. Goddamn government! They'll bullshit you from hell to breakfast.

Dick, his father, prematurely aged, his mind detaching, smiled vacantly.

—Hell to breakfast. My, my. That is a very long way, my sweet.

Mason-Tremblay struggled free of his mother's influence. He was afraid of Julia and had listened to her opinions and advice all his short life. He had followed her directive to attend business school. But then someone else captured his attention. Her name was Pauline and she had expressive lips and wore lengthy, curvaceous skirts. Julia complained that the new girlfriend was "nothing but a gypsy temptress." David reacted by following Pauline across the campus, where he switched his major to the humanities. Then along came Margot and her bed full of delights, and Julia called her "that French tart" while David changed his major to political science. Diane, Mikaela, Kaitlin: bitch, darkie, slut. History, public administration, nursing. By the time he graduated he was enamoured with Petra, who had been selected for foreign service. Petra was the worst of all. Russkie! Bohunk! Polack!

He told her he was of a generation that valued international human rights and freedom above all.

Said Julia, —Generation Freedom, is that what it is? Well, I don't care if you are Generation Bull, or Generation Shit.

He applied and was accepted by the International Development Agency.

II

The old woman maintained a steady and nimble pace and did not stumble the entire day. Mason-Tremblay realized in a dull and sick way that he was struggling to keep pace with a malnourished eighty-year-old. The boy was even hardier, running ahead and back, scouting for the tracks of potential prey. He wore a hat made of rags and woven straw and two feathered wings that extended over his shoulders. During the brightest hours he wore slitted eye coverings of bone, of the type northern people use for snow glare. With a pang, Mason-Tremblay recalled his own Italian shades left behind in the lorry. Nine hundred dollars. He would love to show them to the boy and the old woman, reveal to them his world, the world beyond this sorry place, of Italian shades, bottled water, business class, neoprene.

By the afternoon Mason-Tremblay's head was sunburned and his muscles trembled with exhaustion. They paused under the sparse shade of a thorny tree where the boy offered him a ration of water, then boy and old woman sat on the ground and embarked on a discussion with long intervals of silence during which time they looked upon the foreigner.

Mason-Tremblay looked at them back. He had tried to make a success of it. Everyone expected him to be stellar. After two years behind a desk in a stale Ottawa office tower, he applied for an overseas posting. To his shock, he was immediately accepted. In what seemed a matter of hours he was briefed, documented, passported, bundled out to the airport, the Maple Leaf Lounge, Air Canada business class, Frankfurt, Lufthansa. In a surreal moment, he found himself suddenly gazing from ten thousand metres at the expanse of the Libyan Sahara, then the glint of the Nile, snaking through Egypt in the evening sun.

Before he left Canada, one of his school friends gave him a guitar, somehow having gotten the impression that he was music-al. Mason-Tremblay accepted graciously and packed the guitar along. Perhaps he *would* learn music. When he reached his hotel room in Nairobi he took the guitar out of the case and leaned it against the wall. It was a beautifully crafted instrument, the soundboard delicately grained, golden in colour, the sides and back made of gnarled tropical wood. Every now and again he would pause to admire the craftmanship of the guitar. Each time he had the same sensation — that he was wasting a good guitar and wasting his time.

All the flats normally given to unmarried Canadian govern-ment officers were taken so he was assigned a large house meant for the family of a senior diplomat. It was an old colonial place, luxurious and airy, surrounded by low, green hills. The first days he rested and was comfortably attended by a retinue of ser-vants — two cooks, two maids, a gardener, and watchman. He found the baked goods slightly too rich for his tastes, but the menu was varied and fresh, the laundry immaculately starched and pressed, the floors squeaky with wax, the breakfast table adorned with freshly cut flowers each morning. When he invited a woman for dinner, the staff discreetly vanished.

Through the French doors lay an established rose garden, and beyond that, a vista of the large and open skies of western Kenya. He spent the first weeks unknowing, handsome, languid in the old house, like an aristocratic son of the British Empire. At work he was largely unoccupied, since he was not given any substantial file. He watched the others and looked for promising female company. He was impressed by his superior, the country director,

Anton Kuric, who was younger than he. Kuric wrote succinct, ironic emails, which were read with delighted snorts and chuckles throughout the mission. Everyone thought Kuric was brilliant. He sported retro-styled eyeglasses, a mane of unkempt hair, was seen in the company of an assortment of attractive diplomats, female and male, from other countries. Mason-Tremblay viewed a life to which he might aspire, an international life of good works overseas, glittering diplomatic society, sun-drenched weekends of tennis, swimming, and golf at the European social clubs that were attached to various embassies.

After a month, he was called into Kuric's office and given his first assignment. It was, Kuric explained, a chance for Mason-Tremblay to experience the field. The field, Kuric said, was where the business of development assistance really happened. It was where Mason-Tremblay would have a chance to work with the Kenyan people, the beneficiaries of Canada's aid mission. Going on a field assignment provided the moment that every diplomat and development professional waited for. It was what made all the international agreements, legal contracts, diplomatic language, and dirty political manoeuvering finally worthwhile. Kuric's speech went on for a long time and was more interesting than the minister of international cooperation herself could manage.

Mason-Tremblay was hesitant. He had only been in the country a few weeks and had not ventured outside of Nairobi. Everything still felt new to him. He had experienced some periods of being lonely and homesick. Of course, he was aware that he could not very well object. It was important that he impress Anton Kuric if he was to get on, move ahead into the new life. Kuric concluded by telling Mason-Tremblay that he was being given the task because no one else was available. He said this with such a straight face that Mason-Tremblay assumed he was joking.

Now, here he was, hungry and thirsty and marching across a desert with his eyes fixed on the scrawny back of an old woman. The sky clouded over, and he lost his sense of direction. His guides, his hosts, his caregivers, seemed to follow paths made by wild animals. When he looked down there were hoofprints and scatterings of dried droppings of various sizes and shapes. Finally, at dusk they stopped, and the boy made a fire in a hollow formed between a stony bluff and a flat pan of white crystalline salt that burned the eyes. The woman and child ate nothing that night. They wrapped their faces and turned their backs to him and fell into a guarded sleep that Mason-Tremblay noted could be disturbed by the sound of a passing scorpion, the rustle of a viper, the flitting of a mouse, a sparking of the fire, a change in the direction of the wind.

Eventually he too fell into sleep, but it was a stuporous and deficient sleep of chemical imbalances and electrical misfires. When he opened his eyes at dawn, the fire was out. A cold breeze had drawn away his body heat. There was no comfort anywhere he turned, it seemed. It occurred to him that he might easily die in that place. He might not last through the day. His nose and eyes were raw and running.

The old woman sat a distance away, observing him quietly. She called out. The boy appeared a moment later with a struggling lizard hanging from a snare. He handed it to the old woman and brought the gourd of water to Mason-Tremblay and splashed it in his hands. The woman dispatched the lizard, skinned and cleaned it, revived the coals in the fire, and roasted it. It was no more than a few gristly bites for each of them. Mason-Tremblay thought it tasted of skunk.

They went on like that for another two days, the water replenished from mysterious source. On one of those days the boy came across a cobra but, despite terse instructions from the old woman, was not able to kill it before it dove into a hole. On the next day he went flying after a jackal, which roused the old woman to cackles of laughter.

They climbed a spine of soapy rock that was as black as obsidian and rose abruptly through the sand and broken red stone and acacia like the back of a partially uncovered and enormous sauropod. At the end of the backbone lay a nest of three circular huts made of acacia branches and animal skins and stone footings. That night Mason-Tremblay lay on the smooth black rock. He dreamed peacefully for the first time in many nights, and when he awoke he felt he would survive. They remained at that place for two days. At sunrise each day, the old woman brought the gourd full of fresh water and dried nuts from some source at the base of the black spine.

Mason-Tremblay's strength improved enough that he decided to take his chances and go on alone. One morning, he slept late, waiting for the boy and the woman to be away from the camp. He wished to thank them before taking his leave, but his trust in them had ebbed. They never smiled at him. He lay curled on the ground, waiting for the moment to arise. He heard the voices of men. For a moment, he exulted, thinking his rescue had arrived, it must be the police or military. He jumped up and moved quickly toward the voices. There were three men in T-shirts and jeans. Two carried crude, rusty spears, the other an AK-47. The two loosely pointed the spears at Mason-Tremblay as they addressed him in their language. Mason-Tremblay could only gape at them as he felt the blood rising to his head. A short distance away the old woman and the boy looked on. The woman finally cracked a canny, lopsided grin at him. The boy waved jovially with one hand, while in the other hand he clutched three animal tethers.

Mason-Tremblay swore loudly. He had been traded for three young goats.

CHAPTER 12

Mihret Gebriel
Northern Kenya
April 27, 2016

Her stride was as efficient and fast as that of any country woman. As a child she was accustomed to running the long distance to school without a drop of water to wet her lips. She found her body was still capable, even these years, after childbirth and all her trials. Yet this was not merely a run to school and back. So far it had been an entire day of running at pace in intense heat, under a full sun. She managed to keep an efficient jog until she became aware that she had lost far too much moisture. She slowed to a walk, then finally stopped in the shade of a large termite hill, keeping a sharp eye out for mambas she knew might be near. She had kept her thoughts simple over the last hours, focusing on the matters at hand and keeping her worries at bay. In a while she began to notice fresh tracks on the ground. They were camel tracks, and now that she looked for them, she could see that they went straight and unwavering in a southerly direction. She looked around her once more before she went on, following the tracks.

The tracks joined other older tracks, of camels and other creatures, some recognizable as various antelopes, others old and indistinct. The sun angled down. She felt at once encouraged by the diminishing heat and concerned about the coming of nightfall.

The tracks were joined by another stream of tracks, of goats. Among them was a single print of a human foot, unshod. It was nearly dark when she saw that the tracks led back to a riverbed, at the bottom of which was a muddy water hole. There were camels and eland and, across the riverbed, looking in her direction with their noses sniffing the air, a family of hyenas.

She did not move for a long time, then backed away from her spot and took up a stone and a dried branch. She was fortunate. She was downwind of the hyenas. The water hole would be impossible, or it would be the end of her. It was out of the question.

Mihret felt an upwelling of panic in her chest but she fought it back as she had so many times in the past. As always, she was disgusted with herself, furious with her weakness. This weakness, the tendency to panic and fear, would be her undoing.

Absently she took up a fruit that had fallen on the ground and realized it was familiar to her. There were several on the tree, and she collected all of them before gnawing the outer shell of one and sucking the juice from it. Her head instantly cleared, and her senses sharpened. She felt as though she had been sleepwalking and suddenly woke up. She tied the knobbly fruit at one end of her scarf and the rock in the other, slung it over her neck, and moved away from the water hole quickly.

That night she stayed in the lee of a ridge she came upon just before nightfall. In the small hours she heard the hyenas in the distance, searching for her. She had a visceral fear and hatred of hyenas, the djibb. But the hyenas had always been there, advancing and retreating, throughout the history of Mihret's family. To wander alone away from the farm at night was to commit oneself to the outsized jaws and salivating lips, to the capacious belly of the djibb. She remembered the stories from childhood of hyena armies on the march across the land, stealing healthy adults, even warriors, at will. She had seen with her own eyes the work of hyenas on the weak and vulnerable.

During the long drought and famine, the hyenas had been there too, following the migration due to the famine. The migration came to her family farm while she was there, and behind them came the hyenas. Mihret did what she could. She contacted the police and the army, hoping for men with firearms. In the end, when the police failed to appear and the army drove straight through the farm and away, they were left to their own devices. They made up spears for the migrants to defend themselves, tying any metal to the ends.

Still the hyena armies had their way, even on her own family land. A sick woman who had just arrived, wandered out, searching for a safe and private place to rest. In the dusky light they heard her hoarse voice crying out, *They take me, they take me.* Some men ran to her aid, only to see her carried off by two large hyenas, the beasts fighting as they galloped away, pulling her in two directions. By the time the men caught up there was only a mess of rags left, the remnants of a hand and foot, while, within sight, five other hyenas had joined in to fight for sections of the corpse.

Mihret knew the hyenas would find her eventually. She knew them. They rarely missed a chance if there was vulnerable prey about. They detected the slightest fluctuation in the air so instantly knew everything: that she was a woman, alone, defenceless, lost, dehydrated, weakened. They knew her rough age, her medical history, her sad thoughts. Her fear. They knew all, in unsympathetic depth and detail. It was the way predators of every sort must know.

They found her just before dawn.

Mihret was wide awake when the single large hyena approached her in the half light. The bitch was in her prime, spots distinct in the semi-darkness, eyes aglow, heavy stomach swinging. She was large enough to kill and devour a grown woman by herself. She stopped not thirty metres away to assess her prey.

Mihret prepared herself with her scarf and stone sling and her stick. She prepared her body by hardening herself and summoning all her remaining strength. If it was to be her last battle, she would use everything.

The hyena was noisy and appraising, snuffling the air, vocalizing urgently but low, undecided, it seemed, whether to call her clan to her or to take on this prey alone and have the first take of meat. She was pregnant and ravenous. In this conflicted mood she cast around, taking a measure of the stick and scarf and the way her prey moved. She sniffed the air and sniffed again.

Mihret kept her back to the rock wall against which she had been resting, hoping for a chance to fight. She growled and made threats. Lekek argeng djibb. Beat it.

As the light grew, the hyena took on greater proportions. Her jaws were as capable and massive as those of a lion. She whined and approached, whined and retreated two steps to wait and see how this prey behaved. She licked her lips, sat with her legs splayed and began to clean her phallus carefully, seemingly absorbed in this irrelevant pleasure. She stood, turned, glanced at Mihret, feigning a lack of interest. At that moment there was a sharp eruption of dust. The hyena yelped and sprang sideways.

Mihret did not need to see the triangular head of the viper, recognizing immediately the sudden flaying of dust. With a burst of power she clawed and scrambled straight up a fissure in the rock to the top of the ridge. She paused only for a glance that took in several things: the hyena had taken half-hearted steps after her but stopped in confusion, the hunt having gone wrong, the prey seven metres above her on the ridge and a distracting, debilitating pain burning her hindquarters. Beyond her, in the dell, the other hyenas were alert, having heard the commotion. One broke away and loped toward the ridge.

Mihret ran as she had never run. She sprinted until her lungs burned, then she kept running, only slowing to a jog to collect her breath, then sprinting again. Ahead of her a lazy line of smoke rose against the sky. She ran toward that.

As the sun rose she bounded up a mound of rocks and searched behind her for her pursuers. That she could not spot them was no comfort. She knew they were there. She knew they would not give up so easily. She ran again. When her energy finally flagged she gnawed juice from two of the fruits and continued on, waiting for her gut to cringe in reaction to their poisons. She climbed each kopje she came across, scanning her own trail.

The smoke dissipated for a while, which made her despair. A minute later the breeze subsided and the smoke formed again. She silently cheered, daring to hope. She wondered whether she was being assisted by the Lord, her Father in Heaven, in her hour of need. She would not die yet. *Not yet.* If the fire belonged to herders, they might move on before she caught up. She did not relish arriving unannounced among Turkana herders. She ran and her hamstrings began to cramp and seize so that she was forced to slow to a quick and efficient stride, for she was a walker, no matter what the Kenyan terrorist thought. It was his mistake, his underestimation of her. Her stride was fast and capable of taking her from one village to another, one country to another country. If necessary she would walk all the way back to Nairobi with a spear and stone, with her habesha kameez floating silently around her. *Good feet, good heart.*

By late morning the sun crushed her limbs. The last of the little fruits were gone, and her mouth was as dry as the stones on the ground. She came over a volcanic plateau to look upon a winding riverbed. One arm of it embraced a cluster of brick buildings. It was a wonderful sight to Mihret's eyes. There were large, leafy trees on the banks, and she thought she could hear running water.

As Mihret looked on, she heard the ringing of a handheld bell. Small figures aligned themselves in the centre of the yard, and a freshet of air carried to her the music of children's voices.

PART FOUR

INDICES OF MARKET HEALTH

CHAPTER 13

Hassan, Refugee, Entrepreneur
Turkana
April 28, 2016

Hassan lay awake, thinking of all that had happened. Shapes stirred at the edge of his vision. He knew what these shapes were and he welcomed them.

He rose silently and looked in at the prisoner. Kestner was breathing roughly and sleeping in fits. He had been in bad condition when they found him, and he had not recovered. His was a sleep of exhaustion and illness.

But it was a beautiful night, the moon radiant as though pregnant and ready to deliver. What might the moon deliver? A new world? A better world? The face of the moon this night was scarified like the faces of certain tribal people he had encountered in his travels. It was a revelation when he first saw such people with their rich traditions and long histories. At one time he would have scarcely believed that he might encounter people like that, from faraway places. By now he had been exposed to so many surprising things, so many different people, from all over Africa and the world. It was astonishing. He had come far from the simple farm and community where he had started his life. Yet he still had to remind himself that peaceful, settled families still thrived on their ancestral farms, surrounded by their own people.

The edges of the night stirred unhappily with these djinns that were his constant reminder of past events. Hassan was careful not to look at the djinns directly for they did not tolerate that and might skitter away and not return. After his brother died, he had learned to be careful so that they would stay. Sometimes he could not help it, his eyes would steal a glance, hoping to see the wandering figure in her shredded guntiino as she searched the landscape for the way back, her hand shielding her eyes. There were many others, some faded or distant, stirring in the long shadows made by the moon. Some were the dead children from his community, others the beloved animals from their farm. All faded, and transformed during the time of famine and later. They stirred and watched him as he tried to make his difficult way on this earth. They were there to watch and remind. They were there to warn him about his fate and his choices.

Yet, he kept making mistakes. He should not have given up searching for his mother. He should never have left behind his brother's wife. He should control himself to avoid becoming dependent on the qat that poisoned him each day. His grief over his family and his homeland was blunted by qat and more qat, and when he stopped chewing he felt as ragged as those plastic bags that blow from one end of the land to the other. When he was chewing, his memories were manageable, and he could work like the very devil. But there was a price too: his stomach burned as though he had swallowed a live coal.

It was not possible to sleep. Worries in the lorry, worries in the desert path. Worries, worries. Now the Canadian was sick. Only he knew or cared. The man had dried out too much. Now the light in his eyes had dimmed and his muscles had shrunk. Whatever should happen, Hassan did not want this older man, or any of the prisoners, to die on this journey. Although Rosie would tell him not to mind about the health of the prisoners. *If Allah willed it, then so be it.* Jihad is jihad and people die, he might say. But it was impossible to take that man's religion seriously.

But why did he feel it was he, and not Allah, who was responsible?

He resumed driving, guiding the lorry carefully after getting stuck once and almost tipping into a ravine another time. He kept his eyes on the illuminated area ahead of the nose of the lorry, and he tried not to think too much about what was about to happen.

As a plan, it was simple. As a reality, it was anything but simple. *Simple* disappeared the moment he realized that Money was not a reliable companion. *Simple* was gone like a puff of dust the day Money let the captives escape into the desert. *Simple* shrivelled up each day that they did not find the camp. And now he wondered, what would happen when they arrived? That would be the least simple part of it. Whom else would he be forced to reckon with? Thieves? Murderers? They might decide to murder him outright. Was it as Money had said, or were they honourable enough to pay him the agreed amount?

When he stopped driving, the sun was up, and Money was beside him, shading himself with an empty plastic bag.

—Look, finally we are through with qat. It's gone. So now we suffer like everyone else, like the honest men we are not.

Hassan was weary of Money and his words. Neither his Kiswahili nor his English were up to the task of following that man's twisting thoughts. He suspected that Money intended humour, yet he was hesitant to take up the conversation. His attempted replies seemed to destroy Money's train of ideas. He would say the wrong thing, and Money would be furious. It was important to consider carefully what he said.

—Maybe we are honest more than you think.

—Is that a joke? Or is this some kind of Allah-reasoning? Money sneered.

—Anyway, we can decide how long we chase our jirani about in the dirt. Or we just dump our goods and forget about payment. Go somewhere else, maybe get jobs as real drivers. Maybe no one bothered enough to come find us.

Hassan did not attempt a response. He was struggling to sort which parts were Money-jokes and which were Money-threats. They both went to check on Kestner, their goods to dump. Kestner looked terrible. Hassan drove on, searching the land ahead. Finally, after what seemed many hours but was only two, he saw two dented white Hiluxes in the curved shadow of a broken-walled caldera.

CHAPTER 14
Money Manyu
Ilemi Triangle
April 29, 2016

With the two little Hilux bakkies, it was like a parade. They followed the Hiluxes north and west, along a dirt track, then through sand, then over cracked clay between low hills. They came to a place where one of the Hiluxes diverted, leaving them to wait in the sun. When the Hilux returned, two goats were in the arms of two men in the open back. The men yelled and sang as the vehicle pitched forward.

Hassan watched them as he leaned on the steering wheel. He shook his head.

—These men are not serious. Look, livestock thieves. And even so, they cannot steal a decent goat. At our home, if we catch livestock thieves, we teach them a lesson they don't forget.

—Mungiki. Stoned Mungiki. That's who we are dealing with now. The Terrible. The Hordes. Anyway, you stole a goat from herders, neh? Same as these dwanzi-idiots, Somali. You ate that goat.

—Oh, that. We were hungry that time, yes? Turkana goat had no fat either. All men, including me, forget the code of honour when hunger comes.

—Or thirst. Or they need women. Or alcohol. Or money. Or any number of things. Whatever we want, we drop principles. So easy. Men just follow their hungers, whatever they are. What are your hungers, Somali?

—Me? I could eat one of those goats by myself, in one sitting. But bad-looking goats, these, if you ask me. Also, I want my reward so I can leave these goat stealers and go home to my family. That is all.

—Your reward?

—After they pay reward, we go on our way, leave these people.

—Yeah, Somali. If we get paid.

—Why you say *if*?

—Hard to see that these goat stealers would pay what they owe.

—Yes, yes. Maybe you are right. We will find out when we stop. But what about the prisoner? What do you think will happen to him? Ransom, yes? Then freed.

—You think I'm UN General Assembly? I deliver goods. We hope they pay us, that's all.

—Ah, no. We delivered, so we must be paid. But I wonder what will happen to that man. He is a doctor. It would be better to know, so that I do not need to worry my sleep thinking of it.

An hour later, the men in the Hiluxes raised a cheer and shot rounds in the air as they pulled into a flat-bottomed valley tucked between the flanks of low mountains. In the centre of the valley was a cluster of old huts around an abandoned government dispensary. Mud and blown sand had obliterated the road to the dispensary. Perhaps the dispensary had been abandoned because the road was wrecked, or perhaps it was because the medical officer ran away or because there were no patients. What remained was a square building with cinder-block walls and a zinc roof. The Red Cross symbol on one wall was faded but still visible.

They handed the prisoner to the Hilux men, and these men left Kestner in the back of the lorry while they decided where else they might imprison him. Kestner was watched over by a guard who wore white earbuds and stationed himself on a stool beside a scraggly bush. Near the dispensary the other men set about butchering and skinning the little goats.

No one in the camp said a word to Money or Hassan. Money looked at all this and took the AK and cleaned it and loaded it. They agreed to take turns sleeping in the cab of the lorry. Neither man slept the first night. In the morning a large vat of ugali was brought out of the dispensary, and the ugali doled out in regulation bowls pilfered from some hapless army.

Money sat back in disgust and watched Hassan spoon the stuff. He had cadged the crushed remnant of a pack of Champions and did not venture near the dispensary and their pot of muck. He smoked and took his bearings. There was not much. The lorry with its prisoner and guard, the dispensary and shed, a couple of derelict-looking Turkana huts. The ground around the dispensary was strewn with plastic bags, food wrappers, and empty water bottles. He sniffed the air. A familiar odour. He had come up with it in his nostrils, of the ruinous dump and the lanes around the orphanage. It was the reek of unfinished human endeavours, of struggle against the odds, of wasted time and effort. He did not care to look in at Kestner. He wanted to finish his dealings and leave this place, knowing that things would go against him if he stayed too long. As he sauntered about he carried the AK slung over his shoulder. He took note of the favourite positions of the men in the camp.

The men of the camp wore scarves over their faces, which Money had assumed was a protection against the dust-laden winds. When they drew their scarves down to smoke their cigarettes, he saw that they were young. It explained the poor calculation of food, the wild driving, the burst of excitement over the sight of the camp. Money took his time and picked out the senior man of the lot, then he went to him.

—We should talk. You have a name?

—Me, a name? You can call me Green Man. Or just Green. You can call me that.

—And your friends? Are they colours too? Like red and yellow and blue, all the colours of the rainbow, yah. Like gay flag?

The other man frowned. He had a large, square face and his whiskers were thick.

—You wish to insult? Is that it? You, who are an intruder? What do you want here? You ask name just for joke, is that it?

—We want our pay, then we leave. Me and him. We did our job.

—Your job? Anyway, you cannot leave so quickly. Even in this place we must be careful. Out there to the south, near the lake, is a village and a police outpost. Maybe they start to search because of this business. Better you stay here for a while, hidden away. You can have vacation.

—What is hidden about this place?

—No one comes here. No one comes because this might be Sudan, Ethiopia, Kenya. Could be any. Disputed territory. Ilemi, they call it.

—We just want our pay, like agreed, then we go.

—I know nothing about pay. Maybe it is our boss you want. He pays people from time to time, but I might tell you that in truth, he takes his time. That man feels insulted if someone asks for payment, even if they are owed. He finds excuse not to pay or to pay less. No one can win this battle with him. That is why he is an elephant and we are mice.

The man laughed bitterly.

—This elephant will come soon. Maybe you already know him. Rosie. There, another colour for you to consider. Just stay calm and wait. Take a vacation. You look terrible! This is vacation land, see. Sand and mountains and no water, just as promised.

Green bellowed at his own joke, but his laugh ended in a grunt. He walked away.

Money said nothing more to Green. He fished another broken

cigarette from his shirt pocket and straightened it in his fingers. The cigarette was useless. It would need to be lit by a blowtorch to keep burning. When he looked up, Green was talking under his breath to one of his comrades. Both men turned away, erupting in the same laughter that ended with the same abrupt grunt.

Two days later a third Hilux, as old and beaten as the others, pulled into the camp. When Hassan saw the man in the passenger seat, he nodded at Money.

—There's the elephant. Now we can get out of this latrine.

The man called Rosie had a copper flush to his skin and eyes that looked ready to burst with pent-up blood. He spent a long time talking to his men before he sent for Money.

Rosie sat at the table in the dispensary among bowls of half-eaten ugali and plastic bottles partially full of vividly dyed drinks. Beside him stood a twitchy and ill-looking boy with his finger on an AK-47 that had a butt stock made from a door handle. By Rosie's side were two bottles, one open, from which he quaffed beer. Rosie was old and unwell; he wore a toupée of grey wool that sat on a mottled scalp. He did not try to conceal his face as he invited Money to sit at the table.

—Put your weapon aside. No one will harm you here. And if you sit, this one will be more relaxed.

He gestured toward the twitchy boy.

—My sister's boy. Addicted to everything, that is his problem.

Money remained standing. He looked at the boy until the boy averted his eyes.

—Mungiki. I know your kind.

Rosie quaffed from his glass.

—This dusty place makes me thirsty. Don't mind me. I have old habits. You see, it was my man who hired you. I am a businessman. Some say I am a middleman. I like this term: middleman. It means I am not one place or another, neither here nor there. So, in the middle I am free. You understand? You are also a businessman, yes? Business is the way of the world. You do not need to know more about me or about any others who might come along. Sometimes, to do good business, it is better not to ask too much.

—I won't ask because I don't care.

—You are wise.

—I doubt that.

—On the other hand, you had a mishap. There were three people but you only brought us one. Where are the others? Have they gone to the army for help? Did you kill them? Did they run away into the desert where they will be fodder for the wild animals? This is what I heard. I heard they escaped. You may like to tell me the details of how this happened.

—Details? It happened. That's all.

—Ah, well, perhaps not important, the details. But disappointing not to hear a story like that. Some stories are interesting to me. They have a way of revealing the strange ways of men.

—I do not tell stories. I just do. Others tell.

—So be it. A doer, not a teller. Mzuri, fine. However, two foreigners wandering in the Turkana lands with no water. This is not according to plan. It was not part of the arrangement.

—Only one foreign. The other is Ethiopian. A city woman.

—Worse still. Maybe they will be found before they are attacked by animals. That will be costly, though, you see. So here is what I can do. You were to hand over three, but you instead gave us one. So now I offer you accordingly this, since our arrangement has changed.

He took out a sheaf of currency, US dollars and euros and Kenya shillings, laboriously counted out the equivalent of two thousand dollars, and laid it on the table. Money looked at it for a moment and looked at the twitchy boy until the boy averted his eyes. Then he took what was offered, grasped the AK, and went outside without a word.

He stood outside the dispensary, breathing in the Dandora smells he had not managed to escape, even here in the far reaches of the nation. He searched his pocket for a stub of a cigarette, which he tried in vain to light. Green was standing nearby watching him. Green laughed, the same laugh as before, but then came and handed Money a better pack of cigarettes.

—You see? What did I say? Less than owed, right? What, a third only? What? A tenth?

He laughed his abrupt laugh and moved off.

Hassan was summoned by Rosie's men next. He came to the dispensary wearing a smile, but the smile faded quickly when he saw Money's face. When he came out of the dispensary he did not meet Money's gaze, and Money did not bother to ask questions. He did not want to know details or think details. It had been a huge risk for little to show in the end. He laughed bitterly and aloud. Green and his companions looked at him. He fingered the slim sheaf of bills in his pocket, not a third of what was promised. He squatted on the ground, laughed aloud, and put his head between his knees. It was time to go somewhere and forget.

Rosie's men had moved Kestner out of the lorry and into a shelter of ripped canvas that was really just a hole set into the side of the hill. Money did not want to think about the prisoner Kestner or the other ones lost along the way. It would be best to put the fate of Kestner out of his mind. It would be best if they left this place before Kestner's fate came to pass, whatever it might be. He sensed it, the fate of the prisoner, hovering over the camp, and it was not good.

Yet there was this Rosie and the Mungiki and his own half-empty pocket. One might take up a gun and massacre until the Mungiki massacred back. Or listen to the demands of a noisy knife and go out and hunt Rosie and his nephew as though they were the two wretched goats.

Eight stoned men against one angry man would not be a proper fight.

Money and Hassan huddled together in the back of the lorry, dividing the things they had acquired: passports, papers, electronics, the international bills. Money said he would leave immediately, and he was taking the lorry IN GOD WE TRIST.

Hassan looked dully at the keyboard of the tablet computer that was now his.

—I cannot leave yet.

—If you want to stay here, go ahead. Nothing here but more disaster. You want that?

—I do not want to do crimes. I want to live like a better man.

—Too late, Somali. And by the way, by the way, if you stay here you will not get *more, maybe much more*, and you will not be a better man. If there is a large ransom, if there is *much more*, it will be taken by that thief Rosie and his men, nothing for us. They will kill us before giving *maybe much more*.

II

Money put a long stick into the reserve tanks to check the levels. He wiped the AK-47 and placed it on the floor next to him. A while later, he started the motor, and when the engine rumbled to life, Hassan appeared. He waved at Money, climbed up to the cab on the driver's side, and waited as Money slid to the passenger side so that Hassan could drive.

They left the camp through the north end of the valley. They were neither shot at nor challenged, and as they rounded the hill and the dispensary and camp were no longer in sight, Money felt his stomach muscles relax for the first time in days. He laughed abruptly. Hassan looked at him with alarm at first, then saw that the laugh was neither nasty nor false so he found himself laughing shyly along with Money. He was philosophical about everything that had happened.

Hassan said, —We tried. It did not work. It is like some other bad plans I made. Anyway, it was a chance we took. It was our own choice.

—What choice, man? You think you have choice? Poor and lousy men like us have no choice. We have no control over anything but the humblest thing. Bad meals, bad places to sleep, gangs to do business with. What choice?

—No, I don't believe that. We chose to do things according to our will. Allah provides us with choice.

—So what choice is it if you must wait for Allah to provide it to you? You people and your complicated idea. It is written this, written that. It is written that you are so poor you cannot take care of your children. It is written that the rich choose whatever they please while the poor choose to only survive. If we are honest about it, we are not men. We are just dogs tied to a post, drooling over treats we cannot have, cowering when beaten. Like dogs we have no idea what might happen this week, this month, this year and next.

—But we chose to do things like crimes. I chose myself, but now I can't remember why I thought it was a good choice.

—One thousand now and eight thousand later. Remember that?

—Eight thousand? No, they promised me five.

—And how much were you paid?

—One thousand. Now I have one thousand and four hundred.

—So rich. People with full pockets, they control us. They control everything—the people, the animals, the land, even the water and air. They say, 'Money, go knock someone, because I must not filthy my hands with blood.' You have a choice? No. Why? Because it pays to knock that someone. Otherwise, nothing, no other choice. So I am commanded by the economic system. But the Riches, they have choice. They say, 'Okay, let us take our wealth and make more wealth by getting Money to do something that will help us. Let us make him knock our competitor…'

—Yet they paid you more than me. Why?

—You should have haggled. Anyway, how much does it matter? We were both ripped off, and now we are finished.

—This amount is not enough for my family. I have failed at every plan. I did not haggle with Rosie. He explained that I would be rich. But after we met, I followed him to see if I should trust him.

—You followed?

—In Nairobi it was. I followed because I did not feel settled about him, even then. I followed him secretly, so he would not know. I was like a shadow that no one sees. I followed to his den, a place where the women sell themselves. Then I followed to a café where he took his meal with his men and drank beer. I saw many things. I slept in the street. But on the second day, late in the day, he met two white men. Americans.

A bank of rain clouds had formed in the east as they passed around the hills, and in this way they crossed the Maud Line, the Red Line, and the Blue Line and so passed out of Turkana into what might have been South Sudan. They passed the skeleton of a camel, its long legs splayed. They skirted kraals and the spherical huts of Daasanach settlements and later, the conical huts of Hamars as they came into the Omo Valley. They followed the rambling tracks until the sky blackened at dusk and heavy rain bogged them down, and the river flooded over their wheels. They were stuck that way for two days until they accepted the help of a band of armed men who may have been Didinga or Hamars or another tribe, who laughed and wanted to barter meat for mobile phones. They went on to find the road toward Omorate but stopped when they spotted the Ethiopian flag over a soldier outpost. It was dusk then, and they turned back and went off the main road again onto a smaller road that led them south again, toward Todonyang. And Lokitaung, Lodwar, and on, to Isiolo.

CHAPTER 15

Hassan
Near Lake Turkana, Kenya
and
Jubalaland, Somalia

The two Americans called each other names that only Americans would use: Jeffy, Jimmy, Johnny, Jackie. They were strong and healthy men, even though they were not young. They had smooth tans, greying military haircuts, shirts of expensive cloth. They thought they were inconspicuous sitting slumped in a corner of the café. But after Rosie met them and left, Hassan stayed behind, watching them. There was something wrong about these Yankees. They were too clean and rich to be associated with a Kenyan gangster like Rosie. Hassan ventured by an open door near the table where the Americans had ordered food they did not touch, where they ordered coffee that they pushed around with their fingers while studying the people around them. They focused on the flirtatious and bosomy woman who served them and took great pleasure in uttering coded commentary that puzzled Hassan and stuck in his mind, so that later, by himself, he tried some of the phrases in his own mouth.

—How do you like them apples.

—In all God's glory.

—A piece…

—of His Work.

—Ha.

—As I walk through the shadow of the valley...

—You bet. Hail the magic and wonder of estrogen.

—We are but Witnesses to the Abundant Thing of Life, God Given.

—Let the Thing be embraced. Even by those barely able to contend with the Thing.

—Hey man, I'm only forty-four. I can contend.

—Okay, so let's assume you're still at your peak, bro. But even if not, look, there's more to life. Already got yourself a piece of his work. Already got more than you can contend with. Big house with a pool and three premium cars with incredible sound systems.

—Actually four cars including the dune buggy. And the dirt bikes.

—Surfboards and a condo in Maui.

—Didn't tell you. Bought me thirty-five feet of catamaran. Goes like stink. Catalina.

—So what do you want? A little bit of this, a little bit of that. Easy work, good pay, and a little bit of that there.

—Bro, a man's gotta have variety.

Hassan tried out these phrases in his own mouth, all the while knowing that there were things about these men and their private language and their private world he would never understand. It intrigued him. Men like these he had noticed before. They could be found across the Horn of Africa. Local people identified them as soldiers or CIA or contractors, government men or company men, on the lookout for al-Queda, al-Shabaab, ISIS, the next 9/11. Hassan had no trouble spotting the distinctive outlines of holsters under their shirts.

II

In spite of his other opinions about Money, Hassan was envious. Not for his nine thousand. Not for his quick tongue. Not for the fact that he was Kenyan, certainly. But because Money could read.

More than anything Hassan desired that he could read and so be rid of the humiliation he experienced whenever he was confronted by written language. To read meant joining the world of ideas. To read meant respect. Few in his family had learned to read. Hassan knew of one uncle who had learned to read before he died in the wars. That rumour of the uncle who could read had given the family a thread of private hope that there was not something basically so wrong with them that they could not learn that blessed skill.

He made do with other skills, however. He knew how to survive. He knew how to fight for himself. He knew how to negotiate rugged terrain. He survived the sea. He knew how and when to pray, more or less. He knew how to maintain his private self, safe from the intrusions of strangers. His private self was a powerful thing that could startle strangers. They would think, how could it be that this lost man, this lowly refugee, has pride? They would attack him for the strength that ran in his veins. Strangers, especially those from other places, were not to be trusted.

No, he was not a reader, nor a soldier or gangster; he was not properly a Believer. Had never been religious either, though lately had gone through the old motions, intoning lines he had learned from Mzee Ibrahim, for the sake of those around him.

He was only Hassan, and Hassan was trying to find his way alone, because so many of his people had vanished into a cloud of dust and drought. Wherever his family had gone, he knew they were finished, which meant that the family bloodline would come to an end, not go on to glory and greatness. It occurred to him regularly that it was likely that there was only he, lonesome and illiterate Hassan, keeping alive the dimming ember of his people.

At night Hassan lay awake, listening to the voice of the wind. It seemed he no longer required sleep. Sleep he now considered a luxury meant for the lazy and the satisfied and those at peace with themselves. He tucked his blade along his side, holding it close. At times of late he felt that this knife was his only security and his only peace.

There was a place that was home, a place steeped in the blood of his ancestors. It was important to remember that. Yet sometimes, when he put his mind back there, it was not with the pride that a man should feel for the place that made him. It was an effort now to summon the green and grassy springtime, the herds of well-fed goats and cows. Despite his efforts to cling to that, these memories were overtaken by memories of the pale wash of dust that came with the drought, drawing life from the lands. And the famine and the horror that followed and stayed for too long, finally driving them away.

Other memories were etched so clearly it was impossible to dismiss them, of the very things he wished to forget: starvation and fear. The time of death. The time during which he had the terrible sensation that his young body was shrinking, that his arms were being sucked dry by the wind, and the ache of a belly that protruded like that of an old man. At the time he wondered if he might vanish but for this balloon of a belly. It was wrong. It was not the way a child should grow. He noticed his shadow, that his shadow legs were twigs and his belly was as round and big as his head. He had not liked this new shadow, felt sickened to know that hunger was stealing his flesh away, morsel by morsel, as though he were eating himself. Even then he had known that it was not a thing of which he should be aware. It should happen to a person without them knowing. He remembered trying not to look at his shadow in the hopes he would not know he was vanishing.

During that last drought in his homeland, the water holes shrank, then the well water vanished into mud. The family was forced, finally, to abandon their ancestral lands. His father's herd, the great pride of the clan, was gone, the cattle having wandered away or been stolen or preyed upon in a week-long rage of super-heated wind. Later someone found the remains of the proud herd, some animals partially devoured and others too bony for predators, it seemed.

After that, to return to his father's lands would be impossible. He would not know the place. His claim was weak. What would be a home without people? Who would wish to return to a place of family memories spiked with failure and death?

They had fled with relatives and neighbours, a whole community on the move, following the rumours of better lands nearby, and rumours of emergency food and water supplies. They set out walking. There were bad winds and dust storms. At some point his father and Hanad, his elder brother, were separated from them. Hassan was left with his mother and the smaller children. They struggled on toward the town.

The journey had been impossibly long. He had wanted to stop, lie on the ground and stare at the sky, which is what he would have done were he not driven on by his mother's voice quietly insisting that the lions would like nothing better than to come upon a small child. He kept looking back to see these lions, and he was thirsty and hungry, and his feet were tired. Then he fixed his eyes on her back, resolutely keeping up with her among a group of women and children from their community.

They faltered. He saw his mother's face become hollow. Her eyes went from worry to fear and then to something else that made him realize that real worry and fear were only possible when one was properly fed. In extreme hunger a dull haze overtook them. It was an undefined waiting, for rescue or sleep. There was no energy for imagination or anticipation. The remoteness of his mother's eyes haunted his childhood mind. Any scrap of food she came across, she passed to her children and her men. It was never enough.

The women did what they could for one another. They looked out for everyone's children at first, but after a while these gestures waned. It turned into a fight for survival. They began to die, one by one. Not faceless anonymous people, but names and histories that had been there forever, along with the rocks and hills and the few trees and the sky and the earth itself. He came upon his grandfather's sister by the side of the road, in her repose in the shade of a large stone. He waited with her for a while. She did not speak to him. They sat, saying nothing, garnering energy. She roused herself enough to massage his feet and stroke his back. She told him to go, to hurry along and keep up, saying she would catch up with them by nightfall. Hassan said nothing about the lions. He later remembered this, guiltily. He never saw her again. Where Grandmother had lived was only a hole in which questions echoed.

It seemed they walked for months. It was impossible to know, later in remembering, how long the trek had actually been. After a while their company was depleted, as though some trekkers had taken wrong turns or gone back. In time, they were only a few stragglers along a vast and empty road. Then the smaller children of his family were, one by one, left by the wayside, the first one covered in a goat skin and provided with a simple cairn of four rocks, the next one covered only with a torn blanket. The third, the strong four-year-old named Ismael, whom Hassan had watched over and played with, his mother carried valiantly in her arms. In his starved state Hassan knew something was wrong in the way his mother held Ismael, her favourite child. He could see Ismael's head lolling in her arms. He heard no sound from him.

As they sat by the side of the road under the blotches of shade provided by a thorn tree, he took Ismael gently from his mother and unwrapped the light cloth that covered his face. Ismael was shrivelled and had turned a dark grey hue in her arms. Hassan took his brother away, put him in a plastic bag he found blowing along the ground. He placed the withered corpse in the middle of the ground for the animals to find. Then he took his mother's hand and brought her out of that place. Later, she asked him where her Ismael had gone, and he could not answer but only looked in her eyes until she looked away, knowing what he could not say.

During the last part of their journey, they were alone. They were still together when they came upon a food depot set there by foreigners. Among the thousands of people that had come from the droughted countryside, it seemed that only a portion could be fed and given water and allowed to survive. Many more took stock of the situation. They walked on instead of stopping, pushed forward by vague and conflicting rumours. There came a blank time that he could not recall later, except that perhaps he dreamed it. He was not certain how events unfolded. It was an empty spot that escaped notice, as though he had slept through it. He found himself one day in the refugee camp, in a large white tent, lying on a mat on the ground. He did not know who had brought him there. Later he would wonder why a boy starving and beyond hope was plucked from the jaws of the wild animals and carried across the border and away from the war and famine, amid the sadness of the thousands of dying, amid the raging winds. It could only be his mother who had done this for him, yet she was not there beside him.

He emerged from a fog of dehydration with an ache that extended from the base of his spine to his chest and into his throat. It took him some time to realize that he was being cared for by strangers and none of his family was among the faces that attended him. At first he was alarmed by the people there, people with skin and hair of all different colours and textures. But those people were kind. They took care of him. He saw other children like him, in row upon row of mats on the ground. He heard the wind and sand beating the tent. He dreamed that a powerful creature sought a way in, to feast upon the rows of children. But the tent was a strong one, and the other children were too weak to be afraid.

Someone said to him that he would live a long life, it was not his time to die. They said *marasmus*, but it mattered little to him. He would always remember the word, but he was not hungry. It was more that his body had done a strange thing: it had grown backwards, so that now it was the way it had been several years earlier. Like any youngster, he had been proud of his growth into a big boy. Now he felt shame. It seemed to him that everything that had happened to his family was his fault, although he could not pinpoint exactly how this was so.

Gradually, he recovered, to find his way into the outdoor ranks of listless, stunned, and damaged children. They sat for haphazard classes that he eventually gave up because he kept falling asleep and because he could not achieve immediately what he knew was most important — reading. A while later he was given practical tasks so that he would build strength and be of use at the clinic, which was always short of helpers and space.

Perhaps that would have been his life, drawing water, carrying equipment, erecting tents, doing whatever he was asked amid the complex hierarchies and clans and struggles of the adults, amid the more elemental mischief of the gangs of youths. Yet his nature was one of independence and quietude, and he learned to watch and get along with other people who were not his own, turning aside difficulties, surviving.

Months then years passed. He might have stayed in the refugee camp until the end of his days. The camp kept growing for different reasons, the inflow of refugees surging as Somalia descended ever further into wars and famines that seemed to follow one upon the other with barely a pause. There were farmers fleeing the droughts and townspeople fleeing the bombs and fighters of one sort or another.

One day, as he helped unload the canisters of water that were the lifeblood of the desert camp, he saw an old, bent, and hollow-eyed woman shuffle by. He was uncertain at first, then he said her name. She turned and stared at him. It was his mother. She said not a word. In desperation he began to explain who he was. She stared. After a moment, she took his hand to mutely lead him to the shelter she shared with three other women. He helped her gather her things then brought her to his own place. He found a cot for her and improved the place as much as he could with additional mats on the floor. A month later she still had not uttered a word. She rose each morning to prepare coffee and porridge before he went out to find work and food.

Two years passed before Hanad, his elder brother, appeared. Hanad had searched for them for years, going from town to town, camp to camp, asking everywhere. His beard had grown in fully; it was already flecked with grey. He limped on a badly infected leg. He coughed constantly. It seemed as though Hanad had experienced the whole sad breadth of the Somali famine and all the pain and starvation in it. He looked as though he had suffered along with all of those he had watched die and this had robbed him of youth. When Hassan asked in a whisper what had become of their father, Hanad looked away as though he had not heard. Hassan did not broach the topic again.

Their mother looked at Hanad with her blank regard and accepted him back in the same detached way she had Hassan. They were never sure she truly knew they were her sons. On most days she was capable of her lifelong, ingrained patterns of work, preparing meals on the fire as she had always done. On other days she wandered so that Hassan was forced to search the camp for her, sometimes to discover that she had drifted off into the empty lands around the camp, searching for her husband and family. Hassan would track her down, speak gentle words to her until she allowed herself to be led back.

During this period Hassan noticed that he talked to himself, and this frightened him. He had terrifying dreams of being chased through the desert by invisible things with teeth. In other dreams his father appeared, vividly demanding that Hassan release his mother into his father's care while Hassan, guiltily, was unable or unwilling to do so, selfishly keeping his mother for himself.

The refugee camp grew, year by year. It became like a real town but in the middle of nowhere, connected to nothing, with streets and markets and schools, a hospital and a mosque. People were driven to settle there despite the lack of water, the lack of a future.

One day his mother vanished. Her disappearances into the desert had become more frequent. She would be found at increasing distances from the camp. Hassan had come to expect that one day he would not find her, that one day she would keep walking or she would go so far that she would falter without water or be unable to return before nightfall. They tried to ensure that someone was with her at all times. Inevitably a moment came when she was alone.

When she vanished, Hassan, Hanad, and three other men from the camp went out on the harsh terrain and searched through the long afternoon and into evening of that day. By nightfall the other men gave up and returned to the camp, leaving Hassan and Hanad to search the empty land, their thoughts isolated and pinched in the realization that they had lost their mother permanently this time. They said nothing to each other, then the sun was down and it was dark. They could see the glow of lights of the camp in the distance but went on in a sad and sick silence for a long while. In the darkness Hassan could hear his brother breathing hard. He knew that Hanad was thinking something over. Then Hanad spoke to him.

—To keep our family, we must father children. Otherwise, our people will die away. Do you know good families with eligible girls?

—Perhaps I know of some. They are nervous about young men who are without their own people. But you and I and our mother are a family, better off than some. I know some girls who have lost everyone.

—Yes. We need to arrange a girl for you. These days it is only you and me. We have no one to arrange a bride for you.

They looked across a flat, orange landscape. There was no movement anywhere, as if the entire Earth were a place of desolation.

—What about yourself? What about your marriage? You are my elder.

Hanad stopped walking. He looked up at the dark sky and took a deep breath.

—Listen, my brother Hassan. I already have a wife. She—we —will be a family soon.

—Without a wedding, brother?

Hanad shrugged.

—Just like that. As I said, these days are different. We must do for ourselves, without the traditional things like bride price and a special someone to arrange. This is our situation now.

They spoke nothing more about this.

In the small hours they finally stopped walking and calling for their mother. They were exhausted, cold and far from the camp. They wrapped themselves in the thin blankets they had brought along and curled together on the ground for warmth. At dawn they rose with stiff joints and resumed searching until night came again, and then they were driven back to the camp by thirst and hunger. At their tent a girl Hassan had not met was preparing a meal. Hanad took her offering of rice and beans and served it to his brother. Hanad beckoned to the girl to sit with them and eat.

—This is Waris.

Hanad said only this then looked down and ate his meal.

Over the following week Hassan came and went from his home in a daze. He was aware of a soft voice and a feminine form in the periphery, but he could not bring himself to look upon his brother's woman because their mother's presence was still in the home. At times he was not sure whether his mother had been real or just a ghost of some sort. Or perhaps it was that their own mother had transformed into this other young and pregnant woman.

He observed how kindly Hanad treated Waris. His brother used his words carefully when he spoke to her. His tone was never hard, even when she did things differently than their mother would do. It was as though she were fragile, from injury or illness. Hanad was a voice of reassurance, checking her condition, saying more words to her than Hassan thought was possible from his brother's mouth. He had not seen this gentle side of his brother before. It gave him hope.

Hanad informed him that he would not keep searching for their mother.

—She has gone her way. We can only hope that one day she will return. It is as Allah wills.

Yes, as Allah wills, Hassan agreed silently. He repeated these words to himself as he went each day into the hot sand and low thorn trees around the encampment, searching for her in the same way that she had searched the empty lands for her lost family.

It was the family tradition to do this, he told himself. Every day his search took him farther away from the encampment, and every day the land that surrounded him was more forlorn.

II

When Hassan was first brought to the camp hospital as a child and was laid out with the other starving children, too frail to do anything but take in quantities of plain food, however strange, he had many hours in which to observe those around him. He looked upon starvation, infection, the process of the death of children who should have had their lives ahead of them. He noticed odd details of the way their bodies, their smells and their skin transformed as they recovered or descended into coma. This experience left a mark on his mind. Afterward, it was as though his mind had learned a secret that he could not explain properly. When he saw certain bodily signs and certain behaviours, he was able to recognize illness and frailty, without knowing what it was or what caused it. He saw that the same thing occurred in camels and goats and dogs, in all animals big and small. It became so that he would notice the vital condition of a bird that flew by in the sky, just in the way it moved.

So he knew well that Hanad's days were numbered. It was on his skin and in his movements and the timbre of his voice and the way his mind functioned. Hanad had aged far beyond his years. On the rare occasions when his brother smiled, the smile was for Waris, and Hassan saw a resignation to fate that was that of a person stretched well past their time. His brother smelled of illness. It was a sweet but bitter smell, as though he surrendered to the air that which he should not.

It was the cough that was killing Hanad. It was a rasping dry cough, not constant or loud, but when it came on it made those around look at him with instinctive alarm. They recognized the rattle of an uncompassionate destroyer, a terrible spirit of predation in their midst. Gradually the cough sapped his brother's energy. He resigned himself to lying on his cot where he was able to reflect on the ebb of his life even as his own family was about to begin.

The day approached for Waris's delivery. Politely but firmly, she rebuffed the traditional midwives. Hanad was too weak to help her. She requested that Hassan take her to the hospital instead and to call upon his contacts—the friendly Cuban doctor he had mentioned and the Irish nurses he had befriended. On the day, he waited nervously outside the delivery room where he heard only mild complaint from Waris. The nurses came to find him, congratulating him even though they knew he was not the father of the newborn.

He brought Hanad's wife and young son to his brother. Some community women came around to visit Waris and the baby. They came with glad faces and dispensed with the usual festivities out of respect for the illness of the father of the newborn.

Two days after he held his son in his arms, Hanad passed away in the night.

Hassan was left with Waris and the baby boy, whom they named Hanad. He put no expectation on Waris after Hanad was gone. He brought home food and cloths and blankets for the care of the baby. The mother was healthy and well, despite all that had happened. After six months had passed, she came to Hassan at night, and Hassan accepted her. So Waris became Hassan's wife in the traditional way, and suddenly he had a family of his own. Hanad, the son of his brother, was his son after all.

They settled into a routine for two years, Hassan working and labouring. Whenever there was a spare minute, he tried to learn to read. Scrambling to ensure the survival of his young family left little time, however. The camp was their world.

Waris's belly swelled again, completing Hassan's journey to fatherhood. He thought more about the future. He wondered how his family would negotiate a secure life. The limitations of the refugee camp suddenly began to take on a different meaning. He saw that the children of the refugee camp would learn nothing of the greater world, could not extend their lives into a larger realm.

They would learn that food and clothing is bestowed by strangers from faraway places. They would chafe under the limitations of their choices for education and work. One day they would see that the camp was not only a falsehood propped up by UN money and food and medicine and foreign workers and volunteers but also a human prison.

As Waris's pregnancy progressed, Hassan went through cycles of anxiety, grieving, and depression. He spoke to officials and other men who were worried about the prospects of their families. Father, uncles, grandfathers. Some had applied to be accepted as immigrants to other countries where they could make a new life, learn a new language and culture, and forget the refugee camp. Some had been waiting in long queues for years, hoping for such escape to the United States of America, Canada, the UK, Germany, Australia.

Hassan wondered what kind of life his family might lead in Canada, a place that he saw depicted in photos as expanses of forest, ice, and snow that covered the ground, populated by all manner of people but ruled by the English and French.

One night Hassan awoke with a start. He prodded Waris until she opened her eyes and looked at him—she had become wary of his moods of late—and he told her he had to leave. He would seek a way to make money and come back at the right time to bring them out of the camp. They would travel to Canada or the US where little Hanad could go to school, play soccer, have friends, and find his way.

She listened to him until he was done, then she spoke to him quietly.

—We know no one in those countries. The people in those places are different, and no one knows us. Besides, Hanad can do all those things here.

—But little Hanad and our new one, when he grows, will have no future. There is no place for children to grow here. No one belongs here. It is not intended that people stay forever here. We must find a new place where I can build a home and we will have a dog and a herd of goats. You must only wait here where it is safe for little Hanad until I return.

—And your new son?

He patted her belly and put his ear to hear the movements within.

She was quiet after that and wept a little the morning he left, but she did not object to his decision. It was the will of Allah, and that was all.

He walked out the front gate. No one stopped him. One old auntie who knew his mother embraced him. When he looked in her face it seemed to him that she could foresee his destiny. He stopped himself from pressing her to divulge her wisdom. She wished him strength and wisdom and gave him a push forward.

—Go. Your mother wants you to go.

He strode out along the sole road that led away from the camp. Immediately, he began to see the future more clearly than he had before. He realized he needed to secure, somehow, foreign currency. Then he would find out how to emigrate to the West.

Other young men were straggling out of the camp, all of them full of hopes and fears. Hassan fell in with them on the road. They pumped each other for news and rumours of where it was safe and how and where money could be made. A group of them, including Hassan, was picked up by an open truck heading north. The travellers exchanged information. No one knew much about Europe or America. There was much talk of the roving coastal people, of their boats and how they took control of the large foreign ships and made enough money to build houses and whole villages and bought themselves Toyota Land Cruisers instead of goats or oxen. An older man looked at him carefully.

—It will be a long war in our country. War means there are ways to be wealthy if you can think clearly and you are brave.

Hassan said his farewell to that old man in the city of Galkayo, the first city he had ever visited. For the first two days he wandered through it in wonderment at the solid buildings that held businesses and banks, all of it fine and rich looking, in spite of the war and drought and starvation that swept through the countryside like a huge broom gathering souls instead of dust, piling them into refugee camps.

He walked out to the outskirts, to the airport where he sat for some hours, watching in fascination as machines of all shapes and sizes leapt into the air according to principles that he only dimly grasped. To add to his amazement, people stepped from these miraculous things to walk the earth as though nothing extraordinary had occurred.

He walked all through the city until he came across a construction site where men were pouring the foundation for a large house. The men worked for some time, then they stopped to eat and rest. They summoned him to share their food with him. Yes, they told Hassan, he could work with them, but he should not expect much pay.

—The owners are not big spenders. They are people like us who were poor and then suddenly found money.

The workers were good and simple fellows, but he understood that their welcome was limited because of his unknown clan and people. He took up toiling alongside them nonetheless.

For a time, Hassan went to sleep with sand and concrete and dust on his skin, an ache in his muscles, and hope in his heart. Along with a few others who came from the south, he slept on the building site, in shelters made from discarded tarps and sheets of plastic. The wages he made were sufficient for him to feed himself. He rented boots from another worker who was injured.

As he worked, he thought of Waris and little Hanad. He dreamed that the large house that was under construction was meant for his family. He dreamed that when it was complete, with the windows installed and a beautiful doorway, he would bring them to live the city life in Galkayo. It was the most impressive place he had seen. There were schools where little Hanad could learn to read and a college where doctors were trained. He imagined his son becoming a doctor in this place, while he and Waris lived in the large house with its compound for their herds.

The men told him that the owner of the house was a courageous man. This man was legendary, they said. He was a lion. He had made his fortune on the coast, having seized a large, foreign cargo ship and successfully ransomed it to its wealthy owners. One of the men proclaimed loudly that this was how the brave went about acquiring riches in Somalia. The lion's name was Guleed.

One day this lion, this Guleed, arrived in a sleek new four-by-four with blackened windows. He was accompanied by an entourage of strong men, all of whom wore a type of sunglasses that wrapped around their faces and gave them the cold, efficient appearance of machinery.

When Hassan saw Guleed he bent himself to his work but later asked the other men where Guleed stayed. The next evening Hassan purchased a large bag of the best qat he could find, along with a bag of candy. He made his way to Guleed's lodging, a rented house on the other side of town. As he approached the house one of the men with sunglasses recognized him from the work site. The man stopped him, asked him what he wanted, then searched him and let him approach.

Guleed sat indoors on a beautiful carpet before a television set. He was well mannered when Hassan approached, standing and inviting Hassan to sit beside him. He accepted the humble gifts and invited Hassan to chew qat with him.

Hassan was forthright. He did not bow or scrape.

—As salaam alaycum, brother. With respect, I wish to be like you. Please help me do what you have done. I am bold, and I have already lived through the death of my entire kin so am no longer afraid of anything. I have a wife and children in the refugee camp across the border. I wish to make money for them to have a good life.

Guleed did not laugh or grow angry. He looked around at his men, who were in the background listening.

—Tell me, do you think this fellow has the stuff to ride a boat over water as deep as it is broad, take up a gun, attack an enormous ship belonging to foreigners, all the while fighting the wild seas, the English, the Americans, and everyone else?

One of Guleed's men glanced at Hassan and laughed.

—Sure, why not? We did it, didn't we?

Hassan could see that Guleed suffered severe pain, despite his good manners. Now and again, the blood drained from the man's face and the muscles around his eyes twitched while he shifted in his seat. He was not a large person, but Guleed was as compact and hard as the farmers in Hassan's community. He had the look of a working man, perhaps one who suffered from some past injury, who bore pain because it was necessary.

Guleed said, —Listen, my friend. The ferengi steal our fish and use our waters as a way to transport their oil and wealth. They never think to share with those on the shore. They have no regard for the starvation and suffering of Somali people. This is why, with the help of some fearless men, we act as we can. If you are a fearless man as you say, and you really survived the famine and refugee camps, then come with us to the sea and join us. I know the men of my country. I can see you are bold, to come here without any introduction. Did I not see you working on my building site, my young brother?

—Yes, it was me. You see, I will do what I must in order to survive. I am Somali. My people are of the Majertain clan, of the Darod, but I am Somali.

Guleed nodded and spoke quietly.

—You know, I am not one of these clannish types, Hassan. My men come from many places. You are right! We are all Somalis. Our people populated the world, did you know? Yes, it was we who fathered the others, the Indians, the Persians, and the Europeans. But those people are ungrateful. They hate to be reminded of where they came from. They pretend we are nothing. But we know who we are! We are Somalis, and Somalis must do what we must do to defend our home, yes?

While he spoke, one of the men went out of the room and returned with new blue jeans and a T-shirt and a pair of sunglasses, which he handed to Hassan.

A few days later Hassan was travelling again, this time in the open back of an Land Cruiser, rolling toward the ocean with the hot wind in his face.

When he arrived at the coast, he walked by himself for hours along the sand. He had heard stories of the ocean, but the stories did not do justice to it. He was astonished at the expanse of moving water that stretched eastward to the horizon. Never had he imagined there could be that much water. He kept craning his neck to see the force that sent waves crashing up the beach. It took several attempts before he could step into the water to wet his bare feet. It was only then that he was convinced that it was merely water, wet and warm, as salty as blood. Guleed and his men were nearby. When he saw Hassan in the water to his ankles, Guleed laughed.

—You cannot imagine how much water is out there. When you ride a boat out there, it is like riding an unruly camel, and your boat is as important as your own mother. Without your boat you will never find your way back to land. If your boat sank, the water is so deep it would take a full day for your bones reach the bottom. In fact, out there you learn to forget that there is such a solid thing as land.

Cargo ships stacked high with vividly coloured containers, long oil tankers, freighters with raw things like wood and chemicals—they slid along at the edge of the world, from one rich place to another. Guleed put his hand on Hassan's shoulder. It felt steady and confident.

—We were fishermen before, and we are fishermen now. For centuries we caught fish. Now the fish are gone so those giant things out there, those are our new fish.

During his years at the refugee camp, Hassan had learned to look for people from his own region. He would offer his name and his clan, hoping that they knew his people. Once or twice, someone knew his family. It always caused him to swell with pride when this happened. It made his family real. But he had to give up such hopes on the coast. It was quickly apparent that no others from his place had ever found their way to the sea. Not in the blood perhaps. It thrilled him, now and again, to imagine the shock on the faces of his family members to see the ocean waves.

Guleed set up his campaigns with care, selecting his crews for each boat, ensuring the boys understood what was required and when, and the consequences if things went wrong. Most were young; some were still teenagers. They availed themselves of the plentiful and constant supplies of qat. When the young men chewed qat they were mesmerized by weapons and the prospects of money and power. They were uneducated boys who had not been outside their own communities. They had vague ideas of what money could buy, other than cars. Of cars they had detailed and precise information. They dreamed of being the first over the railing of a ship to be awarded a new car as a gift from Guleed. Some of the men were chosen because they knew boats and the sea and others because they had experience with weapons. Several had fought under various warlords and had to be watched for their allegiances. Some were members of Guleed's clan and family. But he favoured Hassan for his steadfast and quiet manner. Hassan was the only one with a wife and child. He would not do anything rash.

Guleed's boys waited on the shore, smoking, chewing, wrestling in the sand, chasing the girls in the village. Guleed took Hassan aside and told him his chance would come soon.

—I have a feeling that when you come with us, we will successfully take a big prize. You will bring great glory when we ransom that ship.

A morning came when Hassan looked across the water at a distant fogbank that lay like a goat's wool to the north. As the fogbank dissipated in the sun, he saw something he would never forget. An enormous cargo ship parted the fog to emerge in the open light. The ship came on for a long time before the stern was visible. It was the most enormous man-made object Hassan had seen. It came forward without hesitation, without doubt or worry. Hassan looked to the heavens for a moment before he ran to inform the others. This was the ship of fortune, was it not?

—Allah hu akbar.

Guleed's men were down where the boats waited, already stocked with equipment. They ran the boats into the surf and clambered over the gunwales. The three boats raced each other through the surf into the open water, aiming at a point far ahead of the moving ship. Hassan held on, his stomach tight, as they pitched through the swells, the salt spray stinging his skin.

The ship, seemingly unaware of the crude wooden boats closing in, drove forward, bent on a task of monumental importance. It belonged to an endeavour beyond the comprehension of ordinary mortals. Hassan wondered how it was that people could create something so complex and stern and rich, with its brilliantly painted steel flanks that were taller than a mountain. How could steel be made to float on the sea and propel itself over the depths as if the sea were nothing, as if no one would question it, as though no human or natural power could hinder it. It was frightening, not because of the prospect of physical harm in the attack but for the sheer complexity and scale of the machine and

FOUR Indices of Market Health

its endeavour, its implacability as it bore on, its beauty and prowess, its dominion over nature.

As they lunged forward with their puny boats and weapons and his own puny aspirations, he experienced a terrible moment of doubt about his role before Allah and his ability to fulfill his duties in the grand scheme of life, as a father, as a husband. For a moment a profound feeling of fear ran from his feet to his hair: it was a fear of being stretched beyond his capabilities, beyond the destiny that Allah had intended. What was he, and why was he here? Was he not more than a tiny and irrelevant shadow attempting to find its way among other tiny shadows? Now he was being shown that an entire world of wealth, complexity, and overpowering belief was out there, beyond his borders.

A belt of cold sea water hit his face, and he shook away his fears. A water cannon on board the ship bombarded them with sea water. The boats dodged and feinted in the swell and arced in toward the ship. They came near enough to hear the alarm bell ringing and a voice booming out instructions to the crew. The three attack boats approached from different sides, charging forward, surging away over the waves, the way raptors wheel and dive, frenzying a dangerous and dying beast. The ship ploughed straight on. The attacking men put up shields to protect themselves from the water cannons that were unleashed on them from the deck above. They came close in and wheeled away. They had on their side rocket-propelled grenades, AKs, 9mm, a bazooka, grappling hooks, ladders, and ropes. They came close enough to fire grenades, laying the bombs up onto the deck near the water cannons.

Suddenly the water cannons were switched off. Guleed's men threw grappling hooks then moved off elsewhere to throw another hook. There was little need of these tactics in the end. There was no return fire, no resistance other than the brief water cannon. The pirates laid up the ladders. Guleed gave his signal and a first wave of five boys scrambled up in a qat-fuelled frenzy. The older men came after, picking their way up the rungs. Hassan waited his turn on the pitching boat, but when it was his time he did not hesitate. He went up with the agility of a monkey. Heeding Guleed, he looked not down but up, at the rail and deck. His weapon was slung over his back. His only fear was of plunging backward into the sea as he saw happened to one boy. Hassan thought it must the end of him. But the boy, in his life jacket, popped up in the swells like a piece of wood and waved, then dropped away into the wake of the ship to be picked up later.

The crew of the MV *Celestica* was made up of Filipinos and Bangladeshis who were trained as seamen, not soldiers. They abandoned the water cannon and locked themselves in the bridge, there to remain until the door was prised open. They were brought out and ordered to sit on the deck in two queues with their hands on their heads. The captain, a burly and irate Bulgarian, was located in his cabin. The boys may have been rough with him, perhaps because of the batch of qat or perhaps because the captain bellowed curses at them. The boys angrily pulled apart his cabin. The captain pulled a revolver. The boys stopped what they were doing. They backed away for a moment, until someone flipped the safety of his AK and shot the captain on the spot. He collapsed on the floor.

Guleed came. He spoke in reassuring tones to each boy of his crew, taking his time. He embraced the shooter and told him to be still, that God was great. He came to the captain who lay bleeding out on the floor of his cabin. He put his hand to the captain's wrist and after a moment announced that the captain was dead. Guleed looked around the cabin and saw a framed photo of the captain with his family and shook his head.

—This is unfortunate, a man dying at sea, far from his family. I believe he died of a medical condition. We will explain this to the widow.

At that moment a navy jet passed low over the ship. It swept around and took another pass as Guleed stepped to the gangway door to look at the jet's markings.

—The British. Her Majesty's Royal Navy jets. Too late for the British jets or anyone else's jets to claim this ship. This ship belongs to us now. We have claimed it here, in our own waters. Do these British have business here?

The boys answered.

—Somali waters, Adeer Guleed. Somali ocean. The British have no business. The Americans have no business.

—That is correct. As Allah is my witness.

Someone fired rounds after the jet, but the jet was receding into the far reaches of the sky, invulnerable. Guleed, Hassan, and some others broke into the bridge, and the great ship was slowed and turned and redirected toward land. It was anchored in a deep cove offshore of a fishing village. Scrawny figures could be seen on the shore, waving and running, dancing and shooting guns in the air, as though they were all part of it and expected to partake of the profit. A skiff approached the ship, and a negotiator was brought aboard. The men fired their weapons into the air to greet him. The negotiator—a man named Farad—laughed as he came on board and accepted the greetings of the boys.

The hold of the ship was sectioned and secured. It took the men some time to break through into the hold. When it was finally opened, it was found to contain large-calibre guns, two tanks, and a helicopter gunship. There were enough automatic weapons and ammunition for an army. When the negotiator was told of this he stopped smiling and went to his cabin and closed the door. Guleed's boys saw no more of him for a long time.

The days passed. The boys settled into a routine of chewing and going through the food stores, listening to the radio, walking out on the deck, and watching the people on the shore as they resumed their normal lives of fishing, farming, and providing for their families. A week later, fishing boats arrived in the night, and the men broke open the crates so that the small arms could be taken ashore to be sold at the market. The American sailors sent out fast boats to interrupt the flow of weapons and supplies.

The boys grew impatient. Rumours spread that the negotiations had stopped. Someone fired a bazooka in the direction of the Americans, and Guleed came out in his patient way and spoke to everyone, saying that negotiations were always difficult. The Russian shipping company representative refused to believe that the captain was dead. He thought it was a trick and would not negotiate until he spoke to the captain. Guleed sent images of the captain in the meat locker, his mouth frozen open.

Guleed slipped away from the ship one night without telling anyone. Some of the men followed their leader over the next days, swimming out to small boats that ventured near.

Shortly afterward a Russian navy ship appeared outside the cove, the Russians and the Americans making a show of practice manoeuvres. A Kenyan navy frigate appeared and left.

The ship's sailors, meanwhile, had been isolated without communication with the outside world, cut off in the small living quarters around their berths. According to Guleed's code of conduct his boys were not to fraternize with these sailors. But after Guleed left, this code was forgotten, and the boys made friends with the sailors. They passed the time playing table tennis, watching movies, and cooking with the Somalis. The boys allowed the Bangladeshis and Filipinos to contact their relatives by phone.

Farad, the negotiator, finally appeared on the deck, gazing forlornly toward the distant shore. He was a middle-aged and paunchy businessman who looked increasingly anxious as the days passed and his attempts to talk to governments failed, complicated by the presence of an arms shipment that had drawn international interest.

Hassan kept to himself, observing the behaviour of the others.

He knew the younger men would lose their focus and eventually do stupid things if they remained on the ship for too long. Worse still, the ship's food was vanishing quickly. The Americans were constantly interrupting the supply of fresh food from shore.

It had been more than sixty days since the ship was taken over. Hassan decided he had to take care of himself. He decided he would speak to the negotiator alone. He found Farad sitting on the bridge, staring at the shore. Before Hassan could say anything, Farad broke into a long complaint about how he should never have taken the offer that Guleed had made; he was a consultant and a businessman, after all, not a pirate. He went on about his lands and the needs of his camel herd and his wives and the servants that worked in his compound. After half an hour of this he stopped talking, and he and Hassan chewed a few leaves of qat, which was the only thing supplied to the ship without interruption. It was a standing joke that qat would still continue to be delivered as the men starved or died of thirst. Farad shrugged.

—I want to resign this job. Every country in the UN and even the UN itself is now interested in us because of the things in the cargo bay. It is bad. No one wants to claim the shipment, not the Russians, and not the Kenyans. The Kenyans say it is for South Sudan. So now the Sudanese government is insulted. And the South Sudanese are nothing—no government, just bush rebels. And the Americans want to arrest everyone and take them away to Gitmo and waterboard and electric chair.

—So, what should we do?

—We should do as Guleed did. We should run away.

—He ran?

—He told me he would consult his clan and their army. Now he has been gone for three weeks. Maybe he sits in his home and plans another ship that has more luck and less dangerous cargo. Who knows? He has stopped answering my messages.

—And what about the sailors? They are just working men.

—No one cares about workers from poor countries. They have no money and no influence. Their governments do not care about ordinary men. If they were British or French or American or German, their governments would send delegations and soldiers. They would send journalists, and there would be television and books. Maybe even cinemas made about them. Lawyers would come. These shit countries have nothing. They don't care about their people. They are no better than here in Somalia where we have no government at all, and when we did have government, they only used the people for their own purpose. Eh, that is how the politics works, you see? Some people are something, and other people are nothing. So there is one thing left to do. You can think about Allah and perhaps pray properly because the track of your miserable life is written already. Whatever happens is written. There is no reason to struggle against what is written.

Hassan went away with many thoughts. Somehow, with all the disasters that had happened to him, he had not been attentive to faith and Allah and what was written and so forth. Now he thought about what the negotiator said. He considered what he should do. It seemed right that he should think about Allah the Beneficent so that these unfortunate crew of the ship would not be simply discarded as if they were nothing. The fate of the crew disturbed him. It also seemed he should think hard about what it was that Allah would have him do to save his family and himself.

More days passed. He discovered that some of the sailors were Sunnis and had concealed this. Now Hassan brought Guleed's boys together with the sailors, and everyone prayed at the right times and together the way the Quran instructed. In doing this he felt the communal satisfaction of his religious practice, of the brotherhood of praying Muslim men, and it gave him courage and renewed his commitment to faith. It gave him hope for his future and his family. He dreamed at night about the soft skin of Waris and remembered her kind and intimate attentions.

At other times though, the dream of a normal and peaceful family life seemed to retreat to the realm of impossibility. Sometimes he wondered if he were meant to have a wife and children and a home.

He visited Farad the next night and the next. Farad was always glad to have someone to talk to. He said he wanted to discuss the best course of action with the other men and the crew. Hassan suggested that Guleed might not want this, but Farad snorted.

—Guleed finally called me. He said nothing except that we would hold out for four million. Four million! But the owners are not willing to talk. It is as if they would rather pretend the ship belonged to others.

One night Hassan discovered that the youngest of Guleed's pirates, a boy of seventeen, regularly swam to shore to visit his girlfriend and have proper meals, coming back each morning under the noses of everyone, the French, the Americans, the Kenyans, and his own compatriots. He noticed the boy going over the side one inky night when sleep was impossible because of the heat. After that Hassan himself stationed in different places where he could see the boy boldly descend the rungs of a ladder and swim away with powerful, silent strokes.

One night, after watching the boy, Hassan went to the ladder and took it in his hands. His hands trembled a little, and he swore at them for their lack of courage. He took two careful steps down to peer into the oily waters. He could not swim. It was another thing he could not do. He climbed back up to the deck.

Over the next days he grew increasingly restless and unhappy. He went to the ladder often, walking by but not looking at it. Once or twice he passed it in the dead of night and broke into a nervous sweat. The djinns were out in full force around him, clamouring for something, but he knew not what. One night his frustration came to a boil. What did it matter if he drowned? No one would care. It would be better than rotting on a stolen ship.

The air that night was hot and close. Guleed's men were on the topmost deck sleeping under the stars. Every voice and every sound carried across the still water.

When he came to the ladder, he waited for ten minutes to be certain no one was near. He slipped into a life vest and put his foot on the first step of the ladder, trembling. He willed his limbs to descend the ladder silently until finally he felt the water lapping at his feet. He went farther until his legs were immersed, then his body. As he took the last steps, he had to pause to quell his panic and trust that the life preserver would not fail him in the water. For a long time he floated with his hand clinging to the rung. He uttered a silent prayer and let go. He pulled at the water in the way the boy had done. The sea was black as tar. A gentle swell came and pushed him this way and that, then a cool current caught him and swept him sideways and away from shore. He pulled and pushed and kicked against this invisible force he had not reckoned on. Worse still, he could no longer see the dim kerosene lamps of the village. The ship was surprisingly far from him now, the hull looming in the distance. He wanted to curse his destiny and his fate, that he could not swim like the boy, that he could not read, that his people were dead and lost. His destiny, written or not, was not a kind one. He floated in the current, overcome with fatigue. He could do nothing but float and think about everything that had happened. Perhaps it would not be terrible to drift out and die at sea. He thought he heard the splash of something swimming nearby and knew it must be a shark. He had seen many, including large ones, swimming lazily around the ship. He thought that the shark would wait until he had surrendered completely before it attacked.

The ship was out of sight. There was no one to hear him if he called for help. He uttered a prayer and tried with all his might to imagine the greater power that created the conditions and time in which he lived. He heard another splash, and something bumped his leg. It was absolutely dark with no moon. A wave lifted him for a moment and when it set him down, he felt ground beneath his feet. Another, bigger wave came. It lifted him and rushed him forward and deposited him onto sand.

In the days following he wondered if he had been tested there among the waves, and that Allah in his wisdom had taken mercy upon him and directed the waters to leave him on land. It was the kind of thing that people described as a transformation, that converted people into Believers, that they prayed forever after that. Hassan desired that this to be so, but he felt his spirit dragged back by loss of his family and their place in the world. Perhaps he was a Believer of a sort. He made the conscious decision that if given the opportunity, if Allah ordained, then he would try to prove his faith by adhering to the Five Pillars. He would pray. He would go, someday, to Maccah.

Shortly after he went ashore, the British invaded the ship. No one resisted, their spirits drained by the long weeks at sea.

Hassan had made a shelter for himself under a patch of white plastic sheeting on a remote part of the beach, between two dunes. Everyone around there knew who he was and where he was from. The day after the ship was taken over, two young boys sought out Hassan and told him that Guleed was looking for him. They asked if it was true that he was a spy for the Americans. *Let us see your American gun.*

That night Hassan wrapped his head in two scarves as protection from the flying sand, went out. He climbed a dune, and looked down at the flickering lights of the dwellings scattered along the coast. The dusk was purple, the air hot and close. He sat in the sand and thought about his wife and children. It seemed everyone had their difficulties. Everyone in Somalia struggled. In that particular place, after the ship was taken by the British, the local people were disappointed, some despondent. Many had tied their personal fortunes to Guleed and the pirates and the promise of wealth. It was humiliating that the bold plan had not borne fruit. There would be no wild victory party on the beach, no bales of fresh qat. No bright new vehicles and boat motors.

Hassan stood up and took a last look. The coast was beautiful and untamed. It was ancient Somali land and a place of which he should be proud. He tucked his scarves in close and walked away, inland. When it came down to it, the only things he could rely on were his own strength and determination.

A week later, he crossed the border into Kenya on foot.

CHAPTER 16
Money Manyu
Turkana

Nine thousand, maybe more. Maybe much more. Ten thousand at least to do the simplest of things: *collect the foreigners, secure them, bring them to the base, to nowhere, where there are no soldiers or police or farms or borders or government, to a place owned by scorpions and snakes. Not Ethiopia, nor Sudan, nor Kenya. And whatever happens, make sure of the doctor.*

He might have made it. If not for Mungiki treachery he might have shucked his preordained fate like a desert cobra shucks its skin. With the ten thousand USD he might have become a different man with a glossy new coating, a better man in better places. This glossier, better man might be seen to board a jet plane, the perfect man to invade New York City, the United States of Whatever.

That chance had passed. As he and Hassan drove away from the Mungiki base, Money asked himself the question *why-o-why-o-why* and wondered how it was that men ended up with their terrible fates.

‖

Because what was on offer at the Man U Healthy Child Centre was ugali, ugali, ugali and, one day, not even ugali. The place was falling apart. It happened gradually, then suddenly. Children kept coming, but they were listless and sick. The CEO stated quietly that they had no capacity because they were low on funds. He said, *temporary economic shortfalls, soon to be corrected.* In fact, the entire nation and the entire continent had shortfalls. It could not be helped. The CEO disappeared for long periods, leaving the running of the Man U Healthy Child Centre to Matron and the staff.

The economic shortfall went on for a long and dreary time. Each day was a blur of anxiety and discomfort. Each hour seemed stretched to a wasteful length of time, the air burning hot.

In those days of childhood, Money kept his eyes on the dump across the river, where the poorest of the Poors lived. They were worse off than he, and he was worried that they would cross the river to seek what they needed. Then his brain did a perverse thing: he watched the fat people in cars, the people in pictures, and his brain went in the opposite direction, to those who were never hungry and had a choice of tea, bread, eggs, tomatoes, milk, coffee for breakfast.

The CEO reminded the children, —This is your time, your time of great wealth.

Hunger etched its demands into his brain and did not stop there. Like a politician, it wished for control. It invaded organs and limbs, recruited them so that they each independently demanded different things. One leg demanded potatoes, the other rice. Arms demanded meat, meat, meat. Others screamed for oil, beer, mealies, dripping butter, rice, rich milk, mangoes, fried fish in sauce. The list was elaborate.

He put his head between his legs and wept. He wished for sleep. He was terribly thirsty, but raw water felt like a wire brush on the inside of his stomach. Water ran straight through him as though he were not there. Indeed, his insides felt as though there was nothing, just an empty cavern. How had it come to this? There was no answer. Yet he felt guilty, as though he had been careless to let this happen to himself.

The children at the Healthy Child Centre shat worms, Money worse than anyone. His guts veered from emptiness to the squirming fullness that came from parasitic guests. On offer: ugali, ugali, ugali. Not even the worms wanted ugali. So terrible was his gut that the smells of the children and the house disgusted him. He fled, to wander to private places where he could distract himself or at least suffer in solitude. At a place by the main road he counted and sorted traffic into simple cars, square cars, round cars, rovers, Toyotas, complicated cars, vans with passengers, buses, large vans, old vans and new. The large vans with their hangers-on and their paint jobs and their special names: Wet Dream, Abubaker, John F. Kennedy, Karibu, Power Donkey, and Mandiba.

Eventually, if he waited long enough, perhaps an accident would occur, a lucky accident to offer salvation. It had happened once, a crash between a car and a truck, both overturned, and in the ensuing chaos bystanders swept in and stole what they could lay their hands on while the drivers lay stunned, maimed, leaking blood and coins.

Cars flashed by, the fat heads on the fat people visible through the windows. Fat heads that cared not to glance around to see who was by the roadway.

He dozed with the late-day sun in his eyes. His own starved and wormy head was vanishing, along with his stomach. Soon, nothing would be left of him, his head and his inside parts overrun by worms and rot. Yet nothing had happened. He, the other children, they were wealthy with opportunity. In his pocket was his knife. His knife permitted the cars with their fat heads to pass on their way, ignorant of the hazard they had escaped. Nothing happened except the sudden effect of a jar of chang'aa. It was a bad concoction, shot through with all manner of resentments. Part of his brain was eroded away by that stuff. It made the hunger nasty. At times the worms writhed in protest. Could a person die if their worms became angry and rose up? Could someone die of a headache caused by a stomach? Someone as wealthy as an empty and rusted can?

Abundance! Wealth! It filled the senses, stuffed the pockets!

Brothers and sisters floated by, staring. In the distance he heard Aketch, her voice echoing in the lane. Money got himself up, feet below legs, legs below worms. He had the uncontrollable urge to take from her whatever she had to eat. Why was she never as hungry as he?

He tried to shake the smell and the dust from his clothes as he limped forward with his eroding thoughts, his head sloshing full of liquid poisons. Following the music of her voice in narrow lanes. She was there by the side of the main road where vans were stopped. Aketch was bantering with the drivers, giggling, the sound familiar, as of grown women in the tavern.

Money watched her for a moment before going to her and catching her by the hand and pulling her away after him, as though he were her boss, her man. The drivers laughed and went on their way toward the Viagra Taverna with their cigarettes fuming and their hips swaggering with the weight of the coins in their pockets.

Aketch had stopped giggling. She shook his hand away.

—What is it that you want?

—You should not talk to those devils. By the way, the Man U Centre has laws. Ask anyone. Ask the director.

—Your director is not *my* director, and I don't go by laws, whatever they may be. And, *by the way, by the way*, you sound foolish when you try to sound like the director yourself.

He caught her hand again and pulled her along until suddenly she stopped fighting him, burst out laughing, went soft, and let herself be pulled for a short distance before she made a show of shaking him off again.

—Boy! Little man with a little boy! Can you not see when a

girl is busy? What is it that you do not understand? I must eat to survive. So must you.

—Busy? Busy with what?

—Yes. Busy with what.

—And who are these men? Drivers!

—They trade with me. I get food.

—And they get what?

—Yes, they get what. They want me to be their wife for ten or twenty minutes. 'Just a minute of your life.' This is what they say. 'Just one minute,' as if I would be selfish to deny them. As if a minute given is nothing for a girl with a long life ahead.

They went along the main road. Vans flew by, barely under the control of their drivers, plummeting like birds overcome by smoke, down the hill. Others ground their gears in the opposite direction, labouring, thick exhaust swirling behind, strange slogans plastered across their windscreens. Cruel Joke rumbled by. Both Michael Jackson and Moonwalk went by, one after the other, followed by Vladimir Lenin, horn blaring.

—Bastards, these drivers. Mungiki.

—Ay-yah. You are crazy.

They came to the house of the healer. The healer lounged by his door with nothing to do but call out to passersby. He had a mass of hair that erupted from his head like the branches of the wiry bushes by the river. He wore a worn suit jacket and tie and thick spectacles. Around his neck were amulets that moved about of their own accord. He claimed to know old medicines that worked on every person in the community, *including the Cancer*. At one time the healer's place was marked by an ostrich egg propped upon the peak of the conical grass roof. The Man U staff had a throwing contest one day and knocked the egg down, perhaps unhappy with the tips paid for protection. The clients of the healer took this as a bad omen. What kind of traditional healer was so powerless that he allowed his egg to be broken by street orphans? The healer fought back by acquiring a car battery and an electric ambulance light that flashed blue and red. Everyone was quite impressed. The light was a more powerful landmark than a dead egg; everyone could agree on that. Just looking at the light could make a weak head swoon. This was the joke of the healer: his light not only advertised his business but also created several new patients to cure. He called out to Money and Aketch.

—How is it you go by without so much as a greeting. Hey, you! Boy! Girl!

The healer took a close look at Aketch.

—But pardon me, madam. What happened? You are more like a woman, looks like.

Everyone seemed to notice Aketch these days. As they passed by the healer, Money doubled over and rubbed his eyes, feeling as though chang'aa had somehow gotten in there.

The healer inspected Aketch up and down.

—I know girls like you. Independent! Girls like you think they are free to come and go. But I can say, this freedom is a trick and a misfortune. Let me tell you, as a father tells a daughter, that you must avoid men on the road who flash their eyes at you. They have no traditions, no families, no education, no mother or father. Their hearts are ugly. Walking mistakes, they are, with some bright coins in their pockets and nothing else. You must avoid them, otherwise they will trick you by paying for you. Suddenly you will find yourself to be a bought thing, a penny sweet sold in the market, just there for men to taste when they desire a sweet taste. Those men—they have no reason to use moral judgment. Ugly, modern, walking evil is what they are.

Aketch said to him, —How did men get that way?

—When they were young they got the idea of cash money. What happened was this. They set out from their homes to get this cash money. No sooner had they reached the road when they lost their way. After that, they could never find their way home. They roam the country, completely lost. They act as though they are good and faithful, but they are empty banana peels. Banana peels don't think, they just go about making sexual diseases like HIV.

—They can be reported to the international people. Like UNDP. They can stop those men.

The healer looked at her with his eyes glittering.

—UNDP! You young people think you know everything. You get these big ideas from computers. If you keep overloading with big computer ideas, you end with illnesses. Or you make a bad choice and become a healer like me.

They left the healer behind and went on, Money thinking over the things that girls did in the cabs of lorries, the caprices of bad spirits and the tremendous wealth they enjoyed. He wondered what it would like be to drive a lorry. He closed his eyes for a moment, and when he opened them, it seemed as though a period of his life had gone by. Aketch was gone. He had a terrible head to add to a terrible belly. He got his legs under him and sidled back to the house and perched on the stair and stayed that way for a long time. It was getting to the point that he needed to save energy by not moving. Yet a stubborn part of him kept saying things. *Problems. What problems?* Something to do with a meal not eaten, or with ugali, or with chang'aa owning the place where there should have been food. The problem was that his stomach was confusing the rest of him. Or he was sick. Or dying. He could not tell. He tried to remember when he had eaten and what the food had been, and he found he could not. It might have been yesterday or a week ago. Everyone relied on ugali but he refused.

For the twentieth time he got his feet moving. He made his way to the kitchen, anticipating that the door would still be barred. A small child came and stood beside him, saying nothing. A few others wandered nearby, their bellies stiff with porridge, no doubt. He suddenly saw how the ears of the orphans were tuned to the sounds of hope, of adult words or the clatter of pots and pans. He wondered what would happen when these children left the Healthy Child Centre. The boys would go on to become hardened men. Otherwise they would perish. The girls would sell themselves as cheap sweets to be devoured by ravenous drivers. *Just one minute of your life.* He understood this one thing without wanting to understand it: *hungry children wandering into the hungry world without knowing or understanding the bad things in it. Like unknowing fish swimming into a net.*

He hunched over his cramped belly and walked. By the market he scuffed his feet at some half-ripe, half-rotten pawpaws. He took a bite of the best looking one. Somehow it made him emptier than ever. His belly worms rebelled and jittered about, trying to find the way to better places, just like the children in the Man U Centre. He was too nauseated and tired to do anything about it. He knew the hellish business of parasites. He preferred to ignore them, hoping to will them out of his body.

His drifting course took him toward the dump, his fingers playing with the handle of his knife. There was nothing to eat and nowhere to go. He squatted and vomited a clear fluid that he decided was vital stuff that he could not afford to lose. A dog came and sat nearby with its ears perked, licked up the bounty he had vomited, and lay down as though finished. Money stared emptily at the ribs of the dog, at the sores and mange on its hide. It was a ruin of a dog, the things that made dogs great taken out of it by hunger, thrown stones, kicks, and beatings. This dog was his very brother, sick and ruined and starved. Whomever died first would provide a paltry meal for the other. Boy starves, vomits, feeds dog with belly water, dog dies, man eats dog, vomits, feeds dog. The idea went in circles, chasing its tail. The dog was not yet dead, however. Money called to it, wondering what it would be like to kill it. He beckoned it to him with various names: Dog, Brother. Friend, Sister, Boy. When he said Boy, the dog lifted its head and looked at him with bloodshot eyes. It rose unsteadily, hung its head and tail, and slouched over to lower itself in front of Money. The dog understood things well enough. It understood weakness. It understood the knife. It understood what Money was thinking. Impossible, of course, to use the knife on such an understanding creature.

If the dog could move, so could he. Money got up, his shoulders and chest folded over the ache in his gut, the wrecked dog slouching at his heel. They went along the road watching the traffic, hoping for discards from the buses or vans. At times Money felt himself elevate into the smoke-tinged air. Sometimes he floated alone, above the rest of him. The dog floated behind.

Dust blew up as they cast along a pungent wall. Few people were about. He wondered if he stopped, someone would offer him food out of pity. Perhaps they would pity the dog, and then he could steal the food from the jaws of the dog. Surely any normal person would be alarmed to see such hungry creatures walking the earth. They might offer fat bread or a sausage. White bread with butter spread thickly. Hot tea brimming with thick milk, loaded with sugar.

Dog and human. Boy and boy. The two of them lingered before the door of the Viagra Taverna, sniffing the air. The sign read: WHERE A MAN CAN KILL HIS THIRST. Money slipped in the doorway with one hand protecting his ailing belly. He slid onto a stool in a corner, half of him hoping not to be noticed, the other half wishing someone would see his empty belly and help him.

But this tavern was a normal place with normal food for normal people. He had to remember that. He must remember to be normal. The first thing was not to beg, which would get him thrown out. He pictured himself being offered a platter of hot food. In his picture he was normal, nonchalant. He would politely refuse. He went over the picture carefully, as if doing so would make it come to pass. Unless, of course, they were insistent and pressed the food upon him. Perhaps a toasted cheese sandwich with cooked tomatoes sliding over the top. Or a plate of chips glistening with too much oil and salt. He might reluctantly be convinced to take a casual taste or two. Goat meat fresh from the spit—he would deign to take a nibble out of politeness to his host. A modest thigh and leg of fried chicken, a slab of boiled potato slid along beside it. Piripiri, or not. No, thank you. Yes, I will just try. A filet of perch simmered in batter and oil. Possibly. Important not to be anxious. Difficult when his cavernous belly threatened to buckle and flatten him, as though it were the most important part of his being. If only his mouth would stop watering as he sniffed the oil and meat frying in the back kitchen. The dog—it was not pretty—slunk in the door somehow. It glided along the wall and melted into a dark spot at Money's feet.

The owner of the Viagra appeared. His name was Mkande. He was not a tall man but gave the impression of vastness because of his width. He wore a bright shirt that was as large as a tent, with a pattern of sheaves of maize. His head was a melon. Maize and melon. Behind his back people called him the Hippo. He came and went behind the bar, bustling, busy with the customers. Money watched him quietly and hoped the Hippo did not have a temper. Such a hippo! How many children would be improved if they possessed a fraction of the rolls of fat that the Hippo had? Two great rolls on his back, a bigger one on his belly. So much fat. Fat that commanded as much respect as cash in the pocket. Yet, for a fat hippo, the man toiled. He brought a case of Ndovu beer from the back of the place, opened bottles, lay them upon the bar for three thirsty customers, took the orders of the local women who kept the customers laughing, yelled at the girls who worked in the kitchen, accepted money, counted change, yelled at the girls again to be quick with the fried eggs, the goat meat, the potatoes, the rice. The Hippo went out to the back to bring another case of beer. It took a while before he noticed Money. The dog had shrunk himself down into invisibility, tucked into a corner. Mkande the Hippo looked at Money with no hint of kindness.

—What you want here? This is not the place for street boys.

The thick scent of frying meat and eggs came wafting along with the Hippo's words. Money swooned, caught himself. He held himself upright, tried to focus his thoughts instead on the wrecked pungency of the dump, of rotted fish floating in the river. It was important to be as normal as possible.

—One bottle of Ndovu please. And nyama choma. With fresh rice.

—What? You are too young for beer.

Money lay his knife on the bar. He looked lovingly at it and ran his finger along the edge, thinking.

Mkande watched all this. He laughed.

—Very good. Not only a boy but a budding gwangi man. I have seen you and your plague of orphans in the streets. Healthy Child Centre! Ha! Unhealthy Criminal Centre is a more apt name. If I were your director — the one they call the CEO or whatever—I would drag you by the ear and beat you until you became a man. In fact, I might do it anyway. To both you and he.

—I am a man. See, he already beat me enough.

—Ha, ha, said the Hippo without laughing.

The Hippo went back to serving beer and food to the customers. A few minutes later he passed by carrying two empty bottles in one hand and a half a glass of flat beer in the other. He slid the glass of flat beer along the counter toward Money.

—Drink this if you really want it.

Money took the glass and sipped at it slowly and felt a wave of dizziness coming over him. When he glanced down he saw the dog's eyes gleaming greedily from the darkness under the bar. He steadied himself so he would not join the dog on the floor.

—I might be the owner of a place like this one day. Beer and food and tables and chairs. I might have big fat arms and a fat arse. Maybe one day I will have this very place. One day when you are finished with it.

The Hippo stared for long enough that his eyes went red and the veins stood out in his neck.

—What is wrong with you? In fact, what is wrong with me? I should have thrown you out long ago. You are nothing but a starving wretch of a boy. Look at you. You could not get fat even if you ate an entire herd of goats. You are nothing. You come from nothing. You don't even have food to feed yourself. And your CEO and his Man U Child Centre is a failure and no one can help them, least of all me.

—I was wondering, though. Who protects this place from burning down into ashes at night? Maybe the Mungiki?

The Hippo went away with a peculiar and stiff step as though he bore some mishap in his pants. After a minute he came back walking normally and carrying three more bottles of Ndovu for the customers. One of the men at the tables looked at Money saying, —Hey, go home to your mother, she is having my baby.

They were great jokers, those men. They laughed, went back to their drinks and paid no more attention to him or his knife.

The Hippo bustled by, looked at Money and shook his head again, and laughed. He talked to the other men as he went into the back room talking, talking, yelling at the girls. After ten minutes he came back to Money.

—Well, you have nerve. I will grant you that. I try to be patient with children, even the troublesome ones. We were all children at one time. All of us different. So here is a lesson for you: not all of life is about this gang, that gang or this knife, that knife. There are more things. Your view of the world is childish. Look here. Me, I was raised by my father, in a village near the valley. My father was a farmer and is still a farmer. But I wanted to be more.

I wanted respect. I found out to get respect I need to be rich. So this is what I am doing. Gaining respect by getting rich. This is how our country will flourish. Because of people like me.

The veins in Mkande's neck had gone back to hiding in the fat that held up his head. Money still hoped food might appear, although he could not see how. He yawned.

—If I had a different life, I would own a place which I would call the Money Bar, in honour of the great Viagra Taverna by the road, which was always a good and reliable friend of the Man U Corporation, and always respectful, until the day it unfortunately closed.

The Hippo looked closely at Money, his nostrils twitching, his neck veins slowing rising again. He sighed and went quietly to the back. A minute later, the younger of the two kitchen girls came out of the kitchen. She stood in front of Money with her arms crossed, hissing an oath about goddamn orphans. Suddenly Money recognized her as a girl who had left her baby at the Man U Centre some years before. He said nothing, just looked at her out of limpid, starving eyes. She knew he knew. Nothing needed to be said. She turned on her heel and stalked back to the kitchen and returned with a side bowl containing a dollop of rice with pieces of goat meat and gravy scattered over the top. Money stared at the bowl in disbelief. The dog licked his foot. The liquid in his body, his last remaining life stuff, tried to rise into his throat and he had to fight it down. The girl looked at him and said, —Here. But don't eat too fast.

The Hippo Mkande came back in with more plates for the men. More people came in. He brought them beer. He sat near Money and watched as Money took a piece of meat and swallowed it. Money's eyes watered. He did not want to weep. He did not want to be this hungry. His hand shook as he forced himself to steadily take in bites of rice and meat. He concentrated on his stomach, panicking that he would lose what he had taken in.

Mkande watched all this with a frown. The dog was madly licking Money's feet, reminding him of his own empty belly.

Money carefully finished the bowl of rice and meat.

—I might have another of the same.

Mkande whisked the bowl away. He could be heard making a call on his phone as Money waited for more food. He intended, this time, to share his luck with the dog named Boy. What he had done with the first bowl was not right at all. He had not been thinking of the long term, which somehow, in some far reach of his mind, involved sharing his luck.

No one bothered him or brought more food or spoke to him for a long time. He fell asleep where he sat but was nipped on the leg by Boy and woke up. Customers came and went. It grew late. Music was playing. The customers danced.

The CEO walked in. He glanced at Money then went into the back, and Money could hear the CEO and Mkande the Hippo conversing. The similarities of the two men suddenly struck Money as obvious. He listened to their voices and wondered if they were related. Brothers. Cousins. After a while the CEO sat beside Money. He looked at the dog.

—And, what, pray tell, is that creature?

—Boy. His name is Boy. He's hungry just like me.

—Perhaps we can name you Dog, then all will be settled. Boy named Dog and dog named Boy. Ah. Both of you look terrible, by the way. Maybe this Viagra food does not agree with you.

—It agrees.

—How old are you now? Fourteen? In the gap between boy and man.

—Old enough to know wealth from hunger.

—Hunger? With such plenty around? Go fill up on ugali. There is plenty. Your entire life is plentiful enough, even with shortfalls, by the way. But why not in school? You are in this, see. Your body is trying to be a man, but your thinking lags. When you are in that place, immorality comes around, waiting to trip you up. By the way, Mr. Mkande says you threatened him with that knife. Is it so? And where did you get this knife? Is that a good thing for a gap-person, man-boy to carry?

—Yessir.

Money's stomach was suddenly very sore. The CEO chuckled. He called to Mkande to bring more beer.

—Hey Mkande, you get fatter every day. Look, youth like this, with no proper parents or family, they only get thin. Why?

—Him? As I told you. This little dingo wishes to extort me.

—Extort! Can it be true? A thin boy extorts from the fattest man in Kenya?

—Of course, Bwana.

—He acts as if Man U Health Child Place owns Viagra Taverna. How can that be?

—Really. How can that *not* be?

—I stay out of the way of organizations like yours. One day this orphanage, one day that gang. Last thing I need is a gang of orphans to help me, thank you very much.

—Ah, He says, 'thank you very much.' Did you hear? How do we answer when someone thanks us, eh, child?

—We say, 'you are welcome very much'?

Ha, said Mkande. Ha ha, said the CEO, all the while looking at Money. He seemed pleased with this runty, up-and-coming boy he had saved from the streets.

—You know, a young fellow like you can make himself useful. So many are not useful, whatsoever. But you? You could help improve the world.

—How, Bwana?

—Such as you keep a sharp eye and watch that the staff is honourable and do not go join the Mungiki, the Hordes.

The CEO fastened his eyes on Money.

—Listen my boy. When I am away, you must think of me as a

kind of soldier fighting for justice, protecting honour and fortune. I need young people like you, by the way. To oversee our business interests when I am gone. Can I count on you for that, my friend?

—Will I be one of the staff?

—Ah, no. Their job is hard. You must be strong. Right now you are too thin. They would knock you aside as if you were a mosquito. I have no idea why you are so small and ugly. Congenital, it seems. Or perhaps you were infected.

—No. I did not know. Congenital.

—Not everyone is a beauty, by the way. For those who are not, we can only sit back and admire those other ones. One day, as a man, you will see that the beauties need us for some purposes.

—Congenital.

—Do you know what *congenital* means?

—No.

—Means mosquito is born already ugly.

—Ugly mosquitos can have nasty bite.

—What? Never mind that. By the way, use your ears to listen. Use your eyes to see. Henceforth, when I am away, you must be on the lookout for oppression.

—From who?

—External forces. You would not understand. You have duties, we all have duties, to see that our people keep their honour and integrity. The marketplace can be a trickster, by the way, by the way. It can make a fool of people like us. It happens even to entire governments.

His voice dropped to confidential tones.

—Listen my boy, although we do not condone it, if there is not other choice, if the oppressors are arrayed before you, then *violence is sometimes necessary*, you understand?

—Should we kill them, Bazu?

—Well. That depends. Say after me. When they oppress you and nothing else can be said, let violence be your voice. It has an honourable tradition, although we do not condone. Ultimately, one does not need words. Violence must be understood to be an argument and a position. All the great statesmen know this. Say it.

—Violence is a—

—Very good. And by the way, by the way, have you seen irregular activity in our lanes?

Money opened his mouth, but his stomach was still unsafe, so he closed his mouth again. He bent his efforts on forcing his stomach to keep his food where it belonged. As he did so he looked at his bare feet and at the shoes on the CEO's feet, which were shabby for a CEO. Old track shoes, the laces missing. The trousers too were filthy. As he looked at the CEO, words squirmed about inside of him, searching for a way out.

He stepped into a blinding sun with the dog named Boy tagging at his heels. The sun that had been less a giver of life than a bully that knocked hungry creatures about on the ground had finally been banished from the sky. It was quiet now, and cool.

Money lay in the shadow of the urinous wall and slept. The destroyed dog, a stinking shadow too near his nostrils, whimpered in his dreams. When he awoke later, the dog was gone and he was sorry he had not fed it. He remained there watching the electric lights sputter and the vendors close their cubicles and make their weary way homeward.

III

Because of internet. Because not even the smartest of the tech people who invented the internet knew who would see it and what it would mean.

The Hippo, fat Mkande, installed three computers in the Viagra Taverna along with a new sign:

Viagra Taverna and Hotel
Where a Man Can Kill His Thirst

Football TV
Internet Cafe

He meant to charge his customers by the minute. Instead, a chaotic flood of children squeezed in through holes and gaps in the wall, to peer over the shoulders of the paying customers until they were chased away.

After a time Mkande sent a message to the Man U Centre. He summoned Money and asked him to keep the small children out. In exchange he could hang around the Viagra Taverna and learn the internet.

Money took in so much internet, it was as though he were again hung upside-down in the world, his head swollen. For two years he existed in the pixelated brilliance of images, of rivers of new words and sounds and music, beats and dances worshipped across the expanse of the digital world. *Footage* and *commentary* and *porn* and sad and blood and the overgrown, unpruned mess of wants and dreams, far beyond the dingy lane and the dying river and the failing Healthy Child Centre and Mungiki and Dandora dump. Sex, sex, sex, the old and young. Children, even animals. Seeing the seams that hold the world. Deals, sales, video games that take over thoughts, manipulated images, numbers that sucked the life from humans. Fantastic wealth and abundance. Giant ocean waves and the garish confidences of wealthy teenagers who thought their every utterance had importance. Parades of luxuries and obsessions and beauty in dreamlike places, and the rich cities and towns and nations that the entire population of the planet wanted to invade and inhabit and own. Beautiful women and their unwinnable animal bodies, of every skin tone and shape.

And the weak, the confused, the bitter murderers and shit-makers and suicide bombers, the mean-spirited and obsessed, the greedy, the lusty, all exposed before the cameras, on the screens, before his open eyes, crowding into his dreams.

He lay awake in his bed. He made vows into the darkness, to the sleepers who stirred nearby.

When I am CEO, the Mungiki will be dead, the river will be full of big fish. When I am CEO, we will be wealthy with food, special clothes, BMW Mercedes Honda. Everyone will be afraid of us.

Aketch rolled over on her back and yawned, and he was caught in the movement of her limbs, the liquid blackness of her eyes. She sighed.

—Sure, Money-man. Go tell the CEO and Mzee Ibrahim and everyone what you want. See what they say. Maybe they can help.

She giggled at some joke only she understood. Then turned away and went back to sleep.

IV

The CEO and the staff conducted their growing business in the community as though nothing had changed anywhere and there was no world beyond Dandora. They did rounds, collecting orphan donations from shopkeepers who struggled in their stalls, offering partnership in the corporation in return for protection, with the understanding that without them it would fail.

Orphan care: that was the business of the CEO and Man U Corporation.

There was a plastic bag factory, a flimsy shack owned by one Simon. This Simon was young and energetic and good with words. All his ideas were wordy. He had business ambitions about packages. He began by selling ordinary water in used water bottles, sealing it with plastic to look clean, then went on to repackaging food in plastic packets small enough for one bite. He tried repackaging soap and toothpaste for one use, so that the poor people could feel like modern city people and their packages. But the plastic bag recycling was his grandest idea. He collected used bags that were floating everywhere and bundled them according to colour. These bags were the blue and white and yellow and green shards of modernity that blew about all over the nation, all over Africa, everywhere, that sank in the river, lodged in the soil, clogged ditches during the rains. The idea was to collect this bounty, melt them, make new bags, sell. Once he began, his business took off. In no time he had to pay collectors to collect used bags. He had the words to go with the project. *Recycling environment renewable solid waste management.* He put a sign on the shack.

SIMON MANUFACTURING
environmental recycling
bag maker

There were rumours that international aid agencies were interested in Simon, wanting in on his business. It was said that the World Bank had offered international support, but Simon cagily put them off because he was too smart, a *businessman* and an *entrepreneur.* These rumours reached the ears of the staff and finally the director and CEO of the Man U Healthy Child Centre. The CEO and his staff paid a visit to Simon to see for themselves. The CEO made Simon the usual generous Man U offer of a partnership for the purpose of safety and insurance. Later, the CEO was heard to explain how Simon had been sent home to join his ailing father.

The CEO personally took over Simon's bag business. He had a new sign made.

MAN U COMMUNITY SERVICES *and*
SIMON MANUFACTURING
environmental recycling plastic bags

Foreigners came. The international organizations. Two British women met the CEO, looked at the staff and the outdoor plastic bag machine melting and churning out new bags. They went away and did not return. The Swedes came but did not make it to the place because they met a swarm of young Mungiki hopefuls who waved a replica of a handgun.

Then came the Germans. They were led by a woman named Berta who was taller than any man in Dandora. When the same Mungiki hopefuls confronted her with their gun, she told them to go play with their toys somewhere else. She was so unusual the boys did not know how to react. They wandered away and left her alone. She might have been old or young—no one could say. Her hair was as straight as grass and as white as the hair of an old woman. She said she was not a mama this or mama that but more of a sister. She said people should call her Sister Berta. Her voice was strong and loud, her laugh bold, and it was impossible for children to resist staring and following along as she walked through the lanes. She was unafraid of Dandora, unconcerned by the Mungiki. When she met the CEO at the plastic bag place, he mentioned that he was the director of an orphanage. She asked him to take her there.

Sister Berta and the CEO walked side by side through the streets and lanes with a growing crowd of children following behind. They walked around burning trash, balanced on wood planks over the foul ditches, followed a path beside the river with the smoking dump looming opposite, and on past the Viagra Taverna. As they went, the CEO was taken by a made-in-Germany spell. His mind twisted and reversed, even as they approached the hill near the Man U Centre and picked their way through the market stalls of the potato and sweet and onion and tomato sellers. The CEO's eyes suddenly saw through the German woman's eyes instead of his own. His nose smelled what she smelled: a stench he had not noticed before, of the filth that ran in the middle of the lanes. Every now and again they had to step over rotted plastic bags that locals without latrines had filled with their shit. The CEO could hardly recognize his own place. He saw that the place was not wealthy the way he had always insisted. It was an overcrowded, unserviced place with acrid gases that filled the air. When they came to the Man U Healthy

Child Centre itself, he saw that it lacked basic German things like green lawns, reflective glass, stainless steel, pillars of white cement. Instead it was dusty, dirty, the roof broken, the building overcrowded with ill and thin children who had eaten bad food, who carried parasites, who struggled for bare survival.

At this moment the CEO underwent a change before the eyes of everyone. After that moment there were two CEOs: the Before CEO and the After CEO. The After CEO spoke a different language—of a poor man who had struggled his entire life and failed. He forgot to say how it was a time of great wealth and opportunity. He dropped the argument that the staff boys were the luckiest youth in the world, blessed with privilege, if only they were not too blind to see it. If he remembered his old words, he hid them because of the German sister named Berta, with her magic white hair and her tall walk that was like a man's walk.

Instead of making her daily trip to town, Aketch stayed around to see what might happen. The CEO talked gently to Aketch as though she were his daughter and he had only realized it now. He said please and sweetheart and bade her go collect together children from the lanes around and even from the dump itself. *Promise the starving ones that they will be given a meal.* Aketch looked at the CEO and the woman with him. For some reason she understood everything at a glance. She went out and found new orphans and non-orphans whom she lured with promises of rewards. The children came along, the smaller ones with their hopes high, the older ones with their eyes hard, all of them hungry.

Sister watched all this with her arms crossed over her chest like a man.

At first, there were new people and new things at the centre. There was fresh food and a new roof that did not leak. There were piles of wood and coal, bags of cement for repairs. Food and more food. The neighbourhood children who were not orphans hung about. More kids, more babies came in. Soon the place was crowded with more beds with chemically treated mosquito nets, the kitchen had new cooking pots and utensils and plates, and there were children and adults whom no one had seen before. New wires were put in, and better electricity and lights. One day a computer appeared. The CEO by now had a new pocket phone which he spoke into at all hours, as though he were a Nairobi businessman. He spoke with his new After CEO voice and had picked up some German: bitte, willkommen, entschuldigung, ja, nein, mein, kein. During all of this, Sister Berta, the German woman, hovered nearby, near the CEO, so her magic would stay strong. The CEO said *community, feelings, relationships*. He said *future* and *planning* and *development*. Sister Berta's magic was her white hair and her golden skin that looked like a kind of treasure. It was her sporty breasts and her sharp eyes. She used her peculiar way of speaking, which got the attention of everyone, especially men. She brought in German students who made new community projects. They cleared sewage from the lanes and dug new pit latrines in the market and by the school, laughing, their faces as young and bright as new metal. It was as though digging human feces was the best game ever.

After a few months, just as they were getting used to her, Sister Berta announced that her work in Kenya was done. It was time for her to return to Germany. When the CEO heard this, he withdrew to his office, the door to his office clicking shut behind him. The stream of new children and babies coming to the house ceased. Grey hair sprouted from the CEO's head. His massive limbs shrank to the dimensions of a normal man. He was not seen in the Viagra Taverna anymore. Though he still muttered to himself, his passion and violence were wrapped in new used plastic bags and stuffed inside him where they could not escape.

It was around this time that Money first heard rude jokes about the CEO. One of the staff boys laughed and said that the

German woman had taken a lion and made it a goat. Someone else said that she made him into a German, and soon his skin would go white. No one would have dared say these things before. The Man U staff who had always followed the CEO took to doing their business independently.

Aketch predicted that the CEO would follow his girlfriend. When Aketch said this, Money grabbed her, shoved Aketch up against the wall, and rubbed himself against her roughly so that she was pinned in place by his hard and narrow pelvis. He whispered roughly in her ear: —Maybe they are in love.

After that day Aketch no longer spoke to Money as though he were her younger brother. He had grown, his shoulders and arms hard, as though his body had waited, held back, until the moment he was fed. In fact, all the children had grown and put on weight in the months since the German woman had arrived.

The world was tilting, and basic parts of it were falling apart. Money watched from a corner and tried to work through the changes. He had new urgencies that drove him from one thing to another. One night Aketch came to the bed they shared when they were young. She lay without a word, her eyes open in the dark, looking at him, unafraid. He reached across and took her breast and her belly in his hands as if she owed something to him. She let him touch her that way. For a moment his broken sex minded its own business and was content to lie quietly and allow Money to be normal and happy. But it seemed that as soon as he thought about it, the thing swelled into a knot of pain. He drew back from her and ran out of the house as though still mocked by the children in the schoolyard. *Poor Money, his linga run over by a van, now the water comes out all the wrong places.*

V

The Man U Healthy Child Centre came to an unhappy ending. Money was anxious. He was glad. He hardened himself with the thought that he would be betrayed again and again because it was what he deserved. But he would accept that and he would still win, because he deserved that too. He saw the uncertain expressions of the younger children. They were like fragile eggs, ready to be dropped.

Money got stoned on chang'aa and stayed that way for a while, his thoughts boiling below a thin skein of brash words. During the day he heard himself insulting the CEO, repeating nasty things that were circulating about the big man. At night he wandered the lanes weeping privately for what he had said.

—That man is not a man. He's nothing but a worm. We should forget him.

When he said this to Richard, he was gratified for a moment to see the shock register across Richard's face, that his little body jolted as though Money had prodded him with hot metal.

The CEO vanished, leaving nothing behind. This great baba—founder, director, CEO of the Healthy Child Centre, great and triumphal rival of the Mungiki—passed out of their lives, reduced to a faded memory. After a short time it would be as though the CEO had never existed, his endeavours no more significant than the trash that arrived at Dandora dump, once cherished and useful, then discarded into the heap of a million other discards, to rot in the muck.

Within a short time the organization known as the Lethals overran the orphanage. The Lethals were routed by the Mungiki, who were in turn forced to defend against a new and previously unknown horde of energetic youth whom everyone called the Young. The Mungiki became specialized at killing the Young, preying on particular vulnerabilities. So it went.

The Man U name became another memory to be forgotten. Some of the staff boys were taken up by other gangs while others attempted to make it on their own. Without people behind them, they were beaten up or driven away. Two were found dead in the Dandora dump. The orphans vanished.

Eventually, the Mungiki set up a thriving sex trade in the remnants of the orphanage. They brought their own women.

Money and Aketch and Richard left Dandora, walking with their plastic carryall bags stuffed with blankets and a few clothes. They walked until they were in neighbourhoods that belonged to other gangs, and they had to dodge and run and hide their way through. When a boy challenged them, Richard cried out that they were members of the Man U, and the boy laughed and said, *The who?* So they knew they had gone far. They reached a major road with traffic lights where they snagged the side of a slow transport carrying chickens to market.

Except that Aketch did not take that ride. She took her leave easily and without a word, turning a corner when Money was not looking. Months later Money heard that Aketch had found her way to the wealthy enclave of Eastleigh. A foreigner had taken her in after hearing Aketch speak German.

Money was left alone with Richard. It was as though Aketch had planned for this moment from the beginning. For a while Richard drove Money mad by insisting that the CEO and Aketch would return. Finally Money lost his patience and slapped Richard until he promised to shut up about the CEO. This he did until he forgot the slaps then said more and was beaten again.

After that, if anyone asked, Money would say that the CEO had been *sent home to join his dying father.*

CHAPTER 17
Money Manyu
Isiolo, Kitale
May 8, 2016

Money and Hassan drove into the centre of Isiolo and pulled over by a food market. The market was thronged with people and bodabodas and vehicles of all kinds.

Hassan found a duka where he bought brightly coloured fruit drinks and sambusas and fried chicken which he brought back to the cab in paper bags stained through with oil. Money looked out the window at the busy street. A group of armed men walked through carrying old AKs, much like his own. There were Kenyan soldiers in the crowd, but they looked lost among so many other gunmen. Somali words floated in the air.

Hassan looked at the sky to the east.

—I will make my way alone from here. I know this town. I will catch a ride, God willing, east to Wajir. Then I will return to my wife and children.

—How can you go back to your family after all this time, with only that small amount for your reward?

—Yes, it's true. I took chances. I made bad choices. Now it's time to go home.

Money went to the back of the lorry and found the boots that Hassan had not worn. He sat on the tailgate looking at the boots. From his pocket he took out the money that Rosie had paid him.

It made him nauseated to look at it. He stuffed the cash into one of the boots, far down in the toe and then brought the boots with him and handed them to Hassan.

—Don't lose these boots. Keep them and give them to your eldest son when he grows.

—I will keep them then since that is your wish. Kwaheri, my brother, and good fortune. I will not forget you.

Then Hassan turned, walked quickly away, and was gone through the crowd in the market, boots in one hand, his bag of possessions strapped to his back.

II

Money was tired, but he could not stay in Isiolo. He considered going farther south to new places where he might forget about Rosie and his Mungiki gunmen. He turned the lorry around and drove west instead. Eventually the air cooled. The land became green, and there were forests and fields of wheat and maize.

He came to the town of Kitale, where a wave of fatigue made him stop driving. He got down from the cab and looked around at the town. The air was clean. He stretched his legs in the late sun and looked for a place to eat. He went through a door under a sign that said LUCKY DAY CAFE and ordered fried tilapia and curried potatoes and beer. He drank several bottles of beer with his food and became too sluggish to get back in the driver's seat. The proprietor spoke kindly to him. He nodded in the direction of a crumbling two-storey building behind the café, saying, *Four is vacant.* Money took the key that was attached to a piece of wood with Number 4 on it. He weaved out and collected his duffle bag, then came through the café, through a courtyard, through a passageway, and up a short stairway. As he went, he stepped around women and children who sat here and there in the dark passageway eating, feeding the young, grooming themselves, as though they were camping out in that dingy interior place.

Money found a door with Number 4 painted on it, unlocked it with the key, and went in. The room smelled of mildew and sweat. There was a saggy bed, a chair, and a table with a hotplate and a disconnected computer screen on it, facing the wall. As he sat on the bed there were two low knocks on the door. He opened it to find a woman who cradled a baby swaddled in a blanket, in spite of the heat.

—Bwana, I have a message for you.

—What message?

—A personal message.

She pushed her way past him into the room and stood, swaying gently side to side, rocking the infant.

—What message?

—I can do things for you in this private room. Very private.

—What can you do?

—Dance. I can dance.

Money looked at her. She kept her eyes fixed on the floor and swayed the swaddled infant. He waved his hand in resignation.

—Okay, what the hell. Dance then.

She put the baby on the bed. The baby was quiet. It either knew its part or was too hot to cry. The woman pulled off her T-shirt and jeans and began to do an internet dance that featured impossible gyrations of the hips and shaking of the buttocks as she hummed some tune. Her underwear was grey with dirt. Her face was weary and hopeless, her hair dirty. One breast leaked milk. Random thoughts blew through Money's mind. With a troublesome ache he suddenly remembered Aketch. In his fatigue, the memory seemed to pounce on him, like a mugger on a drunk man. He wondered if she was dead by now. Or perhaps she had gone the way of this sad dancer, burdened by a hungry baby, without any easy way to live. After a few minutes he waved vaguely at the dancer.

—Mzuri. Wonderful dance. Okay, stop. Enough.

—You don't like the dance? I have others. We can dance together if you want. Sexy dance is okay too.

—Ah, no thanks. I like your dance. Very beautiful. I am too tired. And I am not a good dancer myself.

—You will sleep peacefully and without worries if you do the sexy dance.

—Ah, no.

The baby began a mewling cry—it was very small—and she went to it, popped out her leaky breast, and let the baby fasten on to it. She sighed as the baby suckled.

—Just wait. In a minute we can do a special sexy dance, then sleep. You are one of those handsome men. Just like the film actors.

—It would be better if you find another sexy dance partner.

He went to his bag and rummaged about for something to give her. He found a stale bun, a dusty sweet, passports, a wallet that once belonged to someone. She looked at all of this with a look of panic.

—Please. There is no safe place for us to sleep tonight.

—What? Why not go home to your people and stay there? Go back to your village so you can have a proper life. Why not go back to the place where you slept before, last night and the night before and the night before? What of the father of this child? Has he no shame to put his child in the street while his mother dances for beds?

—There is no bed in this entire mortal world for me.

Tears gathered in her eyes. Once the tears began, they became a silent torrent.

—Fine, fine. Stay then. Tonight only. Just stay quiet and do not dance or do nonsense. You can sleep in the corner.

The woman did as she was told. Money lay on the bed. When he closed his eyes, he kept seeing the figure of Hassan walking away into the crowd, limping along a road toward a glaring horizon of dunes. He had grown accustomed to Hassan's presence, just as he had grown accustomed to being constantly alert, to constantly checking his rage. He had grown so accustomed to having his knife at the ready that now he forgot to remove it as he lay on the bed. The knife handle stuck into his ribs. He unstrapped it and set it on the floor and looked at it, then lay with eyes open so he would not have to imagine Hassan walking, walking endlessly toward horizons of sand, all the way to Somalia, another Somali defeated by the Mungiki. When he rolled one way, he faced a wall stained with dried human liquids. When he turned the other way, the woman was crouched in the corner, breastfeeding the baby. He stripped off the blanket and tossed it at her. She looked at him without a word. He tossed over the pillow. She said nothing but drew the blanket over her knees, then turned to face the corner like a child who knew daily punishment and accepted her regular punishments so well by now that she knew when and how to mete out the punishment to herself.

Money tried to shut out the sniffling sounds coming from the corner. He listened for a long time before he rose and went to her and pointed at the bed, and she went immediately and lay there with her baby. He spread the blanket over her and sat in the chair for the remaining hours of the night, hearing and not wanting to hear the other occupants of the inn, each sound and utterance passing through the thin walls as if through a computer internet microphone of the Poors in the throes of their private sorrow or passion or commerce. What chances did people have, who owned nothing, not even their own breasts and hips?

At daylight he handed a bill to the woman as she sat on the bed cooing softly to her newborn. It was a twenty euro note, beautifully made, substantial and important with its badges and vivid yellow and green colours. The woman stared at it, her lips forming a perfect O, then scuttled away before this providence was withdrawn. When Money came back to the room at nightfall she was back, somehow, with milk and pieces of roasted beef.

He paid for the room for the week and wandered aimlessly about the town. After that, another week passed, then another, then it was a month. The woman, whose name was Mary, had settled in with her baby on the bed. Money had given up asking her to find another place to sleep. Instead, she stayed out of his way, offering to share the bed, but he declined and bought mats that he placed in the corner for himself. She made faint and weary motions of keeping house in the shabby little room. She attempted ugali on the hotplate, until he stopped her. He went out and bought non-ugali stuff: rice, potatoes, onions, tomatoes, and fish. She was not a good cook, but the meals were fresh, and she said little.

Money was stuck. Eventually, the share of his payment that he had kept slipped away, used for food, for the shabby room, baby bottles, baby clothes, baby medicine, proper clothes for the mother. Babies and women, always needing. There was never enough for all their needs. One day, inevitably, hunger would catch them.

Nine thousand, and, possibly, much more. The words cycled through his mind. How was it not *much more? Why-oh-why-oh-why?*

The baby mewed, cooed, clucked. Its nose ran and it looked at Money with steady eyes.

The loudspeaker at the nearby mosque crackled and the prayer was blared across the world for all to be reminded. Allah hu akbar.

III

He strapped his knife around his back the way Hassan had done. He drank coffee, and went out and sat in the cab of the thing called IN GOD WE TRIST. The lorry was parked on a lively, colourful street of commerce. The town seemed very good. It was airy and rain-washed, and the people looked peaceful and profitable. He looked at all this with satisfaction and a great deal of puzzlement. Despite everything, here was a place where children might grow properly without interference. In the market street, women laughed in the early morning sun as they opened the shutters of shop fronts. Some shops were rich, selling computers, mobile phones, gaudy clothing.

His knife poked him in the ribs from its new position. It was as though Hassan were prodding him. He had to go back to get what was properly owed Hassan. The knife was unwilling to let that go. He drove the lorry to a petrol station and filled the fuel tanks with fuel and the water tanks with water and bought cigarettes and dried meat and a large bag of freshly made sambusas. He bought a strong, battery-powered light and mounted it on the roof. He set out driving again, retracing his route back to the camp.

He was prepared to find the camp abandoned after all these weeks. But when he rolled up the valley, he saw unfamiliar white lorries. There were changes to the camp. The refuse pile had been burned off and an effort had been made to camouflage the vehicles with netting and foliage. When he shut the engine and climbed down, no one came to challenge him. A man wearing a balaclava and faded military fatigues and carrying an AK emerged from the dispensary, looked toward the lorry, and went back into the dispensary. Money followed him, opened the door of the dispensary, and stepped inside. The man sat at the table with four other men. They were eating flowery food that was not ugali. When Money appeared, they put down their food and looked at him. One put his hand on an expensive-looking 9mm pistol. Money put his hands out to show he had no firearm.

—Where is Rosie?

—What is it you want?

—I want Rosie. We have business.

—We know your business. He told us we might expect you. But I can tell you that we have nothing to offer you here. We conducted our transaction with that one you call Rosie, not with you.

—Ah. Business transaction. You bought what he sold.

—Yes, yes, you can look at it that way. What of it?

—Where is Rosie?

—We don't know. We are finished with him. You should go back and forget about that man and this place. Better for your good health.

Money turned on his heel and went out, letting the metal door slam behind him. His knife was jabbing him in the rib so aggressively he thought it might draw blood. He let it jab and irritate. Without thinking about it he found himself standing by the hole in the side of the hill where they had put the prisoner. Kestner was alone in there, lying with his feet outside and his body inside. He was in worse shape than when Money had departed the camp. There was a dirty bowl and a plastic bottle of water, a couple of tangled blankets. Kestner's clothing was wrecked and filthy. Kestner opened his eyes and looked at Money.

—We thought you were long gone.

—Who is we? You are alone.

—My colleagues and I.

—Colleagues? Anyway, *long gone* means *dead*. I am like the Jesus Christ. I returned.

—The Jesus Christ. That's you.

—Who are these new men? Do they not give you food?

—No one goes in for food in this place. Be a good man and get us out of here, will you? If we're going to die, we'd rather do it anywhere but here. You were the one who brought us here. Now you can take us away. Perfect. Look, afterwards, we can be pals and buddies.

—Who is we? Why would I abduct you from the very abductors I sold you to? It makes no sense what you say. Anyway, I don't care for these men. They look like mercenary soldiers.

—Mercenary sons of bitches, yes.

There was, after all, someone watching over the prisoner from the hill above. The man wore a scarf around his head and squatted in peasant position, arms wrapped about his knees and a short, ugly weapon propped against a rock nearby. He smoked and contemplated Money as Money contemplated him back. Kestner glanced toward the man on guard and murmured.

—Oh, yes, him. Saddle Nose, I call him. You know Hutchinson's triad? A lot of cases hereabout. One should be cautious about the behaviour of a gun-wielding man with congenital syphilis. Neurological manifestations, you know. Fits of madness.

—Syphilis?

—I don't understand how people get caught up in these desperate and inconvenient schemes. What can be gained? Don't they realize that people have work to do? Besides, I'm no longer important. Since I arrived here, I've become a nobody. Was a somebody previously. Now not.

—You ask, what is gained? Nothing perhaps. But then, people like you do not know reality. People like you, rich people from other countries, it is like you are not attached to the ground. You cannot learn the reality, even when someone tries to teach you.

—Try me.

—Too late for lessons. These other men, maybe they are teachers.

Just then, one of the men, one of the *teachers*, appeared. He strode up, speaking urgently on his phone in his own language. He put the phone away.

—Get out. You do not have permission to speak to the prisoner.

—Permission? Me?

—Get out. Act better or you will be shot. This is warning. Some want to shoot you already. No one here is your friend. No one likes you.

—Fine that no one likes me. I prefer that.

Money looked the man in the eye and pushed the barrel of his gun to one side.

—You going to shoot me? No? Because if you do not shoot me, I will do as I please with this prisoner. I am the one who captured him. So that makes him my property until you and your people pay the agreed price, yes? Your problem is if you do not shoot me, maybe next time, I hold the gun. Maybe I am not so soft-hearted as you, yah?

Money saw the understanding in the man's pale eyes as they twitched wide in rage or humiliation or surprise. It was satisfying to see that a man had such great understanding. He realized that while these new men were tougher than the first group, they were just as uncertain of themselves. It made him think that their plan was not going smoothly, whatever that might be.

He turned his back on the gunman and looked at the condition of the prisoner. *His prisoner. All of this for one ragged and starving Canadian doctor.* There was some bigger force at play. He could not see what that might be.

Money went to sit on the tailgate and smoke a cigarette. He was sitting that way an hour later when a crushed beetle of an Isuzu farm truck rolled up in a cloud of dust and the other Canadian, Mason-Tremblay, was unloaded, his clothes covered in dirt, his hands bound.

PART FIVE

COSTS AND BENEFITS

CHAPTER 18
Avtar Kestner
Southern and East Africa Regions
2013

Kestner might have remained a practising physician. It was the easier choice in many ways. The challenges presented themselves each day, each hour, a ceaseless stream of the sick and needy. It was a matter of bringing to the moment the observational skill and intellectual agility to duck and dodge through medical science and technology and translate it into the art of individual patient care. It required discipline of mind and soul, the balance of knowledge and compassion, expediency and thoroughness, curiosity and impatience. It required humility in the face of atypical presentations, atypical human organisms.

Yet it had not been easy. In his truthful moments he knew he could not be a clinician. He regretted it over the long term. He did not share his regrets with anyone. He could not, for he felt it as the tiniest anomaly, as fundamental as a muon or neutrino, in his character. He had trained as a physician yet chose not to be a physician. Despite his work in public health, his research publications, the recognition and prestige, his participation in international programs, his stunning remuneration, there was always this muon or neutrino at the centre. *Unable to deal with the mess and fuss of real medical practice, the hard realities of life.* His brilliant medical education and careful clinical mentoring, all a waste.

The clinical work, the art of patient care, the practice of doctor and patient, one on one, came to an abrupt end with a singular patient who never failed to return to him when he least wished to remember her.

Her name was Yolanda Chavez. She came into the ER on her own, a woman who should be at the peak of health, presenting with a slightly elevated temperature, tachypnea, elevated heart rate, agitation, and anxiety. She wiped her tears and said she was worried that she might die. No, she knew how it felt to be over-tired, and she knew how it felt to have flu. This was different. No, she did not take drugs or alcohol. She described the sensation as having a thin blanket of pain laid lightly over her skin.

—It feels like the salutation of death. Like an opening move.

—Do you play chess?

—No. I have kids.

Twenty-seven years old—she was his age to the day. Thick black eyelashes and a mess of silken hair, a loose T-shirt and army fatigues that did nothing to conceal her graceful figure. All in all, Dr. Avtar Kestner, junior resident, examined her, and as he spoke to her, took her temperature and blood pressure, listened to her lungs, drew blood and sent it to the lab. Temperature slightly elevated. Pressure slightly high. The lab results showed elevated neutrophils and platelets, common with stress. Otherwise, nothing remarkable. Something *was* wrong and he did not know what. He *felt* rather than *thought* there was something more. The senior resident was not answering his call, and anyway, he should be able to sort this one out. Her description of her symptoms bothered him. Finally, he discussed with the nurse about admitting her for the remainder of the night for observation. The nurse, who was a matter-of-fact older woman whom he respected, suggested that no, there was no real basis for admission, and besides there were far worse patients and a shortage of beds. *And what was this young thing about after all*, nudged the nurse. *A lonely thing looking for a young eligible doctor to pay attention to her.* It was three o'clock in the morning, in the lost hours in which people give up, subside, are borne away to the basement on a gurney with the rails up, baize covered. It was that time of death, and the emergency ward was as cold as a refrigerator, over-lit and antithetical to hope, wall to wall addicts and drunks and human misfortune.

He heeded the nurse, ashamed that she thought he was not as coldly objective in his clinical assessment as he should be. He explained gently, apologetically, to Yolanda Chavez to take a couple of Aspirins with water and go to bed, to come back if she felt worse. She nodded and looked at him with trust and an achingly faithful obedience that haunted him forever. She went away without complaint. Trust and obedience. Better if she had told him to go to hell. He watched her go with a wince, noting the way her shoulders and chest were collapsed and the way she stepped gingerly. Twenty-seven. It was ridiculous to note her age, to obsess over one patient.

Except that he dreamed of her later that night, as he tossed and turned in his narrow hospital quarters.

He was not on duty when Ms. Chavez returned to the ER the next evening. He was informed later by the nurse — the same nurse — that as she took the blood pressure of this Yolanda Chavez, the young woman collapsed and was dead within the hour, despite heroic interventions. Septic shock. Undone by failed compensations.

His colleagues were sympathetic, telling him it was not his fault, that it was impossible to foresee. The senior resident, though, said nothing as she listened grimly to his account of the case.

At the end of his term, Kestner quit his residency, announcing that he had decided to make the jump to international public health, to the abstractions of populations, data, research. And he was forced to look away when he learned the further details that he wished not to know but could not help but absorb into the deepest part of himself, that Yolanda Chavez had left two young children with a destitute and ill grandmother for whom Yolanda had been the money earner and caregiver. He went to her memorial mass in the cathedral, sat at the back, wept, emptied his bank account, and sent his money to the grandmother anonymously.

He moved on. For a decade or so after leaving clinical care, he was borne along on the noble illusion that public health was a far greater endeavour and that something extraordinary was achievable, like a contribution to groundbreaking knowledge that would improve the health of millions. He embarked on graduate studies toward a PhD followed by post-doctoral research with leading people at the best institutions. He was a talented researcher, publishing in the best journals. Meanwhile, throughout that period his young family remained steadfastly in the background, at the far edge of his great endeavour. The children, his girls, came up even as he was accelerating away, leaving his family behind, ever and more preoccupied with this engrossing sphere of international missions to save the thousands and the millions. It was all a brilliant cinematic dream, except that he had been awake. It was a dream of saving humanity even if he could not save himself. Years flashed by—a kaleidoscope of new countries, new missions, new colleagues—while his daughters grew into young women, and Renate, his sweet wife, grew into a stranger, and he was finally and fully alone, as though he had not been a husband or a father at all. And the exciting colleagues—his co-authors, co-investigators, brilliant friends, in their turns, fell away—scattered over the globe, some ascended to heights, others reduced by misfortunes. Finally, he was left to make his way alone, a lonely sailor far out to sea, trying to find his direction back to port.

It was not that the program director, Dr. Seiko Levigne, physically resembled Yolanda Chavez. Far from it. Perhaps there were certain similar gestures that had lodged in his mind all those years. Seiko was not the first woman who had triggered this reaction. It had happened from time to time over the years, around the world, women of all backgrounds. His was a world full of trusting and compliant Yolanda Chavezes.

He first met Seiko Levigne in her office on a breezy Harare morning. They shook hands, she returned his gaze, and a slight smile formed on her lips, which made him wonder what she knew about him. He fumbled as he made his presentation of the evaluation process, embarrassed because he was overwhelmed by a certain delicate yet penetrating scent, of clean perspiration and other intimate perfumes. He shucked off his jacket, then his tie, breathing, trying to ignore her, bothered. What was it that made his senses suddenly acute, sudden, vivid, his synapses sparking in a long dormant part of his limbic system?

Their roles did not warrant another meeting until the final phase of the evaluation, several months hence. This was laid out clearly in the terms of reference of the review. There was no requirement for her to be present in the field as he visited community-level project sites spread across southern and eastern Africa. She appeared on the second day, at the airport, saying briefly that she would accompany him since she had a round of coordinating meetings in Ndola, Maseru, Maputo, and Blantyre. If it was all right with him, of course. And always she wore the disarming and faint smile, as though she had some a priori knowledge. What was it she foresaw? Was he so transparent? An upturning of the lips while her eyes remained serious, questioning, careworn, even mournful. Was she giving or taking? Perhaps she was mocking him. Perhaps teasing. Perhaps seeing through his self-delusions, seeing the callow man beneath? Mouth one way, eyes another, she provoked unanswerable questions. They were the same questions Yolanda Chavez might have asked.

Kestner got on with his assignment. It was a challenging and difficult evaluation of a large humanitarian effort implemented by 170 community projects in ten southern African countries. Performance indicators, implementation plan, logical framework, outcomes, outputs and purpose, cultural and linguistic bridges, gender policies, environmental impact analysis, and capacity development approaches. A funding mechanism to develop the capacity of communities to prevent and mitigate the effects of the HIV epidemic across southern Africa. There were hundreds of stricken communities in which the epidemic raged out of control, where students and teachers and civil servants were withering into repositories for every known microbe, succumbing to rampant viremia, TB, candidiasis, parasitic worms flat and round, strange tumours, and finally bacterial sepsis that swept up the victims in the prime of their days. Entire families collapsed; young people died in droves. The afflicted wandered away from homes, searching for help where help did not exist. Thousands of walking dead, blowing across the land.

All of this was neatly summarized in the prescribed format, with efforts to quantify the effects of the aid programs on human suffering.

Seiko Levigne and he rode in the project vehicle from one project to another. They rode the central road of Malawi, through a pelting rain that was abruptly switched off to give way to sudden steam and sun. They drove east from the main highway onto smaller routes, through fields of tobacco and cottons and palm groves, all skirted by worn domes and humps of the Vipya Highlands. Storm clouds moved across the landscape. Distant raindrops fell, scattered on the green land like jewels.

Where they stopped, the humid air over the fields poured thickly through the open windows. The driver hailed a herder. The driver was agitated, shouting as though the herder was deaf.

—I'm a driver, not a stopper! I cannot abide to stop! Stopping is not driving!

Levigne stretched her limbs. Her shirt stuck to her in the heat.

—This is where I should stay. I should be lost in untouched places where I can work without being noticed.

—There are no untouched places. Very sorry to break it to you.

—Disconnected and uncontaminated, then. Is that better? Places disconnected from giant corporations and their greedy executives and rampaging technology and uncontaminated by GMOs and pesticides, television evangelists, corrupt politicians, and billionaires. Heaven is a place without billionaires and their abusive schemes.

—What about antibiotics, contraceptives, latrines, water filtration, medical care?

— Can you not see beyond public health? Do you ever take off the public health hat?

—It doesn't come off. Come to think of it, it never fit that well in the first place. The sides flop down over my ears.

—This place is beautiful exactly the way it is. Why does it need 'progress'?

—Well, let's see. So an innocent village woman is bleeding to death during delivery. I wonder how much she revels in her untouched, beautiful village. It's a simple enough question.

Seiko Levigne sighed, hopped out of the car, and set off along the road walking. Behind her, a boy emerged from the brush with a stick and a bicycle wheel rim. He set the stick in the wheel and ran on the road. A mottled dog followed him, attempting to scratch fleas while it walked. Then came a stumping nanny goat who glared with disapproval at the strangers. The boy, flying away along the road with his wheel, suddenly burst into song.

Kestner caught up with Levigne, and they walked through fields of tobacco.

—Don't you ever worry about how much we interfere with these villagers? Even a hemorrhaging mother has her traditions.

—What traditions? Like death? Interference is part of the profession. Interference in human ignorance and backwardness.

—How do you know you're not interfering with other things that are beyond your understanding? Or do you think you have perfect knowledge?

—Evidence-based interference. Humbly, I submit the scientific method. Interference in poverty, infectious diseases, malnutrition.

—Primum non nocere.

—Pardon me?

—I think you heard.

They returned to the vehicle, powered up, roared past boy-stick-wheel (who had travelled surprisingly far), and went on for twenty kilometres before cutting off onto a swampy track that crossed a fallow field. The track led toward a distant grove of trees and the village clinic.

Levigne made the driver stop again.

—Charles, please go ahead. Dr. Kestner and I will walk from here. We'll give the villagers a good laugh.

—Yes, madam. But I will pass by in case you find it too difficult.

—Thank you, Charles.

Kestner stepped out and looked ahead along the rough track through the mud and long grass.

—I know you like exercise, however...

—You say however a lot. Did you know?

—However, snakes. Mambas. This place is prime mamba habitat. Piles of slash, abandoned termitaria. It's not really a question of if. They love nothing better than pursuing lost women who wander near their dens.

—Mambas avoid me. They know better.

—And, secondly, bare legs? You really want to play host to our friend ancylostoma.

—Hookworms dislike me. They're sensitive things. Anyway, I know: schistosomes in the puddles, filarial worms, leishmaniasis, syphilis, not to mention HIV.

She pirouetted away in her sandals and her long skirt. He got out, waved at the driver, and jogged after her through the grass.

They reached the village late, the clinic staff assembled in a neat line, sweating and anxious in the close air of the village square, their safari suits and floral dresses wilting. When they saw the muddy shoes and spattered skirt of Levigne, they forgot their discomfort and shrieked with delight.

A week later they were in the northern end of the project area, in the Lake Zone of Tanzania.

They met in Mwanza. Kestner arrived with Ministry of Health officials by road, Levigne by flight from Dar es Salaam. They drank the first night in the bar of the Tilapia Hotel with Lake Victoria lapping at the shoreline below.

Konyagi, possibly not whisky at all, however; considered the spirit of the nation, the tears of the lions, etc. etc. A buoyant citrusy jolt made perhaps of something called konyagi, presumably distilled but maybe not. Pleasant, non-CVA-inducing and transparent enough to view crocodiles, in hallucination if not in reality. A 5.5, but after two shots, a 7.5/10.

Project sites were scattered on either side of the Serengeti so they opted to tour through the park en route. They hired a local park guide and a Land Rover with a snorkel. The guide was a quiet local man who promised locations off the sanctioned road. They entered the park through the Western Gate and came to the edge of a broad and shallow river where they got down to walk at the urging of the guide.

On the shoreline of the river were rough boulders and large animal scats and old bones. They looked about, wondering where they had come. Nothing stirred. Then a herd of zebra appeared nearby. The herd was agitated, the leaders barking as they came close to the river. The herd approached the water tentatively, then the leaders bolted across, and the herd stampeded across the shallows to the other side and up onto a ramp of land to a grassy rise where they stopped to graze. But for one zebra, a young stallion, who came back to the water with head and tail held high, strutting, circling. He galloped back across the river, neighing loudly, wheeled and turned and splashed across again, shaking his mane, rearing. He crossed a third time, and on the fourth the water exploded beneath him, and his hoof was in the mouth of a crocodile. The zebra fought and stamped and screamed in fury. Other crocodiles appeared from nowhere, then it ended, the river running red with the shreds of the victim fought over.

Kestner and Seiko were stunned. The guide shrugged and picked up a pebble and threw it at the river. It came to Kestner that the place where they stood was among the crocodile grounds, the scat belonging to the predators. He took Seiko's arm, and they backed away while the guide blithely whistled a tune and tossed stones, hoping for further action.

But Seiko withdrew that day. She would not speak to Kestner that day or the next. She was pale and trembled from time to time over the next hours. When he spoke to her, she turned away from him. He heard her weeping quietly once, then she wrapped her arms around her shoulders.

The way that part of their journey went, each day was marked by more blood and violence. Lions that cut newborn wildebeests away from their mothers. Cheetahs that took down aging gazelles. An infuriated bull elephant that charged an African buffalo for no apparent reason, goring it on the ground. Seiko watched all this sidelong, then turned away, vomited at the bleating of the wildebeest calf as it was carried live in the jaws of a lioness. She would not be comforted. In the evenings she refused dinner and turned in early.

Kestner knew he should not have brought her here. After a while he too cringed at the state of nature.

At Ngorogoro she left him, saying she had been summoned

back to her office in Harare. Kestner completed that leg of his monitoring mission alone. In the evenings he dined at linen-covered tables, bought a bottle of Muponene, whisky of Zambia (*a solid 4/10 and notably transparent of manufacture, with ingredients listed as water, potable spirits, permitted food flavouring*). He sipped it, put it aside.

On his last day of that part of his mission, he was the sole client at a hotel on the Indian Ocean coast north of Dar es Salaam. He sat at a table set with silver, a menu card lit by a kerosene lamp, beneath breezy palms, the ocean before him a void, even as the setting sun caught the patched lateen sails of dhows as they were pushed toward shore by the onshore thermals.

Seiko Levigne slipped into the chair opposite, her dark eyes flitting over his face, her smile, as ever, small and mysterious. Kestner started to stand, then controlled himself, sat down and smiled at her.

—You came back. I don't understand you.

—I had no intention of coming back. I left.

—But why? You said nothing.

— I can't tolerate that kind of violence.

—But they're animals. It's nature. It's biology.

—It doesn't matter. Animals or humans, it's all the same, isn't it? It's part of the world I don't want and don't need. Men seem to revel in it. Women suffer it.

—What we saw was nothing more than evolved behaviours. Ecological roles. You know that. Not all men revel in violence. Though I admit I find watching animals in the wild fascinating. There's so much to learn about behaviour.

—Oh, yes, of course. Scientific exculpation.

—It reminds us what we are.

—Yes, precisely. I don't wish to be reminded.

—What happened to you? I'm sorry, whatever it was.

—I don't want to go into it. Let's just say I'm escaped prey.

‖

She stayed close to him after that. She dropped duties, cancelled community capacity development workshops, excused herself from ministerial meetings, garden parties, and the soirees of the diplomatic and NGO set to meet him in obscure locations, across the country, across borders.

They came to the town of Beira, to an old stone place known as the Buffalo Hotel and Bar and were stranded there as a cyclone built offshore. Sections of the roof flew noisily away to clatter in the deluged streets. Palm trees lay flat, squirming before the gale. The power went out.

They found the hotel lounge and bar open, crowded with locals, South Africans, and a contingent of government men who drank and played poker at a raucous table. Levigne and Kestner found a place at a corner of the long bar.

—Here we are, the end of the world.

—Maybe it's the beginning of the world. It probably started like this.

They ordered, drank, took turns composing sentences to amuse one another.

Four Ships Whisky. One ship better, apparently, than Three Ships.

Magic Beer. Ice cold in a tropical bar, refrigeration impossible on account of the absence of electricity.

Benson's of Bottomly: ripe with tannins, rakish hints of sesquiterpenes, reminiscent of certain anti-neoplastics.

She had packed with her two cut crystal whisky glasses, and these were what they drank from at every bar, the angles of the crystal merrily reflecting the intermittent lightning. They came under the eye of the cyclone, lightning flashing; thirty minutes of clear sky followed by dark violence.

In that place the hotel staff bustled between orders, one moment hammering planks over the windows to keep out the cyclonic winds, the next cajoling patrons into ordering food and drink. She sipped her drink.

—I must explain something difficult.

—Are we going to be complicated here? It's been so blissfully simple.

—True. But you probably should know some things about me. I don't want to keep being dishonest. Consider this a warning.

—I am warned.

—Sometimes honesty is self-destructive.

—This is starting to sound like a rationalization.

—It does sound like that, yes.

—Seiko, why don't you just come clean and tell me what you're trying to say.

—I want to. How about we talk about you?

— I can't think of any way I've been dishonest to you, actually.

—That's because you never say anything about yourself. Saying nothing is just as bad as lying, isn't it?

People streamed through the doorway to the lounge, shouting and ducking out of the storm, to discover drinks being served and the cards being dealt, a disaster celebration, a last party. A guitar came out, and a voice rang out a song in Portuguese. The South African mining men made requests of the bartender in Afrikaans and laughed when it turned out he was fluent. The South Africans noticed Levigne and smiled broad smiles at her and raised glasses, saying cheers.

—They know me. We set up an HIV project for their workers. Those are the managers and foremen. They're rough, those men.

—Mining company. Tell me the sordid details.

—They're typical men. They hide behind the unspoken.

—What is it that such men hide? Indiscretions, crimes against humanity? Secret desires? The need to be little boys? How do you know they're not just extremely plain and stupid and obvious and there's nothing underneath but for beer drinking, lewd jokers, a tendency for aggressive pointless games with various inflated balls?

—I've never been privy to the secrets of men. They are a complete mystery to me.

—Okay, so what is your most secret thing? Out with it.

—How about the details of my birth. Official things. My organization thinks I was born in Manitoba. I was forced to provide documents. False ones. It's quite easy, by the way.

He drank his whisky, poured from the bottle the bartender had set before them. Benson's of Bottomly.

—Alright. So what? In the grand scheme of things, it's not such a big deal. Maybe it's important to some petty government official in Ottawa, so what? You were born overseas? Anyway, I would think nationality might be more important than place of birth.

—I have to tell you something. I'm not really what you think. I mean I am, but I'm not. It's been necessary to be creative.

—What do you mean *creative*?

—A person might graduate with an MPH. Or not. It wouldn't be difficult to not and say you did. Mistakes happen. A person is so busy actually doing public health that there isn't time to study it. I doubt that my story is unique. I want to be honest with you, you see, but there are reasons. I was hoping you would trust me. Can we talk about you now? It would make it easier. Tell me something you've concealed from me.

—Concealed? I have nothing much to report. Let's see, I slogged through a baccalaureate, a tortuous MD. Flagellated myself with graduate school, went to classes, sweated over impossible research projects, squeezed out a doctoral thesis, and defended it.

—I'm sure you had to be creative along the way. Here I am, trying to reveal myself to you in the middle of a cyclone.

—You might as well. We'll be lightninged to death any minute.

She ordered food, speaking Chichewa to the server, then went off to the ladies' room. One of the miners said something to her as she passed. She shook her head and slid by him.

When she returned the wind had increased. They sat listening to the storm outside the shuddering walls. They drank the whisky and ate day-old *pao* and strips of meat and watched the fraught celebrations in the room as the wind raged.

—But you do have a medical degree.

—I would have loved to go medical school. It wasn't in the cards for me. Don't worry. I have a broad experience in clinical care and public health, as promised. You must not judge me.

—A graduate degree of some kind?

—Not everyone has that opportunity.

She was quiet the rest of that night, drinking in the eye of the cyclone, flushed, her few words slurred, roof panels madly banging, the miners yelling at each other, the guitar player bellowing in Portuguese and Changana. *O vento é meu beijo. O vento, o vento.*

Kestner was drunk but lucid. He resisted the compulsion to take Seiko in his arms and shelter her. But another part of him remained cool and observant, clinical, analytical, the professional reviewer on the trail of an important anomaly. This part of him searched out the reason and the root and the cause of anomalies. Later, as they seduced each other in a room in which the walls were ready to fall away, Kestner observed Seiko, observed himself, observed all in its anomalous splendour. Finally, she let him catch her by the waist, run his lips along her proud and erect spine, and coax her to him. And still later, in the darkness, he awoke to observe further, as she swayed to her own rhythms, her nocturnal dances, as she slept, deeply mysterious, dancing the dances of Sufis. Later still, his eyes open and his head and throat raw and still full of her while she travelled in her slumber, turning and dreaming, shards of white moonlight breaking through the racing clouds. As he watched over her, his heart pounded. He was flummoxed and observant at the same moment, awash in a cocktail of serotonin, oxytocin, androgens, irrationalities, blind urgencies.

What did he understand of the mind of a pathological liar? Yet...

But the day after, in the light of day, there resolved several unavoidable problems. He was, after all, a contractor. His contract was won based on a reputation for efficiency, for consistency, for completeness. What would happen when Seiko was found out? *When* she was found out. As program monitor, professional consultant to the government, his responsibilities were clear. His task was to report on her project. In order to do this, he needed to maintain his objectivity. He needed to ensure the government received duly diligently acquired, uncompromised information. Now she was a primary concern of that diligence. Her project, twenty million dollars of Canadian government funding, was certain to be scrutinized by the Auditor General of Canada. What was he? *Due diligence*, at the behest of the people of Canada.

Due diligence lay on his back, wet and slick with the sex juices of the program director who straddled and rode him through a cyclone.

She revealed herself by degrees, having opened a door that would no longer close. Not born in Winnipeg, not Canadian. Not thirty-seven years old. Her curriculum vitae, including degrees in arts, medicine, public health, and administration, her professional experience, the scholarships and awards — bases for her appointment to the position of program director — were fabrications. It had gone on for years and resulted in other positions before this one, each position providing a forward momentum to move on to new places and jobs. She remained one step ahead of the questions that arose in her wake. She moved from position to position across Africa, always a step ahead, from country to country. This was her international life overseas. When he asked why, she demurred. Her eyes dropped from his face to his neck, then away. She searched his face for forgiveness, awaiting his judgment.

Kestner felt as though he had ventured into unknown waters and looked down into the depths to see the shadow of something unknown.

She did not mention her real name, even then.

He moved into Levigne's house in Harare. For the sake of appearances, he maintained a small hotel room, then gave it up altogether. If their arrangement was noted at the High Commission or at headquarters in Ottawa, nothing was said. The second phase of the contract to monitor her program was drawn up in HQ and sent to him as though nothing was amiss. There would be no competitive selection process. But he put the contract papers aside, unsigned.

Her place was a rambling colonial bungalow with a large and sunny garden full of birds, dogs, and a goat. In the evening the late sun streamed through wavy windows into an open room bright with local mats and fabrics. They made love late, rose with the morning half gone for mangoes and papayas and tea with scalding milk in the garden amid the purring of rock doves and sunlight that fell in warm stripes through the palm fronds. Out in the field across Zimbabwe, Zambia, Malawi, Lesotho, Mozambique. In the field, they drank, made love in locations that were insecure and risked discovery. In this way they were adventurers, halting the car by the roadside so that the Zimbabwean driver had to wait. The driver became complicit in this game of risky sex, taking them along the lesser, isolated byways and lanes, stopping at village shebeens or abandoned huts and shacks, the chickens skittering at their feet as they took each other standing, guarded by the local shebeen owner, or in a airy bathroom of a city hotel, in the buzzing afternoons, the contemplative dusks, on an isolated beach followed by a sudden plunge into the surf. Then they would be famished, and she would lead him to humble places where fresh local fare was served: hake and chips, a fried egg thrown over tripe with moroho and mealies, nyama choma, sorghum, roasted maize, wild meats with no name, piripiri with *tomate* or not. They drank any whisky available, exotic of taste and name. Boy Buchanan, Village Dew, two bottles of Pig's Whistle or Whistle Pig, or maybe one of each, used on consecutive nights to sluice down—what else—wild boar. Grainy liquors perfused with vanillin, caramel, tannins, esters, heptanal.

His eldest daughter called him with her unerring intuition, her *immense* intuition concerning her father, linked through some unbreakable genetic accord. Carmen, daughter of daughters. The other one, Mars, the subject of much 3:00 a.m. anxiety, never called, had dropped her father apparently, or found it easier to live through her tawdry challenges without him.

By the time Kestner noticed Carmen's message it was late in Montréal, so he waited, plagued by guilt. His daughter's stubborn efforts to stay connected never failed to bring him up short. There was something wrong with him. There had to be. He was unlike any father he knew. He had not talked to Carmen in months.

Carmen, Carmen.

—Daddy, you look terrible. You look older.

—It's your bad connection. Anyway, I *am* older. How are you?

—You forgot Mama's birthday.

—Oh hell, so I did. How could I? Your poor mother.

—You forgot again, Daddy. Yes, how could you do such a thing? How can you be you? Did you forget your wedding anniversary this year too?

—Sweetheart, your mother and I don't actually celebrate our anniversary anymore. I have no idea how I can be me. I have spent many an evening thinking that one over.

—You and Mama are still in love, Daddy.

—Of course, sweetheart.

—So you should display some initiative to celebrate your love by, for example, commemorating anniversaries, birthdays, and other significant family days. That would show the kind of consideration and largesse that would make everyone much happier and better able to cope with hardships.

—How are your studies, Carmen? What hardships?

—I just feel that if more people showed that kind of largesse the whole world would function much better.

—How is Vladimir?

—Valery. His name was Valery. I don't see Valery anymore because Valery moved to Hungary for his post-doc. Valery is ancient history. The Valery period is passé.

—And the contemporary period?

—An insensitive question, coming from the parent of a single adult woman.

—I'm sorry, Carmen. Are you okay for money these days?

—Also, Mars is in rehab. Can you please send Mama a message? Please? She's particular about these things. You may not realize this, but she cares deeply for you. I know this for a fact.

—Why don't you ask me for money anymore? What normal daughter doesn't allow her wayward father redemption. What about Mars? Did you say rehab?

—You never knew your little girl was an addict? Shame on you, Daddy. She'll be all better soon. That's what she says anyway.

Alarming the way this child was a careworn version of her mother, more so each time he spoke to her.

The connection stalled out and after trying for an hour to get it back, he switched off his computer and sat before the dead screen, staring at his mute and colourless reflection.

The deadline for the renewal of the monitoring contract passed and he let it go, ignoring two prompts from Ottawa. He said nothing to Seiko Levigne. All told, not signing the contract meant he would leave her, along with $150,000 worth of work. Instead, he responded to an offer to design a program in southeast Asia, a plea to give a series of lectures in the US, then for another design assignment in Bangladesh. In this way he was able to leave Africa and Levigne in an orderly fashion.

He did what he had done before: abandoned the patient at the crucial moment. Called away to ever more important meetings in important places. A symposium in KL, reviews to be done in Pakistan and Nepal, an emergency consultation in Geneva. A research team investigating an outbreak in Phnom Penh. That took a year. Southern Africa was left behind.

One evening he was packed up and gone. Seiko did not try to contact him at first. As he went, he thought, *She is a mature person and she will think about it and know.* And he thought, *She is a pathological liar, and I don't understand her.* There were placatory explanations he made up for himself as he was deep in his cups, late at night, in remote hotel rooms. Alone in his moments.

She let him go, saying she understood, and that if he found someone else, she knew it was her fault because of her *unresolved issues.*

She sent two final messages, which he would delete from his memory if he could, but he could not, just as he could not expunge Yolanda Chavez. More than a year after he had seen Levigne her text messages came together:

Apologies for everything. Thinking of you during these days of rain and wind.

And moments later:

What a relief it would be to escape from myself and everything else.

Afterwards, after that, there was nothing. He had his sense of duty, that he was a walking manifestation of *due diligence*. And if not, then he should stop working, retire back to a faux winter fireplace in Ottawa, where the snowbanks silenced his rooms over the river.

Levigne quit her post as director and took a new job, then quit that and moved again, a step ahead of her lies. She left the messiness and tragedy of HIV and moved on to other tragedies, of infant mortality, female genital mutilation, maternal mortality, and then the unsolvable morass of the health of millions of refugees. Her experience and profile as a committed and emotionally engaged professional continued to grow.

As for Kestner, he would carry Seiko Levigne along with his other mistakes. His wife and daughters, Yolanda Chavez, and now Seiko Levigne. He carried lies, her secrets, and her trust, foisted upon him in intimacy, skin to sweated skin, under mosquito nets in Maputo, Blantyre, Dar es Salaam, Mwanza, and Ndola, in Lilongwe, Bulawayo, and Beira.

CHAPTER 19
Avtar Kestner
Sylhet, Bangladesh
August, 2015

After he left Africa, the map of his world shrank. But Asia is full of governments in need of health-care expertise. His work continued, juggling multiple assignments in multiple countries.

In the evenings, at the end of fifteen-hour days of travel and work, alone with a meal and a bottle in his room, he reminded himself that he had come to the end with Seiko Levigne. He told himself that at his age, he should be through with affairs of the heart. Except that even after two years, he was not.

Balochistan, Sindh, Bagmati, Khulna, Rajshahi.

Then he was on a long design mission in rural Sylhet. The pre-monsoon heat had been building for weeks. The earth seemed to pant in the laden air. The villagers kept saying that the monsoons would bring redemption, or at least divine judgment.

When the rains finally broke, Kestner was on his way out of the city in the back of yet another Canadian government vehicle. A bolt of lightning split the morning skies, the driver said humdullah, and the torrent that followed arrived so suddenly and intensely that within thirty minutes the road was submerged. They proceeded undaunted in the snorkelled four-by-four, through a new monsoon sea, sheets of water cascading away from the wheels. When they reached the village, the people were celebrating the monsoon even as they set about repairing the collapsed houses.

Later that day he received the message from Ottawa.

We request your confirmation of intent to conduct midterm
evaluation commencing 2016. Refugee Health Project, Kenya-
Sudan border.

He checked the project online to confirm that it was directed
by Dr. Seiko Levigne. She had done this. It was impossible that
she would not have known that he would be requested.

He sent a neutral message. A message of reconciliation. No,
yes, he could, he could not.

There remained the matter of duty, due diligence, his brief
email to headquarters that had been sent two years before, the
message he had thought obvious, a request for a background
check, a simple security confirmation. It had been disregarded,
at least officially.

Weeks later, he was alone in his room—yet another room, yet
another bottle.

Cutty Sark, an old standby, and rating of 7.4, with too large
a volume to be anything but trouble to a solitary man—the
mildew of the room powerful enough to overcome the whisky,
and the whisky powerful enough to ruin the man.

Outside the window, the monsoons cascaded upon the earth,
drowning streets, drowning logic and reason.

At that time he became aware of the Little Doubts, the thread-
like hatchlings of seed and ova, of ambiguity and guilt. It was as
though the community of his organs and tissues knew what he did
not, that he would not have peace, that he would not have Seiko
Levigne. They were threads, then threads annealed into strings
that twisted upon themselves into coils, strings into ropes of
ambivalence, supercoiled, interferers of peace and sleep and rest.
Profound and mysterious, these Little Doubts, auto-suggested

into existence, vying for life. They were at first vague sensations of the abdomen and chest, a nervous tangle of dehydration, mortal anxiety, ulceration, a bruised or broken heart. In due course they grew pearly teeth that gnawed and nipped. In due course the immune system awoke and commenced a feeble hand-waving.

Physician, heal thyself. Physician, seek a physician. He disdained to seek other clinical opinions. Other diagnostic signs would make themselves known in time. He set it aside, prodrome, a spawning crisis, episodic, evolving. A condition, which his clinical colleagues would refer to solemnly as grave, with straight faces, deadpanning words like *innocuous, indolent, irregular, rampant, exuberant, aggressive, benign. Untreatable, multifactorial, idiopathic. A fulminating case of seriousness. A rampant idiopathic disaster.* It mattered little. Tumour, parasite, lesion. An acute inflammation, pervasive and diffuse, a humoral crisis, an established fibrosis, dystrophic calcification, an aneurysm, an occlusion, or thrombosis to lay low the devil himself.

In the morning, with the royal shakes (from whisky, not his disorder) barely suppressed, he stumbled down and had his tea at his usual table in the hotel restaurant, among the consultants and international officials. They were all there, the agricultural assistance programs, the community development programs, maternal health initiatives, infrastructure assistance. They were the top graduates from prestigious schools, the fortunate selections of the multilateral and bilateral agencies: UNICEF, MSF, ICRC, USAID, SIDA. All the acronyms were represented beneath the monsoon thunderheads that boiled up in the sky as the microbes on the ground surged and spawned. He drained his cup of tea, was unable to eat, and joined his driver for the nauseating ride to the villages.

The monsoon rains were ceaseless. Flooded roads swirled and roiled, wastewater spilling through the lanes where children waded back and forth from school in teeming bacterial soup, the air steaming. Roofs gave out and collapsed as the rain poured in, mud walls dissolving. In the fields, dinner-plate leaves gave an illusion of abundance and health. Mobs of children dove into the new monsoon seas. Silicon chips, credit-card wealth, fast-food appetites, obesity, and unconstrained consumerism were mere rumours. Not far to the east the foothills and tea plantations were darkly misted, verdant. A cow lowed and its bell clanged. The district was mud-bound and beautiful, the way Seiko Levigne would have it.

It was another multimillion-dollar rural health program in a place that had subsisted at a constant and uneconomic level for centuries. A place of villagers who sewed their own clothes, milled their own grains, lost children to drowning and infections, were struck down by cyclones and floods, who clung to their traditions of bearing as many children as possible, who beat the surviving children into submission, terrorized their womenfolk into servitude, defecated in the same places their forefathers had, celebrated scriptures written in a distant era in a language they neither read nor understood and so were subject to the interpretations of designated men who were bestowed unearned and holy authority. It was a place of unequalled misery, fear, exaltation. An entire international project was devoted to replacing the awful old life with a modernity that consisted of Styrofoam, plastic wrap, mountains of discarded tires, plastic water bottles dotting the seas, stupidly priced designer sunglasses, Hollywood film previews, pharmaceutical carelessness, profanity-spewing children, internet sex, and mobile music. Kestner stopped and wondered, less convinced of his role and his task each time he took on an assignment.

A young girl in a silwar kimeez bid Kestner come observe the village committee meeting as they began a participatory planning process he had foisted upon them, for the new foreign-funded clinic and school. The committee consisted entirely of excited young women, which meant that their projects would be regarded by the village leaders as frivolous. But foreign money supported it, and government officials were looking on, so the village elders were content to let their daughters play. Kestner performed his role. He listened to the music of spoken Bangla, admired the hopeful faces of the young women, and tried to quantify this life, modern life, his life. If he were an ancient soul, he was a small one, capable only of immediate concerns. He was less than that: a pointless aggregation of cells, a ball of neurons, irritated by light and sound, formed from a melange of genes from ancient places, projected into an incomprehensibly modern circumstance.

There were logistical details to attend and divert. He had to get himself from Bangladesh to East Africa and Levigne Refugee Camp Number Two. Malnutrition and poverty and parasites and young women dying of obstetrical hemorrhage and babies with infantile tetanus and Levigne, Levigne, Levigne.

Weeks later he left the viscous air of the Bangladeshi howers and flew over the subcontinent, over an impossibly azure Arabian Sea, and on to the city of Nairobi.

Journal note written into the margin at this time:

Case history
prepared by the patient himself since there are no other
capable diagnosticians available or even invited

The patient is a middle-aged, Indo-Hawaiian, male, international health consultant. The condition presented with the patient abruptly grown tired of work. The first symptom was fatigue. Patient reported that he ceased to be boundlessly energetic, his hair was no longer stupidly luxurious, the ambitions he long harboured were dimmed. He no longer sprang to his feet in the morning, brimming with optimism. He could no longer reach down and scratch his big toe without a nasty ache in his lumbar. He no longer wasted entire days fantasizing about women. Objectively, the patient was not as handsome, tall, or muscular as he had hoped. He was not as rich.

A paroxysm occurred. He stopped in the middle of a busy workday. Once in a state of stoppage, he immediately recognized that he had a condition.

Diagnosis: The patient suffers Little Doubts. These are chronic processes, diverse, simultaneous. Possibly lumps or bumps. Possibly occlusions, stenoses, contractures, cicatrization, hemorrhages, aneurysms, unresolved inflammations, tissues squashed or swollen, hyperplastic or spastic. Organ or cell. Wrongs not righted. Compensations that have failed. Unremitting exhaustions. Rampant failures. Complications. Sequelae of errors committed by the patient himself. Infection or worm. A tumescent bacterial parasitic virusy malignant septic state. A pulsating mass of dysmorphic dysplasias permitted to proliferate for decades while the patient was distracted by shallow careerist goals, relationships, efforts at a family and other busywork. There is clear evidence of logarithmic decline, or perhaps logarithmic proliferation.

Prognosis: Probability is low that the patient will ever get what he wants. There is a zero possibility that he will ever regain his youth. The probability of death is close to certain.

Treatment: Regrettably there is no treatment for this condition. Sufficient quantities of aged whisky for palliative purposes.

Note: Patient ate a meal of rice, curried fish, subji and a single mango, all washed down with generous doses of J & B whisky (a definite 8). Patient improved dramatically.

CHAPTER 20
Avtar Kestner
Turkana
May 12, 2016

The new men who took over the camp drove in from the north. There were eight men. They wore head and face coverings and fatigues and military boots and came in three Isuzus that announced their arrival with a single shot that echoed against the hill. The men in the camp watched the arrival warily. The Hiluxes were hastily loaded and driven away south.

Kestner sat at the mouth of his shelter. It was far too late to escape. He had become frailer with each passing week. He watched a scorpion scuttle across the open ground. It was reddish brown, and he had no idea if it was one of the deadly ones. It ignored him.

The new Isuzu men looked upon him in his hole in the side of the hill and made no comment. The men were of diverse backgrounds. One looked closely at Kestner and beckoned him to get to his feet. Kestner struggled up, weaved to his feet, and tried and failed to straighten his spine. The man motioned for him to walk, and Kestner scuffed forward, doubled over his sick kidney and spastic intestine. He stumbled forward, gave up, stood catching his breath, gathering himself. He squatted only to endure alarming stabs of pain from his knees. The other men stared. One of them fondled a weathered American automatic. Another had an outline map of Afghanistan tattooed on his neck.

Kestner retreated into his hole, his grotty haven. The men went away. He was left with a jangled solar plexus, even while, curiously, the underlying, mortal, fatal, fulminant Little Doubts, those irreversible specks of decompensation, remained in abeyance. The guards left behind a piece of dough that faintly resembled bread, a greyish lump that smelled of fermentation, and a tin cup of warm tea. It was a struggle for Kestner to get any of this down.

He lay back, watching the sky through a rent in the tarpaulin.

When he looked out later, Kestner noticed a new guard sitting on the ground a few metres away. When Kestner stepped out, the guard stood smoothly and stepped back a short distance, avoiding eye contact. The man kept his face covered. He was young in his bearing, with narrow, thin shoulders, pale skin, and dark hair. His eyes were large and blue.

The guards changed every four hours. Men came by to discuss the business of Kestner with their heads and faces covered in piety or fear, eyes shielded by their sunglasses. They were young, and one caught Kestner's attention for his athletic build and high leather boots and spotless black clothing. During the evening two men sat nearby with automatic weapons laid across their laps.

A Parkinsonian tremble visited that night. Kestner distracted himself by organizing the details of the men who held him, assigning names to each. *Bonobo, Shmendrick, Spider, Shorty, Cool Hand, Hopalong. Klutzkopf.* He wondered if Salim was dead.

On the second day he was shaken awake to find a plate of pebbly rice and beans and a glass of weak tea. He choked it back. Nearby was the jihadi who had guarded him on the first day. Kestner named him Pious, for his careful attention to the arrangement of his prayer mat.

As Pious lay his hand on the plate to take it away he stopped, staring at the few remaining spoons of rice left behind. Kestner looked up at him and gestured at the remaining rice.

—J'ai terminé.

The guard snatched at his scarf. He glared at Kestner with pale, furious eyes.

—Comment sais-tu que je suis français? Juif? Sioniste? Mossad, oui?

—Just a guess. I'm none of those things you say.

The guard looked at him sharply. His blue eyes lost their hardness for a fleeting moment. He was a boy. He stepped back and put his hand on his knife. His face was pale and pitted and patchily bearded. He was nervous. His eyes twitched. With deliberation he wrapped his scarf back around his face and replaced his glasses. Kestner looked evenly at the boy.

—Qu'est-ce que vous voulez? Avec moi et mes amis?

—Amis? Tu n'as aucun amis ici. Tu n'as riens.

The guard lurched away, shoulders slouched. Around his waist was a black leather strap that had once been polished but had become scuffed and dirty.

For a week Kestner was left alone with his discomforts, his Little Doubts. He was given food and water on a schedule, but he did not see Pious again for a long time. He drifted between waking and sleep, a grand debate over whether he recovered or declined humming in his reticular activating system. It was impossible to know without objective information. Once in a while a snippet of his conversation with the guard came back to him, and he speculated about how he might learn more information. The breeze carried voices from different directions, and he attempted to identify each language and accent. French with regional European inflections, Arabic of different tints and cadences, English from Brooklyn, Yorkshire, and Australia. He heard Bangla and Urdu.

His emotions were volatile. He experienced moments of lucidity in which he saw the arc of his life, and other moments when his existence lolled forward into unmarked shadows. It seemed as though the lost, uncharted desert he was in had infested his mind. He detached from his situation and entered unreal states in which things happened to him, people surrounded him, yet he was absent. At other times he observed the guards coming and going and he closed his eyes and wished to escape into a more comfortable past. He was distantly aware of conversations about him in languages he knew. He dreamed vividly when he slept.

His family was with him, and he was exhausted by his work and his travel. He had missed a crucial family event—a graduation, a birthday, a performance. He had left a child waiting in front of the school, or on a sports field on a cold day, or at a party. His wife and daughters were tight-lipped. He was not offered a welcoming embrace. He had missed the event. He had forgotten to bring a gift to commemorate and had forgotten because the mission had been complicated and dangerous and exhausting. His apology was late, feeble, and inadequate.

As he lingered there in his guilt and misery, his professional colleagues arrived, hungry and thirsty, invited for dinner at his home. They were inappropriately joyous. They had been drinking. Someone brought out a Hawaiian party shirt as a gift for him. He put it on. The shirt was clean and cool. On the label it said it was guaranteed to stay pressed and that it was bullet- and knife-proof. Death-proof, it said. Someone read instructions not to remove the shirt, but he found the material itchy. As soon as he was alone, he removed it, and the shirt immediately dissolved, the pieces stuck to his hands. It broke down into nitriles and cyanide, and he was vaguely aware of the fumes surrounding him and then wondered if the fumes might destroy the parasitic-tumour-virus-inflammations, the Little Doubts, that nibbled away at his insides.

Light came on and he realized he had been locked into a room with a cadaver on a covered gurney. He called out to the attendant, but it was late, everyone gone, on holidays, the workday complete or the school term ended, the lab locked, the offices deserted. Only he and the cadaver to spend the night, the weekend, the summer together. And he had no way to tell his family.

He took up his scalpel and approached the gurney, ready to begin.

He awoke to smoke streaming into his hole from a nearby pile of burning rubbish. His airways seared. The oxidized residues from plastics had snagged him from his dream, his nightmare. Little Doubts sang out. There were no guards about, only rubbish that burned badly and emanated thick cords of yellow smoke.

How was it that he had come to this place? It had been a passage through mishap and chaos. Death he had studied and enumerated and analyzed and extrapolated. Destruction had boiled around him, leaving him unscathed, at the eye of the storm, the sacred student and observer of misery. Shiva in the eye of a rampaging apocalypse. Christ meditating on the cross. He had surfed waves of international misfortune. Years of working in the most insecure regions of the world, and he was unmarked. Car accidents, a ferry that sank into abyssal waters. A plane that vanished with everyone on board, that he had not boarded that day, irate, trapped in an inexplicable customs mess. At least two women with whom he had consorted, dead from AIDS. Cyclones, a team of clandestine soldiers on a murderous raid of the trainees who had attended his workshop the day prior —he had departed hours before. Riots, coups d'état, invasions—he was evacuated the week before, the day before, the *hour* before. Others were stricken by infarctions, congestive heart failure, aneurysms in the Circle of Willis, neoplasms of the throat, prostate, breast, lung, uterus and colon, autoimmune diseases, neurological failures, idiopathic everything. Malaria, dengue, typhoid, hepatitis, mamba bite, scorpion sting. Both forms of drowning, fresh water and salt.

What benefit was a privileged background, education, a high professional income, years of experience, if he could not escape the direst of fates? What good was knowledge if it had no sway over death? Here was a consultant of death, of mortality and morbidity and the roads and pathways that death and disease follow. If anyone had influence over death it was surely those who spent lifetimes examining the evidence of classes and subclasses of causes of death, devising points and curves to prove risk factors, rendering the loss of lives as informative, analytical, even fun. Death: a celebration of the aesthetics of causality.

Perhaps it was time to return to Canada. Perhaps he should spend time with Carmen, try to help Mars, reconcile with his wife. Salvation might lie in that direction. Home: it was possible he had one. In principle.

But was it too late to fantasize of home, safety, welcoming hearts? Over the years his visits to Canada had grown rare. His family moved on without him. Surprising that Carmen, after the hurt, the healing, the emotional scarring and cicatrisation, did not ignore him entirely. But the younger one, Mars, did ignore him entirely. After a time he no longer knew Mars, the fallen; Mars, the addict; Mars, the sweet and dreamy infant not made for this sharp-cornered world.

The effort with family would fail. How could one make up for lost years and decades, lost knowledge, lost intimacy? His family, even his mother, were only abstract ideas that he barely understood.

He had launched himself out of the family orbit. Now he was lost, drifting through space, out of the solar system. Work had become his home, and a cold and uncomfortable place it was. Policies and programs and bureaucrats and their endless procedures. International routines in place of rest. No longer did he have a permanent address. The transactional atmospheres of hotels and bars and temporary residences in place of the hearth. Airport business lounge couches on which to lay his head. Government Range Rovers and Land Rovers and Mercedes-Benzes with their particular drivers who knew so well his idiosyncrasies and preferences of drinks, foods, and tailors. Man of status and wealth, he had drifted away to places of roiling, suffering millions, while he himself remained untouched by disease, struggle and unrest, unscathed by wars and storms. Untouched by the complications of people and home and lives.

Two large men pulled Mason-Tremblay along to Kestner's shelter. Mason-Tremblay collapsed bonelessly onto the ground with his eyes closed.

One of the men came to Kestner, dragged him to his feet, and cuffed him about the head.

—Stand straight! You are doctor! Take care your friend!

The men squatted on the ground nearby, lit cigarettes, and watched Kestner through clouds of smoke.

Mason-Tremblay lay shivering, his skin greyish. Kestner removed the blindfold and gag and began working at the tight bindings on Mason-Tremblay's hands. He massaged his wrists and arms so that some colour returned to his hands. A cursory examination found him dehydrated. There were no obvious wounds. His breathing and pupils were normal, his pulse weak.

When his hands were freed, Mason-Tremblay squinted up at Kestner.

—Are they gone?

—Not exactly. No.

—Am I glad to see you. Where the hell are we?

—I don't know. The middle of nowhere.

Mason-Tremblay rose on one elbow and peered carefully around at the shredded covering to Kestner's hole and the two men squatting nearby.

—Those two. Why don't they leave me alone? Always watching, watching. They have no idea of personal space. I'm going to remember those two.

—What happened to you? Where were you?

—Escaped. I ran. I got free. I followed Mihret but got lost. Then...I don't know...some people traded me for goats. After that I got dragged all over Africa. Last place, scorpions. Before that, millions of vicious black and white monkeys. Bloody things kept stealing my food. You can't fight them, you know. They're as smart as humans but more vicious. Never try to make friends with them. Vicious and with teeth.

—Who was dragging you?

—Men. Different men. Rebels. Fundamentalists. I don't know. What happened to Mihret?

—I don't know. No one talks to me. I'm afraid I can't promise you much in the way of information or comforts.

—I was traded five times. Each time, someone turned a profit. How do you like that?

—You're a valuable commodity, it seems.

—People were *bidding*. They bid for you too. They told me you were traded twice already.

—I had no idea.

The trash fires had gone out. Men passed by the door in sullen silence. Mason-Tremblay shivered although it was not cold, and Kestner pulled a blanket over his chest.

—You should rest. A sleep and a meal would do you wonders.

—Is this where we're supposed to sleep? This cave?

—We're not the first inhabitants, I might as well tell you.

—We'll get out of this. They'll get their ransom, and we'll get out.

—Yeah. It's important to keep up hope. You'll make it. I won't. I know it. The kidneys are already done in. It's all right. Don't worry about me. I've had it coming for a long time. All these years of high-risk missions in dangerous places. Simple probability.

—Don't talk like that. We'll both get out. At least we're together. I had no one to talk to. These people—they're not normal. Not a one of them.

—Probability catches up with the best and the worst. It helps if you anticipate the odds.

—How do you anticipate the odds of being abducted? How do you anticipate that your mistress will suddenly disappear?

—What do you mean by that?

—Nothing, nothing...anyway, everyone knows about you and Seiko Levigne. You might as well know.

—Where did you hear that?

—Things get around. You know people in agency—they talk. You know.

—It's in the past anyway. Old news. But no, I did not anticipate that and I did not anticipate this.

—I heard she's back in the US.

—The US?

—Everyone gets jumpy when it's an American, you notice that? But Canadians? No one cares. They think the Canadians carry out *quiet negotiations*. But don't mention any of this to these guys. They're easily triggered, these ones.

The two men who had brought Mason-Tremblay in were replaced by the usual silent guard up the hill, who was evident only by the glowing end of his cigarette. Kestner sat and leaned against a rock, aware of the Little Doubts that had stepped away from his kidneys and now moved down his flanks. Mason-Tremblay had crawled into the hole to lie in Kestner's nest, muttering *In God we triste, in God we triste...*

CHAPTER 21

Avtar Kestner
Northern Turkana
June 14, 2016

Kestner and Mason-Tremblay were brought out of the hole and taken to the dispensary. Isuzus had arrived and departed. The dispensary was crowded with unfamiliar figures. The men were masked except for a leader in clean black Arab garb, to whom the others deferred. He was tall and black-bearded, neither young nor old, wore rimless glasses and polished riding boots over baggy pants. He stood behind the table watching the prisoners come in as the others milled about. His demeanour was of an engineer or architect. In his mind Kestner immediately labelled him the Sheikh.

The Sheikh held his head at an angle, as a man asking great questions about the world. He began to speak in a thoughtful cadence, his accent British and mid-eastern. His followers strained to hear his words.

—You will understand if I dispense with the formality of introducing myself. It is enough that I know who you are, what you are.

He gestured to one of the men, who then offered cups of tea and dates to the captives. They sipped the tea—it was luxuriously sweet and hot—and put the dates in their pockets. The Sheikh smiled.

—My father passed from this world recently. I say this because it is much on my mind. By the grace of Allah, he was a good man. He taught us about the habits and appearances of men. He taught us that every man, good or bad, has a story of good about himself that he carries with him, so that every man, good or bad, lives his life thinking that he is good. My father taught us that the story of every man must be heeded before a man is judged evil or virtuous, true or false. Proud men go about proclaiming their story loudly for all to hear. Timid men say little, lacking some certainty about their story. The ignorant man cannot listen to the stories of others. But women listen to the stories of other women every day of their lives and tell their stories to other women. My father advised that all the stories should be heard. Because I respected my father, I listen to his advice. So I wish to give you the opportunity to tell your story before you are judged.

Kestner responded with a voice barely louder than a whisper.

—You have no right to judge us. You know that. The ones who will be judged, in the end, are you and your friends.

The Sheikh held up his hand.

—But your system of laws is not my system of laws. I will not debate with you on this. Regardless of what we think, we are ultimately compelled by fate. Some say that fate is that which is already written, and then we make the choice of whether to be damned or praised as we fulfill it. Still, my colleagues and I have spent many hours discussing the correct way forward. We have come to the conclusion that your culture, the Western culture, is corrupt. It is a culture that promotes greed dressed as liberty. From a desert camp in Africa many things are apparent. The West has expanded its corruption, pushing into the world, saying it is global economics. But really what they have pushed is global greed. Some argue that this is the culture of wealth and a civilization of wealth, but in truth it is like the fires of hell, a large, unsatisfied mouth with an endless appetite, devouring and destroying people, animals, forests, even the water and the air we breathe. These days scientists lament that the atmosphere is burning, but these scientists refuse to see what is causing it. It is very plain to see from a camp in the desert. Unfettered greed. Nothing more. Even when people know that greed is terrible and destructive they cannot turn away from it. They are afraid, and they are addicted, and they are under the sway of it.

The Sheikh put his hands behind his back, strode one way, then the other, a learned man, a professor of ideas.

—There is another reason for jihad. The West cannot look at the truth and understand it. Many jihadis themselves do not understand. Many just go to battle the opponents of Islam. But the real fight is elsewhere, with the culture of greed that is destroying the entire world and its people. In the West they argue that greed is a matter of *personal liberty*. But this is not logical. If every person on earth is given unlimited liberty, what do they do? The basest, most destructive things — perversity and drugs and sensual pleasures. Men in the West profit from showing on the internet the most depraved abuses of beautiful women and innocent children. They buy and abuse anyone they can to make crude entertainment. They believe that because people pay, it is free enterprise. Where free enterprise is concerned, they think, morality is suspended. They think it is their right to violate and exploit others. All is justified by the drive for wealth. They believe that if they have liberty, everything is right. If their liberty destroys others, or destroys the world, they do not care. So this culture of greed has spread, and now all the world is being devoured. In the United States of America, they want the liberty to own military guns designed only for murder. The Americans even fantasize that they are blessed by God, when, in fact, the opposite is true. They are blessed only by Shaitan, the Fallen One, the Destroyer. He rejoices as children, students in classrooms are shot to death. Mass murders, every day. And what do the Americans say when mass murders occur? They say, 'Personal liberty. We must preserve our personal liberty.' It is more important than the lives of murdered children!

Some of the men in the room stirred. The Sheikh held up his hand for silence.

—You may agree with my view or not. My view comes from a kind of liberty too, but mine is liberty for the innocents to throw off exploitation and corruption and idleness and avarice and mendacity. My liberty comes from our responsibility to God. We signify this by praying five times a day so that we do not forget Allah. In our everyday dealings we are compelled to be just and respectful and dedicated to outlasting the travails of the Shaitan. We must endure hard conditions and accept discomforts with joy and gratitude. And we must always protect our women or children from perversity and corruption.

He made a grand, sweeping gesture.

—Whatever happens, a man must meet his destiny with honour and intelligence. You are here, under our rule. If you make to escape you will be found and brought back. You may think you are safe in your home in the US or Canada or Europe or somewhere, but you are not free. Our people will find you. We see everyone. We see everything. We are everywhere, victims, Muslims and non-Muslims alike. We will point you out and drag you back. Forget about your personal liberties. You are now a captive, and that is how you will remain always, just as slaves remain as slaves and never anything other.

The Sheikh picked up a satchel from the table and pulled out a sheaf of passports and other documents.

—Kestner, Avtar. Is it you? What sort of name is it?

—A Canadian name.

—But a Jewish name, yes?

—My stepfather was Jewish. I took his name. He's dead. I'm not Jewish, if you must know.

—Ah? Do not be afraid. We are what we are. Every person and every creature comes from a place, a people. That is the destiny we must embrace, and not shy from. You agree? You have the look of a man of experience. With experience comes wisdom, no?

—Wisdom is not my forte.

— Even this thing you say is somehow wise. Do you know and understand the destiny of you and your people?

—My people? Who are 'my people'? You must tell me, since you are the dispenser of great wisdom.

—Do you wish to state your story?

—My story is my own business.

—And so you have Jewish name but not Jewish? Is this what you are saying?

—Whatever. I'm a JBA.

—What is that?

—Never mind.

—*Never mind?* Interesting expression, that one. For some men it is hard to choose the right path. Then they eventually pay the price. Like you, for example, a man who tarries where you should not.

—What do you mean?

—It is a choice. Is this choice right or wrong? And how does one know?

—You know nothing about me.

—No? Do you think it possible for modern men to have secrets? In this time of internet cameras? Do you think privacy is your right? Privacy is a childish idea they use in the West to give citizens false confidence. Everything is known, especially those with the means to know. Even the doings of sinners is known. Then the judgment must come. Like the referee in a football match, the whistle is blown.

—I have no idea what you're talking about.

—No?

Someone passed by in the periphery of Kestner's vision. For a moment he thought it was Levi Kestner, watching over him from a distance.

CHAPTER 22
Ali Soudani
Paris and Other Contested Grounds
2014-2016

His birth name was Sebastien. He would have killed and buried that name by now, if it were not for the forces that conspired to keep it alive, such as every time someone spoke to him in French or English. Juge had convinced him that French and English were both embedded with anti-Islamic and heretical concepts that were inherently evil, and they were no longer real languages to him.

—If you speak those languages you are consorting with the enemy.

—Then how do we speak to people? I don't know Arabic.

—You must learn.

He would like to be speaking Arabic or Swahili or Wolof or Dinka. The problem was that he was not good at languages. They had told him so at school. They told him he was not good at social studies, human studies, politics, or languages. He discovered for himself that he was not good at girls. Not bad at maths and physics.

Not good at shooting or running for an hour in the desert heat, for that matter.

Music, yes. He was good at music. He could improvise for an hour, one piece, one mood, beginning, middle, denouement, end.

Merde. The annoying prisoner and his French. The prisoner

had immediately sensed that he was Sebastien and refused to see him as Ali Soudani. He hated to be Sebastien again. It went against his desire, which was to be only Ali Soudani and not think all the time about Sebastien and the things Sebastien had messed up and the things Sebastien was not good at. Ali Soudani was respected, not belittled, and reminded of his car accidents, his failure in the school of engineering technology, his embarrassments and his misdemeanours. Ali Soudani was a comrade in arms, a practitioner and a believer, and Ali Soudani would find his way into paradise one day, despite his wretched history as Sebastien.

He stumbled away from the prisoner in a tearful fury, for he was sure the prisoner did not fear him. *He did not even respect him.* They must execute this man. They would do it, he was sure, and Ali Soudani would celebrate. Perhaps Ali Soudani would even draw his knife across the man's throat, behead the infidel in the way he had been shown.

Sebastien — stupid and weak Sebastien — quailed at this thought. Sebastien could not stand that kind of violence. He thought he should enjoy it, but when they had proudly shown the new recruits videos of beheadings, he had run from the room and vomited. Afterward the other men were standoffish and once or twice he was quite sure he overheard them making jokes about him behind his back.

These were the times when Sebastien missed his piano. Even while Ali Soudani knew music was trickery and a distraction and a corruption and a pleasure of the flesh, Sebastien (now that he was being reminded of Sebastien) sorely missed his piano! How had he thought that there would be pianos waiting around in Syria for him to play when he grew bored of the violence and bored of being a Muslim?

He, Ali Soudani, stood outside the dispensary and took deep breaths. He needed to collect himself and decide who he was.

The cursed and wretched prisoner! How could he have exposed himself so easily to a prisoner? He would request that he be the executioner. He himself would serve as the dispatcher of men.

How could he have thought that pianos would be waiting for him in Syria?

‖

It was because of Juge. Or because of the girls, the girls who thought Juge was everything when he was nothing. It had always been Juge. Juge, his uncle and his brother, the leader, the instigator, the first. The girls had always adored Juge, and he had always followed, driven by the girls.

The ten new fighters had ridden in the back of a delivery van through the Turkish night to the border and were let off there to slip through. Sebastien had counted on being discovered and turned back—another Sebastien miscalculation. The border between Turkey and Syria was not what he expected. It was the middle of a moonless night. The road ran alongside a barren area in which there was merely a shoddy fence, and the fence had been cut and knocked down in places. In the car lights he saw figures moving through the fence toward the Turkish side. Families were trying to leave the country and its disasters behind. He and the others, the young men of Europe who knew nothing yet about disasters, were heading in the wrong direction.

—Juge, wait.

—Wait for what?

—But Juge, are you sure?

—I am sure. But I am only sure for me. I am not sure for both of us. You always like to come along. I never prevented you. Always you come along so you don't have to think about anything.

—I am thinking about one or two things.

—You are finally thinking! Something made you think! What?

—Juge. Maman and Tante Fannie. I told them nothing.

—That's right, kiddo. Neither did anyone.

—And Papa would have been against this.

—Papa! Your papa cares for nothing but himself. Too bad but...

Juge moved away from Sebastien to catch up with the others, and Sebastien stood in the dark watching the families, figures large and small moving across the border, a steady stream, toward him and Europe and safety. Even the smallest of them were silent as they fled.

Juge and the others disappeared into the yellowy dark. He would lose sight of them if he hesitated any longer. His uncle's voice came drifting back out of the darkness.

—And stop calling me Juge!

He hurried along. It was impossible to call his uncle anything but what he had always called him. His uncle's real name was Georges. Except that now his real name was Abu Al Fakir, or Abu Al Shamal — Juge could not decide upon his new name. He said both names made him sound like a teton.

—Juge!

Sebastien said it out loud, defiantly, knowing no one was around who cared, even if they did hear him. Still, he looked guiltily around in the darkness.

A short time later he heard motors. He followed the sounds and found Juge and the other men waiting in two cars without headlights.

It was true. He had always found it easier to go along with Juge's schemes instead of having to work things out on his own. He vaguely recognized this as a character flaw, but the behaviour was so stamped into him that he could barely see alternatives. It was the natural thing to do. Besides, it was Juge who knew more, thought more, had more ideas, more courage. Juge was the one with friends. It had ever been so, from earliest memory. Now they were in Syria, fighting American multinational greed and criminality, taking the side of the oppressed and downtrodden. Juge took the time to explain.

—It will be a new country and a new world.

Sebastien squeezed into the car with the others, and they sped off through the night. The youngest of the travellers—two teens from the UK—were chattering like birds in English. They were full of questions. The driver, a large, bearded head with glasses that caught glints of light, answered calmly, as though he were a father or teacher.

—Will we learn to use automatic weapons?

—You will fight on behalf of our caliphate.

—Will we have our own guns?

—Of course. The best guns.

—What is it like in the place where we will live? Is there internet? Is the food good?

—Best place. Best internet. Best food. All free for you.

—What about video games? We heard there are video games.

—Best games and best gaming systems. High speed. Like a dream. Like video game dream.

The older men in the car sighed and peered out at the Syrian night.

III

—The only time you are your own man is when you play piano.

Tante Fannie said this to him with Juge standing right there. She should not have said it. Or she should have said it to him privately. In a way it was the thing that started everything. In a way it was how he came to join Juge in this scheme to go to Syria. Sebastien laughed uncomfortably when she said it, but Juge did not laugh at all. Maybe Juge needed Sebastien to not be his own man at all, piano or not. The piano was the one thing that Sebastien did on his own, that neither Juge nor the twins could do as well. They had all taken lessons, but only Sebastien kept playing and expanding his musical horizons until he was playing moody, atmospheric compositions that made the others stop what they were doing, Everyone except Juge. Juge found reasons to talk loudly or make noise.

This was in the time after Juge had returned from Pakistan. Pakistan had changed him. He brought with him new rules which he referred to as his personal discipline. He did not laugh as much as before. He took it upon himself to school his nephew and nieces on personal discipline and political topics.

After Tante Fannie said what she said, Juge had the piano taken away when Sebastien was at work. Sebastien stood looking at the empty space where his piano had been. Juge passed by as though nothing were wrong, turned and came back, and looked at the spot.

—More room now. Plus, we can't afford a piano. It is a disrespect to the poor who can't afford such luxuries. It's a mockery. And it is not part of our discipline. It's for capitalists and colonizers, not the oppressed.

—We are the oppressed?

—Music and dancing will distract us from our struggle. We cannot afford to waste our time and energy on these things. You must choose. Are you with the oppressed or are you against them?

—Against whom? Who are these oppressed? And whose piano was it to sell? And how much was it worth?

—Fourteen hundred euros. That is how much. Good money we can use for our family and our cause. To fight the oppressors. And you, my brother, you have to choose. You might not want to struggle for us, but we will struggle just the same.

—What if I choose differently? What if I choose differently than just those two choices? What if I have other ideas?

—Don't joke. You don't have ideas. Anyway, choices get made with or without you.

So Sebastien was left with nothing. Fourteen hundred euros. That was the price of his music, his escape, and his only meaningful skill.

Now there was only his oppressed job at the restaurant (Juge insisted that he was oppressed). The job was terrible. And he had Maman and Tante Fannie and the girls and Juge. And Papa, but Papa was too busy to see them anymore.

He wanted a girlfriend. He wanted to play his piano. He had neither. No music. He had the abusive German chef at the restaurant, and he had the oil burns all up his arm. When he came home in the small hours he could not sleep or play the piano or shower. He would sleep badly and get up by noon for his next shift.

Fourteen hundred. He was not sure if this was a small or a great amount to exchange for musical freedom.

In the end he went to Syria with Juge because he could not refute what his uncle was telling him, that they had no options. Besides, he knew that if he stayed behind, the twins would mock him mercilessly, and the German chef would drive him mad. Or worse, the girls would follow Juge instead of him. He knew they were capable of such a thing. The girls had always displayed a shocking lack of fear.

Why did they go to Syria, really?

According to Juge, there was nothing personal about it. You only had to look at Pakistan and the lies of the French and British and American media and the Western governments and their campaigns of propaganda and their hatred of downtrodden and oppressed people in other countries who were being slaughtered by the thousands in Palestine and Afghanistan and Iraq and Sudan.

—Everyone knows the score.

When Juge talked, Sebastien looked at his uncle's skin and noticed that it was much darker than his own. With his big curls and dark brow Juge could be from any country in the Mideast, or Afghanistan, Iran, or Pakistan. Sebastien's skin was unremarkably light, as colourless as the Paris winter. He was his father's son and looked French. Milk with a touch of olive oil, as Tante Fannie liked to say. The fact that he was much lighter than everyone else in the family was not something that had bothered him greatly. Sometimes he felt he had to prove he was one of them. Was that the score Juge was talking about?

Juge had friends in districts of Paris that were outside of Sebastien's usual ken. Seine-Saint-Denis and other banlieues. Juge was friends with Algerians for whom the 1961 Paris massacre had occurred only yesterday. Moroccans, Maghrebis, Egyptians, and South Sudanese. People with black skin, brown skin, yellow skin. People of colours. Some were schoolmates, others he came across in the street or on the football pitch.

He met the Pakistanis at a match. They were about his age and so he had an easy affinity for them. But these boys were different from the others he knew. They listened to Juge and his politics, yet laughed and bore no bitterness or anger toward anyone. They were full of life and optimism. Boys, they were, and they were humorous and easy and made gentle mischief for one another. Hanif and Chakar and Kamal-Balochi were cousins from near Quetta. They had been brought to France years before on an overland journey that they barely remembered but for a few comic incidents. They laughed about hiding in bags of vegetables and not eating a thing, about not being able to keep Kamal quiet as they hid from the border guards. They claimed it had been an adventure, and they would do it all again. The Pakistanis had many friends around the masjid and in the school. Like Juge they made friends with everyone. Juge was their French brother. They invited him to their home behind a Pakistani restaurant near the auto repair where the father had found work. The flat was overcrowded. Someone was always coming or going to work or school, a child was singing or crying, the smells of parathas or naans or meat roasting. Juge loved it. He fit in easily with his dark hair and moustache. He brought Sebastien along one day. Sebastien could not relax, find a place to sit, say the right thing, use the correct hand, the mother looking at him, a cluster of young kids giggling and running away when he spoke French to them. Theirs was a strange but intriguing language. The father, a man with jet-black locks who seemed too young to be the father of grown children, called Juge his new son. To Sebastien he said,—So you two are brothers?

They returned home with new flavours on their tongues, to their own sad apartment with Maman in her wheelchair and the twins, Sophie and Delphie, out late as usual, and Tante Fannie saying, *les fauves, les fauves.* Wild things. They called themselves that too, giggling.

Shortly after that someone crossed the line somewhere, someone reported, and the police swooped in on the entire neighbourhood, the HLMs, the secret flats. The Pakistanis were deported along with thousands of others, under the orders of Sarko. And the media were complicit with their stupid simplifications, said Juge. Capitalism. Pakistanis and Bangladeshis and Iranians and West Africans of every sort sent back, all poor, struggling working people. From Paris to Karachi, Lahore, Sialkot and Quetta, Dhaka, Rajshahi, Kolkata, Mumbai, Tabriz, Tehran and Bamako, Conakry and Bissau. A spider web of destinations with Paris as the fat spider. Back to their low probabilities, their bad luck. Only the boy named Kamal escaped the cops. He did not return to the flat, kept moving from place to place, spent nights with Juge and Sebastien until the embarrassing attentions of the twins drove him, in shyness, to stay with other friends.

Juge announced that he was accompanying Kamal back to Pakistan. The boy could not live in Paris without his brothers. At first Tante Fannie laughed.

—But Jugie? You are no better than a boy yourself.

Juge explained himself patiently. He had already obtained his passport. He had saved money. Sophie and Delphie insisted they were going along as well.

Kamal, Kamal, they squealed and Juge chased after them, swatting at their derrieres. *Fauves!*

For a time Sebastien thought that he too was going to Pakistan. But Juge took off suddenly. One day he simply did not return home, and when he was well out of the country he posted messages.

Juge was away for months. His messages described the pace of life in the country around Quetta. He described the American F16s that shook the earth as they took off for sorties to Afghanistan. Each jet, he wrote, cost thirty million USD, a bargain.

Juge and Kamal had made their way home to Quetta surely enough, finally riding the dusty bus from Zhob, Muslim Bhag, and Kuchlak. They found Kamal's family living back on the land of their ancestors. It was a rambling farming compound at the base of the rugged Sulaiman range. There were orchards of apricot and pomegranate and almond and sporadic electricity during the day. It was a while before Juge began to appreciate the drought and the three-hundred-metre tube well that others in the valley paid to use. The returned family had saved what they could during their years in France. They were better off than their neighbours. There were plenty of farm chores to do, the family building up the herd as they tried to find their old place amongst the relatives who shared the family land.

Juge worked alongside his friends in the fields, learned about goats and chickens. On occasion they went into Quetta, cadging a ride with a farmer taking his produce or boarding the packed and sporadic bus that rolled through the valley.

It was in Quetta that Juge changed. As he walked near the main bazaar one day, a dark SUV with blacked-out windows barrelled in from the highway. Everyone noticed it because it was travelling too fast for that busy place with children and goats and carts full of farm produce, all scattered over the roadway. Just as Juge was taking all this in, a group of street kids came tearing away from one of the lanes leading to the bazaar, an irate shopkeeper chasing behind them. The boys scattered into the traffic. It all happened in a fraction of a second. Juge felt the collision in his bones, a penetration of steel in the sternum and into the deeper places behind. He ran to the spot and saw that the boy's head had been broken by the impact and lay like a stone. As Juge watched, the boy turned blue. Juge seized him by the face, pried open his mouth, and stuck his index finger into his throat. He dislodged a slimy ball of candy. The boy took a gulp of air at the same moment that blood filled his mouth and eyes. A man rushed over and bore the boy away. Within moments the crowd surrounded the SUV. The occupants locked their doors. The driver put the car in gear and tried to push through. The market crowd became infuriated. They broke the dark windows to find three white men inside. The men had expensive weapons strapped to them. Someone said that they were CIA. Someone else said Blackwater. The market boys climbed on the car while others tried to drag the occupants out. The driver fought. He put the heavy vehicle in reverse gear. Someone fell under the wheels as the vehicle broke free. The mob chased it, then there came shooting. When it was done, four were injured, two with gunshots. One of those shot was Hanif.

Later, strangers met the family and paid reparations for Hanif's leg and his permanent disfigurement. Fifteen thousand rupees. One hundred and eighteen euros.

Sebastien looked into the darkness of Syria and wondered if he had followed Juge one time too many. They drove, stopped in a place and waited for two hours, drove again, pulling into a town as the sun rose. They were in an area of train tracks and warehouse buildings and young men with guns and dark glasses hanging around stolen cars. They were put in the back of a white truck and taken to what looked to be a municipal government building. Outside, there were palm trees and what had once been a thriving flower garden in front, but it was all wasted, dried to stalks. Half the windows of the building had been blown out. They were brought into a cafeteria and given rough but fresh bread, beans, and hot mint tea and shown to a common sleeping area where many mattresses were spread out on the floor. The youngsters were taken away to a room that Sebastien discovered later that day was indeed a video game room, darkened, with large modern screens and a wide array of game consoles, where dozens of boys and young men spent the long hours between their duties, immersed in elaborate games that featured American soldiers in battle. When Sebastien mentioned this to Juge, his uncle just shook his head slightly. He would not be drawn into criticizing the commanders of the army or the administrators of the town.

Sebastien hung about the building and the sleeping area for a couple of days. No one asked anything of him. Juge was busy elsewhere. Sebastien glimpsed Juge now and again, walking in quiet discussions with the older men. He came across Juge in a meeting room one day, Juge expostulating about injustices and wars and the things he believed. A few days later he saw Juge roar off at the wheel of a truck.

A week later Juge came to find Sebastien. He invited him outside, where a cluster of men in keffiyehs and dark glasses waited by two trucks. They were armed with AKs. Sebastien too wore a keffiyeh against the midday sun. He felt out of place without a weapon. Juge climbed in and drove the lead vehicle away with two other men crammed into the cab beside him. The others waited for three minutes then were told to get into the second vehicle and follow. They drove out of the town into the open land to the south. After some time they slowed, as the road was

blocked here and there by blackened vehicles, and the road surface was interrupted by pits caused by bombs. The pits were deep
and wide.

A kilometre or so ahead of them Juge's vehicle was the only
thing moving. The road gradually improved to a normal highway
as they went farther on. The signs of combat fell away behind
them. Their baggy clothes snapped in the hot air. Juge's vehicle
slipped out of sight over a low rise.

They heard but did not see the drone that flew through the
low clouds. There was a flash of light, and the ground shook.
Their driver slowed and stopped and made everyone take cover
in the ditch by the road. After thirty minutes they climbed out
of the ditch and made their way to the top of the rise. In the distance was the smoking remains of Juge's vehicle.

They brought him Juge's bloodied and torn belt, which was
all that was left of him. They told him to forget Juge, forget the
others. They went back to the truck, got in, turned around, and
went back to the town.

—There is nothing left to see. They are martyrs, as so many
others.

Sebastien was alone. He was surrounded by strangers who
barely knew Juge, who had no idea that Juge was his uncle.
Sebastien decided to keep that to himself.

He was homesick. Going home without his uncle was not possible. He could not bear the thought of explaining to the others
that Juge was dead while he had escaped unscathed. For a time,
he avoided everyone, finding places to hide and weep. After ten
days of this he went out among the other new recruits. It seemed,
though, that he had become invisible in his grief. He had lost
weight and looked weaker and paler and more French than ever.
For a time he was certain he was losing his personality. He entertained the idea that he, Sebastien, was only a person because
of Juge, that without Juge there was only a poor specimen of a

human body with no family or country of origin. No identity. He wondered if he had become one of those nameless figures in a snapshot of a mob, an unnamed example of some ignoble human failure, useful to others only as a suicide bomber or battlefield soldier propelled into a hail of bullets. Or worse, not human at all, but simply a bad specimen, an evolutionary dead end.

One of the seniors, a commander, came to him where he sat in his dark corner. He carried a cup of tea and a plate of spicy food.

—Tell me about yourself.

Sebastien could say nothing at first. The man handed him the plate. The man's face was strong but careworn under a thick beard edged with grey. He looked Sebastien over carefully.

—Perhaps you need a wife to care for you. There are many girls waiting to be wives of our fighters.

—My brother died.

—Yes, our brothers die every day. It is part of our fight, and we must accept this. Allah will praise them in heaven. Do not fear for our brothers who are gone.

—What do I do now?

—First, eat.

Sebastien took a bite. There were pieces of chicken in the rice.

The commander went away. When he came back the next day, he told Sebastien to pack. He gave Sebastien a revolver with a shoulder strap and bullets.

—Do not be afraid. They will show you what to do.

It was then that Sebastien's journey really began. Two years later he was in Sudan.

CHAPTER 23

Avtar Kestner

Jihadi Camp

June 29, 2016

They took Mason-Tremblay away before dawn. Neither of the captives had the strength to protest. It was as though a decision had been made and their fate was sealed. The finality of it lingered in the morning air. Kestner was not brought food or drink that day. They brought a basin of water and a cloth. A jihadi with a Brixton accent arrived with scissors and razor and directed him to shave. Brixton cut his hair to a stubble and passed the razor over his skull, chatting like a barber all the while.

—And how's the star of stage and screen feeling today, eh? No need for a long face, right? Your troubles are over, mate. Such a fine-lookin' chap too, eh?

After a time an older man came by and spat a word of Arabic to make Brixton clamp up.

They brought a cotton kimeez and plastic sandals and left him alone. He waited, imagining that they needed to collect their resolve before proceeding from one step to the next.

Kestner experienced a brittle nervousness under these conditions, made worse by chronic hunger, low body mass, infections, parasites, a lack of sleep. Small noises amplified so that he heard them in exquisite, crackling detail. The gnashing of the mandibles of ants and beetles, their feet hissing through the sand, chitinous limbs scraping audibly as they cleaned themselves. A host of creatures came and went. They made various contributions to the orchestra: geckos opinionated and loud, agamas expansive in song, big-eared mice who squeaked with delight upon finding a gift, tiny calling passerines that lapsed into dismay as they flew into his hovel. Each individual life was a marvel, enviably removed from the hellishness of human obsession. He closed his eyes and listened to other, interior sounds: the sluggish turbulence as his mitral and tricuspid pushed shut, the gassy percussions as the Little Doubts skirmished over the cavernous places that had at one time contained healthy viscera.

Days went by. A dog appeared, a creature of random brown and white spots, hair in one place, fur in another. It was young and lost. It poked its snout into his doorway and was there, motionless, for a long time before Kestner noticed it. When he spoke to it, it nodded its head and panted at him, and its tail swished against the tarp. The next day the guards, the new Isuzu men, brought a bottle of water, a packet of groundnuts, a stale pita, and a piece of hard cheese. He shared his food with the dog, and it came and sat by him as it ate. When the guards came near, the dog vanished into the rocky hillside.

Hours passed in which Kestner willed himself to survive. He hallucinated. It was impossible to achieve clarity, estimates of probability, calculations of standard deviation, trend lines, extrapolations. The future might be divined by knowing the movements of small animals as they moved freely from place to place in the camp and beyond. As he lay in a corner, curled like a fetus, he heard voices moving in the air, intruding on his sleep, then fading. This went on for days. At night fluorescent lights illuminated the rocks and hills, and during the day the clouds billowed like enormous djinns, ready to vent outrage upon the endeavour below. Finally, it rained, a brief downpour with sheet lightning above. He stood in it, drenched and shaking with cold, then the dog appeared, skittering in panic until he brought it inside and gave it the scraps he had saved.

He could not muster enough optimism to give the dog a name.
The camp was greasy with mud. It dried into a kind of concrete that fixed the wheels of the Isuzu. At this time men in
the dispensary had loud quarrels. When the men emerged, the
quarrel was still among them, and they stalked angrily through
the valley and up the side of the hill near Kestner's shelter. They
yelled insults at each other in several languages. At one point a
knife was drawn, and everyone was silent. Two men came to haul
Kestner out. They shoved him up the slope to the top of the hill.

The men milled around a video camera on a tripod. One was
garbed in white robes, perfectly clean. Another wore black, his
face covered. Kestner was brought in front of the camera and
given a paper written upon in English and told to read it out loud.
He read:

—*My name is*—oh, yes, I should say my name here?—*Avtar
Kestner, a citizen of the United Kingdom.* But that's not right at all.
Political geography is arguable but...

The guard shoved the paper in front of him.

—*Lisez! Lisez!*

—All right. *I work for government intelligence and pass information to the British and American governments against the people
of*—Terrible fate for a public health consultant. What information and to whom? Why not just be done with it and make me say
I'm an assassin?

—*Lisez!*

—And where's the Sheikh? You know. Puss in Boots.

—*Lisez!* Confess yourself! You must confess. Everything will
be fine and do not worry. Before the Almighty, you must not sully
yourself with lies. Confess!

—Sully myself with lies?

The man behind the camera cursed, and the other men left
off Kestner and clustered around the camera. The argument
resumed. The operation of the camera was apparently in question.

The dog had followed him to the top of the hill. It sat at the top of the hill, on a large rock. It wagged its tail when he looked at it. A gust of wind snatched the paper from Kestner's hand. He watched it soar up and vanish in a spiralling updraft. As he watched it go, he could see over the hill into a stretch of rocks, pale dunes beyond that and in the distance, a strand of brilliant green.

His mind both slowed and accelerated. The men continued to cluster around the camera and quarrel. This went on for some time. It might have been days, as far as Kestner could tell. It was impossible to know time with any accuracy. The dog, his friend, wagged its tail in irony whenever he directed his glance toward it.

They planned to kill him, it seemed. It was a sickening, slow realization. First, there would be the pain, then he would go into shock, and this would be a mercy. If they hacked at his throat, it would be horribly painful. It would take time, minutes perhaps, for his blood pressure to decline to the point that shock set in and his brain became ischemic. Edema, intracranial pressure, herniation. He plodded through the possibilities. His jugulars would be severed first and bleed out. As the cut went deeper into the carotids, blood would eject at pressure. A delay as his cerebral blood pressure dropped to critical levels. Another delay because of residual tissue oxygen. What kind of observation or experiment had ever demonstrated the pathophysiology of decapitation? How long does the brain function without arterial blood? Ten minutes? Fifteen? How long does a head survive after being removed from the body?

At this point he vomited on his legs and lost control of his hands and began shuddering and shaking. He was not having a seizure. He was wide awake watching his body react. One of the men snorted in disgust.

A dark cloud came in. The men paused and looked up. They hated clouds as much as they hated the sun, these men. They hated lightning, night, morning, hot sun, cold air. They perhaps hated the very cosmos. They found their own existence to be repugnant. Later, further quarrels, a blade drawn and wielded. Someone laughed derisively at that. One removed the battery of the camera and dashed it to the sand. Another camera was brought from the camp, but this too was dead. Thousands of large brown moths fluttered in to alight on the men, causing the men to curse the sky. The moths touched Kestner's hair, found it inhospitable, departed on friendly terms. During this time the sun skittered about behind the clouds like a fugitive. It darted to the top of the sky, an ignoble, leaky balloon blown by the gusty wind. A dust storm reared up to the west.

They dragged Kestner down the hill again. His legs refused to cooperate, even as he wished to be upright in the face of these indignities.

After Kestner was back in his hole, one of the men stuck his head through the opening.

—Why is it we have this cheap technology? Why? If this was a business venture, someone would be retrenched! Such stupide!

Kestner lay on his side where he had landed and watched a brigade of ants and a spider, then closed his eyes so that his senses were overtaken by the clamouring of mortal anxiety. The effort to twist away his bindings failed. He curled into a ball and wept, which had the effect of draining away his resolve and leaving his mind as a detached orb, suspended over the hole, while his muscles became sedate.

Later, the camp was quiet, the light neither bright nor dark, the temperature neutral. A beetle struggled along the ground with a ball of dung. The dog returned to lie in the opening, one eye open and watching him, its ears flicking away flies. Kestner spent an hour undoing his bindings. He tried to solicit the assistance of the dog, but the dog whined and backed away, changed its mind, and returned to lie stretched in the opening to the hole, watching carefully as Kestner shed his vomitous trousers and threw them outside, where a host of flies quickly found them. Kestner cursed at the dog.

—What's the prognosis? There ought to be one that doesn't involve death, wouldn't you think?

The dog whined and wagged. Kestner sat beside the dog. Together they observed the deepening of the shadows of the hills. A troop of baboons wandered down the hill into the encampment and settled on the Isuzus. The lead baboon made a show of defecating on the roof of one of the vehicles. A man came out of the dispensary and threw a rock that missed the baboon and hit the windscreen instead, leaving a starry smash. The male baboon howled, picked up a handful of feces, and flung it with admirable accuracy, causing a torrent of angry yelling. The prisoner and the dog observed all this with great satisfaction. The man went inside for his gun, and the baboons cannily scattered, leaving Kestner with an ache in his belly, a dry throat, and a deep lassitude that eased him into a hallucination in which it seemed Levigne was present, sitting against a wall, her arms encircling her knees, awaiting the answer to a question. Unaccountably, his penis became erect. He looked at it fondly. Levigne spoke, her thighs pale brown, smooth.

—You never talk about your family.

—I don't? My wife and I are estranged. My daughters grew up behind my back. I feel as though I missed it. They're women now. I lost touch with my mother and stepfather. I always felt as though I didn't belong with them after they married. I lost touch with everyone. It wasn't what I wanted. It just happened. I gradually lost touch...

—How do you lose touch with your own mother and daughters?

He wanted to explain. You find someone else. You stop calling. You travel. You live far away. You put them away on a shelf for later. Months pass. Years. One day you realize it's you who's been forgotten.

Later a spray of rain on his face awakened him. In the darkness the rain came in gusts, each drop causing an eruption of dust as it hit the ground so that it looked as though the earth leapt up to greet the rain. By morning streams flowed down from the hills and turned the riverbed into a river. By the afternoon the river flooded the banks and swept over the hard-baked land. Animals sought high ground. The snakes came out of their holes.

Kestner crawled deep into his hole. Water ran in and around, and he became wet and cold under his blanket. He was going lower in his life than he had thought possible. He was no more than a creature that crawled out of the ground, a thing whose sole passion was its own survival. He placed his hands between his thighs. The bindings lay scattered on the ground, but it did not matter. He was not free. There was nowhere to go but into an endless land of flood and desert and scrublands patrolled by hyenas.

His hands were cold for reasons that had nothing to do with the rain. That was it: his hands were freezing from within, and he could not fathom this. In fact, looking down at his hands he was of the impression that they belonged to someone else. What had he done with those hands during his life? Had he applied them to good purpose? Anyway, that was it: his hands were foreign.

Avtar Kestner stepped out under the open sky to feel the rain and watch sheets of lightning in the hills. It was another day, another fluctuation of weather, on an Earth that blithely circled the sun.

He went into his hole and sat trying to warm his hands between his thighs, having overcome, finally, the shaking. And there awaited his future.

CHAPTER 24

Avtar Kestner
Turkana County
July 1, 2016

Dawn. The sky a blanket of grey, an unwelcome light. And suddenly Mason-Tremblay was back. He wore a new black track suit and new tennis shoes. His face was washed and shaved, and when he saw Kestner he attempted a smile.

—They fed me. First food in days. Hamburgers. They gave me hamburgers. Not sure about the meat, but I ate them. Two of them.

From his pocket he pulled out a very flattened hamburger.

—I saved this for you.

Kestner took it and stuffed it down his gullet nervously lest the guard object. His stomach was unsure of this unexpected gift, and Kestner struggled to keep it in.

Mason-Tremblay shook. Parkinsonism, it seemed, was getting around.

—Something has happened. I'm getting out of here. I over-heard them. I think they made a deal. Ransom.

—Ransom?

—Both of us must be getting out.

They slept that night in the hole but were awakened, in the wee hours, by vehicles arriving. There were raucous shouts and cheers and celebratory automatic gunfire, then the camp went quiet.

At dusk the next day they came and took Mason-Tremblay away and bundled him into the cab of a truck, in the passenger seat. The driver reached around and buckled Mason-Tremblay's seat belt. There was a roar of motors, and David Mason-Tremblay was gone in a cloud of dust and exhaust.

Kestner could see from his hole the old Mercedes that now lay tilted in the soft ground like a boat run aground, abandoned, and left to rot. Sand and windblown plastic drifted around its wheels.

No one approached Kestner. He dozed and dreamed that he was Mason-Tremblay. He dreamed of Seiko Levigne and Renate and Carmen and his mother and Levi. Among these dreams he envisioned himself walking among endless dunes, away to freedom in death. He was weak in the legs, his energy stores were depleted, and his muscles were shot, atrophied, infected, the infection spreading. Persistent fever was eroding him. Kidneys were damaged, he was sure of it. Nephrons squashed out flat, unable to osmoregulate. He had permanent diarrhea.

The next morning a new guard with an uncovered face appeared at the opening to the tent. He was West African, with skin that shone with health. He had the French-accented English of an educated man. The new guard lay his gun on a rock as though ridding himself of a burden and sat nearby, erect on a camp stool. Unlike the previous guards who had departed with Mason-Tremblay's convoy, the new man looked at Kestner and smiled kindly. He said he was Jaffer, and he came from Mali.

—And you. You look far from your place.

—I am. Far enough that I barely remember my place. But I know about Mali. Ali Farke Toure. Beautiful.

Jaffer looked at him in surprise and gave an amiable laugh. He began to talk about his wife and sons, his parents and brother, and the town he was from, all in the formal way. He described in detail the strengths and weaknesses of each of his six children.

When he stopped talking Jaffer observed Kestner for a long

time, studying him. He picked up his gun and went away and returned with two oranges and a banana in a bag. He watched Kestner eat the fruit.

—And where do they take my colleague, the white man, Mason-Tremblay?

—Le blanc? Oui, he was for ransom exchange.

—Where?

—Je n'sais pas. In fact, no one knows. They will go from place to place, then, when it is safe, they will make exchange. They are expert at this. Anyway, they think they are expert. But these boys, they all want to be part of it.

He laughed easily.

—Then they will come back here?

—Je ne crois pas ça. I know the boys had enough of this outpost. Once they get the money who knows where they go. Maybe they go to fight somewhere. Who knows?

—What about me?

—Sais pas, sais pas. It is the pleasure of Allah.

—It is the pleasure of you and your friends…

Jaffer laughed. He was a humble, friendly man.

—Oui, c'est vrai. What you say is somehow correct. But we are men of Allah, non? That is our belief.

—Are you jihadis or mercenaries? Soldiers for pay.

—Only two choices. Ah, but difficult to answer. Some more on the jihadi side, and others more on mercenary side. Sometimes one side, sometimes the others. We have to live.

—When will I be released? Why was my friend released and not I?

—Ah, you do not know. I can tell you there has been media attention, government attention, even international attention. Your wife campaigns for your release, along with your daughters and others in your country. They are very beautiful.

—My wife? My daughters?

—Yes. I was told of this. It seems, even, that your government made offers.

—Offers?

—Yes. Mais, a complication that I will tell you because otherwise it will sit on my mind. There is, how do you say, *bidding*. An offer, a higher one, competed against your government. Someone with more money. These men are fighters and jihadis, but they have been here in the desert for too long, in one country after another and they are tired. They want to go elsewhere, to fight, make jihad, get education, do MBA, join the motor trade.

Jaffer winked and then looked out at the sky and said, —Merde.

A dark mass roiled on the horizon. It came in fast, filling Kestner's hovel with wind and sand. Jaffer stayed where he was, wrapped his head and face in his long scarf, pulled out a pair of goggles, and put them on. He pushed Kestner to the back of the shelter and then he went around securing the torn flaps and fastening the openings as best as he could. The wind tore the covering of the hole, and when they wiped the grit from their faces ten minutes later, one side of the nylon material had torn completely open.

Jaffer looked at the damage and scratched his head.

After several hours Jaffer went away and returned with more oranges, a piece of roasted meat and two cups of coffee, all of which he shared. He seemed bent on disregarding the protocol of treatment that Kestner and Mason-Tremblay had suffered. He pointed to the sores on Kestner's ankles, festering insect bites, and said that he would summon a médecin.

Early the next morning he returned with another Malian, who wore a shawl over his head and a clinic jacket with a stethoscope in the pocket over his fatigues. He examined Kestner and gave him antibiotic cream for his sores, a handful of vitamin pills, a large bottle of water, tea bags, and a plastic-wrapped package of pita bread.

—I am sorry I cannot do better than this, mon ami.

The médecin went away.

The camp became quiet. Kestner regained a measure of strength over the next days, with the food and fruit and care of Jaffer and the médecin who came and examined him once a day at Jaffer's request. One day the médecin and Jaffer appeared together to say farewell. They offered a solemn prayer that Allah would be merciful in his direction. Kestner did not see them again.

That night the dispensary was brightly lit, and there were loud voices.

In his sleep he drifted and turned, the night breezes taking him here and there, from brilliance and promise to horror and pain. He slept for immeasurable lengths of time that might have extended for days or weeks. One day they came and moved him into a tent with wooden boards on the floor, windows that closed, and a camp cot with a mattress and blanket. He had not realized how luxurious an item a blanket could be.

Three days later several men came. It was a clear day, and the air was cooler than any day so far, as if air from another place had assumed possession over the camp. It made him take hope as a young European boy stood before him. The boy spoke to him in Parisian-accented English. He was agitated.

—Say my name.

—Why would I know your name?

—You know my name. The way you look at me I see you know it. I see you thinking my name. Thinking, thinking. Am I the man you think? No. I am another man. My name is Ali Soudani, did you know? Did you not see? I am not Sebastien. Sebastien is dead. He is stupid and now he is dead and gone. Only Ali Soudani is left. Only Ali Soudani is here. Say my name.

—You are Sebastien.

Sebastien burst into tears. He shoved Kestner out under the open sky. He drove Kestner before him up the slope to the crest of the hill. The boy was hyperventilating and sweating and swearing under his breath. He shoved Kestner forward, and Kestner stumbled and fell, and each time he fell he was slower to rise. He fainted once, and when he came to, other men had come to help drag him the last metres to the top of the dune.

At the top, the camera waited. There was the air of an occasion. Some of the men wore fresh clothing. No one spoke. The camera was running. Kestner looked about at the nearby hills, which wore a pretty green skirt after the rains, and into the skies beyond. The land was open, vast, and promising from the hilltop. He spotted the dog on a bump of earth a safe distance from the men. The dog watched the men intently, ears flickering, tail tucked hard under his belly. Kestner looked at the dog as the men pushed him to his knees. He tried to call out a friendly word to the dog, to reassure it, but the word died in his throat. The dog whined, turned, and slunk away down the hill and out of the camp.

They wanted him to read a statement. Someone pushed papers in front of him, but someone else grabbed them away and threw them to the side.

Sebastien, who called himself Ali Soudani, had wrapped his keffiyeh around his face like the others, and he held his body stiff. Kestner looked up at him and whispered.

—Sebastien, je t'en supplie.

The boy glared, eyes red with fury. The others watched all this closely then came around Sebastien and urged him on. They produced a gleaming hunting knife and put it in Sebastien's hand. They urged him on in Arabic and French and English. Sebastien stared at Kestner all the while, the knife held fast in his clenched fist. It was a good and expensive knife; Kestner could see that it was Swedish with the familiar logo of the manufacturer emblazoned across the blade. The men put a blindfold on Kestner. He felt Sebastien's short breaths on his neck and felt the tense muscle of Sebastien's quadriceps brush against him, and there was a shift in the air as the boy bent over him. Then, a flicker of a sensation at his throat, the blade easily passing through the thin dermis there, so that he could visualize easily the exposed sub-cutaneous fat shrunken with starvation and dehydration and the neat organization of the sternocleidomastoid beneath. Hot wet-ness spread down his chest. He gave into it, powerless and dim, suddenly, at this final moment. He had no understanding beyond the wet and hot pain at his neck.

Oddly, though, it stopped. The boy withdrew, obviously appalled, as any decent person must be. Humanity! What was a man without humanity? It would be impossible to carry through with such pointless brutality. The knife was gone. He was sure he heard it being sheathed. A slick sound of steel in leather. It was over. His blindfold fell away, and he was struck by a wash of colour. He was taken back to his place and given a cloth for his bleeding neck. It was a superficial wound after all. Painless. A clean wound because the knife was of high quality steel. It was a fine knife, that was certain. It meant the wound would heal, quickly and without complications. His other ailments, the pains and discomforts that had plagued him were now diminished to nothing. Even his Little Doubts were quelled. He felt renewed, despite all that had happened.

He lay with his eyes open, mesmerized by the multitude of worlds swirling overhead. An immeasurable time passed. The world spun light and dark and light again in its endless gyrations through the cosmos.

Then he must have slept. When he opened his eyes, Money was sitting nearby, talking in the direction of the dark ridges that loomed against the sky. Kestner had not seen Money in weeks or months. But he was not surprised that he appeared just then. Money spoke in the lazy tones of a person who has indulged, overeaten, overslept. It seemed he was in the middle of a long diatribe. Kestner had awoken in the middle.

—...as if we were corrupt and powerful UN people who somehow negotiate the existence of sick and healthy, rich and poor. But we should never fail our negotiation. NATO versus Russia. US versus Chinese. Jihads versus infidels. Forget the men who make war and violence. They are cockroaches on a shelf. They are hyenas walking in the desert. And Money? Money is a survivor.

He turned now, and it seemed to Kestner that Money addressed him, although Money's eyes looked hooded or shadowed, perhaps because Kestner's vision was weary to the point of failing.

—Your government did nothing for you. Those people care only about other things. Because you are mixed up man, MaHindu, Japon, marginal not white, and they don't know what to do about you, how convenient. Or maybe other reason I don't know. At least you are not African, because then they would pay those jihadis to feed you to the leopards. Ha!

—Where have you been all this time?

—Money was here. Money was there. Money was inconvenient. Imams and mullahs and sheikhs and princes, they make fast and holy talk. According to them Money carried out jihad so now Allah is eternally grateful and will pay off with girls and a comfortable bed after death. I told them if they believed in that stupid story someone was making a good joke on them, maybe even Allah himself. As for me, I am the one with the name of Money, and Money is cash, and cash is not stupid that it believes heaven or Allah or waiting for reward after death. And Money and cash do not depend on the promise of women. Women come and then they go when it suits them, because they also have their own plans. Anyway, that is nothing to me. What I want is something different than what Allah has to give. What I want is to be out of this losing life and into something bigger, a greater and rich life. Money need money. Money need good things to buy. Money need take proper place in the economy of the world because that world better than most people. What Money wants is to be part of America or China, start business, become CEO, make it rich, America-China Dream. I am the man for that place. When the other Riches see Money, they will know he is one of them.

—But realistically—

—This is the beauty of my plan. *You* are my plan. International thinking. You and me only, high-level UN negotiations. You promise by your honour to pay me ransom. You have to give me your youngest daughter, nothing else. Delayed payment plan is okay. Then you are free, get you back to Kenya, Nairobi, airplane business class Swiss Air, home, Canada, white winter, forest lake, snow skiing, blanket bed with wife, hot meals, all of that. When you are safe and happy, back to home, job, money, special friends, then you must remember me, Money, and you must remember our negotiation and your honour and your promise, and then you must pay me your daughter.

—My daughter? I don't think she would agree.

—Only one other thing you should pay me. That thing is due diligence.

After that it was simple, the negotiations brief. Promises were made. In the colourless and dim hours, unbound, he floated out, growing stronger by the moment. An unknowable amount of time had elapsed. The hour and season were tropical. The ground he stepped on consisted of jelly. He wondered if, after all, it had rained in his absence. He rose out of his hole and walked away. He left his ragged, deathful hole, his grave, behind and did not look back at it. He skirted the steep slope, walking on an angle. Then came to the abandoned lorry, IN GOD WE TRIST, with Salim perched at the ready behind the wheel. Kestner clambered up and into the cab. He lay down on the bench seat taking breaths as mechanically and airlessly as a faulty ventilator. He cringed to hear the tremendous racket of the diesel engine as it came to life, and he resisted the urge to look out the window as he rolled slowly away from the camp.

—Salim? Why can't we drive faster?

Salim turned and handed him a lump of something in a package. It might have been food—bread or meat, a fruit or root vegetable. It smelled of nothing, as neutral as dried dust. Kestner sat up, took a piece of stuff out of the package and put it in his mouth and chewed as Salim nodded in approval.

—Ah, no, Sah. Fast is not in the SOPs, which we must follow for religious reasons and insurance purposes. Do not worry. No one can follow. When they realize you are gone they will celebrate. They will thank us.

A dark terrain flowed past in which dim forms gyrated. In the distance, empty spaces beckoned. The threat of thirst, fatigue, illness were trifles. The future was at a curious remove and did not concern him. The place of future worries was occupied by endless space, endless liberty.

He was free. His body was free. He floated as he sat on the familiar bench in the back of the cab. Salim drove through the hills, then along the lake. He stopped and switched to the reserve fuel tank. As Kestner breathed, he felt cool oxygen drawn into the evacuated spaces in his lungs. He counted each molecule as it passed through his alveoli into his blood and watched as each molecule went through him unused. His breaths were of no use on this day. They did nothing. When he drank, the water was neither cool nor warm. He did not speak to Salim since speech was unnecessary, a waste. Salim benignly gestured to the empty lands as though he had achieved mastery over it as he navigated over gritty hills and through winding riverbeds.

A storm blew up, and rain fell suddenly and hard, filling the riverbeds. All about them the parched hills drank. Flowers erupted colourlessly from sand and stone. The lorry surged through the raging waters until it was forced to climb to higher terrain. The storm passed through and left particles that danced in the air without settling to the ground. When they stopped, the silence roared.

How long did they drive? It might have been hours or weeks. It was as though a small region of his brain—he thought of the hippocampus—were injured in some way. He had lost his ability to gauge correctly the passage of time. He looked hopelessly at his watch, but it too had failed. The hour and minute hands had corroded away somehow, leaving only an erratically advancing second hand. They came over a rise to see a ribbon of black tarmac laid out over a broad plain. In the distance, a white UN vehicle sped along, glittering in the sunlight that emerged between the rain clouds. In a while they were at the road, which might have been comforting but was not. Instead, the road disturbed him, for there was something profoundly wrong as they rolled steadily forward through a long day in which the light faded only in the tiniest of declinations. The twilight was endless.

They arrived in a large town, the lorry lumbering through throngs of thousands or perhaps millions of people who looked to him purposeless, their faces two dimensional and indistinct, like badly contrived digital extras in a film production. It was still twilight. Many vehicles had been in recent accidents and lay overturned or on their sides with their wheels still slowly spinning like the legs of overturned turtles. Farther along in the town, other vehicles stood upright, burning. The flames cast an orange, flickering light on the crowd. He detected the glint of steel of a hunting knife he knew very well, and he noticed the gleaming, perfect teeth of the mob.

It was good that he was not alone in that place. With him was Salim or perhaps Money, although whoever it was by his side hid his face from him and had little to say, so he could not tell. Perhaps it was David Mason-Tremblay. But he was accompanied, and this was a relief. They stopped and got down among the two-dimensional figures who rushed about in a peculiar bent-kneed way, their feet at times sliding along the ground so that they seemed to skate. He cut through a band of looters, into a crowd of children who had found enough space for a soccer game, using an empty whisky bottle as a ball. The bottle rang over the pavement, leaping at the keeper who parried it away, flashing in the light and dark. Behind the goal a woman seemed about to assaulted, her skirts drawn up and tied over her head. She spun about, though, was pushed from hand to hand, the assault rejected, as though it was not what was wanted or needed. Two youths fought, egged on by a dozen women dressed in natty airline uniforms. It was impossible not to associate the cause of the fight with the uniforms.

The bottle soared between the goal posts to shatter against a rock. Kestner stopped and gaped at the puckered thighs of a fat man who danced in vulgar contortions, his head entirely enclosed in feathers, his face transformed into a beak. The crowd swelled with men and women of every creed and colour, many appearing as large birds and wild animals, dancing in monstrous costumes and ritual masks that were worn down by centuries of use, the eyeholes blank pits, the expressions locked and horrific. Vehicles were aflame and passengers ran helter-skelter until they became caught and dragged into the vortex of dancers. A Mercedes car was rocked until the doors popped open and two men and two women spilled out. Someone seized the wrist of one of the men and tore his watch away. Another pushed a woman down while another wrested her bag away from her desperate grip. Then her jewellery. The woman decided to fight. She took up a stone, swung it, and threw it wildly so that it caught someone on the head. It bounced off harmlessly, and the man laughed.

How the people celebrated! Yet he had no clue as to what they celebrated or who they were. It did not matter. Others went by in the curious bent-kneed run, skirting fires, accidents, fights, gardens, animals. He had no idea of where he had arrived. He sensed that nearby was the Rift, the great rent in the crust of Africa, the chasm painted in ink shadows made by moonlight. Beyond that were the wild spaces of the Mara plains, where predators roused themselves and listened to the sounds of the night. For a long time he wandered without direction, until he found himself in a wilderness of shadows far from the city, and he wondered that he had become so disoriented and lost.

He came to a low building with a broken door — a café or informal eatery, with the unmistakable ripe scents of decaying, raw meat, old oil frying, and human fatigue. A metal sign read, URGE YOURSELF ON. Another read, SAD HOUR IS NEVER HOUR. He took a seat facing the door and was alone; he looked for his companions but found that whoever they were, they were now lost. New companions awaited. He was detached. He could be the companion of any man or woman. He was ordinary, a man with appetites and ordinary instincts. A large bottle was brought, and he tipped it back and tasted nothing, not even warmth or cold. He could hear each individual synapse of his nervous system click off, one at a time. He had never heard that before. In his chest his heart was a silent and solemn witness, the contractions remote and quiet despite the human mess that surrounded him. He opened his gullet and drank from the bottle in the dull hope of reward.

He wished for his senses to dilate into the largesse of inebriation. Yet nothing happened.

He could not feel his bones. His senses whispered messages that he could not decipher. He was suddenly tired of his own failings as a man, his lack of ambitions, his misplaced confidence in friends and family, humanity as a whole. Was it not time to move on to a new phase of life? What use was he? He no longer had real connections. His emotions and sensations were dead. He no longer thought. Around him there was only a falseness or a thinness or a liquidity of unfamiliar forms. What did he possess? Why could he not be sated? He was a creature of the deep sea, gasping on a gorgeous beach where others frolicked. Tasteless brine or temperatureless fluid or air or nothing spilled into his throat. A few steps away, the formless others passed around him like ghosts, and beyond that, flaming cars, the racket of chaos, glass shattering, voices cheering while others screamed in agony.

He found himself further afield, wandering an empty and wide road in the outskirts of an unknown city. There were minarets and churches and temples of all kinds.

An old man in an elaborately arranged wedding turban stopped him and spoke to him in a tongue he recognized as Hawaiian, but he could not understand the meaning of the words. He tore himself away and walked on and was surrounded by a familiar, coppery aura, a glow like a tropical dawn. He felt he was near Renate, she of the thick tresses of copper hair that he so admired and had wished always to caress but had desisted doing so. If he had not desisted, would that have made it better?

He recalled vividly a moment, a crystalline winter day in Ottawa, the colours shifting with the passing lights, even though it was far from dusk. Walking, feet uncomfortably damp. Winter coat. Winter and nothing but imperfect shades of white that led to a door and a table where his wife waited. She should have been his hearth, his crackling heat, his welcoming harbour. He was relieved to see her, yet something was wrong. No, they were no longer husband and wife. They were separated, and this was the aftermath. Still, fleetingly, he was triumphant that she was there as promised and had not decided to spurn him. It was he who had broken their home and vacated, after all. She had not wanted this. For a long time she had been saying that she would not see him again, that she preferred to be left alone to mourn their failed family and perhaps find the heart to begin again without obligation to him, that he at least owed her that one thing, to be released cleanly and forever, because she was still young and desired to be properly loved. That was how she had stated it. Yet here she was, waiting for him, sitting in a pool of warmth of her making. For a moment he basked in the expectation that she would plead with him, and he toyed with the idea that he would harden himself against her. But he was wrong. She did not plead. She was calm and beautiful, her eyes clear and not at all mournful. He looked away for a moment, into the street, as though searching for someone else. Unfamiliar faces emerged out of the snowy street and vanished anonymously. He knew no one else there. All around were cold shades of white but for Renate, who was the only colour, a glorious island of copper and red where she sat and watched him. When he looked at her, he suddenly realized his error. He would not admit it to himself or anyone at the time. Too late, he looked up to see a receding and salvational light in the winter sky. He pretended not to notice. She was talking, playing with her tea cup, talking about their daughters and their concerns. It was not about him. It was over, and then she was at the door, smiling kindly, her coat fastened. It was too late.

Maybe it was not too late, after these years. Perhaps he would go back, apologize, make up to her. Surely she would embrace the husband who had had travelled so far and endured so much. He would settle near his daughters, learn about them, let them into his life. They would forgive him. He would resume his role as father.

But the moment, the vision, was coming to an end like the ruined celluloid of an old movie. The faces of his daughters slipped sideways, jittered about like flies, in and out of focus in the murk—his memories could not root themselves properly in this bad light. Now Renate jittered too, one part of her eye gone, then the mouth. He struggled to keep his family but they slid away, leaving fleeting black and white celluloid, streaming past at speed, of babies, diapers, cries in the night, girls in birthday clothes, a woman presiding over dinner, homework, sports fields, piano and violin recitals, and a dark shadowy presence, he, father as interloper, unexpected guest, late, busy, caught up, on his way to an airport, just arrived in a gust of sour wind that blew the decorations asunder, his presence temporary or partial, his life in other places—Geneva, Cairo, Hanoi, Rome. His family had grown up. But when? He had nothing to reach back to. There were line sketches of awkward adolescents, the older one and the young one indistinguishable in height and complexion, but the elder one smart-mouthed and the other, the younger, watchful and mysterious. How old were they now, his daughters, his flesh and blood? Where were they? How could he get back there and what would he say? How would he find them without recalling their faces? Carmen, Car-moon, Car-mean. Marcia, Martian, Mars.

See Daddy? Mommy still loves you.

All those fragments were swept away by a puff of wind, and he found that he was simply sitting on a rock surrounded by tall men in scarves who covered their faces from the blown sand. They chewed and offered him nothing. They chewed and talked among themselves in a language foreign and undecipherable. Or perhaps he could not hear properly because their mouths were covered.

Ah, but suddenly he did hear clearly one thing.

There was no point to her life, so we took it.

They were talking about Seiko or Renate or Carmen or Mars. Even as they said it, he looked about for Seiko. After this searching and trouble, she was finally with him, he was certain. He craned his neck to see her, but found he was restricted. He could not see past the men who surrounded him.

The second hand on his watch leapt forward, so he glanced at it. It was getting late. Events had occurred from one moment to the next, in one country to the next, one woman to the next. He felt an enormous relief, then a moment of ecstasy, then this too passed, and he was anxious again, horribly anxious because he had failed at these moments of life, of living. It would remain ever so because he could not change. The time for change had passed. The idea and possibility of redemption was a mockery. It had been beyond his capacity to take the hand of a woman or a child. His wife, his Renate, valiant in her effort to sally forward, hide her injuries, avoid dwelling in her pain, her family, her father, the old gun in his hand, the letter that failed to mention his daughter, his wife, anyone in his family.

Shadows accompanied him as he moved along the dusty road under a broad sun that occupied half the sky yet produced only the dullest of light. Spectral shadows: his own father, indistinct; Levi Kestner, shambling and large; Renate's father Jaap De Jong, revolver in hand, brain matter exposed for a daughter to find. These figures had been hanging about all along, he realized. He had not acknowledged them before now. It was his mistake.

Strangely, the deep and gnawing pains in his abdomen, in the first, second, third quadrants, had been purged. He had come from his pain and become a floating mist of thought, memory, regrets, and wishes. His Little Doubts were defeated, scarred over into a scirrhous lump. There was peace in his body, yet his mind battled on.

The dawn dissolved to dusk, an entire day deleted, the light dulled further, the pleasant copper and amber hues crushed and smeared over by a premature murk. He walked through the shards of his past mistakes. Always the mistakes, never the triumphs now.

He heard Salim in the hollow distance.

—*Nothing matters, Sah. Nothing! What matters is that we must not worry. When we worry, the problem is that the predators smell it. When the prey is worried, it makes mistakes, and that is a good time for hunting. It is the way of the predator. They know no mercy. They never pick one side or another. They only care about blood.*

—And Dr. Levigne?

—Ah no, she is just here.

Kestner looked around but could see no one.

He walked again, passing along a familiar road toward a refuge that was not sleep. He felt Levigne's presence, although she uttered not a sound. It was late, and she was at the point of vanishment. When he listened, he heard the echoes of disturbing messages that were difficult to grasp at that moment. It was the voice of Money or the Sheikh or Salim or perhaps a stranger on Kenyan television. He could not be sure. It was a speech, political, important and trivial, threatening and familiar.

—The wealth of the world is death! It is forced down our throats! It is plastic. It is a poison taste in the air. It is sewage. It is dead, an unloved corpse. Beauty murdered. Grace murdered. Corpses on corpses of those murdered by wealth, filling the natural land, rotting the land, while the monstrous wealth is forced into open mouths. The people grow sick. Wealth spills out of their stuffed mouths. It sticks in their throats like a bite of plastic food too big to swallow. A greedy bite that cannot be chewed, the mouth stuffed and stuck with the deadness of the wealth that cannot be spit out and cannot be swallowed. What will happen when the world fills with the dead sewage of wealth? We are surrounded by corpses on corpses.

Kestner looked about for the speech maker but saw instead hundreds of faces, all faded and featureless. Money, Salim, the Sheikh, Levigne, the politicians, the revolutionaries, the drivers and farmers and lawyers. The public health officials and doctors. The lovers and students and children. He walked quickly, looking all about at these faces that milled about in a grey twilight. There was neither sun nor moon nor cloud, only the dun tones of unpolished gun metal. Various voices rose about him.

—They take their lives and bring their famine to the rich.

—They arrive at our border with mouths open, ready to be stuffed with death, while corpses are stacked on the land.

—They come with bellies willing.

—Whomsoever can refuse the bountiful gift of death?

He ran on before the voices, through the half-light under the gun-metal sky.

—The darkness is in the sky because there is nothing left.

Finally, the voices faded. It was quiet. The road and land he crossed seemed to settle. The world was suddenly exhausted and ready for sleep. Only Kestner moved along the road. He alone remained awake. It was appalling to think that he had arrived here, only to be burdened by the task of bearing witness to the strangeness of it. It would be important that he remain sober and duly diligent.

He could hear a phone sputtering. It malfunctioned, transformed into a transmitter of cosmic chatter. Someone out in space was trying to call.

The road ahead was unclean, beset by a septic apocalypse. Microbial messes had spread thickly along the ground on which he walked. His feet trod in filth. He was mired, his feet struggling through infectious material. He had arrived at the epicentre of contamination. The road, the city, the country in which he walked was overwhelmed by sepsis. It burned with fever.

A cloud of moths fluttered about his head and landed on him to avoid the septic ground. He put his hand up to scatter them, and they moved effortlessly away, taking with them the remaining light. He was aware of someone nearby, a woman. Through the darkness her face was pale and indistinct. He knew her murmur so he reached out. She shifted away, though, so that he barely touched her sleeve. Her sheer, slippery silk slid past his fingers. She gave off no scent.

He skidded forward on the bacterial scum, into an airless and cold night.

All about him were pools of pathogens that fluoresced and winked as he trod through them. Pseudomonids and serratias, bacilli and mycoplasmids and cocci and vibrios and spirochetes.

Makers of slime, quiet invaders of mouth and eye—they formed a primordial muck through which Kestner struggled. No one would call this slime a home. It was the bottommost way station to better places. No one could possibly own these lanes, these ditches, these thrown-together shacks with their dirt floors.

He came to a low entrance lit by a kerosene lamp. The place was familiar. It had the scent of the origins, a starting point from decades earlier, in the midst of a family. Generations of family members moved dreamily about in the interior, preparing food, eating, engaged in half-hearted quarrels and reconciliations. A young woman breastfed an infant while three older children scooped handfuls of porridge from a black pot. They did not seem perturbed by a newcomer who arrived stunned at the door. In fact, no one seemed to pay him any notice in the dim and smoky light. It was a single long and narrow room with irregular sides and corners in which nests made of piles of clothing and ragged blankets were piled. As his eyes adjusted Kestner could see heads poking out of the nests. It was late. Despite the activity and noise, people were sleeping. Gradually, as the hours went on, people slumped over where they sat, or simply dropped to the floor in the area near one of the nests and went to sleep. The chairs were filled with some oldsters and a couple of drunks who slept upright. Parents crashed down near small children, arms and legs grasping at their loved ones. The smallest ones rolled and tumbled in their dreams until they came up against a warm back or belly. A youth burst in and swept the remnants of meals from a table and flopped upon it with his arms and legs dangling from the sides. In the small hours, well past one, two, four o'clock, the last of the adults was down and out so that a stillness reigned, broken only by the shifting of sleepers and the meandering conversations of dreams.

But Kestner would never sleep. He knew it even as he wished for that bliss. By now sleep was barely imaginable. It was an abstraction, an innocence he no longer possessed. There would never be sleep.

He watched the lamps burn down, heard the gentle and chaotic ramblings of slumber, and was reminded of the ties and complications, the warmth and smell of shared animal needs. He was reminded of the life of families and of the joy and pain of nurtured and growing children who would one day break away. There came a sharp pang as he suddenly saw that he had missed that, that he had passed it up without understanding its significance. Ultimately, everyone, poor or rich, came from this place of shared sleep, of family life, of dreams.

He was walking again, or moving somehow, and he found himself at the familiar, polished portal of the High Commission of Canada. He stepped through the door as a man hesitant, as a man undeserving of redemption and return, passing uneasily through one world into another. As he went in with his wrecked clothing and shoes, unshaven, bloody, and gaunt, the receptionist and security guards were jaunty in their salutations. *Jambo! Habari Bwana!* The receptionist winked at him with some secret knowledge. He stopped and stared at her, unwilling to let it pass, even as she turned away.

But there was nothing wrong. In fact, nothing had happened. The mission had been a disaster but, really, in the grand scheme of things, it was nothing.

And after that, there was nothing at all.

CHAPTER 25
Ali Soudani
In Blood
July 1, 2016

His clothes were ruined. He stared down at them as he walked away, letting the knife drop from his hand. No one had warned him that this would happen to his clothes.

The other men stared at him and he realized in a flash that he had done a thing that they could not do. *He* had done it. Only he, Ali Soudani, finally and completely. He staggered away from the scene and did not look back. He could not. As he went, he vomited, fell, staggered up, and went on. Blood had soaked through his clothes, stuck to his skin, and dried in the hot wind. Immediately he saw that this blood would never wash off. It was drying into a skin upon his skin. He tore the clothing off and threw down each item in a fury. He tore at his boots. Bloodsoaked boots. He was naked and coated with bloodskin, as though he had just emerged into the world, a newborn. Sure enough, he could not shed the bloodskin, just as he could not shed the image of the head with the eyes still alive, staring at him.

What had he done?

The sun was still rising. He plunged on in a revulsive, furious trance. He hated this Ali Soudani. Here he was, finally and fully arrived, only to find that his destination had all along been a new, utterly abhorrent person. His chances were used up, ruined, and he had destroyed another human being in a moment of unfocused hatred. It was obvious. His entire life had been full of hatred because he was misbegotten, of a people and a nation who knew from the beginning that he was misbegotten.

How had he deserved this? He held up his blood-soaked hands, threw down his head, vomited again, and staggered on, trying to distance himself from the horror he had created.

—Pourquoi moi?

He screamed into sky.

—*Pourquoi? Pourquoi?*

He plunged on toward the sun as it mounted the sky, where it would assume its seat over Sebastien, and over Ali Soudani.

CHAPTER 26
Money Manyu
Sudan and Kenya
July 1, 2016 and before

Money Manyu had hung back and watched without reaction or comment as the man he had abducted, the man he had then rescued from the desert, was brutally dispatched. No one had asked Money's permission. He had held himself back. He fooled himself at first, thinking that he did not care, and this entertainment was nothing, and this man was nothing. Yet, as the gore flowed, his own sharp knife lay trembling beneath his clothes like a live organ of his body, shifting as he shifted, thinking its own thoughts, pulsing warmly against his thigh to remind him. He had not used the knife, even in his growing fury at the jihadis as he watched them laboriously and amateurishly kill the prisoner for no good reason but to make a video.

After it was done, they milled around like excited children. Oh, they had done a great deed! How great were they! How great their cause, whatever it might be! Jihad, profit, adventure!

Money turned away in disgust. He scuffed the sand back down the hill to the camp. As he descended, he became aware that a jihadi walked near him. He did not care to look at the other man. He was ashamed, and the shame was boiling into rage. He did not want it, the boiling rage. He needed to keep it, but it made his muscles so tense he thought they might snap like wires. He felt the knife grow warm against his leg.

Finally, he stopped and turned and looked at the other man, and at the same moment the other man stopped and looked at him. The man was a poorly made thing with pasty skin. This man was jumped up as though he were on something worse than qat. Instead of speaking in a normal voice he cried out at Money.

—Et toi, qu'es tu? What do you want?

Money went still. His knife was heating up. It wanted out of its sheath.

—Nothing. I want nothing. From nowhere. Want nothing. Or maybe from anywhere. Maybe Africa. Maybe America. Maybe some other where. So what?

—America? And what is this America to men like us?

The man threw his arms up as he said this, his gestures exaggerated and his voice cracking. It was difficult for Money to listen to such a strange, white creature, with his weeping voice and panic-stricken eyes. There was something wrong with him. Money shrugged and wondered why this thing of America had popped out of his mouth.

—Nothing. America is nothing.

The other man uttered an animal cry, turned his back, and walked on down the hill. Money looked at his back and suddenly he realized that this was the executioner, the wielder of death. He was soaked in blood, and he looked as though he would burst open with the death he had just delivered. Money called out to the executioner's back.

—Hey, you think you are a kind of god, a kind of millionaire, to kill a man that way? You are not a millionaire! You are a cheap servant, nothing more! A cheap servant of death! There are many cheap servants like you, and you mean nothing! You mean nothing to anyone! Was there a good reason to kill that man? Was it necessary? He was a man, nothing more! Only a man!

The executioner let out a loud sob and fled from Money, away from the camp, off into the sand and scrub. Money watched the man tear off his bloody scarf, then his shirt, then his trousers.

Money's knife was burning his skin now, and his rage, instead of subsiding, seethed in his chest like an abscess.

It was past the time for him to leave this disaster behind for good. He had spent the time waiting for something, a chance, an idea, revenge, he knew not for what he waited. He thought of Hassan, out past the border, traversing deserts.

Violence is a tool.

Violence was a knife burning a hole in your leg to make sure you did something.

He went back and sat in the shade, his hands shaking. Those bastards had shamed him into climbing the hill with them, had not told him what they were about. Wear this, they said, and proffered a scarf with which to wrap his head and face.

—*The winds are hard. But if you are a man, come with us and we will show you a nice entertainment. Better than video game! Better than internet sex! Better than anything!*

And then he had stayed because he could not tear himself away from the brutality, even as the scalding rage brimmed up from his fruitless balls all the way to his brain.

His knife came out, but there was no one in the camp. They were at the top of the hill. The bawling thing of an executioner had fled into the desert like an escaped chicken. Money was alone. He went into the dispensary first. He splintered open the lockers he found there and slashed open the bags and possessed himself of everything of value: a sizable quantity of shillings, USD, euros, and other currencies he did not care about. He took the currencies he did not like, swept them into the middle of the room, and lit the pile with a lighter he found. He took the other cash, the passports, the documents, and scooped everything into a bright red shoulder bag. Two laptops, one pair of good shoes, a bit of dried food. He went to the main tent in the midst of the camp. It too was empty. There was a box shoved off into the corner, and in the box was a wooden case that he prised open with his knife. Inside were the passports of Kestner and the

Ethiopian woman along with credit cards and a few thousand in euros. He stuffed everything into the red bag.

He went out quickly and found the two remaining Isuzus, opened their hoods, and let his knife slash as it wished. Fuel and water ran out of tubes. It was not the same as blood, not the same as slashing a person.

He went to the old lorry and sat there for a while. IN GOD WE TRIST. What did it mean? Yet this had become his home. He hit the starter, and the engine rumbled on the first try. He shoved it into gear and clutched out slowly, the way Hassan had advised, and the lorry swayed and resurrected itself, hauling itself out of the sand like a wounded dog climbing out of the river.

When he rolled out of the camp, the jihadis were atop the hill shooting rounds in the air in front of the camera, taking turns, rolling back the video they had made and playing it over to see their fame and glory. They did not notice the noisy departure of the lorry.

He drove south, his head roaring with voices. Director, New Matron, Aketch, hundreds of lost children. But the roar gradually died down as he drove and as his mind was diverted to the chore of finding a way through without tipping the vehicle into soft sand or over a cliff, both of which he encountered repeatedly. As he went, he was alone, as he was always.

II

Because of Richard. Because of Pelé, the hero of the World Cup.

Who went his own way in Nairobi. Who left Money, thinking himself as bright and free as a flying bird.

Money did not make such mistakes. He knew what he was and what he was not. He was not a bird, nor was he free. He was dirty and earthbound—perhaps he was a large rat. He would always be stuck on the ground, and he knew that.

Richard, he thought, could not survive without him. Aketch would survive—he knew that. She would do better than survive.

But Richard? Richard was nothing on his own. He only existed as a shadow, Money's shadow. So what happens when a shadow discovers it can fly like a bird?

It would have been better if Money had invaded the city lights of Nairobi on his own. Money often thought that were he alone when he arrived, he would have carved a place for himself among the rich and creamy and unknowing people. It was impossible, though, with a sniffling shadow at his shoulder, watching his every move, his every mistake. Richard had glued himself to Money, always two steps behind with a lost and hopeless face. There was no need for him to speak. With his weepy eyes he asked question after question of Money, silent questions that were far worse than said questions. The only answer Money had for Richard was a solid beating to shut up his eyes.

Even homeless and hungry and sad, Richard had grown. He somehow dodged the ravages and the crookedness that had been Money's lot. One day Richard would be the taller one, the stronger one. That was fine. He would never be able to stand up to Money. He would be one of those gentle things who never find out how strong they are because they are afraid to try. So he would suffer beating after sickening beating without fighting back. Worse than this, Richard would never hate anyone because he was incapable of it. He would always dream that the CEO and Aketch loved him, and that Money was like a brother, even as Money told him often enough that, no, he was not his brother and would never be his brother. Even as Money stood over him cursing him and cuffing his pretty head, first on one side, then the other.

—You are just a dirty baboon, walking behind. Not brother, not sister.

Money took a clear account of himself. Unlike Richard he would not be soft and stupid. This was the way he would not be easily tricked.

Money and Richard stood close by the side of the road in the centre of Nairobi. They watched with listless curiosity the important and busy cars that swept by. Where were they going that they were in such a rush that if a person came in their path, they would simply knock the person down, the wheels spinning onward to their more important thing? What was it that filled the lives of the people of the shiny cars? Money watched carefully, trying to make sense of this world. He saw that there were battles to be won, riches to be taken, money to be spent, other people to mislead, to scare, to beat. Of course, Nairobi was busy. This was the *economic* life. The CEO had taught him something about it. The internet had taught him. Money tried on the fake smile, the confident mask he saw being worn by these others in their shiny clothes, in their shiny cars. He tried the fake smile, knowing it was ugly when he did it because it could not hide very well a person with a burning belly.

Richard noticed his smile and started to smile too, stupidly, so that Money had to work to hold down the urge to give him a full beating right there in downtown Nairobi in front of the uniformed marhinos. Instead he said, —What are you grinning about, baboon?

—I am not that animal.

—If I say cat, you are cat. If I say baboon, you are baboon.

—Maybe I grin when happy. I must have felt happy.

—You felt happy? Only stupid people feel happy for no reason. And I know for a fact there is nothing for you to be happy about. You are too stupid to know otherwise. Why don't you just say you grinned because you felt stupid.

—I felt happy because I thought maybe I could learn to be a doctor and ride in a private car like these. With a driver. Doctors have them. Look. Are all these people doctors? They look like doctors to me.

—What do you know about cars and doctors?

—Baba was a doctor.

—That man was never a doctor. Just the owner of orphans.

—Doctors give people a good life, and the people are so thankful they hand over money and respect.

—What makes you think the people in the cars are doctors?

—Look at them. They must be doctors.

Money shook his head and swivelled to give Richard a smart cuff, but Richard ducked away without looking at all perturbed. It was another infuriating thing—Richard had become quick.

—Even for a baboon you are stupid. These people are bankers. Anyone can see that.

—Still, if I was a doctor, I would help the ordinary people when they are sick and hungry. I would help people like us.

—How can the sick and hungry help the sick and hungry? One plus one is only two, not five.

Three marhinos watched the two figures slouched along the curb across from a major bank. The figures were conspicuous, standing inches from the spinning wheels of the cars of the doctors or bankers or whatever they were that roared to and from important business meetings. Eventually one of the cops moved toward them. Money and Richard did not wait. They darted into the moving traffic, barely avoiding being knocked down by a bus. They gained the other side of the traffic circle, pelted down a narrow lane, dove into an empty shed, and lay on the wooden floor, breathing, waiting to be discovered. They fell asleep.

They woke at the same instant to the sounds of voices, then a gang burst into the shed. Without saying anything they commenced a game of booting Money and Richard about on the ground as though they were practice balls.

Money took the kicks and waited until the gang boys tired themselves out. It did not impress him very much. He made his body as resistant as a brick, so that it hurt their feet to stub their toes on him. While the force of their assault waned, he thought about touching Aketch's breasts.

BECAUSE OF NOTHING AT ALL

They finally stopped the beating when they ran out of breath. The leader pointed at them.

—Who the *fuck* are you and what the *fuck* you doing in our place?

Money felt around his body where the worst kicks had landed. The pain had already dissipated. He would not have so much as a bruise. They had dealt him a minor dusting—a mere kiss and hug by his book. He made a quick calculation that determined how he could fight his way out of the shed. The calculation was five against two plus he was in the wrong and Richard was a hopeless fighter. He had broken some rules by entering into a strange space, trespassed on a strange gang, which is trespassing of the worst kind. He had only been in Nairobi a few days and had entertained the illusion that the rules of the street were different or did not exist, though he knew well enough, really, that such rules are universal and applied in every neighbourhood the world over. No numbers of doctors or CEOs or bankers would ever change that.

One of the boys picked up an empty box that lay in the corner.

—Why the hell you eat our food?

He showed the others the box and beside it an empty mealie sack.

There was no point in denying it, even as Money's stomach was as limp as the mealie sack. He shrugged. Richard looked forlorn and held his head in his hands, although Money doubted that Richard was hurt. If he were really hurt, he would be weeping by now.

Money looked over the gang members individually. They all wore the most stylish blue jeans he ever seen. Their T-shirts were identical, with big letters in black and the profile of Bob Marley.

Richard opted to speak.

—You should be nice because, to tell the truth, I am the son of Pelé.

Some time before, after the CEO vanished, Richard dreamt up this story of the miraculous and great Pelé and his courage and skill in the 1962 World Cup. Money had no idea how Richard had learned about Pelé. In fact, he himself would not have known about Pelé but for Richard. But it was weird because there was this wrong thing about Richard: he was not at all discouraged by his terrible lack of skill with a ball. He had no talent as an athlete, despite his smooth muscles. What he had was an obsessive story about the greatest footballer ever. This story was nurtured like a tomato plant every day, so that it grew leaves and roots. He told the story to anyone who would listen: the story of a poor African man who had led a country called Brazil to World Cup glory. How he had a son when he came to Kenya, and that son was none other than Richard.

But it was hardly a good moment for made-up fantasies. The gang boys might be in bad humour. They could as easily laugh and treat it as a joke, as they could knife the intruders, Pelé or no, and leave their bodies of their hapless victims to rot along with an empty box and empty sack. No one would care. The leader of the gang looked at Richard in mock seriousness, as though seriously impressed.

—*Really?* Son of Pelé? My God. Which means you are also Pelé?

Richard nodded eagerly, thinking he was a fine thing. One of the gang stepped outside. All he could come up with was an empty soup can. He brought it in and tossed it at Richard's feet.

—Pelé. Hokay. Show us the Pelé skills you learned from your Bwana.

Richard confidently picked up the can. He tossed it up in the air and attempted to juggle the can on his feet. He kept it in the air for all of two kicks and that was it.

One of the gang snorted. He toed the can adeptly from the ground up onto his foot, flipped it to his thigh, bobbed it up to chest, then thigh, foot, foot, thigh, heel then caught it on his foot and let it come to rest there.

—And you? You also the son of Pelé?

Money stayed down, shook his head, put his head on his knees between his hands. He was tired. He needed a moment to think. Knife beckoned weakly from its place by his leg. He might use it, but the calculation was unchanged. He watched carefully the smallest gang boy, the one who said nothing and wore a sneer on his face and whose muscles were hard as knots. He was a major reason Money did not like his chances. The others were puffy and lazy and a bit stupid or stoned, and their blows had been weak. But not the small one. The small one was a killer. He was the one who pushed everyone else to do worse things. They were just another gang, and Money knew about them as soon as they had walked in the door.

Meanwhile Richard kept talking, blithely doing what he did to survive, which was to play the fool. Somewhere along the line Richard had come to realize that people eventually took to him, just as most people take to puppies and injured kittens and lost babies. Perhaps he had known this from birth. He squirrelled away gifts people gave him when he hung about the main street and the market. Clothes, chocolates, fruit. He pretended to ignore the ladies who put out their hands, greeting him with little touches and hugs and sweet names like darling and dear. Young women fawned on him. But Money had watched all of this. The bestowers of love were the same people who turned their backs on Money with worried looks on their faces. At first Money thought it was because Richard had his own name, not a name given him by the CEO. At first he thought he had been a victim of bad naming. He realized it was more than that. He had to harden himself against Richard and all Richards and take on the responsibility of showing the Richards of the world that hardness and toughness were stronger than cuteness. Richard, stupid, cow-headed Richard, had no understanding of reality. He was always looking for love.

Now, in the presence of a strange gang, boys who might be perverse or criminally insane, Richard had the same dumb faith that he would be accepted sooner or later, even though they had beaten him with some pleasure, and despite the stupid story of Pelé and the bad show of juggling.

Money kept his face hidden, his head on his knees. He needed to get away, to do something that was not hemmed in by the rickety walls of the shed in which they were trapped. He had goals. Outside the shed, the heart of Nairobi waited to be invaded. The heart of Nairobi was beckoning him like a sexy woman, saying, come, I am easy. Yet a part of him stayed aloof from that too, knowing that sexy women were tricky where he was concerned and the heart of Nairobi was false, that he would never find it. He had his instincts. He knew plenty about lies and tricks and delusions. He might spend his entire life pursuing the easy thing, and he would not succeed because it was a trick. Because between the large cars carrying the CEOs and bankers and doctors, he noticed thousands of people wandering the streets who were like him, disowned and dispossessed, clawing the earth with dirty nails, scrambling to find the lost key to unlock the door, never realizing that behind the door was more nothing. They were shadowy, these thousands. They were the badly paid and the never paid, and they were the petty thieves and servants who went about on their knees if they had to. And year by year they wore out and faded away until they were gone. The promise of Nairobi was a trick. It was not open to him or Richard or Aketch or any of the people from Man U Healthy Child Centre. It was a mockery and a trick. He saw it the first day he arrived and watched the businessmen in pinstripes and the women in their jewellery and saw at the same moment the ranks of the failed.

Richard laughed, already making friends with the gang.

Lessons were coming to Richard. Lessons given by a dutiful Money. The lessons would happen later, when they were alone. They would involve a necessary measure of pain so that Richard might weep. Necessary in order to fight the trickery and lies.

Because of Richard he was forced to tag along with the five beaters. They followed the gang on a long tour that ended in a street outside an expensive club. By then it was late in the night, and the rain had settled into a monotonous cold soak. The gang paraded their blue jeans and the athletic shoes they had used to kick people, steal wallets, plastic cards, sunglasses. They swaggered about, drank beer, finally forgot about Money and Richard and went into the club, and a short time later were ejected into the street, in a fight. It was as though the nightclub had eaten the gang and then had indigestion and spewed it back out.

The fight started with pushing, then blows, then knives were drawn. A burly someone collapsed into the gutter.

Money and Richard looked for what they could lay their hands on, which was unfinished bottles of beer that the fighters had put along the wall while they fought. The beer was fresh or warm or flat, but all of it good after the first two. They stood aside and drank quietly, observing the pushing match and enjoying the brawl.

As if on signal, the fight ended when a wave of newcomers arrived, sliding up in expensive cars. The newcomers wore clothes that were far better than the ones worn by the gang members. The newcomers were tall, expensively perfumed, their hair straightened. Money looked them over, bothered. They were his age, like him but not like him. It was not only their clothes and perfumes and shoes and tended hair that bothered him, not only their cleanliness but their accents and their gestures. It was that they seemed completely unafraid of what would happen to them in the next hour, the next year. They were not worried about anything or anyone. They passed into the club, and everyone in the street followed, except for Money and Richard.

The rain blew down in fits. The air in the street chilled. Money and Richard leaned against the wall, watching the cars come in and the clubbers celebrate. Late in the night the streets were a slickened scene in which drunken patrons came and went while another world of poverty and humble living things struggled below the surface. The door of the club opened and closed. Painted girls came outside and smoked.

Richard looked wistfully at these girls. His eyes shone with pure and raw yearning.

—Look at them. Such big and long legs, those girls.

—Look, baboon. If you want those girls, you either have to wait until someone hands you a better wallet, better clothes, better friends, or you just go ahead, take what you want without asking permission. Anyway, it is the duty of people like us to inform them that in the end of their life, they will also be big losers.

Richard shuddered and answered more into his own shirt than to Money.

—Who said I care about them? Under their big joogz they have no hearts.

The night rain slanted down and their clothes stank.

Money looked upon Richard's pinched young face and torn shirt and wistful eyes. That poor, disowned orphan boy went to the wall and sank down with his head on his knees. After a while he departed into sleep.

Money shook him awake.

—You want to sleep in the rain or ride in a warm car?

Richard stood up, soaked and groggy and shivering. He trailed behind Money as he followed two women as they left the club. The girls were too young and clean to be alone in a rainy, late Nairobi street. They should have been home in their fathers' houses, wrapped in dry sheets and pillows, sleeping. Adventures were what they were after. Adventures and fun. They went unthinking along a dark street followed by two shadows who wore shoes that were so bad the rain had saturated the paper stuffed inside. Richard stumbled behind Money, his feet slurping and his teeth chattering. But the girls did not hear or see their followers. They came to their car, just as Money stepped up to them. He made it simple and friendly.

—Ah, ladies, but I need your daddy's car.

The women turned and took in Money and Richard, and a kind of horror dawned on their faces. They opened their mouths and turned and fled into the deserted street. They screeched for help but began laughing at each other instead, drunk, unfazed by street thieves. Their high heels failed, and they were hilarious on broken heels and curved haunches that had only been used for dancing. The keys were left hanging in the door of the car. A purse had been dropped, and Money calmly rescued that too.

All this time Richard watched, his shoulders slouched, his eyes round and sad, his clothes a mess. Money had to push him into the passenger seat of the car before he searched out the slot into which to insert the key. He turned it, and the motor hummed to life.

He had trouble mastering the car. It finally went forward only to knock into a wall. But after a few minutes, he was able to achieve control, and they drove away in the rain, comfortable in the dry leather seats. He turned on the heat, and they drove for hours through the rain, through narrow lanes and out into main streets where late taxi drivers cursed at them, then down a side road where the car suddenly went dead and drifted to a stop. They saw a police Jeep, ducked below the windows, and curled up on the seats for an hour or more. Richard had not said a word. He did not sleep but lay with his eyes round, as though having a nightmare. It made Money want to shake Richard to wake him.

When the downpour paused, Money got out of the stolen car. He hated everything. He was exhausted, even as he dragged Richard out by the collar.

It rained again, heavier now, a deluge of piss, the streets awash while the unreachable and beguiling heart of Nairobi was silent. They were cold and wet as ever, the glow of the beer they had taken transformed into a bitter aftertaste. A confusion of lights wheeled around them. They came to a place where the smell in the streets burned their nostrils. It was as though they had stumbled backwards through the rain, all the way to their old home across from the dump. Heaps of rubbish were piled up against walls and got in their way. Foul liquids streamed along the middle of the lane. Nearby, steel pounded on steel as an unseen creature or process of the city went on without regard for any human feeling. Richard stopped and he finally spoke. He was shaking, and his eyes were on some future in which he was warm and dry. He cried out.

—How can people be working now? They should either be asleep or dead.

Money stared at him.

—Shut up. You know nothing. Those workers are hungry Poors like us. Poors will do anything, at any time. You might as well learn this. Poor people sell themselves, day or night. They labour in the death of the night. It is death labour for death wages.

—What happened to us? We should be football players. Or doctors, or CEOs. Why is it we belong in Poorland?

Money laughed although he wanted to weep. He stopped walking. Damn Richard.

—You know, baboon, when Aketch left us, it cracked your head.

—Who is Aketch? Who is that? Do I know someone with that name?

Richard began to sob so much it turned into hiccups.

—Look, shut up that wailing and weeping or I will beat you into stupidity.

Money pulled out the abandoned purse and dug through it until he found a clutch of bills.

—Look, if you shut up I will find you beautiful hot food and a warm place to sit. Your cracked baboon head needs warming.

They came to the place where the steel work was going on. Strong men were battering red-hot rods while others hauled the cooled and finished steel and strapped it to pallets. Money spat.

—Compared to these wajinga, we are rich, just as the CEO said.

—I don't think of the CEO anymore. That man is nothing. Not father. Not brother. Not doctor. Maybe he was your father, maybe he was just a drunk mlevi.

—So. You dispense with Aketch. Now you dispensed with the CEO. Amazing. A massacre of everyone.

Richard walked away sobbing heavily.

It was hopeless. There was nothing Money could offer Richard to divert this sorrow. It welled up from an infuriating, hopeless depth. The wet wad of bills was still clutched in Money's hand. Pathetic. He riffled through their bag of possessions. He found stolen purses, two old blankets, two old shirts, and two pairs of smelly trousers. He also found a water-stained note that Aketch had written and stuffed into their things. He unfolded it and read it by a street lamp.

To Whom It May Concern:
Maybe you are poor in Nairobi. Maybe even poorer than my
family. So we are together with no difference. Please, these
are my sons of Money and Richard. But Money is more
my son than Richard who is beautiful by himself. Money is
named in honour of the Money in the world that can be found
everywhere we are not. We are modest and with no power and
no money. So this son is Money as we are poor, and may he
pass through your place in peace. Both of these are orphans

with no father and they must find their way through all the
evils. Please help them as they are your brothers.

Richard blundered out into the Nairobi rain, and Money followed with his head boiling in anger and shame. They stumped on through the early morning hours. A dim and foggy light came up and the rain stopped, leaving golden mist hanging in the air. The sky cleared, and the sun edged up into the sky. An entire clan of brown rats boldly crossed their path, the adults carried the pups by the napes of their necks, and the young ones scuttled to keep up. It looked as though the rats had decided to move to a better part of the city.

Money and Richard continued on through the streets. As the morning came on they picked up the scent of baked food, which they followed until they came to a bakery. They went in and then stood in the street eating meat pies as they watched the corral and slaughter of the first cattle of the day in an old abattoir.

The next day Richard walked away as Money shut his eyes and dozed by a sunny wall where they had stopped to dry out. Richard did not return.

Money saw Richard one more time four months later. Money had been casting about for weeks in a dull rage because he had suffered one humiliation after another. On this particular day he was in a fury and prepared to fight, steal, die, throw himself at his foes. Nothing was easy—he had bounced from one corner of the city to another, by turns uncomfortable, afraid, cold, sore, hot, intoxicated, bitter, and lonely. As he moved along the street he felt this fury in his blood, simmering, and he knew it was a danger, and he wished it felt better than it did. It was not holy or noble or just. It was a terrible, ruinous force to be feared.

And just then, Richard appeared. Richard popped out of a shop directly in front of him. Money hardly recognized him at first, but there was no mistaking the smooth muscles and beautiful skin. Richard was clean, his hair clipped short. He looked well-fed and relaxed. His short pants and shirt fit beautifully, the kind that wealthy people wear, of soft and thick material. Behind him came an expensive woman with huge eyes. She spoke into the air in an unbroken stream, like a bird at sunrise or perhaps like an entire flock of birds. She was a beautiful and expensive woman, not a girl. She was not a member of a family, nor was she a street girl, nor a gang girl, nor an addict. She was from the world of the internet that Money had glimpsed, in which beautiful people go about their days in comfort and warmth. He saw it all in a quick glance.

Richard was the pet monkey. Such a handsome monkey too, that Richard, lapping at the milk and warmth while she petted his smooth skin. Money wanted to laugh even as a lash of sharp words came to his tongue. He stopped himself. He realized something else at that moment: Richard was free. He had freed himself. He had realized there were choices. He had chosen to walk away from the gnawing uncertainty and hunger and Money's beatings and the dump and Aketch and the CEO and his wealth.

Money pursed his lips, and his heart surged in his chest as he watched Richard walk away with his glorious mother bird. His eyes burned, and he hated that his eyes burned so. He knew he would never see Richard again. How he hated that boy with smooth skin. He hated Richard's stupid Pelé story and his regular muscles and perfect head, his wet eyes, his needs and yearning and his weeping. His unfulfilled expectation of love and trust.

Richard did not notice Money that day. But perhaps he did notice and pretended he did not.

Later, whenever Money thought about it, when he recalled the last time he saw Richard, his blood felt as though it stalled in his veins, and his eyes burned, and he hated it.

III

After a night and a day of driving, he slept quietly in the darkness, protected from man and beast by the steel walls of the cab. When he awoke, he drove until he found himself on a southerly track which eventually led to a road, then a highway, then a town, then a bigger town, and then he was back in Nairobi.

IN GOD WE TRIST rumbled unwanted into the city like a bastard son returned home.

It came to pass that Money had no conscious destination. He drove as though he were part of the machine, without mind or heart to stop him. He only stopped when he came to a massive traffic jam that was so entangled it was impossible to skirt around. The lorry became locked in on all sides by more and more traffic. After a while nothing moved. He turned off the engine and fell asleep where he sat.

When he awoke nothing had changed and no one had moved. He briefly considered the market value of the lorry. It was a rugged, indestructible machine but stolen, so he gave up the idea that he could enrich himself that way. He took his bag, abandoned the cab in the midst of the other trapped vehicles. He strode out, wending his way through the vehicles by foot. The enormous traffic jam stretched backward and forward as far as the eye could see. Engines were off and people were doing as he did, leaving their vehicles to find a place to drink or eat.

His destiny, if this was it, was not adequate for what he had done, what he survived, and what he had witnessed. Now he found himself back in a familiar place. He laughed at himself. How old was he? No one had told him, and he had no record. He could be as old or young as he preferred. The things he had done were lined up behind him, and it was hard to forget. Behind him were the jihads with their bent ideas and deeds that he now had to drag along with him like an unwanted and noisy child.

He realized he would have to drag it all behind him forever, stupid brainwashed jihads, severed head dangling from a badly butchered neck, flat and ruinous eyes still alive, staring like the worst death medicine possible.

Yet he did not fear evil. He knew the devious ways of it, and he was not afraid because he was quite sure he came from evil's house, played in evil's streets, made friends with evil, eaten of evil, shat it out.

His bones were heavy with fatigue. It was a new thing, but he recognized it as a thing that happened to men like him eventually. Evil demanded too much energy. It sucked away excesses. He wondered if he could become good and righteous. He snorted to think of it. He laughed out loud.

On either side of the traffic-jammed road, shanties rolled up, looking as arid and unpromising as the mile upon mile of dunes and stone of the Turkana. It was about five o'clock. Out of habit he glanced around as he went. No one pursued him. No one challenged him or threatened him. There were people all over the road, but no one knew who he was or what he had done. Every now and again he thought he saw a familiar face, but he was not sure. He picked out the touts and gang boys who were concentrating on the opportunities presented by the many rich people who streamed along the roadside. The skies glowered overhead. He heard the distant buzz of machinery or traffic or of a man complaining of his unexpected and impending demise. All the soft stuff, the pain, the obsessive human struggles — it was small shillingi compared to the constant striving, the relentless struggle, the desperate clambering for survival and dominance.

He weaved through the stuck mass of cars that were so close together he had to vault over fenders. He squeezed his way past hundreds of vehicles pointed in every direction, many abandoned, while others blared their horns at nothing. He lost his bearings here, perhaps because of changes in him that had taken place in jihad country. He saw no familiar landmarks. He thought he was moving toward Dandora, but there was nothing he recognized amid the confusion of jammed cars and the thousands of headlights in his eyes. It was too glaring, too noisy, after the silence and blackness of the desert. It was a traffic jam of a kind that was never conceived of by the inventors of cars, yet a storm of cars that was inevitable, with motors so thick and so many and so dirty that in desperation they spilled over into ditches and tiny lanes, to stick like coital dogs partway into shacks and houses along the roadside, unable to reverse or go forward while the inhabitants of those shacks — large, angry shop-keeping ladies with formidable limbs — bellowed in outrage. He never imagined there were so many cars in Nairobi. It was a traffic jam that threatened to spread its tentacles throughout the entire city and beyond, into the country and the towns and the villages, across the borders into other countries. Drivers were mad with frustration. All the while the evening deepened, and the roar of the striving poor ebbed and flowed.

He pushed on ahead through the night, past wailing buses and enraged taxis and a clot of official cars with drooping flags, sirens, lights flashing, and horns blaring to announce that they carried important personages. It made no difference. All were equal now, stuck where they were, pointed in odd directions but unable to progress. Over the road hung a pungent and sour cloud, of exhaust, rotting rubbish, of excrement and human regret.

Shadows shifted about before the low slanted walls of the shacks and the ghosts of dead children stared from the corners, awake with disappointment, sucking at a night thick with engine fumes.

Money found himself in a narrow lane, in front of a familiar sign that had been overwritten:

VIAGRA TAVERNA
WE WELCOME MALES AND FEMALES OF ALL KINDS

An extension had been erected, shoddily, to accommodate the expanded vision. The place was packed with custom. They arrived thirsty with their new-earned money, with digital music wired to their ears and festivity in mind. A giant screen was fastened to one wall; a football match was about to begin. Here was a soupy mix of the classes, the inhabitants of sleek motors alongside haggard refugees, all sweating and demanding beer. Mkande was in his usual position by the till, his face concentrated on coins and bills. He called out the back for food and beer. He yelled, —These people drink like frogs! Like frogs!

At the doorway, passengers from an overcrowded bus quarrelled with the driver. The driver had enough of the fight. He descended the bus and slipped into the bar. After a moment, the passengers followed behind, the last of which were fancily attired women on their way to a funeral. They sang holy songs and laughed as they promenaded in, grand and delighted with all they encountered. They made eyes at a few promising men who sat along the bar with sleek mobile phones before them. The women were missionaries of the Church of Desire and Lust. They flashed loaded glances and swung themselves about as though they knew only dance and rhythm and no other kind of motion. They were sated and drunk from the moment they arrived but free and generous too. They hugged strangers and extracted themselves from wandering hands. A stately and tall woman entered and immediately drew the attention of every man in the place. She said little, but her smile was a stunning flash of sun followed by a coy moon. The men were fixated, mesmerized. A few of those in better clothes jockeyed for position, offering to buy her food and beer. Someone loudly offered a gift if she would just sit by him and pretend to be his girl. Voices could be heard:

—She should be the queen for our nation.

—Yah, queen for this special day.

—It will be Queen Day. And all of you drinkers are the subjects of the queen and Queen Day.

The traffic chaos pressed against the door of the bar, as though a tide were pushing in, swamping the place with strange fish from the sea. Money and suits were washed ashore. A man in a business suit turned around. His mouth was brilliant with English, his words clipped and expensive. He wore spectacles framed in delicate wires. He was not the only suit in the place— it was one of the changes to the Viagra.

—Perhaps she already is queen. But what I know is that queens need kings.

Several suits laughed at this brilliance. They were in accord with Brilliant Suit while the workers and drivers and wageless others looked down at the bottoms of their beer bottles and were aggrieved not to be wearing suits too.

Money stood in the doorway and surveyed the place. He went forward, and someone looked at him and gave up his seat. Money sat, and after a while he looked at the queen and decided that indeed she was a fair and just ruler: she heard all and saw all and understood all. She looked upon the lesser men and women; the ragged, the sweat-stained and dirty, the shaved and perfumed. He wondered, as he had now and again, what might have become of that other, Ethiopian queen he had tried to sully. It did not matter; it was too late to think about her. He could not imagine that something as simple as a dry wasteland would cause that Ethiopian much concern.

But he fancied that he had a chance with this present queen. She had returned his gaze steadily and regally, and it was clear that she understood about him. After that, all he wanted was for her to look at him deeply, smiling or not, but it seemed there were many people and things for her to look at, and she looked at all of them.

What was he? Evil or righteous; a decent man; a reformed and converted man?

Maybe she would look into him and see the deeds he had done. Maybe she would realize that he had no choice but to commit those deeds. That he was forced by his anomalous life, the flaws in his circumstances. Because of this, because of that. Because of his difficulties and his fraught character, stamped by the instinct for survival and market share and profit. She would understand. She would forgive him for what he was. His eyes fastened on the queen, and he suddenly felt a grand and warm and tender hope toward this woman. He wished no harm should come to her this night or any other night. Perhaps he would watch over her to make sure. He remembered Aketch, and the feeling expanded and washed over him like wave of strong fresh qat. What had become of Aketch? Did she ever save a thought for him? Was it possible for Aketch or any other woman to forgive his broken and unworkable manhood, his murderous humour, and his dented body? He was not a nothing. He was a strand of the fibre of life stuff and man stuff, damaged, trapped in his poor body and poor prospects.

In the desert a new kind of desperation had assailed Money. It had come over him as he waited simmering in the heat, agitated by the constant wind, impatient, and finally with too much time to think, he fell prey to the ravages and fears of days past. Alone in a sleepless night, wandering lost in dark lanes. His thought was that hunger, his old companion, would arise again. Loneliness and hunger and age. The reward for his efforts would not arrive; his risks were for naught. He was nothing but a dull pebble cast from one obscure location to the next. He was forgettable, illegitimate, unofficial, dispensable, unpaid. Anger was futile — he knew this too — but it was there of its own accord, exposed. So he had boiled away in old fears and dull angers in the wild land while noisy winds blew around his ears, speaking to him the facts of his existence. Only a month before, he had cared nothing for comforts, those trappings of weak men. He would have said that those urges were the product of manipulations that were part of the plot against the poor, another case of brainwashing that he had to resist, no different than the conspiracies of the mullahs and missionaries. The wind that blew around the empty distances of the wastelands—it blew here, and it blew there, and then it blew in his ears, speaking about the things he had done, and things he was and was not, and it made him think about his past and future. And so he wondered what it would be like to have a woman waiting for him at the end of a dusty and fraught day, at the end of battles, at the end. It was impossible. That wind, that hellish wind. It leaked into his blood with dire messages that he could not ignore.

In the Viagra Taverna he felt a movement beneath the table, and his hand shot out and seized a child who had squeezed in through the same gap in the wall that he had used so many years before. The scrawny thing looked at him defiantly, perhaps expecting to be dragged out and beaten. He let it go, and it scrambled away on hands and feet, into the murky places under the tables.

Money heard the voice of Brilliant Suit uttering brilliant words. No doubt this brilliant man had a brilliant wife waiting, and brilliant children in school uniforms. Perhaps a brilliant mistress too, an inexpensive and low-risk mistress. Brilliant Suit had all the things women desired. All the things that were a mystery to Money. Brilliant Suit had no need for Queen, yet still made plays for her that she half-resisted, even though Queen had no need of offers. Brilliant Suit came up with devices to attract her. He cooed like a dove, crowed like a rooster, made baffling statements. He made her laugh. He talked like a radio, this Brilliant Suit.

—I recommend this woman for Nobel Prize!

Other quick mouths came back.

—For what? Nobel Prize is for different things. Medicine, physic, politic, football, music, film, philosophy—

—Eh, not philosophy. No Nobel for philosophy.

—What about Nobel Prize for Drunk? They give that, they must.

—Ha, ha. No, that is not Nobel. It is World Cup. You go to group round, round of sixteen, et cetera, et cetera, then you can get World Cup for Drunk.

—Looks like you already won group round!

—Fondling. You can get Nobel Prize for Fondling. Or even Wishing to Fondle. But Nobel Prize for Sexy Queenship is another department.

—Maybe me. Maybe I get Nobel for Sexy. I know sexy better than any man here.

—Oh, yes? Okay, maybe you then. Or you could get Nobel for Self Deception.

—No, but *she*—the queen—she gets Nobel for Sexy without a doubt. Women are always the ones to win that thing. Not men.

—You could get it too. You just need to practise so you will gain proficiency.

—Why do you say that? How you know how much practise I do and how much proficiency I am having?

—Just a guess. Looks like you need to study the thing and then practise.

—You say?

—I say.

—Ah, no. It is the beginning of tribal times again. Luo versus Kukuyu. Et cetera, et cetera.

—And what et cetera are you?

—Modern. Modern of the city. Et cetera of nothing.

—Ha, et cetera and Masai. Here's to et cetera and Masai.

—Okay, Masai. But maybe I don't like tribal fight.

—Maybe you no warrior.

—Jah, or maybe just a herder-farmer.

—Or maybe *lady* farmer.

The expected war did not erupt. Everyone laughed deliriously and then toasted and tilted large bottles instead of throwing them. Bad feelings should have been created, and Money was mildly disappointed not to be entertained by a fight. It was like being shown a meal but not being permitted to take a bite.

He fingered his knife. His knife had been bothering him as he watched the people in the bar. With his head down as though he were weak or ashamed, he sauntered toward Brilliant Suit. He moved thoughtfully, and then he seized the fine material of the suit and hauled the man onto the table and held the knife to his throat. Mr. Suit had nothing brilliant to say about this. He blubbered and waved his hands and finally choked out words.

—But why, brother, why?

Money spoke calmly because he was calm. Now that he had done it, he was calm, and his voice showed him to be a patient man, really.

—Why? Tell me. Do you tell the truth? Who did you sell in exchange for suit and watch and all this rich stuff?

—No, brother. I work for the UNDP, sometimes UNICEF, sometimes the British or the World Bank. I'm just an economist.

—What is a World Bank economist doing in a taverna in Dandora?

—Stuck in traffic. On our way north. I came in to wet my whistle just like any other man. Nothing more. Here, take this. A gift.

Brilliant stripped off his heavy golden watch. Money palmed it and looked at it.

—What should I do with this? You think it is easy to simply buy a man? You think you can use bribery to bring justice?

—It's not what you think. I'm no different from you, my brothah. A long time ago, I also came from a place like this.

The man's eyes were wet. In a moment Money would be forced to kill him, just to stop him from weeping. As it was, the sharp knife only nicked the fat skin around his neck. It made Money furious to see the fat blood oozing over his blade. He would have to wipe clean the blade before he put it back against his leg. The man might have HIV, hepatitis, Ebola, any nasty germ.

He dropped the watch on the man's belly and stepped back. A circle had formed about them, but no one said a word or made to interfere. They could see what Money was. They instinctively knew about calm men with knives.

He looked at Queen. She had gone quiet and suddenly lost her crown, transformed into a timid and frightened and ordinary witness, her chest collapsed, all the impressive shapes shrunken into an unobtrusive ball. She could not look Money in the eye as she had done before. Instead, she kept her eyes down, and her breath came quick. It was clear what she thought. She did not see before her any sort of hero, nor a complex and superior man of action and thought. No. She saw what he really was — an angry and twisted and dirty and bent orphan-man. But so what? She was obviously not really a queen after all.

Money stalked out of the Viagra in disgust. In another minute he was overcome with fatigue; he squatted on the ground to catch his breath. He stayed that way in the shadow of a familiar wall near the roadway, watching the traffic jam. In his hand, he held his knife.

Behind him, inside the Viagra Taverna, the voices had grown loud, then a scuffle commenced, generated from the heat left in his wake. Brilliant Suit strode out and away into the cars with a handkerchief clutched to his neck. Queen slipped hurriedly away. After that, bottles broke and the fight flared through the confined space, in and out of the corners with grunts and thuds. There was a pause in the action—perhaps because some last bottles of beer were located and consumed—then the fight resumed. Someone ran out to bring more fighters from nearby. There was a desperate drunkenness at this end of the world. Between the loud voices roared the television; Liverpool versus Chelsea, the commentators' voices urgent. The fight might have aligned with the football sides. The front wall of the tavern swayed, and the door banged open. The fight spilled onto the road, with men down, women screaming, others laughing drunkenly, visible blood, pieces of roofing for shields and the testicular dance of fighters.

Yet Money was not sated or even interested. He was low, his nerves shredded. He wandered away without further comment. Mkande had not recognized him; no one there knew who he was. He was unremembered, even in the place he had grown up.

The yellow glow of kerosene lamps lit the neighbourhood. The unofficial power supply was broken; darkness held sway but for a flicker in the sky that emanated from distant reaches of the city. He required a deeper night in which he could think clearly. He passed down the old lanes, the homes to his old fears. By his side he had a knife, nothing more. And now, suddenly, this knife and the blood that stained its blade were burdensome. He stopped and pulled it up and looked at the dull gleam of the blade for a long moment before he cast it away. The knife clanked against a wooden wall and fell to the ground. For a moment he waited, his chest heaving. He might just as easily have killed Brilliant Suit. Death meant nothing. One less suit in a world of suits.

But a figure slipped along the wall and retrieved the knife. It was the child from the floor of the Viagra, or some other child who did not belong in this forsaken city night, wandering the lanes.

—What do you want there? Are you in need of a beating? Why you not asleep in your place by your mother and father?

The figure froze for a moment then came hesitantly forward. The knife was held up in the outstretched hand, as though Money had lost it. Money turned away and walked, but the child ran along beside him, insistently holding up the knife. Money peered at the child.

—Take it. Learn from it. I no longer want it. Take it, small kid.

You found it. Now you own it. See, the edge is sharp. Protect yourself with that. Keep you safe.

The child answered in a voice so clear and high that Money wondered if the child was human. The voice was like a dash of cold water on his skin.

—Ah, no, Bwana. That would be wrong. If I take it, they will steal it from me. Maybe they will beat me. Or if it is left behind in the road, another child will find it. They will take it from that finder. Every way, every possible way, the end of the story is sad.

Money stared at the child, at a triangular face with large, serious eyes. He quietly took the knife back and slid it into its sheath. The knife weighed ten kilos or more. He could scarcely manage it, but he turned away, to shuffle away with the child following. After a while the child melted into the darkness, singing in its high voice, and he found himself walking near two women who trailed a cloud of cheap perfume and alcohol. In the lanes where the darkness was thickest, they called out fond words, calling him *my brother*, so he knew that they wished for his protection. They had no idea that he was a man who had only a knife that was too heavy to carry. They had no idea that he was the last person on Earth who could be protector of the lost and weak. But he did not care any more. He let them talk, let them converge on him, to stumble against him along the rocky path. He heard their sleek hips sliding against their garments, sniffed the scent of their heated skin, and that was enough.

In the distance the electricity surged, and the city lights flared against the night sky.

EPILOGUE
Susan Seiko Ono
San Francisco, USA
January, 2017

She did not learn of the fate of Avtar Kestner for some months. The story leaked out, and parts of it were stitched together into a story by a Canadian investigative journalist who attempted to follow up on the abduction, the return of one Canadian and the demise of the other. There was the political issue of whether governments should pay ransoms to terrorist groups that abducted Canadian citizens. There was the bureaucratic issue of the failure of intelligence and security services.

But she knew better. Her ex-husband would never stop. It was not in his nature. To him, everyone has a price.

The two men sat across from her on the private flight to San Francisco. When they had appeared at Refugee Camp Number Two, she knew who they were. She avoided them at first, until they cornered her in her office and explained that she needed to go with them, telling her that her husband and family needed her. She sat in silent outrage. But then, when they started in about Fumiko and named her children, went into details of her mother's medical condition, she gave in. She packed her bag and left, without telling her staff, without telling anyone. Suddenly she realized the length to which Marius would go. They had somehow compelled her mother and sister to divulge her location.

So she went with them, abandoning her new life, abandoning her returning lover, capitulating to Marius and his twisted possession of her. She went with the two men. Don't worry, they said. He even sent his private jet. Your husband, he must miss you bad. And they laughed the laugh of affluent men.

When the opportunity arose, she would leave again and cover her tracks better this time.

What had she done to Avtar?

At some point, sooner or later, she would find his daughters and explain. She promised herself that at some point in her life, she would at least do that.

—Fin—

Acknowledgements

N, Nt, and T for travelling beside me along this road.

My deep gratitude to those who worked to make this story come to light. First and foremost, Bethany Gibson for her highly attentive and perceptive editing. My friends Mark Baker and Elisabeth Finch for their unfailing encouragement. Marilyn Biderman for her effort to steer this in the right direction.

I am grateful to Susanne Alexander and the people at Goose Lane Editions. This publication process was a real pleasure, from beginning to end. Thank you so much for making it so.

Lastly, I would like to salute the many outstanding people with whom I have had the honour to work on health-care projects over the years, at times in places remote and harrowing. The nurses, medical assistants, drivers, community workers, managers, government officials, students, physicians, and scientists in Mwanza, Dar, Dhaka, Sylhet, Rajshahi, Lahore, Karachi, Bangkok, HCMC, Addis, Bahir Dar, Nairobi, Harare, Bulawayo, Mutare, Lusaka, Ndola, and Ottawa—you know who you are.

Notes

Chapter 2: *Only a medicine man gets rich by sleeping.* African proverb.

Chapter 2: *Small deeds are great in small man's eyes, and great deeds, in great men's eyes, are small.* Ahmad ibn al-Husayn (al-Mutannabi), trans. Geert Jan van Gelder, "A Victory Ode by al-Mutanabbī: The Qasīdah on Sayf al-Dawlah's Recapture of the Fortress of al-Hadath in 343/954" in *Classical Arabic Literature: A Library of Arabic Literature Anthology.*

Chapter 2: *Deep in a man sits fast his fate.* Ralph Waldo Emerson, "Fate."

Chapter 7: *And they feed, for the love of Allah, the indigent, the orphans.* The Holy Quran, Al-Insan, chapter 76, verse 8, trans. Yusuf Ali.

Chapter 7: *And from the evil of darkness when it overspreads.* The Holy Quran, Al-Falaq, chapter 113, verse 3.

Chapter 7: *Awake, arise, or be for ever fall'n.* John Milton, *Paradise Lost,* bk. 1, line 330.

Chapter 7: *It matters not how strait the gate...* William Ernest Henley, "Invictus."

Chapter 7: *Better to reign in Hell than to serve in Heaven.* John Milton, *Paradise Lost,* bk. 1, line 263.